THE
LITTLE PEOPLE

Barry Swan

Valley Press

DEDICATED TO

THE BOGLANDS

The Little People, vanquished and demoralised, took to the sea in ancient times and found a final refuge in a remote, rain sodden land on the edge of the western world. This last great flight, preceded as it had been by a history of successive migrations before the advancing multitudes of noisy, destructive and technologically superior tribes known collectively as the Giants, was called the "Last Flight of the Heroes". The propensity to flee was so inbuilt into their culture that they had made a virtue of fear, defeat and running away. All their heroic tales and sagas concerned mythical warriors renowned for their immense lack of physique, for "courageous" cowardice, "steadfast" weakness in the face of adversity and admirable physical ability not only to run away very fast, but to hide in the most unlikely spots. Whilst it was forbidden by their druids to write down anything about their history, the Last Flight of the Heroes was remembered in all its sorry detail in oral tradition, in sad songs, extremely long poem-dirges and soulful religious ceremonies.

Perhaps to compensate for this overly pessimistic side of their culture and history, ordinary recreation mainly took the form of ecstatic communal trance dancing. This was more or less approved of by the normally puritanical and clear-headed druids despite the participants' dependence on psychosis-inducing mushrooms. (The Little People would dare each other to consume larger and larger quantities of the most poisonous fungi.) The shamans recognised that at its basis was perhaps a holy, inexpressible worship-ritual with roots far back in antiquity that they reckoned must have had something to do with the original worship of the "real god" – the god whom they so studiously and piously had sought since time began – and whom they had not yet found.

Then there were those individuals who had never seemed to return in spirit from the world-of-trance and be useful members of society again. These had a special name encapsulating the respect in which they were held by both shaman and commoner – the Forgetful Ones. (They often disappeared into the world of the giants, sometimes even deliriously attempting to insinuate themselves into giant affairs, perhaps forgetting their true origin.)

The Little People mocked the customs of the giants. These Morons (their pet name for them) seemed to spend all their free time rubbing body oil over their muscles, challenging each other to duels to the death, or participating in loud, boastful arguments after their competitions of physical endurance, at least one of which had to take place in the morning and one last thing at night. Their most absurd sport was their war-cry competitions, whose words the Little People learnt off by heart and repeated to each other with glee and laughter during those long nightly interludes before they slept (they really only slept properly in that restless last hour before dawn – and they mocked the giants for wasting a good portion of their lives in sleep). There was not one single, significant or insignificant thing about the giants that the Little People didn't know or laugh over. They knew all of their bodily habits (being keen, inconspicuous watchers) and heard all their whispered confidences. They could read their minds like magicians. They knew of their every move before the giants had even thought about them. They could see all the end results of every giant plan, enterprise and dream. Indeed, it was the dreams of the giants that interested them most, and caused them the greatest mirth.

Yet most giants never seemed to be aware of the existence of the Little People, those (normally invisible) folk who were, at least sometimes, their sworn enemies. They knew nothing, or pretended to know nothing, of that hidden world that was so at odds with their own.

They were not aware of how their own supposedly harmless, every-day activities, honest, work-a-day endeavours and even personal habits (pleasant or unpleasant) could cause havoc in the lives of multitudes of little folk. Activities that were humdrum, productive and quite satisfying to them were crushingly and thunderingly disruptive in the world of the folk of the sídh, the hallowed hills; dispersing all the "blessings" (features of every place that were never to be touched) that constituted so much of the world for the Little People; who wanted nothing more or less than some small share in the earth's bounty, to be able to walk openly in the sunshine and talk out loud without having to whisper or speak in coded language all the time, and, of course, not to have to make such a great play of concealment, both of themselves and their activities.

Certainly, there were in the giants' store of knowledge many stories, tall tales, legends, myths, queer beliefs and all sorts of fables and ethical viewpoints concerning a much hyped underclass. It was talk that filled the empty hours of the giants after they had become exhausted through excessive activity and loud arguments, and had nothing useful or more important to talk about. This talk – of "undesirables" and "outcasts" whom they had never actually met, conversed with or had any direct experience of – appeared all the more obsessive and childish for being very much in contradiction to giant philosophy that considered the visible world to be the only reality. What could not be seen, heard, smelt, felt or tasted did not exist. Their main perception of the mythological undesirables was that they were outcast simply because they could not be seen, heard, smelt, felt or tasted.

When it came down to it, if anybody was asked whether he or she really believed in such things, denial was always the wisest and easiest recourse.

The expansion of the Greater Giant Empire, which had already succeeded in extending its civilisation over all the continental landmass, threatened now to expand even further – beyond the sea until it had reached to the very end of the known world.

Then – it was said – the Little People would have nowhere else to flee to.

They hadn't been very long in this "last" outpost when, sure enough, their worst fears were realised and the giants, whose wide feet could squash whole forests and mountains, whose monstrous heads were always stuck up in the clouds so that you couldn't always easily see their eyes or read their minds, appeared again on the scene. It was not known how they could have got there so quickly, for the watchers had reported no sign of giant ships along the seashore. It was believed that they had come over by walking straight across the sea, driving their cattle, women, children and other livestock before them.

The giants had made a huge encampment at their baile near Átha Cliath, (now Dubh Linn in the nomenclature of mortals), a place that had never been settled by the Little People. Indeed, it had always been assiduously avoided by them. There had never been a clear-cut reason why they should have cursed this place (that is, if the absence of their approval inevitably meant that there was a curse on the spot); but one obvious factor (though

3

whether it was cause or effect was anybody's guess) was the absence of blessings at Átha Cliath.

Strangely, although the "baile near the crossing of the hurdles" has, since the time of the giants, been the main gateway for all sorts of predators, braggarts and undesirables to enter the country, adjoining as it does the main sea routes from the nearby landmasses and with a deep, open bay and flat, deep-soiled hinterland guaranteeing both food supplies and easy getaway to all parts of the country, north, south and west, neither the Little People nor the giants themselves had originally entered the island here. The accepted points of entry to the country for the first inhabitants were in the southwest and west. And it was not as if that was the easiest option, for the landings there were on very difficult, inhospitable terrain indeed and showed that the giants were capable of making the most stupid decisions and tactical errors.

The giants' encampment had grown inexorably over time. Descriptions of how they erected huge buildings which, against the laws of nature, adjoined each other with no open space between them (they were actually stuck together), as well as other wonders, were brought to the ears of the Little People by various giants whose conversations they overheard. Massive, stupendous, amazing, unbelievable were the words used by these "country" giants of what they saw in the big encampment.

The earliest generations of giants built a high wall around the camp, restricting both entry and exit. This certainly showed a less than courageous side to their character. Inside their highly defended HQ they became introverted, and began to indulge in those eccentric, even unnatural activities for which they were now notorious, such as giving themselves the title "Rulers of the Earth", "Official Speakers", "Qualified Thinkers", leading to that strange behaviour that was so hard for Little People to understand – arguing and quarrelling over every single subject in existence, often where the less important the matter, the more serious the quarrel. Sometimes it appeared that the quarrels were over nothing more or less than the actual words of the quarrel! The obsession with thinking had then led to something called "meaning" – another fatuous giant invention. There was no such word in the Little People lexicon (and hence no serious quarrels. Little People did argue and even hit out, such as when one individual inadvertently might knock over another slightly smaller individual, or when the "sign of some important thing" was being awaited and there was uncertainty over the time of its arrival – but these arguments were always solved either by running away or, more sensibly, awaiting the unfolding of events and thereby preclude the need for any prolonged dispute). All this giant discord, that led inexorably to bloodshed and internecine wars, was inevitably over some such "meaning". Disputing became more endemic as time went on (one generation of giants never learnt from the mistakes of the previous generation, whereas Little People's knowledge increased incrementally from one generation to the next). The eventually victorious Baile Átha Cliath debaters and thinkers went around imposing all their "ideas"(which in fact were simply thoughts generated by those violent, subconscious, hereditary impulses of mortals that constituted "thinking") on weaker giants over the extent of the land.

They also took to inventing "names" for everything, which immediately had the effect of destroying the integrity of whatever it was that was named. For names were imposed in the hope not of uniting the name-giver and named but of establishing a definitive, mutual exclusivity – an infinite distance – between them. It was evident that giant language (and in time mutually incomprehensible dialects) was another device used to separate themselves from reality and the natural world around them.

Succeeding generations continued this preoccupation with, and speaking in praise of, the big encampment, which increased in size over time. Every country giant had to make a pilgrimage there. Whole woodlands were cut down to erect habitations. Later stone was dug out of the ground and incorporated into the buildings, so that as time went on their abodes became increasingly gigantic and grotesque. It seemed that their contempt for the natural world also increased in time – as though the natural world was an inferior abode. Everything they did in the encampment – build, work, move about, social activities – was considered more advanced and satisfactory the more distinct and separated it was from the natural world. The interior of their homes, roadways, public places were designed in such a way as to exclude the world of nature. Their way of life as well as their mentality was directed inwards in an intricate maze of convoluted, *furtive and complex intercommunications and lines of transport that turned its back on all that was "external" or natural.*

Giant preoccupation with the Baile at Átha Cliath was considered the reason no other great settlements rose up in the countryside. Many of the country giants, instead of developing their talents and channelling their energies into utilising what was around them, looked to the great Baile for all their values, laws and sustenance. Consequently, they all believed that there could only be one Baile Átha Cliath. And since they could not understand much of what went on there, they had to bear another humiliating burden in being given the name of country ignoramuses.

A particular feature of the inhabitants of the Baile, which caused great puzzlement to both giants and Little People in the rest of the country, was the assertion of their moral and cultural superiority by means of what they called "humour". This humour was unknown elsewhere. When country people laughed, it was usually because of some accident, or the failure at some feat that is beyond the capacity of the individual attempting it. Such gut-shaking laughter was always either very close to – or indistinguishable from – tears and sorrow. All Baile Átha Cliath humour, however, depended not on some tragic mishap but simply on long sequences of words, spoken quickly, that ended in something called a "joke". Country giants were unable to understand these; not one Baile Átha Cliath joke ever made them laugh. It seemed that Baile giants went around all the time joking. They could not have a serious conversation, as everything had to be said in such a way as supposedly to make the listener laugh. If a joke failed, the joker felt sad and inadequate.

Little People humour was different, again, to all giant humour. When something humorous happened, they remained silent. Their laughter, when it occurred, was ironic rather than humorous. Their practical jokes were initiated not to get a laugh but to teach a lesson. They also had a "long term" sense of humour, suddenly seeing the funny side of something that took one, two, three, four hundred years, or even a thousand, to take place. Words, even when used constructively, were seen by them as divisive and at best necessary evils. How they could be employed in humour was beyond their understanding.

The Little People had a wonderful civilisation which they did not talk about at all. It was based on allowing every single individual to use his or her talents in any way that they thought fit. Negative strictures were few and far between. There was no such thing as eccentricity in Enchanted Land. It meant that the frustration level there was very low indeed, and it would take a very serious matter to make them lose their temper. The chief merit of their culture was that they were all allowed to indulge their whims. One important activity was the collection of all sorts of interesting objects, found or picked up over thousands of years, which they stored in their cellars and hiding places. They also had skills in metallurgy, woodwork, leather work, silk, fibrous materials from plants and the remains of dead animals – all of which produced the most wondrous, beautiful objects. The characteristic feature of these creations was their minute size. Each object was considered more beautiful the smaller it was – miniaturised (even by their standards) clocks, musical instruments, saddles, shoes, riding boots, hats, overcoats, hair combs, cooking and eating utensils – the list is endless. Their repertoire of song, poetry, short and tall tales and their skills of erudition were literally "out of this world". The more one looked into their civilisation the more wonderful and complex it became. It was as if reality was responding to imagination by creating the results and effects that one wished to see. Therefore there was no end, or limit to the things that they created. All of this civilisation, of course, was invisible to the giants.

Little People rule extended over nearly all the country (unlike the rule of the giants) and into all five dimensions. This rule was facilitated not by diktat, but by the carefree passing on of ideas, opinions, suggestions, praise or occasionally criticism by each and every individual to the next in line (so no personal offence or pride could be taken) and actions were put into effect by whoever happened to be on the spot. The punishment regime for recalcitrant or rebellious little folk was temporary banishment to "visibility", which had a one-hundred-per-cent effective non-re-offending rate.

Their official king (that venerable individual who had always claimed that he was the first to come into existence and everybody believed him) was seldom seen. He ruled by example, living an ordinary, common life amongst his people without their knowing of his presence. His greatest pride was his skill in hiding his real identity as he went about. *The queerest thing about their kingship was that any individual could become king for a time when the real king was away, unavailable, or just not around. It was thought that the position was, in fact, shared and passed around between different, unknown individuals at different times and places.*

Although they sometimes went hungry when there were shortages of vital foods and drinks – for they too depended on nature – this was never a time of sorrow but of increased pseudo-religious activity. They left it to the shamans to deal with all economic and social crises. These ensured that no discord or instability entered into society, by preaching that shortage times were not so much a curse, as a gift of the unknown god, a sign that they should busy themselves temporarily in some anti-social activity, such as helping a nearby giant in a practical way, forgoing co-operation with all mischievous powers – and thereby influence the course of nature.

Although the shamans had never found their god, they kept the Little People metaphysically content by teaching that their exile on earth would end one day; that having to share three dimensions with the giants was, in fact, some sort of training for another, greater task, far ahead of them.

One

OLD FARMER MURPHY was driving the cows home though the rushes of the lower wet field. He was making customary heavy work of this task. His old, heavy hobnail boots were sticking in the mud, whilst progress was further slowed by the weight of his rain-sodden, mud splattered "all-weather" overcoat. He pulled himself along with an unsteady motion, his red, gnarled hands wielding a blackthorn stick that threatened more to upend than steady him. The rain was falling heavily on his unprotected head, his long, white hair coming over his eyes and obscuring the view.

What irked him was that the cows were refusing to hold to the trail, making "breaks for it" and kicking their back legs up in the air. He swore for sure that he could hear laughter in their grunts and bellows.

He was beginning to lose patience. It was always at that same spot that they played up; and always at that same spot that he began cursing.

'Streepigs! Oinsigs! Get back! Get back in fecking line!'

He had been attempting, yet again, that seemingly never-to-be-successful task of making the cows walk a straight line to the shed for the evening milking. This waywardness was the one thing that really got him down. To call his beloved cows prostitutes and fools was out of character, and he would always be remorseful afterwards. On any other subject he was completely easygoing – indeed on most matters he couldn't care less. Animals, farm, life itself, nothing had ever troubled him much. Then, a few months ago – for no apparent reason – at that exact same spot he had suddenly felt a vague, troubling discontent. An unfamiliar, and uncharacteristic anger rose in him; and he had to take it out on someone or something! He decided, for a start, that it was about time that he asserted his mastery over his cows. They would no longer be allowed to wander this way and that way.

The contest of wills soon became a daily ritual, with the cows apparently no longer willing to obey any instructions whatsoever. Even milking time, normally an interlude of peaceful somnolence for man and beast, was proving increasingly problematical.

They *would* get it right, even if it was to be over his dead body!

It could not be that difficult after all. Wasn't there a clear pathway in the field, the result of years of continual walking by both man and beast along a line so straight and perfect – taking the shortest, easiest and most mathematically accurate route back to the yard – that it could be imagined that a genius had devised it?

(It would be some time later that Patsy would come to realise that the Little People were only trying to tell him something, through this "interference" with the cows.)

When he got to the yard he saw the young vet from town waiting for him. He had come about the TB. (Murphy had to be grateful for small mercies – the fellow was only nine hours late.) Instead of treating the cows he proceeded to counsel Patsy. The existence of that straight line was all in his head, the vet advised him.

Murphy swore and shouted at him, waving his fists and kicking the ground like an enraged bull so that the fellow fled out of the place even before the job was started, leaving the farmer standing there, weeping in rage and frustration.

The so-called "farmer's friend"! What use was all that education? If it was not for these government laws he would never allow him or his kind in the place at all. He did not know one end of a cow from the other!

Afterwards, the vet consulted with his boss over the alarming change that seemed to have come over the once easygoing Farmer

Murphy. He was advised that the only way to deal with such farmers when they became truculent was to hit them with an extra large bill. That would preoccupy their mind. He would then see a great change in the man's manners.

(This humiliation of the vet had been seen and enjoyed by the Little People. They had an inveterate hatred of vets over and above any other mortal or expert, for this type of specialist had run them out of more business than the rest of the scientific community put together. What was more, vets along with other various "experts" were turning up all over the place these days, even on the most insignificant, humblest of farms. Murphy had always been someone of immense interest to these hidden watchers, and they regularly observed his everyday activities.)

His house was of particular interest, for it was not his abode alone. It provided refuge for quite a number of different natural species – spiders, bats, mice, a rat or two. A frog dwelt beneath a kitchen flagstone. Patsy always warned visitors not to walk there. He did not know what he could do about the state of the floor. The damp was a great problem but he and his late departed old folks had lived with it, and it was certainly not worth spending money on. Cobwebs had grown in such profusion that they did not look like cobwebs anymore. They were like curtains of fine silk extending from corner to corner and room to room. Murphy used to blow his nose in them when he had a sup of drink taken. One room upstairs could not be entered so thick were the cobwebs. Every species of spider was in long-term residence in the house. The building was still as originally built, with a decaying thatch roof wherein rats resided. The thatch was good stuff and he would never change it. It was cheaper than those modern roofs. His water came from a hand-pump outside, and although a bit rusty it was at least fresh, natural water, not like the stuff they were putting in pipes these days. He had lots of places to go to the toilet although it was a bit of an awkwardness at night, having to deal with such things as buckets and cleaning up. To look at the old whitewashed house from the outside, you would say that the walls were giving in. But they were the best walls in the world for weren't they his own! Murphy was proud to be living in such a fine farmhouse when others down the road lived in those "modern" hovels that had no upstairs. After all, wasn't he from a respectable, long established farming family? He didn't just love his house. He respected it. Nobody was going to interfere with it, or with him. He had his pride.

Would he ever forget the day the government man came up the path to talk to him about a grant!

'What! The government want to give me money to do up my place? Money for nothing? They will just hand over the cash and not ask for it back, with extra? What sort of a fool do ye take me for?'

The council official tried to explain about agricultural improvement programmes – you heard about them on the wireless all the time – there was nothing underhand about it. Hadn't his own neighbours taken up their grants? He only had to ask them. They had lovely shiny sheds; some of them, an indoor toilet and taps. Electricity might not be far behind either. They would tell him.

'I have known your likes before you were ever born. It is not from being gullible that I am still the proud owner of Toberbeg farm. We know all about your kind around here. Be getting out of here now, before I lose me temper.'

Patsy was going to town the next day for tobacco. He had decided that whilst he was there he would mention the cow problem to the parish priest. He had always kept himself to himself as regards religious matters, leaving everything that was spiritually problematical to the good Lord – such as did his guardian angel really hear and see everything; were bad thoughts wrong; or was the beggar who came up the lane one day and gave him a long spiel on how to cheat the government, the church and the neighbours just a well-meaning sort of fellow or the devil?

He had had a bad night of it. He was accustomed to sleeping in his clothes, for a number of very good reasons, mainly for keeping warm and being always ready to go on an out-and-about during the night, should that be necessitated by a number of eventualities. This night he had tried to get out of his trousers as he had to get ready for the important visit the next day. It wasn't often that he called in on the priest. He was sure he had a best pair somewhere in the house.

Getting the trousers off was a lot more difficult task than he had imagined. It must have been the case that he had forgotten the technicalities. It was some time before he realised that he would have to take his jacket off first. The braces of his britches went over his shoulders and were catching in his sleeves. He knew that before he could take his jacket off he would have to undo the thick baler twine that was tied around his waist to hold everything up. This job proved next to impossible. He could cut it, but in a moment of sudden clarity, where consciousness goes blank and one scarcely seems to be thinking, or even alive, he made a wise judgement. He somehow knew that it would not be safe to go downstairs in the dark to find a knife to do the job. He struggled with the twine and managed to push it downwards, freeing his jacket to some extent. It should now clearly be an easy matter to remove his jacket, as it had no buttons, and he commenced doing so with a certain amount of bravado. Then he discovered that his jacket had a sort of inside jacket sewn on to it and he soon realised that there was no way that this piece of attire was going to come off easily. The whole thing was an impossible job and it was as he was balancing himself there pulling at his clothes that he fell over knocking the slop bucket, which fortunately contained *fual* and not *cacha*. He gave up the job with relief, and went to sleep in his clothes. The strange thing about this business (and it had not occurred to Patsy) was that he was accustomed to taking down his trousers at least once every day to obey the call of nature, and he had never had any problem with the task. It would seem that panic, now, had for some reason affected his thought processes.

So, disappointingly, it was in his everyday work clothes that he headed off to town. Father Murphy was in the presbytery garden doing the thing that all parish priests in the land had to do – pick up the odd bits and pieces left lying around on the parochial grounds (often the strangest things) by visitations from God knows who or what – without getting his hands dirty. Murphy, coming up from his first port of call, the tobacco shop, called out:

'It's Murphy saying hello to Murphy.'

The farmer was a shy man and he always opened even small talk by a circuitous, somewhat detached route. The spitting out of the tobacco juice that accompanied his greeting was pure bravado on his part.

'Anybody dying, or just plain sick?' said the other Murphy without looking up. He had the local man's way of talk here down to a fine art.

'Nobody sick yet, Father, that I know of, although of course there could well be. I want to talk to you about a serious problem of mine.'

'I expect it is a problem with the cows,' said Father Murphy, looking directly now at the farmer, who from the looks of him had not washed for many a long year. He recognised him at once as the man who always gave only one shilling a year to the collection.

(Murphy would later triumphantly point out to Father Murphy – after he had begun imbibing some of the book knowledge that the same priest had introduced him to, and which he had previously scorned as "education" – that this "twelve pence" was in fact a token of ancient authenticity, based on the Sumerian practice of duodecimal calculation and imbued with a long-since-lost religious meaning. And what importance was a shilling anyway to the Kingdom of God? Wasn't the church itself merely a holding operation, pending the return of the Lord?)

He could be forgiven his miserliness, thought the priest, for wasn't he just an old bachelor farmer who had had to stay put until his old folks died and he could inherit the few weedy acres he called a farm. He could be forgiven everything. Even his sins.

The thing that enraged him, he said to Father Murphy, as they both sat with a cup of tea in the parlour, the tears pouring down his face, was the fact that *he knew* that the cows walked that line perfectly straight when he wasn't there. He knew this for sure, for he had spent many an hour spying on them through the hedge. He knew for a fact that they were well aware of the existence of the line. It was always on rainy, miserable days when they knew he was in a bad mood that they made a point of playing up and running wild. He had worked that out long ago. They behaved like this always – and only – to annoy him.

The priest nodded his head, staying very quiet. After a long silence, he asked in a philosophical tone:

'Is somebody trying to tell you something?'

'Who?' asked Patsy, surprised.

'Somebody.'

'I don't know...'

'Or asking?'

Another silence.

'Come in here till I show you,' Father Murphy said eventually.

He led old Murphy, who had recovered his composure, into the library as a sheep is led to the slaughter.

'What is that?'

'My library. I am very proud of it. It took me fifty years to build up. Every book you would want to know about is there. In those books, Mr Murphy, is all the knowledge of the universe.'

'Begorrah, it's a fine sight.'

'Without those books mankind would not have got to where it is today.'

'That's a sure thing.'

'Have you ever read a book?'

Murphy thought a good while on this.

'I read a book at school when I was a young fellow. But nothing since.'

He said this with an audible sigh of relief. He could not be accused of any wrongdoing in that area.

'Books – good books – come to us from...God. It is said that they are all first written up there in Heaven. Then the Lord sends the book down to earth where some poverty-stricken scholar sitting alone in a tiny, sparse room somewhere puts it all down on paper, unbeknownst to his neighbours or friends. The writer is the tool of the Big Brain.'

'Could they help me with the cows?'

'God – the author of life – can. You have only to ask Him in a nice way and He will do it. But there is another way that might better suit a man like you. Do you see this book?'

'Yes.'

'This is the history of the great men who conquered and ruled vast areas of the known world and huge multitudes of unruly people. Rameses, Alexander, Caesar, Charlemagne, Akbar, Napoleon. Sure, what are we compared to them? It makes one know what humility is when one reads a proper book. So much! So many! Such bravery! Strength! Determination! Foresight! Most of us would not be fit to kiss the shoes of these great men. What is looking after some cows compared to commanding an army of fierce, blood-thirsty men, and to leaving your mark on history in glorious, golden letters in the skies? Imagine if you had to go out to your field and instead of having a docile herd of mute beasts to drive home, you had the awesome task of amassing, motivating and leading hundreds of thousands of disciplined, energetic, single-minded, ruthless warriors not to a simple cow shed but into a battle that they know will result only in their death – or at best painful, grievous injury? Try doing that with your cows with a blackthorn stick! As the great leader leads his men – leads and not drives as you would cows – and not along some level, grassy field but over endless tracks of wasteland, across treacherous gullies, down deep, awesome ravines, across fords in flooding rivers, ever-alert for ambush by men or wild beasts – would he wish for the peace of mind of a man leading his mild beasts sweetly home for milking? No! He prefers death and glory! So the next time you find you have to curse some dumb beast, think of the mighty effort of will, of oratory, of the needful, learned and emotive allusions to classical exemplars, the wise and uplifting sayings and irrefutable home truths with which a strong, bold, wise leader has to encourage his men in the thick of battle against overwhelming odds, so that they all feel the passion and zeal of the victor even as they face – not some snug cowshed – but defeat. Think, as you amble happily and carefree along, of how he has to haul each lustful, rapacious, avaricious, self-centred individual out of his selfishness so that, face aflame with zeal, personal survival is no more an issue and all that he has left behind, including family and kin, are not even a memory and all is sacrificed to the greater cause, the nature of which he may not even be fully aware.'

The priest paused to catch his breath.

'Begorrah,' said Patsy, much humbled.

'Take this book home with you and try to read a few chapters. Even a few pages will do you good. Ask a kind neighbour to read it to you if needs be. When you have read of what has been done in the world, come back to me and I will give you a book that has been written about none other than your good self!'

'About *me*?'

'Yes.'

'What book is that?'

'That would be telling you. First – you must read this book.'

It was only when he had left and was on the way home on his bicycle, happily chewing his tobacco, that he realised that the problem with the cows was not so much on his mind anymore. Instead he was thinking about all those great men, and how he himself might someday, too, rise to such greatness.

Whether it was the fact that he had on the carrier of his bike a paper bag with a huge book that told the story of all the great men of the world, who had done things that he had never even dreamt of doing, a book that would make him see, as things stood at the moment, his own very small place in the greater scheme of things; and the contradictory fact that there was a book in existence that had been written about *him* – and that one day he would get to read it – there was a noticeable change in Patsy Murphy at that moment. For the behaviour of the cows seemed a long way away now and it did not bother him at all. His head was buzzing with thoughts.

To those people he passed by on the road there was another, more radical difference in Patsy Murphy. The once consummate, extremely careful bicycle rider who took great care in keeping to the left and much pride in maintaining an unvarying distance from the margin, was wobbling all over the road. He was riding, as one gossip in town put it, like a drunkard.

It was this riding of the bicycle in an erratic manner all the way home that (for the second time this week) brought him to the attention of the little folk. Word went up to the higher echelons in Enchanted Land that the easy-going giant who inhabited one of the few remaining places in that region that still retained most of its blessings, was suddenly showing signs both of great promise and great peril.

A watcher was delegated to find out what was in the brown paper bag that Patsy had on his bicycle.

Father Murphy pulled heavily on his pipe and determinedly blew out the smoke like a man who knows what he's about.

'A pipe is like religion – smoky and very good for the mind,' he thought. He felt pleased that he had been able to help old Murphy. He always waited for them to come to him. Now he would set about the next step – finding a wife for the man.

He went over to the television set in the corner, muttering: 'I'll see what is going on with this new-fangled craze that's sweeping the country. Television! I suppose a thing like it had to come one day. It could be a force for good or ill. As long as it doesn't change our people, everything will be all right. Our people still believe in the One Thing. And always will.'

He turned the switch and eventually moving images appeared on the screen. Three cowboys on horseback were chasing and shooting at a band of a thousand fleeing Indians.

'Good old cowboys and Indians! There's no harm in that. Like all good fairy tales, they lift the spirit. It's only the factual, serious stuff that does the damage. Bishop de Bruin says that if the television ever gets down to dealing with real life – that is when the danger will come. But our men on the board are ready for any eventuality. Two years now the television has been in the country. Already I see changes in the young folk. They are doing more talking. That is good and it is bad.'

The Indians were all shot except for the one who appeared to be a friend of the cowboys and as the advertisements came on Father Murphy went into the library with an advertising ditty ringing in his ears of a never-fails-to-arrive bread van with the freshest loaves –

The world is in a state of chassis, and so is my butter crust van.

The library was the only room his housekeeper, Mrs Dunne, was not allowed to clean. He was inordinately fond of it, calling it his sin bin. He opened a locked cabinet and took out a Baby Power (a very small bottle of whiskey). He would never keep an ordinary sized bottle of whiskey in the parochial house, deeming such an item inappropriate for a parish priest. When he went back into the living room the six o'clock news had begun.

There had been great excitement in County Monaghan that day, the newsreader announced. Just outside Monaghan town a local man had sighted a leprechaun in the bushes. His cries brought others running to the scene, until the whole population of the town had converged on the spot. Everyone saw the leprechaun, which was sitting in a small bush across a river. Gardaí, soldiers, journalists, clergy, schoolteachers, children – they all clearly saw the little fellow.

Flash news from Cork city! With newsreel footage! Another leprechaun has been spotted by thousands of people along the quays. It has taken to the rooftops. A newshound attached to *The Cork Examiner* has hired a helicopter and this has taken to the air with the purpose of capturing the entity on film. The footage was now being examined and would soon be available to all of Radio Telefis Eireann's viewers. Another flash! The leprechaun appears on the film!

Father Murphy took in a long, deep intake of breath and held it for a very long time. Then he slowly exhaled with a loud, prolonged whistle.

He lowered his eyes and said a short, though forceful prayer that all the country – and especially the vulnerable therein – would be guided wisely by the kind hand of fate in the coming, challenging times. For he knew that such a "manifestation" was a sure sign of something wrong in the country. Then he rose up and finished the bottle in one gulp, for fortitude.

The last thing he always did at night, before retiring to his bedroom to say his prayers and thence sleep, was to lock the backdoor. This particular night (perhaps because of the third Baby Power) he had forgotten this job, and had fallen asleep rather more quickly than usual, *as no one straight line of thought would stay in his head and so enable him to say his prayers.* Instead, his head had become a jumble of mixed, irrational thoughts.

He was awoken suddenly by a loud knock on the backdoor that reverberated through the whole house.

Thank God Mrs Dunne is away, he thought as he made his way downstairs, for she is easily frightened by unusual or unexpected noises in the night. It was then that he discovered that he had not locked the door.

He opened it slowly and carefully. There was no one there, only the night air and the blackness of the town.

Father Murphy's mind was elsewhere next morning as he ate his hastily prepared breakfast of half-fried sausage, runny egg and fatty rasher. The poorly cooked fare did not give him even passing occasion to mourn Mrs Dunne's absence. She had gone to Galway to visit her daughter who had lately had to be taken into the Home for the Alcoholic Demented. It was a solid character reference from Father Murphy that had obtained for her one of the few vacancies there; another manifestation of the great, though covert power a humble parish priest could exercise not just here and there, but far and beyond.

So totally were his thoughts taken up by a new, disturbing realisation, however, he did not even finish his breakfast.

He knew, intuitively, that the worst sort of crisis, a spiritual crisis, was at hand.

He stopped chewing, spat some gristle on the floor, and held his head as one does when a severe headache strikes. But this was worse than a headache. It was spiritual anguish. He could scarcely put the dreaded thought that was coming to him into words.

There! He could see the words right in front of him. Even say them –

A challenge to the power of Mother Church.

And this would happen not on some foreign, infidel ground, but right here in her own territory!

The signs were all about. Even the Little People had been warning him, it seemed, leaving those cryptic messages around the presbytery grounds. Only yesterday he had intercepted a piece of paper blowing by. It was a faded page from an old newspaper and the only legible words were:

You won't regret it.

He had taken this to be a "thank you" for those Baby Power bottles that mysteriously disappeared occasionally from his large stockpile in the shed. They knew that he did not begrudge them; in fact he even secretly sympathised with the good folk. He had always wished them the best and gave them their due in the greater scheme of things.

But now he took those enigmatic words as possibly referring to something else – something of much greater import. The words seemed to be anticipating some decision – or deed – that he might shortly be responsible for. And other happenings, particularly the increasing number of petty, mainly harmless accidents that were plaguing him lately, and which he had put down to age – cutting himself at shaving; tripping up on the pathway; knocking over the vase of flowers in church; dropping valuable things but never breaking them – took on a new significance. He realised that these could be warnings to be more careful and wary as something momentous was afoot.

Some other "messages" that had come to him, he suspected now, signalled by their "jocular" nature the dawning perhaps of an era where respect for properly constituted authority, awe for the sacred, and contempt for the profane and downright malign would be no more. For instance, on more than one occasion recently he had found himself waking up suddenly in the middle of the night to the sound of his own laughter. He had tried to reprise the humorous material that caused such a peculiar happening, but to no avail. All he could remember was his own loud, guttural laughter. And something told him that perhaps it was no harm not to be able to remember. There was that period, as a young theological student up to the teeth in the books of Aristotle, Augustine and Aquinas when he had regularly awoken everybody in the dorm with his loud sleep-talk and strange, hollow guffaws. He had been informed by more than one of his peers that many of his uttered words had been risqué and at best, gibberish; and that he had better not let the Prefect hear him!

It came to him now that all sorts of little jokes, visual and verbal, were passing through his mind in recent times, especially when he was most relaxed – say after 'another' Baby Power – and particularly at night. He had put this down at first to "humours" – the effluence of the mind that affects every human being as he or she is dropping off to sleep, especially when little else is going on in the head and life and times are rather mundane. But some of these semi-conscious jokes were a little too ingenious for that simple explanation. Why would he see the bishop in jockey gear, for instance, riding the big winner at the races? Where was the sense in that? Or the Pope himself, engaged in a fistfight with some shabbily dressed opponent? Or even himself in church, lobbing handballs off the heads of the men, women and children of his own congregation? The weirdest one was himself in Duignan's pub telling farmyard jokes at the top of his voice, and the customers falling over themselves with laughter. The Little People were most likely putting these things into his head. Sometimes this was the only way they could communicate to people whatever it was they were trying to say, by distracting their minds from solemn business and affairs.

The fact that they were making their presence felt again might on its own be insignificant – a throwback to a more innocent, happier time when faith was the bread and butter of the populace. Normally such excitement would have been put down to some brouhaha over a local matter – the hysteria of a hot-blooded dispute between neighbours or close relatives; or a crisis in communal consciousness when some formerly respectable local bigshot is exposed in some sordid scandal. Such disgraces, insignificant though they may be on the national scale, could cause strange things to happen in people's psyches in remote, rural communities – and have reverberations even in the underworld.

However, something told him now that this thing that was afoot here must be on a larger scale; more than just local, national even, perhaps international.

He had better ring the bishop!

He stood up abruptly and went to the telephone. The operator put the call through (only after a long, friendly chat with Father Murphy with whom she was on most friendly terms, discussing the ins and outs of the trials of Mrs Dunne and her daughter and lots of other gossip).

The big man himself answered. Father Murphy could barely contain his excitement and agitation. The bishop must warn all his priests to be on the alert. And whilst being careful not to alarm the faithful, they should keep a close eye on church buildings, interior and exterior, the grounds, cemeteries and so on. He said that the bishop might, in particular, tell the clergy to keep a watch on their holy statues, for he had had a dream in which persons of unknown provenance were making fun of them, even to the point of desecration and blasphemy.

The bishop listened patiently. In reply, he admitted that he was detecting disturbing signs too, what with all this new, loose talk that seemed to revolve around Hollywood films.

Father Murphy interrupted to say that he was one step ahead of the Episcopal Palace. Whilst he congratulated the prelate on his esteemed wisdom, he was probably not aware that what was happening was due to *below-the-surface currents, bringing things never before experienced or dreamt of.* This was the meaning of the signs. These disturbing, subterranean movements were unsettling the customary sangfroid of not only ordinary folk, but even the little heathens of fairy land. God bless the mark! Hopefully, the little heathens weren't eavesdropping on the phone call. They too liked nothing better than to exploit just for fun the vulnerabilities of susceptible people, or to worsen human difficulties generally in a sort of philosophical fashion. But they were really little conservatives at heart. In a different, more constructive world, they could well be employed by the Church in the pursuit of its enemies.

No, instead, the powers of evil were on the loose. The old ways of combating them, through the execution of good deeds, would probably no longer be enough. Whatever good did it ever achieve anyway, continually exhorting the faithful to a plenitude of good deeds? Most people's idea of a charitable act was to character-assassinate their neighbour, or bring an opponent to court over some minor issue. In any case, the most marvellous, self-sacrificial of brave deeds would not be sufficient, but only mark the beginning of the battle. More complex methods would be needed. But he, himself, would begin the battle immediately with the tools of the exorcist: prayer, fasting and a good deed.

The bishop could hardly get a word in edgeways.

'That poor fellow Murphy is getting worse,' said the bishop to his right-hand man after the phone call; 'he has been talking to me about leprechauns and the end of the world. I was trying to reassure him that I had my finger on the moral pulse of the country and not to be worrying himself; that nothing could happen in the diocese without my saying so. When I was explaining to him that the real challenges were primarily to the virtue of chastity, and to the faith of the youth, he has been telling me to watch out for our statues! I think I had better have a word with that professor up in Maynooth, the one who is an expert in this new-fangled subject they call psychology – but which we old-fashioned codgers call the disturbed mind. You know – Canon Carey. I will see if he can arrange to have a bed put by for him at St Dymphna's, if the need should arise. The Baby Power has a lot to answer for.'

Where would he start in the matter of implementing a good deed? Father Murphy asked himself the following morning. With that poor Patsy Murphy.

Never was the good will of the clergy more in evidence than when helping members of a benighted flock to get to do what they should be doing; especially those things they thought they didn't want or need to do. For some time he had been mooting over the predicament of Eileen, Widow Rafferty's daughter. The poor girl was stuck with looking after her mother, left behind while all the young men went off to greener pastures. He believed now he had found her a husband. Why else would Patsy Murphy have come by his way yesterday, if there hadn't been something more important than cows the matter? It would be a marriage made in heaven, literally. He could kill two birds with one stone and execute his first special good deed. He would be on his bike and down to Bailebreoite straight after Mass.

It is a strange phenomenon that in such a community as Father Murphy's, where events and time seem to move exceedingly slowly, if at all – so that nothing much seems to change from one generation to the next – that regarding some vital matters things move faster than anywhere else in the world, faster than in the biggest, modern city, faster even than the speed of light.

The conversation at midday between the parish priest and a certain single lady who lived up a remote rural lane in a district called Bailebreoite, so named for the reputation its people had over the centuries for falling sick – was immediately common knowledge throughout the region by late afternoon.

Word went around that Patsy Murphy had entered the marriage stakes. Jealousies and rivalries of all sorts now came to the fore –

and a great, hectic air of sporting competition, ancient feuds and long-lived hatreds, forbidden loves and new, unexpected loves now appeared (or re-appeared) in a society that had been, for some time, quite socially moribund. Names spoken openly or indeed publicly, as well as the names or identities of various candidates either kept back, or mentioned/suggested only covertly or elusively were put forward, at the behest of those who could "best speak up for them" as suitable, even better candidates than anyone else imaginable for a marriage partnership with the good man, Patsy Murphy. Local derbies in football, hurling and handball, cross-roads chats, upcoming céilidhes or visits from famous showbands took second place to the fun and sport of hearing about the wish of Patsy Murphy to marry with prolonged discussions and louder, even aggressive debates about who would make him the best wife. The number of fights in the county increased. Schoolchildren upped their misbehaviour in school so that even the strictest master could not control them. Women fought openly in the streets, roads and lanes. Dogs and cats fought their own kind and each other. The crows and jackdaws would not stop squawking. There was also a huge increase in tears of joy and sorrow. People found themselves laughing, or crying loudly at this, that and the other thing for no good reason.

The best thing was that everybody – and that meant everybody in the county without exception (everybody that is, except of course Patsy Murphy – who up to this point was unaware of the controversies surrounding his person and quite oblivious to all the excitement) – had his or her own favourite candidate whom they knew for sure that Patsy had already chosen. For many the keeping of this lady's identity their personal secret was the greatest fun and boast of all. Never had there been such unity of purpose in the country, not since the days of the Black and Tans.

When Father Murphy's plan came to the attention of the Little People, alarm bells also rang in Enchanted Land. The simple one was about to be shanghaied by a woman and a priest! But they knew better than to start an all-out war. Determined, straightforward opposition meant certain failure. Human affairs were always outside their immediate or direct control. Their power was curiously limited; their ability substantially to affect events, people and the material world had a funny way of failing or turning sour just when it might seem that they were on a winning track!

This was the problem that for aeons Little People philosophers had worked on. It had got more difficult. In recent times they were studying a new quandary – the materialization of a strange dichotomy. Things that had once been similar realities in both fairy and mortal worlds and which still looked the same – now were changed into something new, alien and mutually incomprehensible. It affected even ordinary, simple things such as water, moonlight, a field of grass, a bucking bronco, a stubborn ass. These were no longer what they used to be. Water, for instance, turned out to be no longer the pure, magical stuff with which they had always felt at home (some of their compatriots, the water sprites, actually kept their homes down at the bottom of lakes or even under the sea, and even these were complaining) but a foul-smelling, bitter substance that was no longer palatable or useful.

What they had originally thought to be an adaptation of moonlight, lighting up habitations and even the darkest parts of the countryside, was discovered instead to be a strange, new energy field, utilising some unknown energy to produce light and heat out of nothing. They had no influence over this, and had learnt to be wary of it as it was known to frighten the life out of more than one of the sídh when it had sparked up and flashed and gave out flames when they had meddled with it.

And how many times these days had an inviting field of beautiful fresh grass, covered in daisies and buttercups, become overnight barren, desolate pavements of stone?

Bucking broncos – the giants called them horses – had all now been replaced by contraptions of a similar size but of a totally different constitution, made of metal, emitting foul fumes and a continuous roar and never ceasing in their galloping as they destroyed all that got in their way.

As for the dumb, stubborn jackass that was such a favourite of the mischievous sídh in particular, more often than not these days it was no longer a reliable beast of burden but had become instead an idle, wise-cracking know-it-all. He usually took human form now, though inevitably betraying his dumb ass origin by wearing clothing that looked totally incongruous as well as ill-fitting, with a silly cock hat on an over-sized head, covering elongated, pointed ears, a long face and a generally misshapen body. His real nature was always inevitably given away by his loud, raucous, braying laugh that would break out during conversations at unpredictable but regular moments.

Who was to know for sure what marriage, or other such important social events, now meant to these giants?

Despite these new limitations to their power and understanding, they would try to settle this matter between the priest, the farmer and the woman to their own satisfaction. If the worst came to the worst, they would find their own wife for Patsy. They already had someone in mind.

The Little People's favourite, however, didn't even live in the district. Their attention turned now towards a certain inhabitant of Baile Átha Cliath, Bridie Murphy, whose relatives lived close-by Patsy Murphy. She had always been a person of some interest (if only from a distance) to the fairy folk for reason of her eccentric, disgruntled nature. She was that sort of mortal who did not behave as other mortals did. Her values were determined not by accepted conventions, but by her own, irascible nature. Her very eccentricity and petulance, allied to Patsy's simplicity would guarantee a chaotic household to the liking of the Little People. Their idea soon became a determination that Bridie Murphy, and not anyone else, would become Farmer Murphy's wife.

Bridie had been taken up to live in the Baile as an infant by the disgraced Sheila Murphy (the shame of the unwed mother). Everyone in the district had heard much, however, about her exploits in the big smoke since then. Their exile only served to increase interest, casual gossip and curiosity back home. Indeed it increased over the years, as her case represented the only native scandal and source of deep notoriety and shame that they possessed. Her various relatives had all sorts of names for her, the favourite being little Miss Misery Guts. Thoroughly spoilt by the good times in Dubh Linn, she was. She didn't deserve her soft life. Not appreciating her good luck in living up there where there were opportunities galore – especially such as they did not have down here.

'How could she be so ungrateful, what with all the easy living and the comfortable circumstances that she is so lucky to enjoy?' said an uncle who had once visited her in the Corporation Buildings. And wasn't there a great view out over the whole city! You couldn't get that in the country unless you went up on the top of a very high mountain. If her poor, dear mother had only lived to see the luxurious circumstances her daughter was now enjoying! She was well-off in the city, and better off to stay there, for the girl had none of the good humour or ability to chat, sing and socialise that characterised country folk, qualities that were so necessary for survival in the countryside. She was an odd, city child, who could never live anywhere else.

'I said to her that it must be great to be able to go to the Gaiety Theatre and see all those famous actors and singers in the flesh. She said that she would never waste her money on the likes of that. *Gaels of Laughter* was on the wireless and she turned it off. She said she could never understand Jackeen jokes.'

(These were famous all over the land. Weren't they all used to trying to laugh at them when they heard them broadcast on the Jimmy O'Dea and Maureen Potter show. Even if they didn't understand them, they laughed because they knew they must have been funny as everybody in Dubh Linn was laughing.)

'No, she told me, she had never once laughed at a Jackeen joke, not even with false laughter. It is no wonder that the people up there think her a little mad.'

In her letters home (these were all read by everyone in the community, even before they reached their destination) she would say how much she hated her job. According to her relatives, she had a cushy number as a respectable servant, with a uniform, to a member of the rich nobility.

In reality, she was a skivvy for an impecunious shop-keeping family. She was forever saying in her letters how she wished she still lived in the countryside. How she could still retain memories of her birthplace was anybody's guess. Her only wish, she said, was to get out of the noisy, smelly kip of a slum that she had grown up in, where the only fresh smell was that from the Liffey at low tide in the early morning. There was no future for anyone in the city. How she would love to meet and marry some solid farmer down-country!

Because of these threats of imminent return, they were forever sending her messages (via travellers on the Dubh Linn bus) to for God's sake stay up there and never show your nose down here again. It would be bad luck for everyone.

The more sensitive little folk used to cry, mimicking the giant emotion when they recounted some of these conversations. Her dislike of Dubh Linn and her simple tastes had greatly warmed them to her.

How could they not compare her many admirable qualities with those of the other colleen "in the frame" – Eileen O'Rafferty? They knew her well, too, especially from the loose talk of her mother.

The first thing that other woman would do when she moved into the house would be to order Murphy about and make all sorts of improvements around the place. Eileen was someone who paid great attention to new ideas. She discussed men's affairs with much aplomb and worst of all, tuned in to domestic science, husbandry and even farmers' programmes on the new picture-information gadget that the giants now were becoming preoccupied with. That thing was worse even than the listening box, which had been disseminating harmful ideas all over the place for the last forty years. The people took it even more seriously than the sound box, and thought that once something was seen, said or done on it, it was the best thing in the world.

Eileen O'Raftery was also a great keen one for money matters. She had been clever enough to work out – her mother proudly boasted to every passing stranger as she stood on the lane outside the cottage – that you could easily con even the smartest bank manager by walking in cockily and saying you wanted some money to "improve the business". As long as you had property, such as a farm, to back up the brave words. The more money you asked for the more likely you were to get it. This money would then be used to improve the farm, drain the lower fields and level the hummocks. Eileen and her mother had many such schemes of personal, economic and social self-improvement up their sleeves. All that was wanting was for a "suitable" man to appear on the scene.

Such foolish talk and vain ambition had indeed taken up much of the very first conversation between Eileen and the parish priest, when he went to see her that day, in her little cottage by the stream that she shared with her mother.

Father Murphy had beamed with pleasure at the practical level-headedness of Miss O'Rafferty, and knew that he was wise in his choice of Murphy's wife.

The little folk usually approved of – or at least were neutral about – clerical influence in the giants' lives. Especially as it prevented the giants from meddling in the magical arts that were their own responsibility. This was why strict clerical control of, for instance, the reproductive activities of the giants was encouraged by the little folk. They well remembered the time when marriage and intermarriage was only too easy and loneliness amongst the giants was a rarity. Loneliness was such an important ingredient in allowing leeway to the Little People to get into things and places that would otherwise be off-limits. But at other times they fumed at this influence; in particular when the clergy came to organise or re-organise the everyday lives of individuals in whom the Little Folk had some vested interest.

Instead of responding, now, to this emergency by sending

important emissaries – or even whole hostings of mounted folk in full battle dress and chanting spells – the Little People decided to take the matter in hand coolly, slowly and with much careful consideration, trying as always to ensure that no one or no thing was physically harmed or practically disadvantaged in the process.

Their most radical action might be to call in the best watchers for advice. Instead of working on a grand scale, undermining or confronting whole groups and trying to untangle complex situations, they would concentrate instead on a single individual.

And the more unimportant, humble and insignificant this individual, the better the chance for their plans to work.

Two

SEAN MURPHY WAS a quiet, somewhat unsociable lad who these days kept himself to himself. To his relatives, school companions and mentors he was an unenthusiastic, even dull gasúr with something of the slibhín (sly fellow) about him. He had faded into the background of the social scene in recent times – lost in thought, seemingly oblivious or indifferent to all that was going on around him. So well did he exclude himself from most gatherings that eventually nobody even noticed his absence; or if he was physically present, his mental non-presence.

His uncle, Patsy Murphy, had certainly detected the change in him. From that young, enthusiastic lad who got up out of bed every Saturday morning no matter what the weather, and came down the lane to help with the milking, he had become the strange lad he was today.

On the rare occasions old Murphy met him now and had a few words, he got precious few words back. No enquiries about the cows or how things were about the place.

'Too much education. And he's heading to where there's more of it,' Patsy had muttered to himself.

Here was just another instance of the heavy hand of education causing nothing but trouble and sorrow in life. Why was it that something that should only be good and a blessing, something that they had all been brought up to value, especially as it was only available to the chosen few, should also be a curse?

He also felt sad that the lad had never – not once – mentioned the offer he had made, not so long ago:

'When my day is done, lad, and it may be sooner instead of later – the farm is yours. You would make a great cowman!'

The buachaill was on his way to take up the study of philosophy at the Coláiste Ollscoile, Dubh Linn, the highest institute of learning in the land. He had only chosen this subject because it was the one everyone had warned him against – with his teachers in particular attempting to persuade him against it and to take up a more "realistic", less controversial field of study. One that might be of some use to the nation and guarantee him what was certainly not guaranteed to most of his contemporaries – future employment and a role in forging the destiny of the nation.

He had finished his time of learning in the school in Dunmor with some relief, after many years of rigid school mastering by the Strong Men. These dedicated schoolteachers did not tolerate laziness, foolishness, weakness – or indeed any of the seven deadly sins. They put moral and physical prowess (so closely interrelated as to be almost identical) before academic knowledge. They believed in one thing only – the truth. Sean, however, had somehow developed not a desire for truth, nor a sense of firm moral purpose, but a strong penchant for doubting. He looked around him at the world and decided that he did not want to know the truth. Instead, fantasies and fairytales began to occupy his mind even, or especially, as he listened to the Strong Men propound. The more fantastic the tale or fancy his imagination brought up, or he heard or read about, the more did it successfully perform the healing task of driving away the truth.

Initially, his doubting had been simply about what others said. However – and unbeknownst to his school companions, family, Strong Men or clergy – he had already arrived at a state where he did not believe in anything at all.

(The Little People had already given him a title – Seanín, the Doubting giant.)

It seemed to him that all that fervent induction into the moral and physical certainties was in vain. For one thing, hadn't he already broken the highest, gravest moral taboo so highlighted by the Strong Men – "to think virtuously of oneself and others"? His mind, instead of being drawn to noble, virtuous, or positive thoughts was drawn towards the prevailing sordidness that, whatever the Strong Men's assurances to the contrary, seemed to constitute life. His body, supposedly that "most noble mechanism, imbued with a soul and privileged to be the abode of the divine" – preoccupied him now only for its grubby, unhygienic aspects, a squalor which seemed to constitute its most compelling features. His preoccupation was not with breathing the "fine air of heaven" (a favourite exhortation of the Strong Men) but in feeling, sensing and reflecting on the most unquestionably earthy, non-divine forms to be found on this downtrodden earth. Whenever he tried to imagine the much vaunted pains and joys of paradise, he could only visualise the baser delights of hell.

He had also failed to make the mark in those ordeals of strength imposed by the Strong Men such as football, hurling and athletics. Initially he had been good, though not very good, at running, jumping, chasing, dodging and hitting but soon, even here, his doubts began to interfere with his performance and he slid back to being a mere timeserver; and eventually a mere spectator. Finally, he was reduced to the shame of being one of those "not interested" in physical sports; not even in being a mere spectator. He became a non-participant.

Seán went into the fish and chip shop for what, he told himself, would be his last meal ever in Dunmor. The girl told him to take a seat and she would bring over the plate of chips and Coke. He sat down and looked out at the falling rain. So heavy and thick was the downfall and so poor the visibility, that he found himself doubting that the world existed at all – apart from the rain. The senses, after all, were all that he had for establishing what was there. And however much one depended on the senses – however acute were those five senses – there was still no way of knowing if what the senses perceived was real – or a dream.

He now even questioned his own reality. It seemed to him to be a reasonable possibility that in fact he did not exist.

'Yer chips an' Coke,' said the girl, hardly looking him.

He thought, from the detached way she was acting, that perhaps she, too, realised that he was not there at all; that maybe she thought that she was serving someone else; or that she had in fact not served anyone at all.

Maybe she did not exist. Nor the plate of chips that was before him.

And what did it matter anyway?

Wasn't he off out of the town and county for good on Monday?

As he stared out the window, he saw a gigantic black shadow coming down the street, blocking out even the gloomy rain. It was one of the Strong Men.

The one known as Finn McCumhail for his boastfulness and fighting spirit, and for claiming to be the leader of the vaunted band of warriors – the Fianna.

Suddenly the memory of his last game of hurling came back to him, bringing back again the gloom.

It might be considered as his last farewell and goodbye, having being quite a debacle. He had been having no luck in getting, holding or pucking the ball. It was like being in a race where everyone is passing you out. It was also the case, of course, that nobody was sending him the ball.

Finn McCumhail was giving him some verbal abuse from the side-line.

'I could beat a thousand of yez when I was yer age. I once hit a ball that went all the way to Dubh Linn and back. Aren't I famous for saving Erin back in the old days, when I sent the last Englishman packing? Who can stand up to me? Murphy – ya little tyke – ye shame me like no man of Erin could. Yer no man of Erin!'

Sean felt the blood run up to his face. At first it was shame – then anger.

'If they think I am useless, I will show them,' he muttered to himself.

He made a determined effort to get the ball. As he ran after the crowd of players and began to swipe hard at their legs with his camán, a remarkable change came over him. It began with a kind of hum that came out from every pore of his skin. The hum became a roar louder than a stormy sea and filled the world, so that all else was silence. His body increased in size, doubling, trebling, quadrupling. He trembled and whirled about inside of his skin. His frontal features became turned to the rear. One of his eyes withdrew back into his head; the other opened wider even than the width of his head. His jaws were bared to the ear. His lips were drawn back to the eye teeth and gullet. His hair, standing on end, was on fire – or was it blood that spurted from every bristle? His features had become unrecognisable even to his own team members. He did not know it, but he had entered into the warrior frenzy such as that Lug, Cuchulain and Rameses underwent when facing overwhelming odds. He commenced attacking everyone now, friend and foe alike, until not one person stood erect on the battlefield apart from himself.

Finn McCumhail entered the fray and took on the young warrior.

'Hold it there, young fella. Whoa! Whoa! A bit of spirit in ya, there? Well that counts for something. But ye are no match for the great Finn McCumhail.'

It was said to have been the first time ever. The first time a lad had been ordered by the Strong Men never to return to the sports field (though it was said that Finn had spoken in praise of the lad's "mad spirit"). To be barred forever from the game of hurling, and all Gaelic games generally.

He opened his eyes and saw that he was still sitting at the table in the fish and chip shop, waiting to start on his chips! Finn McCumhail, or at least the shadow of his gigantic frame, had gone. The memory of the effort of being Lug, Cuchulain, Rameses, had momentarily taken the strength out of him so that he could only breathe in short, quick bursts and his face was red and hot. It was with a laborious effort that he began to eat the now nearly cold chips.

As he gulped his food down the girl subjected him to long stares. A few moments before she had observed him staring out the window, as if his attention had been taken by some important matter. His face had become red and strangely contorted. His body seemed to be shaking or trembling.

His sort were nearly all like that – nervous types. He was one of those boys who had just finished the Leaving Certificate. He was off to greater things. The likes of him would become famous leaders, professors, explorers – that sort of thing. He had probably been thinking just then what he would accomplish in some exotic, faraway country. He would find himself in some savage land amongst the wild men. He would be teaching them the ways of civilisation. That is, if they did not kill him first. He would become famous and wealthy from the gold and treasure he would get there and would not even think back once of that poor place – that humble town – that little restaurant where he had been given a plate of properly cooked chips by a simple girl who had not had much of an education, who did not think such great thoughts or have any ambitions of her own, or had any chance of getting out of the place, unless she went to England. And it was a problem to get to England. You had to be sentenced to go there first by the courts for committing some serious offence. The likes of him would never give a thought to the likes of her – especially when he would only be thinking all those fine thoughts of brave deeds such as she could never herself be thinking or doing. What must it be like, she wondered, to have a great brain? She sighed, feeling envious at the thought of the great life that lay ahead for Sean.

He left his seat and walked out the door. The rain was still thundering down and he decided to head for the library to wait for it to stop. He saw Finn McCumhail walking towards him. He immediately turned to cross the street. With a bit of luck he hadn't been recognised.

'Cuchulain? Is it yerself that's in it? Come here, Cuchulain, till I give ya another beating!'

Sean pretended he had not heard. He did not look back.

He knew that he would only be remembered in Dunmor, by all his contemporaries, as the one who had made a great fool of himself on the sports field that day. He had indeed put the fright into his surprised peers by "going mad", but had come off second best in the end to the great Finn McCumhail. He turned around now – there was no sign of the big fellow. Deeming it safe, he entered the library. Just to make sure – he positioned himself at a reading table in the far corner with a view of the door. He then opened a book he had grabbed from a shelf.

He spent some time gazing at this unusual book – it was by an Irish author, but hadn't been banned. *Ancient Stories of Pagan Ireland*. His interest was held by the opening tale of incest, debauchery, treachery, duels to the death, massacres, decapitation with display of severed heads. It held his attention so that he did not feel the passing of time, and before he knew it the rain had more or less stopped. He closed the book, put it back on the shelf (not bothering to ensure that it was in its correct place) and went out the door under the eyes of the disapproving lady librarian. Yes, the rain had more or less stopped and it was time for the long walk home.

He heard a shout:

'It's the beardless boy wonder again. Come here till I have a chat with you!'

He decided the best thing to do was to move away fast. As fast as he could, for he knew that Finn McCumhail was very fast indeed. The whole town might be watching, but (he told himself) the day was not yet in it for him to display his own full power. If he showed his power now – here he was fantasising, as he had lately taken to doing in moments of stress – without the formal permission and blessing of the "gods" – it would be bad luck. The innocent too would definitely suffer for any pre-emptive use of his "hidden" powers. He could hear rapid footsteps behind him. He saw the shadow of the giant come over him (though it was a sunless day) and felt the breath of Erin's greatest warrior and heroic defender on his neck. It was a great temptation to turn around and face his foe head-to-head. That would be the easiest thing to do. Honour would be saved. But pride was never a weapon of Cuchulain's! Modesty and humility belong to the brave! Victory would be all the sweeter for being postponed!

To say that he could walk fast when he wanted to would be the greatest understatement ever made. He could walk faster in an emergency than the fastest athlete in the county could run! The speediest walk is faster than the fastest run for those who have the knack. It has its own way of conserving energy, to be re-channelled into the effort to escape. No waving of arms, blowing, panting and sweating that inevitably takes from the strength of the runner. Heroes never run – he reflected. They just take huge steps. The dignity of the fast walk away is greater even than the dignity of the mightiest warrior running to join battle.

But the taller, older Finn McCumhail had longer, more seasoned legs than the boy Cuchulain. To his immense surprise, the Strong Man appeared suddenly before him, as if he had alighted there from above.

'What's wrong with ye, lad? Aren't we pleased with the results of your testing. Yer mad deed on the field of play – yer fast walk that is quicker than a run – makes ye a worthy one. A skilful mind is greater by far and more pleasing than the brawn of the greatest strongman. A cunning way is more saving of bloodshed and for the establishment of peace than the brave acts of a great warrior. Ye are welcome to join us in the Fianna!'

The Fianna! He had never given them a thought before. The renowned Giant army who prided themselves on alertness to danger, ease of mobility and proficiency in battle. Wasn't the Fianna the proudest band of warriors in the world? Entry qualifications included – being able to defend oneself with only a shield and length of hazel rod – from within a hole in the ground up to the waist whilst nine warriors let fly with spears from ten furrows away. One had also to be not only a prime poet in the twelve books of bardic literature, but able to compose rhymes oneself – good, bad or indifferent, it didn't matter. Made up of members of different tribes, they travelled in bands around the country protecting land and people. Their system of watch guards and signals alerted them very quickly to a danger in any part of the country. Their average sword was three feet in length, the hilt comprising six inches of the total length. It was used to cut and hack rather than stab. If a Fianna spear penetrated, however, its withdrawal caused more damage and pain than the original infliction of injury. Greatly to be feared was this spear. Their armour was made of the toughest leather of hide of a cow not younger than three years. The Fianna was made up of three classes of giants – aristocratic, disinherited, outlaw; each under obligation to give a certain number of their days in service. In return they were granted free bed and board by their local chieftain. After a fixed period of service they could return to their normal duties. As well as defending the island from external enemies, such as the Formorians, ordinary peacekeeping duties were also under their jurisdiction. Indeed, law-making and keeping, very important in Giant culture, was very much part not only of their official duties but also their recreation.

'I...dunno, sir. I haven't thought about it.'

'It is a great honour to be asked. Terrible will be the harm that may befall ye if ye don't join after being asked.'

'I will think about it, sir. I have to go now, sir, and help me uncle with the milking.'

'The milking is it? Ye will be doing greater things than that. Ye can leave the milking to the farmer.'

Finn left him, happy in the knowledge that he had placed the young fellow under a *geas* – an unbreakable injunction or taboo – with regard to his joining his outfit. It was an old giant belief that if someone in authority asked you to do something you were, basically, obliged to do it or else pay some unspecified price or penalty. It was made doubly binding by the fact that the lad had told a lie when he had said that he had to go help his uncle (for wasn't every answer, excuse or explanation ever given to a Strong

Man either an elaborate concoction or a simple untruth?).

Already – even before he had set out on the road of life – even before he had read or heard the first word in that great new subject "philosophy" – Sean had become deeply immersed in the powerful, mysterious, hidden "currents" that lay beneath ordinary life. He was no longer a mere surface performer; nor was he a simple observer or accidental participant in hidden things. He was already starting to be a major player in the inexplicable – in things of immense import, sacred, even tabooed that underlie what appears to be ordinary, normal or tediously humdrum. He was already in the throes of the condition sometimes referred to as being "caught up in"; a state that at other times has been confused with – or deliberately associated with by the envious or ignorant – either the ecstasy of the mystic or the less salubrious condition of those who are said to be "barmy".

This feeling, that he was now under some mysterious obligation to an unnamed power or powers, made him feel disheartened as he went down the country road. He was entering into that worst of all doubter's fates – to become a double doubter – doubting his doubts. It was a sense of being out of his depth – of not knowing what was going on inside his own head – that made him decide to pay an impromptu visit to his uncle, Patsy Murphy. Perhaps he hoped to experience again the comforting sense of everyday, normal life, the sweet simplicity of the already past.

But it was too late for that. All was changed – he realised as he walked up the lane to the yard. He had no more interest in cows.

Eileen and her mother were busy at the table sorting out for sale the week's eggs from the hens that ranged over their one-acre garden, when they heard a noise at the little wooden entrance gate.

'By the saints it's...a priest!' Eileen had cried, looking out the window.

Her mother dashed over and exclaimed, 'It's the parish priest...!'

She fainted and fell on the floor.

She was still lying there as Eileen nervously opened the door and genuflected before the awesome presence, stuck for words.

'Don't you know me, Eileen? It's Father Murphy. I baptised you, gave you First Holy Communion. And I intend one day, not too far in the future, to see you married.'

'Oh yes, yes, Father. Oh, I'm sorry for the state of the house. I'm sorry for my poor dress and my general bad appearance.'

'Whist, woman. Hold your peace. Will you let me in? I have some good news for you.'

As he sat himself down at the table with Eileen flustering and fustering around him, he proceeded to give a short, well-tuned homily on the merits of the married life over that of the single state. Eileen listened attentively. She did not take in a single word. She only knew that she must agree with everything he said. After a while, he stopped the sermon and asked:

'What is that? For crying out loud! Is that your mother lying on the floor?'

'It was the shock of seeing you coming in the gate...'

They both helped Widow O'Rafferty to her feet. Father Murphy sat down again and the widow yelled, 'No! Not in *that* chair! Father must sit in the best chair!'

Eileen brought out from the bedroom a chair with a soft cushion. It had been obtained from the second-hand shop for the sole purpose of being employed – in the extremely unlikely event of one ever arising – on exactly such an occasion.

They looked at him and were filled with a holy fear of this man of the cloth. Seated there before them was all the power and mystery of the unknown. This being – he was not really an ordinary man – knew the secrets of life and death. He could read their hearts, their hidden thoughts, past and present. To say anything that he disagreed with; even to think contrarily to what he said; worst of all, even to consider for a split second arguing or contradicting him would be something that was not just bordering on madness, but was madness itself. Both women could not get themselves to really believe that this august presence was now gracing their own home! The parish priest was actually sitting there before them in their own best chair!

'Make your mother a cup of tea,' he said, 'look at how pale the poor woman is.'

'Don't you go making a cup of tea for me, Eileen,' said Widow O'Rafferty; 'surely it is more than a cup of tea that you'd be taking, Father. Eileen, bring Father a drop of something decent.'

'It is yourself that needs looking after', he said to Widow O'Rafferty as Eileen offered him a generous drop of poteen.

It would normally be a young curate that would have been sent to such a home – at least on any other business. They did not carry the aura, power or mystique of the parish priest and did not frighten the people so much. But this was too important a matter to leave for a casual chat in the street, or even a formal talk in the presbytery.

'I will get straight to the point. There is a decent, honest, single man, a solid farmer, who lives not too far from here in Rathcloon, whom you might even know or have heard of, by the name of Patsy Murphy. He needs a wife. Now, no offence meant, but the single condition is no state suitable for a good-looking, healthy woman like yourself, Eileen. It would be your duty, in the eyes of the Lord, to marry this Patsy Murphy, unless there was a good strong impediment against it. And I can guarantee you here right now that there isn't.'

'Ah, that is good news, Father,' said Widow O'Rafferty; 'it would be a heartbreak if there was an impediment against it.'

'That it would be. Now is there any good reason why Eileen here shouldn't be married to Mr Murphy?'

The priest was looking straight at Widow O'Rafferty, ignoring Eileen who, at this moment, didn't know what to think.

'None at all, at all.'

'Is that right, Eileen?'

Eileen had considered the proposal in the interval and decided that it was a great idea.

'That's right, Father.'

'And what does the good man Murphy think about it?' Widow O'Rafferty asked.

'I haven't raised the subject with him yet.'

'And when will you do that?' the widow asked.

'In time, Mrs O'Rafferty. In God's good time.'

Widow O'Rafferty, mother of the bride-to-be, a thin woman with dark hair and piercing eyes, was insistent:

'Well, Father Murphy, if you ask me...'

Her point was going to be that the sooner old Murphy learnt of his fate the less chance he had of escaping it.

Eileen intervened. 'Doesn't Father know what he is doing? Hasn't he fixed thousands of marriages over the years? He is fairy godmother to half the country. He knows it would be bad luck for me to see Mr Murphy before the wedding announcement. When will you tell him now, Father?'

'These things have their own momentum, Miss Eileen.'

Both the elder and younger O'Raffertys were now beginning to feel some increased excitement over the whole matter. The sight of Father Murphy enjoying his poteen seemed to lubricate the social atmosphere. He didn't seem half so daunting now as when he first appeared. The prospect of Eileen becoming a farmer's wife had already wrought a change in them. They wanted to know more immediately. They wanted things to get a move on, in case something untoward or unfortunate should intervene to upset arrangements.

Eileen, who had inherited the freckled face, brown hair and blue eyes of her many-years-since deceased father, allied to the single-mindedness of her mother (but not her dark looks), could not hide her own enthusiasm.

'That poor man probably doesn't have a head on his shoulders at all. From what I hear, some of those bachelor farmers are like children. He'll not know what hit him by the time I'm finished. He hasn't the faintest idea that he is probably sitting on a crock of gold. The first thing I will do after the wedding is make an appointment with the bank manager. I can see that house now, in my mind's eye, not as the hovel that my sixth sense tells me it is, but as a sparkling new house with a proper roof and new front door. A clean, modern kitchen with a brand-new, electric cooker! A telephone in the hallway! A washing room with sink and lovely taps. New carpets on every floor! A nice television in the spic and span sitting room…!'

Father Murphy, his large frame twisting uncomfortably in his seat which was a bit too small for him, tried to curtail her enthusiasm, putting her to the test:

'Hold your whist, girl. And how are you going to pay for all that? What do you know about farming anyway! It is a hard life, with little money in it. You've been brought up in a simple cottage, the daughter of a poor roadman who died from consumption long before his time. The only livestock you have ever looked after is that old dog there by the fireside, or the hens in the garden.'

'I am a farmer's daughter,' interjected Widow O'Rafferty, proudly. 'They would not be wanting of a bit of advice from me. I know all about cows, calving, the AI man! He will have the best of both worlds with me living there, too.'

Father Murphy looked around the cottage kitchen. The house was bare enough, though he had been in worse. Walls whose original plaster had never seen paint, stained dark brown now from sixty years of turf and wood smoke. A small dresser on whose shelves stood just three old, cracked blue plates facing outwards in a pathetic "proud display". An ash and birch-bristle broom in the corner by the fireplace, that had clearly seen long service in both inside and outside sweeping. A holy picture hanging lopsided from a loose nail on the wall. A dry holy water container on a nail just inside the door. The bottom of the door rotted away, allowing entry to rats, mice, cats, and small dogs on occasion. The window broken in the lower corner, with cardboard taped on to keep out the elements. The smell of the paraffin lamp everywhere. A large tin basin on the sideboard used for all the washing. A bedroom probably no better. The toilet, the little shed outside. If it was not for the small takings of Eileen from her cleaning job at a more substantial house in the neighbourhood they would be "for the poor house".

There was no possibility of the likes of them getting a grant from the government – or a loan from the bank! Suddenly, he found himself sympathising with Eileen's unashamedly material ambitions – her grasping at the chance of a better life. And with herself approaching thirty, time would be running out, too. He made a vow to himself – he would let nothing get in the way of this match!

He stood up and said the next thing was for him to go to Patsy Murphy bringing along with him the good news of the consent of the whole O'Rafferty family. Along with the undoubted blessing of the good Lord Himself on the arrangement. For if heaven did not look down in favour on the match there would surely have already been discovered some impediment to the marriage between Murphy and Eileen O'Rafferty.

He had never felt so fully in command of himself, so content in his calling and so sure of his wisdom than at that moment as he began to take his leave. He bowed gracefully to the widow as Eileen went on ahead to leave the "adults" to have a last few, private words.

'I have reached a grand old age myself. And if it is the last thing I do to see your Eileen settled down in a happy marriage, and yourself looked after in your old age as well, I will die a happy man.'

The widow gave him an intense look. The strangeness of this was that she looked deep into his eyes, whereas previously this was something that nobody – not even his own relatives – would ever have taken the liberty of doing.

'Ah, Mikey, ye'r not that old! Sure, you have a good few years left in you yet.'

She put her hand on his and held it there.

The shock of this went through Mikey Murphy.

For one thing, how did she know that his name was Mikey?

'Come back and have a drop with me soon,' she said in a voice now full of gaiety.

He laughed and said that he would. He continued laughing –

for no apparent reason. He felt extremely uneasy at the same time.

Then they both laughed together.

Was it mad the woman was? Was it mad he was himself?

He asked himself these questions as he struggled to keep a straight line on his bicycle on the way home.

His heart was thumping. All sorts of wayward, haphazard thoughts were coming to his mind. The wobbling became more severe. Before he could get his thoughts collected again he fell off the bike. He hit the side of the road, landing on his side quite hard.

Nothing like this had happened to him since he was a boy.

'Thank God nobody saw it,' he muttered as he lay on the ground. He looked around. There was nobody in sight.

Holy, holy, holy, Jimmy Maloney.

Now he wasn't sure if he had just thought, or said these words himself at that moment – or if he had heard them coming from some extraneous source.

'I feel quite…light-headed…bewitched,' he muttered as he got up off the ground. At the same time he wondered why he should ever even think such a thing.

Garda Fintan O'Hourigan was sitting at his paper-littered desk in the Rathcloon garda station. On a close examination these papers would reveal themselves to be nothing more interesting or sinister than the announcement of some local event in or around the village – the GAA match on Sunday, the Irish Countrywoman's Association meeting, another plea for flower planting on the outskirts of Rathcloon by Muintir na Tíre with a view to being allowed to enter the Tidy Towns Competition (a plea that had been turned down or ignored for the last five years), an educational talk in the local hall on breeding chinchillas as a lucrative source of income, organised by Macra na Tuatha.

O'Hourigan had begun writing up the annual report for the statistics department at Garda HQ.

Once again there was no change from the previous year:

Crimes committed

Murder = 0
Death under suspicious circumstances = 0
Death by own hand = 0
Robbery with violence = 0
Theft = 0
Fraud = 0
Assault minor = 0
Assault grievous = 0
Incidents of domestic violence = 0
Traffic offences (car, lorry, tractor etc) = 0
Traffic offences (bicycle) = 1
Malicious acts = 0
Crimes against the person such as acts of indecency (major) = 0
Similar (minor) = 0
Drunk & disorderly = 0
Disturbances of the peace = 0

He was wrong – there was *one* offence this year, though it was still waiting to go to court. That would be Patsy Murphy on his bicycle (no lights). Although it was daytime when he stopped him, Garda O'Hourigan was sure that he had committed an offence – i.e. that it was obligatory that a bicycle have lights front and back, in operational condition, even during the hours of daylight. However, he supposed only the judge would know for sure. Still, he would put it down as a crime. What did they think of him at HQ? That he was a great champion law-enforcer with the lowest crime rate in the country? Or the laziest guard around? There was no way of knowing. In the long hours of enforced inactivity he had been dreaming up lists of new crimes that he would be able to book and prosecute. He had written down a quota – something that he might present to the inspector the next time he came. It would show that he was indeed very much "crime-aware", whatever the signs to the contrary. That he hadn't been moved or promoted for over fifteen years meant that something was up.

List of new crimes for Rathcloon & Surroundings

Leaving gates open, loud shouting, singing & carrying on, kicking balls onto roads and other places frequented by the public, walking in the middle of the road, the braying of jackasses, pedestrians on the road in the middle of the night constituting a danger to passing traffic, weeds of whatever kind in fields, unsupervised dogs, cats & other mammals, failure to control the noise of crows in treetops adjacent to one's property, useless and senseless arguments, failing to keep vermin under control, failing to prevent smoke from fires entering adjacent premises, cow and horse dung anywhere except on one's own farm, fishing or hunting game on Major Moore's lands and river, talking loudly to oneself in a manner likely to cause alarm to others, slandering husband, wife, neighbour, church or state institutions, being found wearing unusual, inexplicable, or exotic materials or dress without a satisfactory explanation, poisoning of lands, water, animals or people leading to a strong supposition of malice aforethought, drinking hard liquor on the top of Foirnocht hill just before or just after midnight, non-genuine Wren Boys, the placing of spells or curses both for good & bad reasons on one's enemies real or imagined, acquiring the expertise of a well known wise woman for the purpose of placing such spells or for the execution of other deeds of that nature, the killing of livestock in a sacrificial manner, the holding of unauthorised religious services/ceremonies on Foirnocht hill, being conscripted into, or conscripting others, into local secret societies, being found in the possession of inappropriate materials or substances, specifically, skulls, bows & arrows, hand-made spears, masks, spades & shovels out of season, holding others against their will in a manner devised to create a sense of insecurity and subsequently sending out information liable to mislead relatives, friends and the security forces.

Garda O'Hourigan was proud of his list. He was enjoying the exercise. Other, worse crimes came to mind. He could think up the most atrocious of previously unheard-of crimes. But he had better not write them down! What would be the chance of getting his list into law? Well, banning all weeds was a definite starter.

At the moment, however, another grave matter had come up. In fact he was now involved in his first important investigation in many a long year. The previous night someone, or some bunch of hooligans, had pelted stones at the door, window and roof of the station. He had been reading a novel, had his legs up on the desk, a cigarette in his mouth and a glass of whiskey at his side. The immediate shock was great, so sunk was he into his book. When he fully realised what was happening, he crept carefully to the window and peeped out without revealing himself. He could see nobody. The stone throwing had stopped, so after the passage of a number of minutes he deemed it safe to check outside. Devil a sign of them there was when he went out.

Meanwhile, Michael Fitzgerald, top scholar of the year, had proudly accepted his invitation to join the Fianna. He prepared to undergo the ten entry requirements or "trials" with complete confidence that they would be a "walkover". His confidence in himself had always been his strongest point. When his parents handed him over at the gates of the castle and assured Finn McCumhail that Michael was no longer their son and that the Fianna could do whatever they liked with him, the first test was successfully completed. This meant that in the event of injury or death no claim for compensation would be laid by them against the Fianna.

'I promise ye, whatever harm he does when he is with us shall be no concern of yer's,' said Finn and thereupon the second test had been completed.

Michael was taken to a bare cell and Finn made a sort of supercilious gesture at the surroundings.

Michael knew that he had to say something in verse:

This room is not like the vain boasts of the Fianna,
In that it has more in it.
If this room was as full as it is empty,
It could not display the full array of the brave deeds of the
  Fianna.
I would wish to spend an eternity of lifetimes
In this bare room,
That would not be long enough to contemplate the wisdom of
  the Fianna.

Finn slapped him on the back and took him out of the room.

The fourth test took place in the afternoon. Michael defended himself successfully against nine warriors from his hole in the ground. It was the test that they nearly all pass, for its fame is such that they come well prepared for it.

Tests five to ten were of a kind, and took place in the woods. Michael's fair hair was woven into many braids and he was set at a run through the woods, while the ones seeking to wound him were sent after him, there having been just one forest bough between them at the start. If he was overtaken, or wounded, he was not to be allowed entry to the Fianna.

He was not overtaken or wounded.

If his weapons quivered in his hand, he was not taken in the Fianna. His weapons did not quiver.

If he cracked a dry stick under his foot as he ran, he was not taken. He did not crack any stick whatsoever.

He also had at full speed to jump a branch level with his chest and stoop under one level with his knee without breaking stride, or else he was not taken. He did all this with the ease of a skilled, seasoned warrior.

He had to extract a thorn from his foot without pausing in his stride, or else he was not accepted. This he did with a smile on his face.

He returned triumphantly and expectantly to Finn.

Finn looked at his hair. One small part of his hair above his right ear was disturbed out of its braiding, which had occurred when he had smiled.

Finn took Michael to the gate of the castle and booted him out with a kick to the backside.

'Next,' he shouted.

In came a small, thin wisp of a fella, already going slightly grey, Liam Lawler, known as Caoilte, son of Ronan, who proceeded to insult Finn to his face:

'Ya long piece of sheep's cacha – get out of my way before I hit ya so hard ya won't even remember it.'

Finn laughed and shouted at the top of his voice:

'Ha ha ha! You'll do! There's no need for *ye* to do those useless tests.'

He took the wiry fellow into the main building and led him to a glass display cabinet.

'Ya see that hurley in there? It's the champion of all Erin. And it's mine. There is a saying in the Fianna – that if Finn's hurley stick is ever captured or broken, that will be the end of the Fianna. And the end of Erin.'

''Tis a fine camán, sir,' said Liam; 'but there is one better in Erin than that one. It is my camán.'

'One day we will have a trial of strength,' said Finn;

'There is one thing I want to ask ye. That Sean Murphy, who was in your class. Do ye know him well?'

'A bit. He was from the country. They aren't as civilised as us. He seldom spoke. Give us Dunmor boys a topic – we can give a spiel on it till the sun goes down. The country goms – Sean lived five miles out – are always dead quiet. They look as if they are asleep most of the time. Or else they roll their eyes and look up at the sky as if something is going to fall out of it. When they open their mouths, they talk strange. And they wouldn't know a settee from a donkey's arse.'

'I want you to write to him. Tell him all the great things that go on in the Fianna. He should be back here.'

'I don't know about that. I have heard it said, I hope I am not committing a calumny on him – that Sean Murphy does not believe in God. He is an…atheist.'

'No, Liam. He is better than that. He is something neither you or I are yet. A state that we should all aim for. Only the saints achieve it in their own lifetime, at the end of their days, when they detach themselves from everything in this world. Sean is there already – he doesn't give a shit.'

'What is he doing now?'

'He's off gallivanting to Dubh Linn. No doubt he will do the round of the pubs. No harm in that. If he meets up with a mot though – that could be the end of him becoming a Fianna warrior. However, he is under a *geas*. He will not be allowed to forget that. Be a true Fianna and write to him as soon as he gets up there. The Lord knows he will need a friend.'

'As my first official duty, I will write to him, Finn. I will bring him back here where he belongs, to defend Erin from friend and foe alike.'

'That's the way.'

(The name Caoilte would become immortal in later times when the Árd Rí, concerned by the Fianna's increasing rebelliousness and arrogance, came to imprison Finn in an attempt to dilute the band's power. It is the archetypal story of how Caoilte obtained a royal reprieve for Finn and the Fianna only after eschewing violence – his campaign had laid waste to the whole country – and taking up once again those ascetic, disciplined exercises of humility, obedience and poverty that had imbued inner strength and discipline into the Fianna in the early days.

In this case, after debasing himself in front of the king by wearing humble, gloomy, colourless clothes he had undergone the standard penitential exercise of doing the rounds of every lake, mountain, valley, plain, seashore, wood, bog, tree, bush and river in Ireland in order to bring back, for the Árd Rí's inspection, a bribe of as much gold, silver and copper that could be found on land, water and air. This difficult task was made all the more demanding of

Caoilte's resolve and moral fibre when he had to refrain from showing hurt or disappointment as the High King more or less ignored his achievement, ordering the loot hidden away where no one could ever trace it – without so much as even looking at it, appearing greatly unimpressed and ungrateful.)

Sean was delighted to be leaving. His parents and sister came to see him off at the Dunmor bus stop. There were tears in his mother's eyes. She was, as usual whenever a difficult or challenging situation arose, speechless.

The grip of his father's hand was as tight as a vice. No matter how hard Sean pulled, he could not release his hand.

His sister giggled continuously.

He was made to promise that he would wave out the window at them, until they were gone from sight. After much muttering, he agreed to do this.

He saw them waving. He gave them the benefit of the doubt with one small wave just before the bus turned the corner. He then settled down in his seat to prepare for what would certainly be the happiest journey of his life. He was leaving behind forever the Strong Men, all that laborious work on Patsy's farm, all that having to assure people that you heard and understood what they said to you, or that you agreed with their views, their beliefs, prejudices, their dreams even. And of course that puzzling entity called a family as well.

At the back of his mind, fending off the expected happiness, was a niggling doubt – for the bus might break down, leaving him stranded on the outskirts of some bleak, minor town or remote, forsaken spot.

As the bus went along the road that ran behind Rathcloon a leprechaun (a solitary fairy) seated on top of Foirnocht Hill was attempting to mimic a giant "emotion". He first tried laughing. Then crying. He then got the two sounds mixed up so he didn't know which was which. He decided he would try for the one that he imagined would describe what the giants call "grief". He cried out *ho, ho, ho!* It sounded to him like laughter. So he tried *hoo, hoo, hoo!* That sounded more in keeping with the noise giants made when they were in the throes of what they called "sadness".

Hoo, hoo, huuuu!

He knew that they also liked to "relate" their sorrows. This was easier –

Desolation in the land. Huuuuu! A curse has been on us since the time of Dermot McMorrough. Huuuuu. We were doing all right till then. Didn't Brian get rid of the Danes? And then came the time of unbelief. Huuuuuuu!

The little individual was crying to himself as he sat on Foirnocht Hill, watching Sean's bus passing down the road on its way to Baile Átha Cliath.

Sean, along with many more of the flesh-and-blood of the country, was leaving, their suitcases stacked tightly at the back of the vehicle. Sean himself was, in the scale of things, quite well-off with a "postal check" from Uncle Sean in America tucked away inside his jacket. Many of the others with him were even more fortunate – for they were heading further away – to foreign lands – where they said the streets were paved with gold.

The leprechaun had given up counting how many of the young and not-so-young giants had left over the years. It made for lonely times for chaps like himself, who depended for company more on mortal folk than his own kind. His little frame shook, his tears and cries increased as the bus went further and further away. Blades of grass, white, yellow and blue flowers, nettles, thistles and the wind itself bent and swayed with his crying. The bees, flies, horse flies and midges were unable to land, scurrying away in all directions. His cries engulfed his entire body, causing him to bend double, to sway sideways, to lean backwards so that he saw only the empty sky. It was all that he could do to stop himself falling over. His crying became a wild screeching. The birds around took notice. A lark descended. A swallow came sweeping unusually low. Crows, jackdaws, magpies came squawking and fluttering by, perching on treetops and field gates to see who or what was causing the disturbance. A fox appeared on the rim of the hill – saw the leprechaun – and turned immediately to go on about its business. A hare came next, stood on its hind legs, rubbed its fists and twitched its nostrils. It too, after a quick glance, swiftly went away about its business. Like the fox, it knew not to interfere in little folks' affairs. They were only too well aware that they were liable to be shanghaied into doing all manner of menial jobs – into slavery – if they were not careful.

As the bus disappeared around the corner the tiny creature's cries reached a crescendo, blowing up a whirlwind, carrying bits and pieces of loose vegetation, fluff balls and detritus into the air. The convulsing sobs eventually became fewer, turned into short, rapid intakes of breath and more subdued groans. The little fellow then became silent.

He congratulated himself for having, he believed, at least to a small extent, successfully experienced a mortal emotion.

It was just before the bus went around the corner that Sean felt his attention drawn to the hill. The excitement of departure had gone and he felt somewhat despondent. His attention became focussed on Foirnocht (Bare) Hill. The unremarkable landscape feature had been a part of his childhood. Many were the times he had run up it to view the surrounding area. People had always joked about it, wishing that it had been a real mountain, or at least had the height of a decent hill! Yet this very lack of noteworthiness caused an unfamiliar emotion in him now.

There! He was sure he had heard his name being called. He heard it again –

Doubting Sean! Doubting Sean!

Even as the hill disappeared from view he was hearing a soft music from out of nowhere whose beauty gave him a strange joy. Yet he was so tired now that he was already asleep, even though it was still only early morning and the journey barely begun. He dreamed vividly, of multitudes of Little People in green jackets and red corduroy britches dancing merrily in circles to fiddle and flute tunes, his good self in the middle of it all. Uncharacteristically, he found himself enjoying being at the centre of a crowd, dancing like the best of them. It was obviously some great occasion! There must have been hundreds, perhaps thousands there.

And the reason for his being the centre of attention was, it appeared, his ability to dance athletically, with boundless energy and consummate skill.

He never knew he had it in him!

He was also singing an unknown song. Better than any professional artist! And he had always been a poor singer!

The fact that the song he sang now was completely unknown to him only added to the fun. The words just flowed, the meaning irrelevant.

A tiny fellow came up to him who, from his ornamented attire and dancing eyes was no doubt a member of the minstrel caste – and handed him a fiddle. Sean played like a maestro. After a few hours he changed over to the flute. It danced in his hands.

He experienced what could best be described as a great "transfer" of emotion, thought and sense of secret purpose between himself and these noisy, dancing diminutive figures. Neither he nor the other musicians and dancers ever got tired. Instead, the jumping and music were increasing both in speed and intensity as the hours went by.

When he woke up he discovered to his surprise that he was no longer in the bus but lying on a bed in an unfamiliar, room with a small gas stove in the corner, next to a sink. It had dull brown wallpaper with faded red flowers and showed every sign of having being inhabited for some time; unwashed cups, plates and cutlery, clothes that he recognised as his own thrown carelessly over a chair, the after-smell of a fry-up. His suitcase was on top of a clothes cupboard. There were books that he did not recognise on the floor. To his even greater surprise, right at the side of the bed on a chair was a cup emitting the vapours of piping hot tea! Outside was the sound of heavy traffic, the siren of an ambulance rushing injured, dying or mother-to-be to hospital, the bells of a speeding Garda squad car, the whoom and whaam of traffic echoing in a world of concrete and metal.

His breathing stopped for a moment. His heart was beating fast. Perspiration was on his forehead and his hands trembled. For some reason, he felt disorientated.

Three

AS THE INEXPLICABLE unease gradually subsided, he raised himself up and sat on the edge of the bed, stretched his arms and scratched his hair. By the looks of all the books, he was already well advanced into his studies, although he had difficulty recalling now anything in philosophy, ethics or moral theology – words that appeared in the titles of the books on the floor. He took the cup of tea into his hands and sipped it. It was still hot.

He seemed to remember something about a shop. Yes, there was a shop downstairs, and he owed the shopkeeper lady some money. He remembered now. She declined to talk to him anymore, unless it was absolutely necessary. The ultimatum concerning the rent had come via the house help, Bridie Murphy.

Bridie had appeared to have taken a great shine to him, as she came from the same part of the country. She treated him almost as a long-lost brother, and it was she who had found him this accommodation. However, she had to be careful that she wasn't seen to be "familiar" with him, as it would surely cost her her job. Mrs Byrne was always keeping an eye on the morals of others, especially of those who were socially inferior. And especially the morals of Bridie Murphy.

The girl from Corporation Buildings was not the slightest bit grateful for all that she and her family had done for her, providing her with a good job and a sandwich every day. Of course, she never moaned, but you could see the defiance in her eyes. What else would you expect – coming from those flats? And it was on her recommendation that they had provided board and lodging for that fellow from her own place down the country!

What a queer lad he was! He never, ever, finished the healthy breakfast of fat-fried bacon, sausage and egg she sent up every morning. He left so much over she always had to send it back up to him again the next day.

He was supposed to be a student. Yet he kept very unusual hours. She could hear him creaking up and down the stairs nearly every night, long after he should have been fast asleep in bed. It seemed, also, that he could spend many a whole night in his room just walking about. And then there was the matter of his spiritual duties. Only yesterday it had been enforced upon her once again to talk to him about this matter.

'Did you, or did you not, go to Mass this morning?'

'Of course I did, Missus.'

'Well, I didn't hear you go out.'

'I go about very quietly.'

It was obvious that he was slacking in the matter of religion. She warned him that his "soul" was in danger.

'And don't be talking to that Bridie Murphy! We don't want tongues wagging. She goes up there to collect the plates and tidy up, not to be wasting time chatting. Did you ever meet Father McDoon?'

'Oh yes,' he said, another fib being called for; 'I have indeed. A very nice man.'

'Well, you can meet him again this Thursday. He is coming here to see you.'

Sean thought now that Bridie must have made the cup of tea. That was strange because today – Monday, it was, he reckoned – was her day off. Slowly, very slowly, things were coming back to him. He knew that he should possibly be somewhere else now, or at least on his way there. He would ask the missus. He put his head out the door and shouted:

'Missus! What day is it now?'

Mrs Byrne, at the bottom of the stairs, shook her head in exasperation. Once again she found herself having to advise the annoying fellow.

'Monday. You should be off to your classes at Elfsfort Terrace.'

'Thanks very much.'

'And while I'm at it, you just remember what I said – and do not be chatting with Miss Murphy.'

Sean tried hard to remember where the university was as he walked up Rathmines. He was heading along a route whose landmarks he vaguely recognised. In this way he was able to tell himself that he was going in the right direction, which in fact he was, into Harcourt Street and thence a short cut through the buildings where they hacked up the dead bodies. He spent a few moments looking in at the human remains in the anatomy department. It was all coming to him in a rush now and he went through familiar doors to find himself in a concourse full of students. It felt right. He looked again at the notes he had made on foolscap paper and saw there "Prof. Smith (Room U12) – rough notes". He looked up at the wall clock and saw that it was one p.m. He could ask somebody.

'Hello, if it isn't the philosopher.'

He didn't recognise the voice, or even the face that appeared before him.

The Dubh Linn natives, Dennis and his friend Thomas, were sniggering over some private joke.

'I was wondering if I should be in a class now. Is there a lecture by a Professor Smith in Room U12, would you happen to know?'

'The morning lectures are all finished. Why is a fellow like yourself bothering with that subject? Only Dubh Linn people, or the clergy and intelligent classes should be doing that sort of stuff,' said Thomas.

Sean had been slowly coming to the strange belief that when he was talking to people they were not really there. He was discoursing with what were figments of his imagination. Therefore, he proceeded now with a certain careful carelessness, as if he was talking to himself.

'I don't know why. I'm only doing it because everyone was against it. Nobody where I come from had ever even heard of it before. Maybe that is the reason why! I don't see any point in studying anything practical or useful for a career, for that would be believing – and accepting – that there is a reason for anything, or a point to something. I want to do a meaningless subject – and obtain a useless qualification. That is the way I can best keep my sanity.'

'That's absurd,' said Dennis.

'Two absurdities doth common sense make,' replied Sean, remembering a similar quotation by a great philosopher he had come across either in a book, or in his dreams.

Dennis gave Thomas a knowing look, gesturing that in this instance there was a "screw loose" somewhere.

'I'll lay odds of two hundred to one against him passing the first exams,' he said to Thomas after Sean had departed with a quizzical look on his face looking for the way out.

Michael Fitzgerald was soon to become the young whiz kid about town. Rejection from the Fianna had only given him a greater determination to prove himself. In no time he was expanding his business interests. Business affairs would be the main route to success, but politics would also be employed. He would become the wealthiest, and then the most powerful man in the county – and then in the country. He would show them – though he knew deep down that no worldly success could ever compensate for not having been taken into the Fianna.

His first investment was a new suit. His second was a moustache. His third was a second-hand, former undertaker's saloon car. He took over his father's occasional auctioneering business and gave it a new name: *Michael Fitzgerald and Partners*. His main partner, his father, a many-times bankrupted builder, provided the reassurance that only the sight of a well-dressed, stout, cigar-smoking mature businessman can provide, whilst Michael became the leading edge of the business, espousing smart commercial ideas by means of shamelessly optimistic or pessimistic (as the case warranted) forecasts of the Erin of the future. This land would either be a desert abandoned by all, where nothing was worth a farthing (if his client was selling something), or a land of such fantastic wealth that people would not only not be emigrating from it, but would actually be flocking in from the corners of the earth to partake of its new, incredible wealth (if his client was someone he wished to borrow money from).

A half-share in the yearling "Fast Lad", by Thor-out-of-Maeve, both renowned more for their names than their abilities, neither having achieved anything better than runner-up in moderate races, was his fourth investment. This was in lieu of fees for auctioning off heirlooms of the cash-strapped Major Moore, a prominent member of the poor-gentry class. It was a brilliant turn for Michael to advertise his business as *the only auctioneering firm in Ireland which charges no fee*. He would just go around and select some useless, ancient object that the owners were simply delighted to see the back of. Business came flooding in; so much that within a year he was hiring an experienced employee of one of Cork's biggest auctioneering concerns to take over and do all the running for him. He was now able to concentrate on furthering his "empire".

As he awaited the day of Fast Lad's first racecourse appearance (he was with a well known local trainer, who had agreed to waive a year's training and boarding fees for Michael's promised year's supply of fresh hay), he went around looking for fields to rent, preferably on the outskirts of towns along the main roads. These were surprisingly easily available in quite large acreages at low rent. The farmers could not believe that they were being given money for nothing. Within a year or two, with the money he would be making from selling hay to stables all over the country, Michael would be able to offer these same farmers previously undreamt of sums just to take the fields off their hands. He intended to hold on to all the land possible with a view to the date when they might bring him in a few quid in that – still imaginary – time when land might be worth a bob or two. The persistence of this delusion of a wealthy Erin of the future some put down to a harmless mental eccentricity which, considering the faults of other great men of the world, should be no bar on the lad's climbing to the top of the ladder of success. The Established Party (Cumann Na Naofa) were already asking him to stand in the next election as their – and the country's – youngest TD.

Everything was going amazingly well for Michael – and he still only at the onset of adulthood! It was almost as if a blessing had been bestowed on him for having spent even that brief time with the Fianna.

Somehow or other the press had got wind of the fantastic performances of Fast Lad on the gallops. The rumour was going around that he was the fastest thing ever seen, not only in Paddy Fox's stables (admittedly a minor player in the racing world) but ever, anywhere. Controversy started when the local press had turned up for a photo. The journalist/photographer was given a good beating and his camera film was destroyed in front of him. The case went to court, where Paddy Fox made a "speech from the dock" defending all and any methods necessary to defend from all those that would wish to destroy that rare thing – a one-in-a-million racehorse. "Every man of Erin is beholden to a good horse…" His speech earned him applause from the big crowd in the public gallery. The national press took an interest. It was rumoured that some businessmen in America and the Near East had made "tentative bids" of staggering amounts for the as yet un-raced, untested two year old. The owner (identity unknown) was holding firm – for the honour of the country. It would race as an *Irish* horse. And it would stand at stud in Ireland. Already, the papers said, stud bookings were being lined up.

Fast Lad was never to race. Unfortunately, he sustained a serious injury when he was galloping at a speed believed to have been unsafe even for a brilliant racehorse. He went straight to stud – the new stud farm of Michael Fitzgerald who, in an act of great patriotism, was turning down all foreign bookings and accepting only Irish mares, at least for the first season.

The brochure claimed that just by having Fast Lad in a horse's pedigree was enough to quadruple its value.

And the biggest surprise of all – an almost unbelievably generous gesture – the fee for any Irish mare's first booking would be held way below that of established Derby winners currently at stud – a meagre £500, no foal, no fee.

When he eventually addressed the selection meeting of the local Cumann Na Naofa, Michael gave a speech explaining that the one blot on his record – his rejection by the Fianna – was due not to his having failed the Fianna initiation tests, but because he had shown off whilst successfully performing them. This, he said to great applause, had taught him the most important lesson in life – the need for humility, an essential attribute in any politician.

Father Murphy had been standing outside Patsy Murphy's door for at least half an hour. He had knocked and shouted and the dog inside had been creating a racket – but there was no sign of Mr Murphy. He knew that he was in there because he could hear him moving about.

'Are you in, Mr Murphy? It's the parish priest,' he shouted for the umpteenth time.

He waited another ten minutes. He was walking back to his bicycle at the entrance gate when he heard the door open. The farmer was gesturing to him to come in.

'It's a great honour,' were Patsy's words to the priest as he led him to the low stool beside the fire, the sheepdog snapping at his leg and biting him, though its teeth did not penetrate the flesh. For some reason (most likely he was merely oblivious to the dog's antics) Patsy made no attempt to restrain the animal. It was now sitting on its haunches, baring its teeth at the priest and growling.

'Have you ever,' asked the clergyman, 'thought about getting married?'

'That is a thought that does be on my mind from time to time. But I usually give it short shrift.'

The dog gave a loud howl whenever the priest spoke, and went dead quiet whenever his master spoke. Father Murphy did not know if it was his imagination, but it was as if the animal was trying to stop him from having his say.

'Maybe you give it too short a shrift!'

He had to shout these words to make himself heard.

'Is the shilling a year I give all right, Father? Is that what you have come about? Do you know I read in that book you lent me how the ancient Sumerians did everything in twelves. Twelve pence in a shilling, twelve months in a year and so on. Not to mention the twelve apostles!'

'Begob, you have learnt a lot in a few weeks.'

'You'd be surprised what I understand now, Father. Did you know that the French Revolution was supported by the lower clergy? And opposed by the bishops. Now that is a quare one. It wouldn't happen here in Erin, would it?'

'What are you saying, man? That is not what you read books for! You read books in order to learn to read properly, and then go on to read devotional works that provide uplift and help on the way to the eternal life. The French Revolution, I ask you!'

'I'm making it my business to get more books. I am writing off to Dublin for them. The town library is next to useless.'

'And what sort of books would they be, Patsy?'

'Political books. History. Social sciences. Factual stuff.'

'Patsy, you told me that you never learnt to read at school.'

'I couldn't believe it, Father. When I opened that book you lent me I could read and understand every word!'

'Look. I will give you a list of recommended books. In fact, I will give you some extra decent books for free. Don't be bothering sending off to Dublin. Now listen here, my good man. Be forgetting all about this reading nonsense, and think about getting a good woman for the place. I have the very one for you!'

However, Patsy was still preoccupied by the subject of books.

'What was that book you said I was going to be in? Does it have a name?'

The dog was howling, growling and snapping at every word and indeed at every movement of the priest. Father Murphy was beginning to lose his patience.

He had meant "the book of life", kept by St Peter at the Gates of Heaven. The poor fellow thought that *his* earthly life was of sufficient interest to merit recording in an earthly book! Well, he would not disillusion him now. That would be unfair, a bit cruel. He would prolong the misapprehension, but to suit his own purposes.

'The first chapter is going to be called "The Greatest Romance Ever Told". It will be the story of how you came to be married, Patsy.'

'Married! To who?'

'Eileen O'Rafferty! Don't you know her? The most comely colleen in the county. She has agreed to marry you, my man.'

The farmer gave a puckish grin and his eyes seemed to do a dance in their sockets. He got up off his chair at the other side of the fireplace and then just as suddenly sat down again. Then he jumped up once more, his limbs moving abruptly, his eyes no longer dancing but fixed in a gaze of horror.

'Is this a trick ye're playing on me?'

'No trick, Patsy. It's as good as done. The young lady in question has assented, and there is no going back.'

'Can I go back on the deal, at all?'

'To go back on the deal would be worse than anything. It would not only break every code of honour. It would break hearts. The whole community would be affected for the worst if you failed to keep your end of the bargain.'

Patsy sighed heavily and shrugged his shoulders. At least it was not as bad as one of his cows dropping dead.

'Sure what's done is done. She could keep the house clean and help me with the odd jobs. And there is a spare room upstairs that she can sleep in.'

'She is your wife. She must share your bedroom, Patsy. And your bed.'

'My bed! There wouldn't be room for two in that, Father.'

'Do you know the facts of life, Patsy? How babies are brought into the world?'

'What! Are you telling me I have to have babies? What sort of a man do you take me for?'

He paused, in deep thought. The dog was now as quiet as a mouse, emitting only an occasional low whine. Patsy spoke in a pleading voice.

'I am too old anyway.'

'No man is too old for that, Patsy. That is one good thing that has kept this country going over the years. I have known men twice your age to bring twenty children and more into the world. And raise them all up as stalwart sons and daughters of Erin. Such a thing is to be encouraged. The Good Book says so.'

Even the dog seemed to be taken aback by the priest's talk, for it had gone completely silent.

Old Murphy signalled his surrender by sitting down again, slumped with his face resting in his hands and elbows resting on his knees. Staring at the floor, he spoke in a barely audible voice.

'There is one thing that you must answer me, Father, before I give my final word.'

'And what is that, Patsy?'

'What do I have to do to see to it that she is – you know – in the baby way?'

'What are you asking me for, man? Is it a lecture on the facts of life?'

Old Murphy's embarrassment was great; his face had partaken of a deep, strange colour.

'They say that married people do it the way – you know – it's done on the farm.'

'Well! What then...?'

'You will have to instruct me how to go about it all. From beginning to end. I would make a hames of it on my own. There is no way I can marry her until I'm sure I know all about what I'm going to have to do.'

He looked ready to cry. His body shook and trembled.

The priest knew that it was up to him to build up the unfortunate fellow's confidence somehow. He would have to present and explain all the details of married life to this man in simple, un-daunting, friendly, non-technical, positive terms such as how one might explain it to an innocent child. It was a task that he would have to prepare himself for, with careful pre-planning not totally dissimilar to the intense manner in which one would prepare for an exorcism: much prayer and fasting, clearing the mind of all distractions, retaining a sense of one's own fallen state and total dependence on providence.

'I will be back in two days, Patsy. Be ready.'

Father Murphy could no longer conceal his agitation and state of excitement as soon as the farm was out of sight. His poise and élan had disappeared. He was sighing, huffing and puffing and shaking his head from side to side exclaiming, 'Sorrow, sorrow!'

This time he rode steadily and swiftly. One would have thought that he was on a racer instead of an old bicycle. He rode with the determination and strength of a man demented.

Immediately he got home, he was on the phone to the bishop.

'Something is definitely up, Your Lordship. A farmer – to whom I am providing spiritual guidance – has learnt to read overnight! Before he came to my house a few weeks ago he did not know a book from a pint of porter. There is only one way that it is possible to obtain such hidden knowledge. Well, in these modern times we are not supposed to pay any heed to, or even mention, such things. But I still hold to the old fashioned beliefs. Patsy Murphy has experienced a fairy stroke. It appears to be a beneficial one on the face of it. But it could also be a trap of some sort. What is more – they have been working on me, too, lately! An attempt has been made to bewitch me. Something has been putting persistent thoughts into my head about a widow. Prayer doesn't make them go away. It is something like what they used to call a spell...'

'Take it easy, Father Murphy. It's just imagination. You need a rest. A short spell in St Dympna's would do you the world of good.

When you are in there I will come over and talk to you. And have you ever thought about retirement?'

'I know I enjoy a sup now and then, but I do not think I am a suitable case for St Dympna's. I am insulted!'

'At least let my man come over to talk to you. There may not be a need for any hasty decision about your future. Expect him on Saturday. He will have a good long talk with you, just to see that you are all right. Forget all about fairy spells and what not! That is all rubbish. What is going on I am sure has a logical explanation, and is all in the mind.'

'I am trying to get through to you,' said Father Murphy in exasperation, 'that the Church is facing a challenge of unknown provenance. I know I am only a simple parish priest, but I feel I am in the front line of this battle – a battle with hidden, dark forces. The least you can do is give me some encouragement.'

'Wait till my man gets there on Saturday. Don't do anything of your own accord. Wait for a bit of professional advice. The best advice I can give to you now is not to mention any of these matters to any third party. We can't have people saying we have a priest who believes in supernatural beings interfering with our day-to-day thinking and decisions.'

When he had put the phone down, the bishop turned to his secretary.

'Get me the psychologist again in Maynooth.'

Garda O'Hourigan mounted his bicycle and headed slowly but steadily out of Rathcloon. He couldn't remember the last time he had gone on "patrol". Perhaps it had been in the early days, when he had first arrived and he might have gone out once or twice to get to know the terrain. Another one was certainly due, even if only to reassure the population that he was still "on the job". Of course, being a person never to expend energy unnecessarily, he was at the same time on a second, more secretive mission. That was to visit Mr Murphy, the farmer. He would enter the premises when he was sure nobody in the area would see him. This was why he had headed out at dusk, timing his entry to Murphy's farmhouse for the onset of darkness. He turned off his bicycle light, dismounted and carefully made his way up the pot-holed, muddy lane into Patsy Murphy's. Patsy was already at the door waiting for him when he got there.

He put the bike against the wall of the house and stood in front of Patsy, their faces barely discernible to each other in the darkness.

'Hello, Guard. Can I be helping you?'

'Mr Murphy. I am here about your upcoming court appearance.'

Before Patsy could say anything the guard continued in an officious tone, 'It is the no small matter of your being in possession and control of a bicycle without lights on a public highway.'

'Guard, what do I care about those rules? They are the Englishman's rules. The law is an alien imposition on the people of this land by the foreigner. And it was the middle of the day when ye stopped me, anyway.'

'Ah, don't be taking it like that! Can I come in? I have a proposal to make that might get you off the charge. Before things go any further.'

'Come in,' said Patsy, for it was going to be another long winter's night and he would welcome any company to pass the hours. Sure, hadn't he once as an experiment tried talking to himself all night to see if it would cure the loneliness and cheer him up. It had gone well for a good while, and indeed he was beginning to think that it was the answer to all his problems when he was startled to find that there was a voice answering him back – encouraging him to keep up the conversation and even to steer it in other directions. He got the fright of his life and stopped the talk before it went too far.

They sat down by a dying fire, which Patsy attempted to rekindle by kicking it. Guard O'Hourigan asked him when he was going to get electricity.

'You must be the last man left around here without the electric.'

'In time,' said Murphy, 'in the Lord's good time.'

A fresh block of wood on the fire and the sheepdog silent and out of sight in the far corner, the guard commenced to explain his business.

'Us guards are the most honest, hard-working civil servants in the country. Doesn't everyone know that? Oh yes, we do have little tricks up our sleeves at times to catch the bad ones, but that sort of dishonesty is for the good of the country. But I can tell you, Mr Murphy, that up till now I have never resorted even to one little trick. Until now! As regards the serious charge you are facing, I have a plan that can get you off.'

'I will listen to that,' said Murphy, for he was indeed worried about a fine, which he would definitely be unable to pay. And the word of his humiliation would get around.

'My plan will not only get you out of trouble, but it will put you in my good books, and the good books of every Garda Siochána in the country. You will never have to fear the law again. Not even if you commit a very big crime.'

'What do I have to do for that?'

'This place of Rathcloon has a bad reputation up at Garda headquarters. They even talk in the Dáil about how backward we are. Some Dubh Linn TDs have a habit of making fun of us.'

'Oh, we can't let the blackguards do that!'

'We won't! We'll show them. We are as capable down here as they are up there, with their big criminals and their famous court cases. Do you know they write books and make films about Dubh Linn criminal big-wigs?'

'No!'

'That they do. You would think that we are all simple little children down here.'

'That we are not!'

'Well, they will soon see the light. How would you like to be in my great plan, Mr Murphy?'

'I would do anything to be in it, if it means we show those big heads what's what.'

'Well, here it is, for what it's worth. You confess to a murder and I will let you off the bike charge. I will make my investigations and send my reports to headquarters. It will be a clever, devious murder that no great detective sent down from Dubh Linn will be able to solve. Only yours truly here will finally solve it. And you yourself will be cleared by me at the end, and you will be a hero throughout the length and breadth of the land.'

'That is the best plan I have heard for ages! You are a clever man, Guard.'

'Call me Jim, Patsy. Jim O'Hourigan.'

'Jim. Would you like a sup?'

'I don't touch the stuff normally, Patsy. But there is always a first time. And an occasion such as this calls for a toast.'

He was given a mug full of poteen. From the way it went down smoothly it was obvious that he was well used to it.

'I will explain to you about the murder,' he said when he had recovered his breath; 'but to be honest I don't think I should have any more of this stuff. Me system is not used to it. But go ahead yourself and drink as much as you want. Let me do the talking, and I will take any questions you might have at the end.'

Guard O'Hourigan had already made a mental note of "manufacturing, possessing and selling of illegal substance" for inclusion in his record book when he got back.

He proceeded to explain that the way to do these things was to turn up at the barracks and confess outright to the crime. Notes would be taken, but no charges would be made at first and the confessing murderer would be free to go back home to milk the cows or whatever. An investigation would begin, with regular visits to the farm by local garda (O'Hourigan) to look for the body, or what remained of the body, so that charges could be brought. When the Dubh Linn detectives appeared on the scene, the fun would begin.

'No body, no crime,' said Jim, 'and that is the beauty of it. Is there any remains of an old cow, sheep or dog around the place, that could fool them for a time?' he asked.

Patsy thought hard but couldn't say.

'I could manage something though,' he added, as if afraid O'Hourigan might lose interest and drop the whole proceedings.

'Good.'

'Will I be really famous then?'

'More famous than any man around these parts since the time of…'

'And you will forget all about the bicycle lights?'

'You have my word on that.'

'I'll drink to it. Can I ask ye one straight question?'

'Go ahead.'

'I'm due to get married soon. Do you think being charged with murder could make…the other party…change her mind?'

O'Hourigan paused, reflecting on Patsy's conundrum. It was a bit of a surprise to him that the man was contemplating marriage. After some moments – and the offering of congratulations to the prospective bridegroom – he said, 'You know, you could use it either way you want. The manliness of being on such a charge would impress any woman. On the other hand, if the time came and you wanted out of it, then the same thing could be used as a good excuse for her to go back to her home.'

Garda O'Hourigan took his leave at midnight. He got on his bicycle – and then remembered to switch on the lamp. It was not a dynamo affair but a straightforward battery-run lamp with a knob at the top and a brand new battery.

No matter how many times he turned it, the light would not come on!

In the end he rode off into the dark, his eyes trying to get used to the conditions so that he could get a general idea of where the ditches were. It was one of those moonless, starless nights. He rode very slowly, cursing his "official issue bicycle" and thinking of all those guards who went around in cars. Suddenly he let out a yelp. The bike was accelerating, even though he was not pedalling any harder, and was carrying him off at an immense speed. There was nothing he could do to bring it to a stop, or even to slow it down. The brakes did not work either! He went at such a speed that he had to cling on; his hat had already taken off into the air. Up the road he went, down the next road. It turned left, then right, then at a speed equivalent to that of a motor car along a road that went on forever. He had no idea where he was, or where he was going to.

'It's that damn poteen. I should have known better than to have taken a sup.'

He tried to engineer a soft landing at the side of the road in the vicinity of the grass margin. At least that would be safer than heading into a busy, major road.

He could not get himself to come off the bicycle no matter how hard he tried. He would later say to himself that it was as if he was glued to it.

The wind blew so fast past him that it whistled in his ears. Then came the rain, battering his face with such force that he felt the blood coming up and his skin burning. And no doubt those hard objects that were striking him were sticks and all sorts of debris that you often find lying on the public highway. It was almost with relief that he found himself and his bike entering into a road that appeared to be much wider (a main road), and this was confirmed when a car went flashing past.

There might be some help here. He called out. Another car was coming. It was going to be the end of him. Each car that subsequently passed by – he must be nearly in Cork or Limerick by now – appeared to be on the verge of running him over. He was closing his eyes nearly all the time now. The bike began to career this way and that way whenever they were on a straight stretch, with different parts of O'Hourigan's uniform coming off as he struck bushes, branches and even the trunks of trees. Time passed but the guard, fearful and thunderstruck, was not aware of time passing. After what must have been hours, for the light of dawn appeared on the horizon, he looked up and saw what he thought was none other than Foirnocht Hill ahead. The speed of the bike increased. They turned to the right up a rock-strewn, pot-holed lane, through open or half open gates, across fields and he could have sworn that they circled Foirnocht Hill at least three times. Then the bicycle did a sudden u-turn (this must have been where the guard lost all the contents of his pockets, including his all-important notebook), and he realised to his horror that they were now going to circle Foirnocth Hill *from the left* – that is, anticlockwise.

'No,' he shouted, 'no, it is bad luck! Stop!'

They went around the hill, through lane, track and field, over stream, ditch and hedge a further three times, and O'Hourigan knew enough about country legend to know, now, that by circling the hill anti-clockwise he had immortally insulted all the visible or invisible inhabitants, be they spirits, fairy or whatever, that lived or had ever lived in that spot.

Dawn had fully broken when his bike thundered into Rathcloon village. The group of women heading for the church for the Rosary before Mass (in other words, daily mass-goers, the most pious folk in the district) watched in shock as the shouting, cursing Garda approached at great speed, heading straight for them and causing each disbelieving lady at the last moment to jump back as the bike hit the pavement and a tattered, battered Garda O'Hourigan tumbled onto the ground before them.

Bridie Murphy always went down Moore Street late on Saturday afternoons to get cheap fruit and vegetables. Some items would even be given away for nothing, if they were far enough gone and you spoke in a sad way to the stallholder. They were well used to beggars, and often showed them little patience, so you had to pretend that you were doing it for a poor old man and woman living in a one-room hovel who were unable to get out and whose children had deserted them. In her case, the old couple were her father and mother. She had built up an impressive CV for them over the years. Her dad had been old enough to be her great-grandfather when she was born, and her mother was at least fifty when she gave birth. The dad had fought in five different wars, in the uniforms of five different nations, and the shooting had gone to his head so that he now talked only gibberish. He walked on one leg. To top matters, he had been denied a pension by the government as all his wars had been foreign ones. Her mother had been born at the tail-end of the famine, which had lasted till modern times despite what the books or the government said. For the purpose of giving a decent impression, Bridie always put on her Sunday best so as to assure the stallholders that she was not a nobody but a lady of some good standing. She carried on in the same way at the meat market in Meath Street. The north ring road, too, was usually her destination on cattle market days, to beg the farmers for the odd penny or two. This was especially effective at five o'clock in the morning when business was at its height and, as she had discovered, resistance was low. No decent Dubh Linn people ever went near the cattle market, so her blatant begging forays were safe from exposure to the likes of Mrs Byrne.

Today's visit to Moore Street had been particularly important. She had invited Sean Murphy up to her home for a meal and she would have to put on a good show. The best bacon and cabbage, with good bananas after.

Sean arrived apparently under the influence of alcohol, although he had only drunk one pint of Guinness. He clambered up the stairs in a stop-go fashion, resting against the wall when he ran out of breath and muttering to himself strange philosophical words he had been trying hard to understand all week. He was repeating them now more to keep a hold on sobriety than for any reason of learning. Some young lads passed him on their way down, staring not because he was seemingly drunk but because he was wearing a black suit and tie.

'He's a culchie,' said one youth. 'Hey, Mister. Where ya from?'

Sean steadied himself against the wall. He was beginning to feel unwell; it seemed that ordinary stout and beer were destined always to have a deleterious effect on him, whilst he could drink large quantities of the hard stuff without any ill-effects. He had difficulty pronouncing his words.

'Do you know about phil..osophy?'

'Wha...?'

'Did you ever learn...philosophy?'

'Will ya listen to the culchie! What's that word?' asked the tall one.

'It's a fancy word,' said another.

'A fancy word! Better not be! What does that word mean, ya eegit?'

'It's a subject that every learned person talks about, but nobody knows what it means. If anyone knew, he would be wiser than all the clergy, all the professors, all the governments in the whole world...'

'Will ya tell us what it means, Mister?'

The tall lad had become somewhat cagey.

Sean had dropped down to sit on the step. They moved closer to hear more words of wisdom. He began to tell them slowly about how he had come up to the big city in search of knowledge. Where he had lived people knew very little. That was why people in the city called them by many insulting names. Up here in Dubh Linn it was supposed to be different. The amount of ignorance here was on an different level altogether – far worse than in the country, for the reason that city folk did not know that they were ignorant. They thought that they had all the knowledge there was to be had in the world. But real knowledge and wisdom are secretly hidden away. Nobody has yet found them. That is why they invented something called schools, learning and philosophy...'

They were interrupted by two men coming down the stairs.

'What's going on here?' asked one of them loudly.

'This fellow is telling us the meaning of some big words. He is a genius. What is that word again, mister? Phil...?'

'It's one of those heretics purveying false wares,' said the first man.

'That suit and tie. You can tell them a mile away,' said the second.

'He's drunk,' said one of the youths.

'Then he can't be a Bible basher. He must be a dirty fellow. Out to corrupt the youth,' the first man said. He proceeded to pick Sean up off the floor and held his face so close to Sean's that neither could distinguish whose alcohol it was that they were breathing in.

'Get yerself and yer dirty talk outa here before ya get what's comin' to ya.'

He gave Sean a punch in the stomach for good luck.

As the group went downstairs the first man asked, 'What was the word?'

'Philisophy.'

'I knew it. A dirty, dirty word.'

The tall youth said that he had to go back for he had dropped something. As he passed Sean, he said in a low voice, 'Come back again, Mister. We'll be here. If yer selling something, we'll be interested.'

Bridie, hearing the commotion, came to the door. She led Sean into the flat – being careful to keep a certain distance from him. Not because of the state of him (he had been sick on his jacket), but because physical contact between the sexes (unless already legally contracted to, e.g. in marriage) was forbidden in that culture. Physical touch was a power with magical qualities. This was extremely useful – and dangerous – to those who knew how to use it – hence the many rituals, taboos, beliefs, superstitions and phobias surrounding it. In this instance, she had long observed a difference between city and country folk. The former were more prone to ignoring taboos. In Dubh Linn the unwary were often liable to find the uninvited hand of a complete stranger being laid upon them. (Hence the physical touch of a Dubh Linn native had no magical qualities.)

With country folk it was different. Just to get to know such an individual, much less manoeuvre oneself into a position where one could be comfortable at least in offering a handshake, one had metaphorically to wade through many "fields" of long grass, nettles, thistles and briars, across treacherous marshes, up steep hills and down low, mist-enshrouded valleys before meeting the real person. Sometime it was as if they were under some sort of protective spell. She had detected a strange "atmosphere" about Sean the first time she met him. He gave the impression that he did not quite live on the same plane, or in the same world, as others. There seemed to be an unspoken "warning", or hands-off, about him. Yet there was nothing cold or stand-offish in him. She had heard enough of these kind of things about country people from her mother to know to tread carefully in his case. In particular, she should not pry into that person's private thoughts. Nor ask too many questions. She also knew intuitively, and perhaps regretfully, that married life with Sean back in the countryside would somehow be an impossibility.

'Better take off your jacket,' she said. 'That's telling those bowsies. If more people stood up to them the way you did, it would be a better world.'

It was amazing how big his appetite was some little while later, and he ate up all she put before him with gusto. It was as if he hadn't eaten for years.

'I can get you good food for nothing,' she said when she had an opportunity to put in a few words between the stream of talk that was coming from him. The books were obviously doing him no good, as indeed he had once admitted to her when they were in Byrne's shop. As a country lad he had no understanding of life in the city. If it was not for her he would know even less about the place; where the Pillar was, how to get around, how to make the pennies last and get free things, how not to talk to too many people, especially the rough, idle sort who frequented every street corner. She spoke quietly, in an interlude where Sean had clearly become a little tired from too much talking about a false doctrine called existentialism which was leading half the world astray.

'Free food?' he replied abstractedly, still trying to get his mind around another conundrum (if the "Spirit of the Modern Age" meant a total reversal of man's ancient, innate inability to understand or believe in anything – and hence the age-old invention of "faiths" and "mysteries" – to a modern era of doctrinal and scientific certainty on any number of once indeterminable matters, thus dispensing with that prehistoric, ingrained human characteristic that some called honest scepticism, others the highest idealism, and the wisest saw as the only road that can be taken in this world – honest-to-goodness doubt about everything in existence).

'What's the catch?'

'There's no catch. I get loads of grub at the markets. I even know where you can get lunch for nothing. The Salvation Army.'

'Salvation Army! A good name for them, if you're starving. What do they want for that?'

'Nothing much. They say they just want "your soul for the Lord". All the wasters go there.'

'Sounds like the place for me! Uncle Sean's allowance is quickly used up, especially with the price of whiskey up here. Do ye remember, now, how you were telling me that you wanted to go back to the country to settle down? That all you were waiting for was a good man. Well, I got this letter from an old school companion, Liam Lawler, who has joined the Fianna. He tells me my Uncle Patsy is in the marriage stakes. After all these years! Now there is a good man for you! He is a bit past his prime. Still, he is a farmer. Will I write to him and tell him you're interested?'

Sean was more or less having a tease at Bridie's expense.

Bridie tried to hide her interest, indeed her mounting excitement. She would play hard to get. She took a few moments to ponder her answer.

'Oh, I'd be interested. Is he a real farmer?'

'Yes.'

'Does he go gallivanting?'

'No. He is a home-loving man.'

'Does he smoke or chew tobacco?'

'He does.'

'Is he fussy?'

'Doesn't care less.'

'Is he neat and tidy?'

'Not in the slightest. His place is a huge mess.'

'Well! He is the man for me. I thank you, Sean, for giving me the opportunity to meet a real countryman. Will ye write to him and tell him I think it would be great to meet him?'

Sean was taken aback; though also quite pleased that, at least for once since his arrival in the city, he had done something useful.

'I sure will. And I'll give you the best recommendation in the world. I will tell him that you have everything the country woman has, and also something the country girl doesn't. The sophistication of a city woman. That will be enough to persuade him.'

Sean took out Liam Lawler's letter and opened it.

'He says it's great in the Fianna. They practise hurling all day. And their brains are being challenged non-stop to think up ways on how best to defend Erin. I will always be a Fiannóir, too, he says, for I received the invitation and did not fail the testing – as I never took it. Unlike Michael Fitzgerald, he says, who failed a basic psychological test. He says Michael is now condemned to a miserable life making of a lot of money, to settling down to a happily married life, the bringing up of a family and dying peacefully in bed of old age. He feels sorry for him, he says. No chance now of receiving the crown of glory – martyrdom! He says: "The chance of being a martyr for Erin is still there for you, Sean. Just write to me and tell me how you are getting on. Don't forget."'

Sean laughed but it was a hollow laugh. Those last words felt more like a rebuke.

They listened a while to the radio programme *Songs for Night Time*.

'I will send that letter off first thing tomorrow, Bridie. Thanks for the advice about the food. I will go down there for some. And if you ever get extra yourself, I'll share it with you! Now I'd better get back. I told Mrs Byrne I had a late lecture tonight, but I will have to think up a good one to explain why I am still out at one o'clock in the morning!'

As Sean walked slowly through the city streets, he was thinking up great words that he would use in his letter to Uncle Patsy. He found the proposed letter far more interesting than any of those course essays he had to write. The words would surely come to him, he hoped, as if sent from above, when he went to write them.

No sooner had he given mental expression to this thought than, sure enough, the words started to come to him out of the blue.

Dear Uncle Patsy

You've been so good to me since the days of my youth letting me help you out on the farm, forming in me all those good habits of life and also of the mind that I can say that I now walk on the road of experience out in the greater world a more assured and confident individual than I would have been had I never met you or had you as my <u>most</u> informative influence from my earliest days. In short, you are a king to a slave, a master to an apprentice, a hero to a humble, weak upstart, a good fellow to a poor creature such as is my good self, Sean Murphy.

You will not believe who I have met here in the big smoke. Bridie Murphy, from near our own beloved townland, a young woman whose only desire in life has been to marry a good man like yourself and settle down to a life of hard work on a farm. Bridie has all the sophistication of a Dubh Linn girl – the life of the theatre, concert hall...'

He could not stop the words pouring out. By the time he had turned into O'Connell Street the letter was finished, with umpteen recommendations as to why his uncle should marry Bridie forthwith. It only required the signing off –

And I know, Uncle Patsy, that you will do the <u>right</u> thing – and become engaged to Bridie Murphy immediately. To make sure that on the great day when you first see the sight of her, and you nearly faint at the sight of the beauty of her, you will not have to say, I delayed, hesitated, doubted, thought about marrying another, and now to my great sorrow I have lost the beautiful, sophisticated Bridie Murphy forever.

Your dearest nephew,
Sean

Sean was so pleased with himself that he muttered, 'Thank you, thank you!' to nobody in particular, only to that Muse that had made the writing of the letter so easy.

As he walked under the immense outcrop of Nelson's Pillar he felt suddenly annoyed about the sight of such a monstrosity in Erin's capital city – a grotesque obstruction glorifying a conquering hero of an imperial power. He wished that somebody would blow it up.

He had no sooner made this wish when he saw large sections of stone falling slowly to the ground, landing at his feet. He heard no sound. He looked back and up and saw the last pieces of the pillar crumbling to earth. He was wondering straightaway about the coincidence when he distinctly heard in his head the words: *In gratitude for services obtained that is your second wish fulfilled.*

Sean walked the rest of the way home a sober fellow. He knew that however much he might doubt the objective reality of this "message", or whether any significance of any kind should be attached to it – even if only from curiosity or the academic interest of a psychologist or psychiatrist, he could not doubt that the next time he made a wish there was a possibility it would come true – and therefore he would have to take great care in future with his mental deliberations.

The following morning he was not sure at first if he had imagined all that had happened on his walk home the night before. (A new propensity of Sean's to "blank out" recent events in his life, though alarming at first, soon became his most cherished ability. He found that he could get through everyday life with a minimum of stress, without having to worry about anything in the past, present, and even in the future.) He heard Mrs Byrne shouting up at him.

'Sean Murphy! They have blown up Nelson's Pillar! What did you get up to last night?'

'What? Are you telling the truth? They blew up the pillar?' he shouted down.

'I have it on good authority that you left Bridie Murphy's in the early hours and you were seen at the pillar when it was blown up. Where there is trouble, you will find Sean Murphy!'

That evening, at about four o'clock when Sean had got in from his afternoon lecture on logic (he had already posted the letter to Uncle Patsy) there was a garda waiting for him in the back room. The guard asked could they go upstairs. Mrs Byrne and her husband were nowhere to be seen. They both sat down on the two available chairs and the guard opened proceedings.

'So you are from near Rathcloon are you? You don't by any chance happen to have had dealings with Garda O'Hourigan? He tells me that they are all a troublesome lot down there. He has a murder case on his hands right now. You are a bit of a tearaway, I hear. Poor Mrs Byrne is at her wits end. She has asked me to tell you to pack your bags and leave the house as soon as you have found alternative digs. Well, your alternative digs will be the cell in the station, at the rate we're going. You have treated her quite badly, haven't you? Now tell me, what did you do at the pillar last night? Before you answer, could you just give me a nod or a wink in response to anything I suggest regarding how you might be involved in the explosion or, more likely, who or what it was you saw there. Nothing to incriminate you, for I cannot record a nod or a wink in my notebook. So you may feel safe as regards giving evidence against anyone who may be, or may have been, a friend or acquaintance of yours. Your evidence will only be for me to hand over to the big boys in the branch. Remember now, a nod or a wink. Did you see them?'

Sean shook his head. The guard threw down his unopened notebook on the floor in a flamboyant gesture. It was hard to decipher his mood, but it could be interpreted as imminent impatience.

'Did you hear, see, notice anything? Anybody?'
Another shake of the head.
'Do you know how it happened?'
Sean gave a nod.
'How then?'

Sean winked.

'Not a word goes out of here. I will ask Mrs Byrne to keep you on till the end of the month.'

While all the big boys were chasing the supposed bigger fish, here he was, a humble guard on the local beat about to break the biggest case for decades.

'It was the gentle folk. They did it. On my instructions.'

Sean paused, and then gave two deep nods and a big wink.

By six o'clock that evening Sean was in the city's major psychiatric home, under sedation and a twenty-four-hour watch.

And that was the night of his first "big dream" – wherein the *geas* under which he had been placed made itself felt.

In front of him was the Árd Rí, a golden crown on his head, seated on his throne, hearing a charge against the Fianna of "conspiring to be a rival power to the state". Upon the outcome depended the future fate of the renowned band of warriors. The high king was addressing their unchallenged leader – for Finn had entered second childhood – Caoilte, whom Sean immediately recognised as Liam Lawler. The Fianna stood before him in very tattered, rough attire, worn and torn. They looked very downhearted, unshaven and unwashed, shuffling around uneasily like a gang of beggars caught up in a police swoop. He knew and understood their skill at self-abasement – an attempt to pass themselves off as a harmless group of idealists who had no ambitions or prospects of temporal power, or indeed any interest in material matters.

Caoilte was speaking boldly and with bravado, beating his chest and holding his hand to his perspiring forehead, denying that they had ever attempted to overthrow the state:

'And there is that Judge Sean Murphy there. You yourself are one of us, for I have it here in your own handwriting. You have written here' – he held up a piece of paper – 'that there is no finer body of men than the Fianna. That no wrong can ever be done by the Fianna. That those who accuse the Fianna are false. That the Fianna will always suffer tribulations and unjust charges brought by their enemies. You state that your full allegiance is given over to the Fianna for all their days without end – that you will always be a Fiannóir at heart. Do you deny your own words? Or are you the greatest charlatan, the smallest minded man in Erin?'

'Let me see that letter.'

Sure enough, it was all there, in his own words. To rid his mind once and for all of the *geas* – or moral obligation imposed by Finn McCumhail he had – in this letter written so many years before, promised them his prayers, good will and support over the coming years. If they were ever in need or trouble, they could come to him. If ever they were short of a man, they could call on him.

He felt his heart drop.

He was no longer the young Sean Murphy. His limbs were less limber, his mind more clouded and dull, his heart heavy, as of one who no longer had any dreams or ideals. He felt he was carrying the burden of guilt, not of the Fianna, but of the powerful, rich and successful.

As he listened to the talk – complex legal talk about constitutions and constitutional rights, political talk about subversive activities and treason against the state, talk about personal failings and the weaknesses of different Fianna warriors, talk full of bitterness about hard lives lived dangerously defending Erin without reward – he knew that he was not just witnessing the fall of the Fianna; he was an active participant in it.

As he listened to the haranguing and the listing of innumerable Fianna crimes, there was a loud shout.

"Have mercy!"

Sean tried but could not discover the source. Until he realised that the deep, hoarse voice was his own.

The high king, in a deep, lyrical, even musical voice, sentenced Caoilte – in lieu of a sentence of death – for he had heard the call for mercy – to go the rounds of Erin and bring back a tribute worthy of a king. Tribute. Mercy. That would be enough to secure the release of the Fianna.

Caoilte and the Fianna were unrestrained in their thanks, bowing their heads –

'Buíochas duit, Árd Rí, buíochas duit, a hSeáin.'

Their thanks ringing in his ears, Sean fell into a dreamless, untroubled sleep.

The next day he woke up feeling on top of the world. He felt pride and joy in his incarceration, for wasn't it all in a worthy cause – the removal of an eyesore from the centre of the city? So uplifted was he that he did not feel the need to eat or drink all day.

He also came to an important realisation about the nature of that "hidden" reality he had lately been wondering about. When he asked the doorman whether the Fianna or the Little People had called around, asking for him, to congratulate him on his great deed, the doorman had replied in the affirmative, saying that both had called by and sent their regards.

Sean no longer doubted.

Four

NEWLY ENGAGED FARMER CHARGED WITH MURDER

SUSPECT LEADS GARDA TO BONES IN FIELD

THE HEADLINE IN the *Cork Examiner* was big news. Garda
O'Hourigan had become somewhat concerned, as he had not
expected an insignificant, local murder to catch the national
headlines. He had spoken to three reporters that day alone, defending
his "old friend" Patsy Murphy before all-comers.

'An innocent man, if ever I saw one.'

'It will all come out at the trial.'

'None of this business will stand in the way of the marriage of
a good man.'

That evening Garda O'Hourigan (now the famous Garda
O'Hourigan) admitted to himself that he was feeling a little out of
his depth. He had already nearly forgotten why he had instituted this
murder in the first place. And he had no idea where it would all end.

Father Murphy was talking to Patsy in the kitchen, before the same
turf fire which had burned for as many generations back as far as
one could go, like the old Pascal fire – indeed pagan fire – of old.
(The sídh prized this fire and became consternated whenever Patsy
let it get too low. They had all manner of tricks to get him on course
again to see to its replenishing.)

The priest was feeling pleased with himself. The bishop's emissary had come and gone. The man could not report anything back to the bishop for, on being requested to answer truthfully a number of questions, he had tricked the fellow into letting him hear his confession.

'I'll tell you everything,' he told the man in truth.

Thereupon he fully confessed to drink, superstition, contempt for those who did not pay their dues, dishonesty in his relations with a number of parishioners and a host of other sins delightedly drawn from the deep reservoir of memory and hindsight. If the monsignor had felt anger upon realising that all revelations were forever secret under the seal of confession, he did not show it.

'Sure no woman would want to have anything to do with a murderer. Much less marry one,' said Patsy, a degree of relief, or hope, in his voice.

'Never mind the murder. How are you now with the facts of life? As I've explained them to you.'

Patsy trembled as he contemplated once more what Father Murphy had called "the marriage act".

'Oh, it's horrible, horrible!' he said for the umpteenth time.

'Now, Patsy, calm down. Eileen is a patient woman. She will give you all the time in the world to overcome your…scruples.'

'The facts of life are very fine. But you can't expect an old man to be facing them. Anyway, as I said, it is not right and proper for a murderer to be getting married.'

The priest had spent many hours trying to reassure him that physical relations between a man and a woman were very natural and proper. He had prayed for inspiration in this difficult task. He had re-read the manual. He had – much against his better judgement – even tried imagining what it would be like for Patsy on his wedding night, placing himself in Patsy's shoes, feeling the trembling and fear, preparing himself as a soldier would for battle, noting all the subtle snags and logistical problems. But he had put a stop to that experiment when he realised that he was in danger of losing control of his "wandering" thoughts. The tricks the devil played!

Even now as he remembered he coughed and spluttered. The redness and perspiration began to appear again.

An idea came to him.

'Patsy, are you still reading the books?'

'That I am to be sure.'

'There is a lovely love story that goes by the title – what is it now? *Helen of Troy*. The love that launched a thousand ships. I will find you my copy. I read it as a young fellow and I will never forget reading how the memory of that woman's beauty haunted those poor bewitched men all their lives. They were ready to kill for her. There was nothing more admirable in classical times than that. To be willing to kill for love.'

'By the hokey!'

'And what is the book these days?'

'Oh it's all politics, legal wheeling-dealing, how to get around the law. *Great Crooks of Our Time* is the name of the book. You'd be surprised who is in there, Father, but I will not mention names. From the sound of it, your book about love might be the better thing. This *Helen of Troy* sounds the one.'

'It will be no trouble for me to get you that book.'

Even as he spoke Father Murphy was beginning to think along a different track. *Helen of Troy* would not be enough to do the trick. Indeed, there were two tricks that needed to be done. He had not only to get Patsy reconciled to the married life – he also needed to wean him off his apparent, recently acquired addiction to sensationalist literature; dangerous, subversive literature. No matter how harmless or learned it might present itself to innocent readers, always there in the background of every so-called "intellectual" book was an attack on the Church.

Helen of Troy was too milk-and-water for the job in hand, he now decided. He needed to make Patsy so besotted with his fiancée, so lovelorn that he would not only race as fast as Lester Piggott to the church on his wedding day, but he would also dispense with all the books he had accumulated and forget that he ever did read; that he ever *could* read. It would have to be what they called…a saucy book. Not a dirty book, mind you. Just a saucy one. There was no other hope for poor Patsy, for whom the yearning of the flesh was a long-dead passion, if it had ever existed at all. It would be no sin, but a creditable act of charity to arouse in the poor man the God-given physical desire for a woman. Now where would he find a book like that? He had no experience of such things. He would be ashamed to have any knowledge of such books. He would play it safe and ask the bishop himself to recommend such a book. He would be on safe ground there.

'We'll give it three more weeks, Patsy, before we arrange the introductions. In the meantime, you will have some good serious reading to do!' he said as he stood and faced the doorway.

Patsy jumped up and stood between the door and the priest.

'Before ye go, Father – can ye tell me – what does she...look like?'

'Ah, don't be worrying yourself. It is the marriage nerves that you've got. You can depend on me that you will be the best looked-after man in the country. Your house will be the pride and joy of the neighbourhood. You won't have to worry about having to deal alone with all those grants and taxes that are becoming so important these days, for they say a burden shared is a burden halved. I wouldn't be surprised if you ended up a wealthy man, sitting back in the lap of luxury with nothing to do all day. It won't be a shilling a year that you will be putting into the collection plate then, Patsy!'

After the priest had left Patsy went back to the fire and sat down. He hurriedly pulled a sheet of notepaper from his pocket and read it again – for the umpteenth time.

It had come in the middle of the night. There was a knock on the door. He went down and opened it. Although it had been a quiet, calm night there was a screeching wind outside. Nobody was there. Then he heard a little voice piping "look down at your feet, Patsy." And there was this letter lying on the step, with his name on the envelope, but no address and no stamp. He thought at first that it might have something to do with the murder.

He read it by candlelight. It was from his nephew up in Dubh Linn.

URGENT

St Dismal's Institution,
Dubh Linn.
20th July 19—

Dear Uncle Patsy,

They have locked me up in this place, saying that it was me who blew up Nelson's Pillar. I told them who it was, but they don't believe me. I have been doing a lot of thinking since I came in here. I am quitting all this philosophy stuff. It is totally meaningless and is not good for the head. I am writing to you because I have a message for you from the Little People. Nobody here believes in them. In actual fact, to tell you the truth, they have lately been doing some jobs for me. I don't know why they have placed their confidence in a young cynic like me, but there you have it. As the saying goes, never look a gift horse in the mouth.
They tell me that I have more wishes!
And they have been teaching me tunes and little bits of song which I hum to myself all the time.
They have given me a message for you. They say that you must not make a rash decision and rush into marriage with one Eileen O'Rafferty. If you have to marry against your will, then they have found the wife for you. She will save you all the trouble of having to act the husband, father and grandfather, and yet still have all of the advantages of marriage. Bridie Murphy of the Corporation Buildings is the greatest girl in the world, Uncle Patsy, and her dearest wish is to live in the countryside. She keeps me in grub up here. She has put me wise on many things. When I told her about you she said that you were a man of great wisdom, the surest proof of this being the fact that everyone

laughed at you. Isn't that a great wise thing to say? She has visited me here in this prison and her words have led me to make some great discoveries about myself and the world, some of which I will share with you in time. When I told Bridie about your engagement, she said wouldn't it be a great thing if you and she could pretend to be married and then nobody could say boo to either one of ye. A pretend-marriage, with no calls at all on either side. She will be happy to just walk around the fields all day and keep out of your way. The fairy folk approve of the plan. That is the important thing.

  Well, that is all for now. Don't forget to keep the home fires burning.

Your fond nephew,
Sean

'Can you believe it?' muttered Patsy to himself; 'I am all the rage in the country now.'

There was desperation in his laugh.

It was a bit rare for his nephew to be introducing him to women at this stage in his life. When he was already engaged, and so on. But if the murder rap couldn't get him out of the tight spot he was in, then he would look again at Sean's suggestion. The idea of having a wife to fend off the world and yet not have to be a real husband and father had already begun to appeal to him.

'The best option is to give him his head on this,' said Bishop de Bruin. That way we can keep tabs on him. Now, what banned book should we tell him? The list is as long as your arm.'

'Ah, now ye're asking. I'll go and ring Maynooth.'

'Choose a good one, my man. A "saucy" one, as the poor fellow puts it. The ethics theologian in Maynooth is on the Censorship Board. He will know where they keep them. Be careful to explain the background – as to why we are enquiring and asking for the loan of a copy.'

'I say – one of our most solid PPs is going off the rails. He is in the throes of a passion he has no idea how to control. We think it is best to let him have the book in the first instance. It will hopefully cool down his fancy and then we will call him in for a talk.'

'More or less correct, Monsignor. But don't give it all away. The last person who must hear of what is going on is the archbishop up in Dubh Linn. We will make our reputations by sorting out this thing ourselves. We will let them think it is just a matter of impure books. The last thing they must ever know is that we have a parish priest on our hands who talks about the fairies.'

'That's right. By the way, as you know, I didn't get too much information out of him that day. Would it be an idea to send someone else over to the parish – incognito like – to look into things?'

The bishop had a deep intake of breath. He thought deeply of what he was going to say. He spoke slowly, as of one making a most important statement.

'If ever I sunk to that, to not trusting one of my own parish priests, no matter how bad, drunk or mad he may be, that will be the day I give up being a bishop.'

'That's right.'

Life in the main town, outlying villages and farm lands appeared on the surface to be as normal as ever, despite all the recent controversies, scandals and excitements. Hurling matches, the assorted Gaelic games, fighting, drinking, singing and talking went on as if there had been no late community upset, no undue challenges to the status quo, no alien intrusions from unexpected quarters. The flight from the land of the young, fit and able, the steady slowdown and downturn in economic activity, the recycling of the same old tales and talk, the burying of the dead seemed to be the reassuring, permanent feature of life there. Only the sight of young Michael Fitzgerald in his motor car racing around the roads and lanes seemed oddly out of place.

Even with the prospering of his business ventures, his rising status in the county, his steadily rising money savings, he felt a sense of dissatisfaction. This car for instance, the most admired vehicle around and the object of envy of every person was, as far as Michael was concerned, a crock. As he sped along the main road outside Dunmor he imagined that it was not a second hand car he was driving but a brand new Mercedes.

And what a road! He was doing 120 k.p.h. along a wide, well-marked dual carriageway with NO POTHOLES. He was confused by the fact that the road sign he passed showed only kilometres. He was feeling somewhat strange. There was something tight and uncomfortable around his belly (itself a heavy, unfamiliar bulge) and he saw that he was strapped in. He looked up in the mirror and saw the face of a grey-haired, suntanned, middle-aged man with a cigar between his teeth. He did not recognise himself!

And instead of heading to a business meeting with a farmer in a pub to buy 500 bales of hay, he was instead off to the airport at Rathcloon and a flight on his private jet to the great city of Brussels. There he would meet with his international business partners to discuss new building contracts for his construction firm. In his strange-looking briefcase (it was thin, flat and seemed to be made of metal) were the plans for the new European capital, BailenahEoropa, to be built in the heart of his constituency. The choice of this location had been the greatest achievement of his political career as Ireland's forward looking Minister for Enterprise. Everywhere there were For Sale signs advertising sites for residential and industrial development. He thought back to "the old days" when that land, destined now to be the nucleus of what would perhaps be the greatest city in the world, was considered only a "bog". He had been so quick all those long years ago to see its potential value – on the main route to the provincial capital – and to persuade so many farmers to part with their "useless" land.

He pulled suddenly on the steering. There was a screech of brakes. He had nearly run down a man. He looked like a tramp. He must have lost concentration for a moment. He was lucky to have avoided him. He could have ended up in the ditch, his car a wreck, as well as knocking down someone and having to face a breathalyser. He should not have had that last whiskey. His mind was playing tricks. He looked out the window and saw the tramp walking ahead. As he slowly drove past the unkempt, bearded figure he caught a glimpse of his face. He thought he recognised him! Sean Murphy the nay-sayer – who had once believed himself too good for the Fianna. He had stared back at Michael in recognition! He seemed to be cursing him! Cursing the great Michael Fitzgerald, the economic saviour of the nation (even prospective Taoiseach), and his great plan for the development of Dunmor and region. Sean's bearded face was up against the window! He braked suddenly, then he pulled away and accelerated.

What did they put in that whiskey that he had drunk in the pub? Who could you trust nowadays, even amongst "friends", especially when you were a politician. They laid all kinds of traps for you – even your friends. Janey Mack, he had headed out on an ordinary, simple journey and here he was hallucinating. He had been seeing into the future! That marvellous Mercedes that he had so lately felt at home in was now the familiar old crock once more – and the road was an uneven, pot-holed lane again rather than the modern highway of his dreams. It was due to that spiked drink. It had worn off now. He felt better.

It was just some old tramp.

And "BailenahEoropa" was one hell of an idea…

When he slept that night he had a dream. He saw the tramp again, his face turned away, walking along the verge. As he passed him, the face had changed and he could have sworn that, just before it disappeared, he saw the face not of Sean Murphy, but Michael Fitzgerald.

Eileen O'Rafferty woke with a start. She had just had a vivid nightmare that they had hanged Patsy Murphy. She was due to go to the courthouse that very morning for the reading of the charges. It would be the first time that she set eyes on her beloved Patsy! She was going as moral support. Father Murphy had instructed her to bring extra toiletries, a foresight that she would later marvel at.

She wiped off the perspiration and sighed in relief. It had only been a dream! Her Patsy was still an innocent and free man. Until proven guilty. And everyone in the community knew that Patsy Murphy, if found guilty, must have had a very good reason to commit murder.

And the enumeration of these "good reasons" became the great diversion, almost a sport in itself. Some said the victim was an unknown, long-suffering relative whom Patsy had had to put out of his/her misery as an act of charity. Others were of the opinion that Patsy had once been tricked into marriage by some "morrigan" of a woman, who had proceeded to make his life a misery. So ashamed was Patsy of his wife that he had hidden her from one and all. Finally, he had ended the charade, with one quick flourish of the hand. Yet others speculated about Patsy's identity as a wise man, cleverly concealed beneath his apparent simplicity, innocence and other-worldliness. He alone, perhaps, would have been aware of some great troublemaker – or potential troublemaker – in the townland, and had forestalled much harm by finishing off the brute beforehand. And there was no use in looking up the identity of the missing person, the proponents of this theory said, for who could account for the millions – also – who had emigrated?

They set out before dawn to walk the three miles to town. There they boarded the early bus for the regional capital. Unbeknownst to them, Patsy was on the same bus.

A few, innocuous yet noteworthy words passed between Patsy and the O'Raffertys, who were seated immediately behind him. They were annoyed by his tobacco-chewing and spitting and powerful smell of the farmyard – his general air of decrepitude accentuated by his unkempt appearance, his leathery skin, dirty coat, ragged boots and hole-strewn hat. Widow O'Rafferty was the first to voice her complaint.

'Can you stop that disgusting spitting? There are other people on the bus.'

'Any decent man would have washed and dressed before heading out on the road,' admonished Eileen, 'much less get on a bus with decent people.'

Patsy paid no attention. In fact, although he heard the words, he assumed that they were directed at somebody else. He continued munching and spitting and thinking to himself what he would say in court. A man had called on him a few days previously claiming to be a "solicitor", but he had given him short shrift.

He began to organise his thoughts now in order to have his case ready for judge and jury, ignoring the continuing barrage of reprimands and insults that were coming from behind.

"My lords and justices – I am not a wealthy man. Just a poor, respectable farmer. My only hope is to avoid the rope and return to my farm that has been in our family for countless generations. The cows do not know how to manage on their own. As regards this murder, I made a complete breast of it to Garda O'Hourigan, a fine policeman worthy of the uniform. He assured me that I would not hang as I was cooperating fully with the gardaí, saving them months if not years of costly investigation, and that I have expressed remorse, and that there is only a small chance of me doing the same crime again. If everybody in the country confessed to their wrongdoing like you have, he said to me, us guards would no longer be needed and we would be living in the next best place to Heaven. On the other hand, if you sentence me to the ultimate penalty, every criminal around will take the message and continue to hide their crimes."

He stopped thinking and gave out a loud laugh. His whole body began to shake with laughter so that the bus itself seemed to shake and roll. He was laughing in surprise at his own wise choice of words. His suddenly acquired ability to argue it out with the best legal brains in the country! He never knew he had it in him. He felt supremely confident, smarter than the most experienced, trickiest lawyer. Previously he had been a man of doubt, insecure, inadequate, a failure, bearing the burden of unrepented, minor sins (mostly imaginary and the more troublesome for that) hanging heavily on mind, body and soul.

Now he was a new man, a man of the world, a genius. The whole bus was shouting at him. This was, he decided, because they were in wonder of him and his new abilities. They were shouting his praises. Then the shouting stopped and everybody started to laugh. They too, apparently, found his transformation to be a marvellous, if preposterous thing. He was so pleased with their laughter that he increased the loudness of his own laughter. He waved his arms around in gestures of camaraderie with his fellow passengers. The bus driver and conductor were laughing too. The laughter continued as the bus pulled up in the county capital. They were all unable to stop laughing even as they disembarked onto the street. Passers-by now joined in the merriment and Patsy himself – the centre of attention and no mark on him for the fact that his bulky, twine-held clothing made him look as if he had come straight there from the barnyard in attire certainly not appropriate for a respectable city – led a merry procession of happy folk around the streets, city folk joining in, past a number of dark, dirt-splattered statues that appeared to stand back in horror at the behaviour of the crowd, by various public buildings whose neat and tidy clerks came to the doors and windows to see what the fuss was about – and eventually to the courthouse.

'I have seen this before,' said an old man, observing what appeared to be the whole population of the city marching and laughing; 'in days that are long gone. They are under a fairy spell. God bless the mark. Who would have thought that the Little People would show their hand in this city in these modern times?'

Then he felt himself being pulled into the procession.

They all crowded into the courthouse. The O'Raffertys were guests of honour, directed to their seats provided courtesy (the clerk whispered) of Father Murphy.

Judge Moran strode into the courtroom in his usual sombre manner. He was the only one not laughing. He sat down, settling his black gown as he did so, and stared at the gathered folk with bafflement, as if he was surprised to see them there. He pretended he did not notice that everyone else had sat down before him, nor the general hilarity that infected even the legal teams. After some warnings and issuing of directions that he conducted with all the aplomb of a professional MC and bully, the hubbub died down and a quiet of sorts settled over the room.

"Here I am again," he thought, "having to deal with another sordid peasant crime. Am I to be stuck in this forsaken town for ever? Will I ever escape from these lamentable people?"

This was a man who did not believe in things such as the fairies (for it had been whispered to him that there was undue fairy interference in the case before him); a no-nonsense individual with a practical mind. He was someone with the power to dispense life or death. Descended from a long line of respectable landholders who had retained their lands through the Cromwellian hard times, itself a feat calling for qualities rare and special, it was said that he had inherited all of his ancestors' virtues but none of their vices. His physical presence alone, with his round, large face and thick, black eyebrows not to mention his elegant black gown, gave him the look of a Brehon of old. The ability to speak unceasingly on any topic, his knowledge of untold volumes of scholarly works, his air of assurance accompanied by a permanent, if subtle smirk, ensured such respect that it could be said that there were no limits to the power and influence he was able to wield in society – or the things he could get away with.

His refusal, or inability to laugh, his determination to hold out against the "climate of current opinion" and to ignore the generally accepted tradition of the need always to take into account in judgements the prejudices of the people; his reputation for straight, direct thinking – made all the more surprising what happened next.

He had just taken a first look at Patsy Murphy. He felt a gurgle in his throat and to his horror he realised he was going to laugh. He feared he might be losing that for which he was most noted – self-control when all around were losing theirs. He felt himself going into a daze that progressed to that level of sub-consciousness where one becomes aware of one's own absurdity. His previously solid character – his conservatism, dogmatic religiosity, his refusal to countenance mercy or to see "the other side", his defence of the status quo, his acquiescence to higher authorities – all threatened to go by the board now as he fought the strange light-headedness. Before, prudence had always ruled whenever fantasy appeared. (Oh yes, there had been the occasional wild flights of fancy, of idle daydreaming in court, but he had always recognised this for what it was – the detritus of an overworked brain, more a reason for sorrow than shame.)

Now he found himself struggling to hold back a whole series of vulgar and jocose remarks aimed at the unfortunate yokel in the dock. Crude and even obscene words formed on his lips. He greatly wanted to ridicule publicly the idea of such a person deserving even a hearing, much less a trial, in a court of law.

And then just as he had somehow succeeded in restraining himself from laughing or speaking out, he started daydreaming.

Darn this stale, tedious process. Why shouldn't he throw caution to the wind and abolish the law itself! He could restore the original legal codes of Erin, if he had a mind to it. He would become the greatest innovator in legal and social history, remembered in intellectual circles for all time. His judicial genius would put all of old Erin's immortals in the shade. Up in the gods, he would be the envy of the heroes Finn McCumhail, Brian Boru, St Columcille and Eamon DeValera, who would all look down and applaud his brave and genius-inspired innovations! He would end all this placating and ingratiating of the lower classes, abolish equal rights, and establish a hierarchical system that recognised the superior merits of a new aristocracy that would soon be established in the land.

When they looked again at the judge he had left his seat in some agitation and his appearance had undergone a remarkable change. His face was lit up by some interior excitement. He was pacing up and down deep in thought, thumb in his mouth. He had thrown off the black gown and rolled up his sleeves. To the bemusement now of everybody he started to speak in the Gaelic language, addressing his audience on various points of Brehon law.

Not since the day, long ago, when he had had to "speak a few words" in order to pass an exam had he attempted to speak thus. Initially, in the minds of those present, this retrograde behaviour was down to the prevalent habit of the time of calling on the ancestors and their traditions to compensate for some personal inadequacy, or problem in presentation, to cover up a professional flaw, or injustice blatant or covert, in one's dealings with the public. Usually everyone went along with the charade for the sake of peace, and because nearly everyone themselves had resorted to the practice at one time or another. However, it soon became apparent that Judge Moran was not play-acting this time; that for some reason, known only to himself, he had decided to carry the ruse of "being a Gael" beyond make-belief and into the realms of reality. For he was, amazingly, speaking with total fluency, something usually impossible for a non-native speaker.

As soon as this mysterious speech ended, Patsy Murphy began to mutter something. He had not got out more than a few words before he was interrupted by the irate judge.

'For your own sake, hold your peace. You will not say one more word during these proceedings.'

Instead of sitting in solemn stillness (he had finally taken the chair), Judge Moran was agitatedly fiddling with his shirt collar that seemed to be fitting too tightly around his neck. Over the course of the next few hours this collar would give him much trouble, seeming at times to choke him. After a while no word would come from his mouth without his first checking the tightness of the collar, thus greatly slowing up proceedings. It was also noticeable that a red flush came on his face whenever he struggled with some minor decision or judgement, or when he displayed impatience with Patsy.

(To most there, these were just the marks of a shifty, guilt-ridden braggart, but to any who knew its ancient code, it was a punishment decreed in Brehon law.)

Eileen and Widow O'Rafferty were greatly surprised – and pleased – when they discovered that the man on the bus and the defendant were the one and same Patsy Murphy. They cheered and clapped and shouted:

'Good on ye, Patsy!'

Their disgust at the smell and spitting now became transformed into something like a glorious light about the man. It was as if he had become one of the ancient heroes; that beneath the heavy, musty coat and rustic appearance lay concealed the powerful, athletic body and muscles of a giant.

Patsy, cheered by the applause, and ignoring the judge's injunction, stood up and shouted, 'I have a few strong words to say here in me own defence. I've been caught up in a spot of bother, and I have been a little bit confused lately about things. I have been taking advice [referring here to the stream of letters that had been mysteriously arriving from Sean], and I now have my own solicitor who is unable to attend here in person but who, via a third party whom I have been asked not to name, has been advising me lately. They have told me to say nothing more about the murder. There is much worse than murder going on. Worse even than lying on oath, worse than rape and pillage, worse than crooked judges and crooked lawmen, worse than making vows that you don't intend to keep!'

To everyone's amazement, Patsy was shouting and waving his fist.

'And they are happening in Rathcloon right now – or worse still – in the days soon to come. That little warning I pass on to ye now.'

There was a loud cheer.

'Hooray for Patsy Murphy! Hooray for the Little People.'

Judge Moran was enraged. They were all in contempt of court, he shouted. He could have had them all hanged! He alone would be the judge of Patsy Murphy. How dare the "rabble" challenge him! There had been too many cases lately of people getting ideas beyond their station and questioning authority. There was no way, he said, he was going to give in to ignorant peasants, or allow himself to be influenced by those ludicrous little tykes whose supposed ancestors had retreated in shame and defeat before civilisation and true religion, exiled to the gripes, thorn bushes and muddy cesspools of the backward places.

Who was the God-appointed judge here? He or they?

There were gasps and much shock in the courtroom, for the judge had gratuitously insulted the Little People. People blessed themselves.

'Me apologies, yer honour,' said Patsy.

He sat down and a short while later took a book out of his pocket that had been given to him by Father Murphy. He became absorbed in it as the trial proceeded, only his chewing and spitting disturbing the quiet, studious air about his person.

The Little Peoples' official representative at these proceedings was a grey-haired, tiny, wizened old man who had slipped in unnoticed and whose name nobody knew, standing at the back of the public gallery.

Judge Moran had spotted him and took him to be a civil servant from Dubh Linn secretly making notes on his (Judge Moran's) suitability for promotion to the "top bench".

If this "official" had not been there reporting back to the nether world on events in the courthouse, the fairy folks' influence on these proceedings would have been even less than it was. In recent times their ability to "tune in" to giant affairs had become greatly diminished due to the many developments that had afflicted life in Erin, as everywhere else. For instance, the speaking and picture boxes continued to preoccupy the population and worse still – capture the attention of the young. There was less room in the giants' minds for imagination. Giants, young and old were no longer letting their minds idle in "enchanted land", but were beginning to ask questions that should never be asked – why the earth went around the sun; why water is wetter than clay; why children know more than adults; why dogs chase cats; why invaders never cease to arrive in Erin; why the wind blows sideways; why the earth is under the sky; why the sky is so high that even utilising the superior technology of eagles, little folk had never been able to reach the top; why night gives way to day; why some on this earth don't have to work; why giants prefer praying to the unknown god than to known ones; why female giants are stronger than male giants; why real fire is better than artificial fire; why it is always best to conceal one's deeds; why laughter is better than sorrow; why talk is more worthy than deed.

Questioning and arguing not only about familiar, inconsequential local matters but about issues that were unfamiliar, of great complexity, even incomprehensible and of no concern to oneself or one's local community, appertaining only to those who lived great distances across the sea, who spoke foreign languages and did their thinking in a manner that would be alien and unfathomable to the giants of Erin – was now the business of every smart-ass giant in the country.

It had been their recent preoccupation to ruin Patsy's reputation in the eyes of the respectable, thereby adversely affecting his marriage prospects. But the murder charge, which had come along as a god-send (and they had rewarded Guard O'Hourigan by giving him a terrific ride across the country, whilst at the same time warning him to tread carefully), had only increased his credibility and the respect in which he was held. These days murder, rampage and every form of criminal act had become not punishable deeds but entertainment, being the main fare channelled through those sparkling boxes. They could not understand why the criminal had become the new folk hero. Now here was poor Patsy in the midst of a huge crowd, being treated like a hero instead of as an outcast, the prey for every unwed maiden and charlatan in the country.

They were on a watching brief here. Taking note of the little grey man's presence, Judge Moran knew that he had to put on the show of a lifetime. There would be no doubting that he was worthy of the highest judicial position! That they were in the presence of someone who did not kowtow to mere mortals or sub-human entities, whose mind ranged high above the common mind, even to consorting and conversing up there with the great immortals.

The light-headedness was gone. He was now in control of himself. There was a capital case before the court. Murder, he reassured himself, was a crime that could not be tolerated. Primordial crime – consorting with beasts, rampaging, lying before God and man in the matter of quality of beasts and chattels for sale, usurpation of the natural order, were all endemic in the countryside. It was necessary for there to be the sternest application of law and order in the backward areas. At least until that day when everyone came to live in decent houses, in decent towns and cities.

Someone shouted, "Patsy is a hundred times better man than any man here."

'Remove that person,' said Judge Moran.

The offender had disappeared. The crowd was laughing and talking.

Judge Moran was lost for words again. He called for order in an unnaturally quiet, pleading voice.

The first witness was called.

Garda O'Hourigan commenced giving his evidence, but not without firstly praising the character of the defendant in glowing terms; describing Patsy's fulsome confession and his facilitating of the finding of the bones in the far corner field of the farm. There was not much else to add, he said, other than the fact that the accused was penitent and a gentleman.

'Has the victim been identified?' asked the judge, still trying his best to recover his proper, customary voice (for he was still talking in a strange, alien, even unreal accent).

'Mr Murphy says that he can't remember the person's name, age or sex. He states, further, that he is not at liberty to divulge the reason for the murder. He is under the power of the Little People,' said Mr O'Connell, a solicitor who had been appointed by the court to speak to matters appertaining to Patsy's case.

'The Little…'

The judge tried to complete the words but he could not. His face had gone pale. He felt weak, nauseous. He wondered if he might be catching a bug from the country people. But the worst thing was the strange sensation in his throat, as if something was caught there. Or worse still – a *thing* live and troublesome had entered through his mouth and had stuck in his gullet. He was alarmed now at the thought that he might be "possessed by an evil spirit". There was only one solution – a heartfelt plea to the God whom he had never before taken seriously. He tried to pray but no words would come.

Now he felt angry – with himself – for being so superstitious.

There was no holding back the explosion of fury – it was as if the words were being put into his mouth; that he was indeed under a form of possession.

'I have been hearing more than enough about the *giccle gopul* today. I have heard the whispers – that they have come to town and that I should watch my words. Where would that leave the impartial judiciary, I ask you, if I heeded such advice? They have no status in law, not even in Brehon Law. Their position in society is lower than that of the lowest human being. They have no rights, no obligations, not one good thing to offer society. What have they given back for the right to live in this green and pleasant land? Nothing but tomfoolery. They have always taken for granted their tenure in dear Erin, not appreciating, I am sure, that St Patrick or Brian Ború could have removed them for good at one stroke, should they have so wished. No – they did not do that, for they felt sorry for the little bothersome craythurs! Well, all I can say is that all that they have given back to society is bad luck and misfortune! Damn those mean spirited, small minded, jealous sprites that don't know what's good for them. I have never had the privilege of meeting one of them, but if any are of a mind to show up here they would get what's coming to them! Sure, they don't even really exist at all, if you think about it. They are figments of the ignorant, superstitious imagination, playthings of the stupid, the drunken, the mad, the bad. Sure, you couldn't invent them and their antics if you tried. Have you ever heard of one of them doing anything sensible? They call them "the gentry" and fear to speak ill of them, these little perverters of the course of justice! Well, this judge is not afraid. I declare them to be in contempt of court for their interference in this case. Furthermore, I call upon their legal representative to appear before me forthwith, or else a harsh sentence on the whole tribe will follow. I declare proceedings adjourned until one of their spokesmen, or representative, appears before me. Now ye are all free to go to the pub.'

The crowd left the courtroom in a rush and headed for the nearest pub. Patsy remained in his seat, engrossed in his book. Judge Moran was left wondering what he could have said to have caused such a chaotic exit from his normally dignified, orderly court.

It was remarked upon, a little later, that Judge Moran had not shown up for his usual pint of porter with the lads.

'He looks a bit off colour today,' said Mr O'Connor, the solicitor, downing a second glass of Jameson's; 'it's as if something about this case has got to him. It's not like him to be putting on the style for a mere "murder trial".'

'We could be seeing him going upstairs any day now, after that big speech about the fairies! They say the top appointment is late in coming through,' said Mr Flanagan, the prosecuting lawyer; 'attacking the Little People may be a sign that he is appealing to a wider constituency.'

Their laughter was all the deeper for being low and restrained.

'Well, if he gives this man the rope, it's number twenty. Then he has the quota,' said Mr Flanagan, referring to the rule that anybody who had twenty hangings under his belt was guaranteed the ultimate accolade – a reputation for fairness and a seat at the top bench.

'There is only one way to make your reputation in this land', said Mr O'Connor; 'find the innocent guilty and the guilty innocent. A solid record in this builds up a man's reputation no end. It appeals to people's sense of justice when you let the popular man off, and put the unpopular scallywag down. I am still trying to get my head around this Patsy Murphy case, though. Is it the usual land-grab job?'

'Or the Church making an example of a miserly man for not contributing his dues,' suggested a legal clerk.

'Don't be talking!' said Mr O'Connor. 'The Revenue, too, has been known to set up people. But my own opinion is that it's a ruse by *certain* political powers to undermine confidence in the government, and simultaneously erode morale at the grass roots, by destroying the moral reputation of a well known farmer bachelor. For they are the backbone of the country. It has been tried before. In the eastern countries. We should stand up to subversion by foreign powers!'

'It's worse than that,' said a second legal clerk who had come over to join in the discussion; 'everybody knows that there is always a sin against chastity covered up in these sort of cases. The charge on which the defendant is indicted is just a diversion to trick the unwary mind and prevent it from discovering the real…disgrace…'

'Which in this case is…?' asked Mr O'Connor.

'Oh, you never know!' said the clerk, pleased that he had seemingly annoyed the well known senior solicitor; and enjoying the realisation that his suggestion was now causing various imaginations to deploy in uncharted waters whilst their purveyors could only be in a little awe of the clerk for his possibly having the definitive answer to their ponderings.

'I would say it is not a sin of the flesh that is behind the shenanigans here today, but good, old-fashioned money – the lifeblood of Rathcloon as of everywhere else,' said Mr Flanagan; 'and it is my humble opinion that there are financial shenanigans going on over there, and by the end of this trial Mr Murphy, or someone else, will be a very rich person.'

'I have heard it said that he is not entirely untainted by druidical things,' the first clerk went on. 'His farm is jinxed for every honest individual who goes there. So I am told by no less a person than the famous Garda O'Hourigan! He had his own bad experience, I believe. More than one visitor to his place has never been the same again afterwards. Just ask Mr O'Connor here!'

Mr O'Connor went quiet as he recalled the incident when he had visited the farm. After a tirade of abuse from Patsy all his papers were blown up in the air by a sudden gust of wind. He had spent the next hour chasing them – and not retrieving one single sheet.

'Now all *that* is the first real evidence I've heard in this case,' said Judge Moran, who had come in and had been listening, unnoticed, to all the talk. 'So this fulsome praise on his behalf by Garda O'Hourigan is just so much codswallop! I thought so. When a policeman praises someone, you may rest assured that something is up. If that is the case, he is for the rope. No mercy. Straight down the hatch.'

With that he downed a treble whiskey (that had appeared miraculously in his hand) in one gullup.

The third legal clerk came rushing up: 'The fairy legal representative is here, Your Honour.'

He winked at the others.

'Where is he?' asked the judge.

'Outside the door right now. The little man told me.'

'Let's go and have a look,' suggested the other two clerks in mock excitement.

'Not on your Nelly,' said Judge Moran. 'You would not see them if you looked, and to do so is bad luck anyway. Let him wait his turn like everyone else.'

It goes without saying that the 'legal representative' of the fairies was both annoyed and embarrassed. To be summoned to a mortal court was one unheard-of thing already. The king had said that he should go. In these trying times it was best not to make too much trouble. Try and obey the giants. But to be made to stand and wait like any mortal…! There would be many regretting this day – or that they had ever heard mention of the Little People. Before he would be through with them they would be begging for mercy. Mercy! Ha! What a fatuous idea – like so many others employed by the giants to cover their tracks. There was no "mercy" for evil-doers. Why should there be? And there were plenty of evil-doers around this town this morning. Oho, there would be ructions! As for this foolish judge of the many foolish words – he would pay!

The crowd in the pub were very excited by now, and they all stood to one side as Judge Moran approached the door. He went outside and looked up and down, sideways, backwards and up and down again.

'I will be waiting for you in court,' he said eventually, making sure it was more of a whisper than a loud command, for he did not want to become a laughing stock (and certainly not at this juncture in his career, with promotion waiting just around the corner).

When the court had re-assembled they all looked at the empty space in front of Judge Moran. Here there stood, apparently, a fairy or leprechaun that nobody but Judge Moran could see. They took his word for it that the little fellow was there, for not only Judge Moran but the small, grey man who had busied himself acting as concierge ordering people about and moving chairs and clerks to "make room for the royal representative" – also was certain that the chap was there.

It was apparent to some that the judge was surprised that he had been taken up on his command to the sídh (he had only been speaking metaphorically when he had issued the injunction), for he was displaying an uncharacteristic humility, uncertainty and respect.

There was a brooding quality about him; what could be termed a "haunted look".

'I will ask you, dear sir, seeing as you have honoured us with your presence here, to forgive any harsh words I may have used previously about you or yours when addressing certain problems caused by your, apparent, involvement in this case. I ask for mercy and forgiveness for any insult, slight or slur I may have made on your character, way of life, beliefs or racial characteristics. It was not my intention to put you in a spot, but only to ask if you can throw any light on this case that I am trying here today.'

He became silent. It was plain to everyone there that he was listening to someone – to whom he responded at intervals.

'Yes, I made a mistake.'

'I'm sorry you feel that way about harmless words that were only uttered as an oratorical device.'

'If you do, I will call in a priest of Holy Church.'

He crossed himself (which example was followed by everyone else there).

'I can only say that I will take your views into account.'

'Any such objections will be overruled. I will see to it that Patsy gets a fair trial. But I should not be told how to do my job.'

'Yes, I know his character is at stake here.'

'Nobody's character has been taken.'

'Even if I should find him guilty, that will be no reflection on his good name.'

'There are worse penalties than death.'

'Have it your way, if you must. Do your worst. I have a job to do. I will not be spoken to like that.'

The last utterance he had shouted out, as if keen to let everyone know that he was still his own boss.

The trial resumed with Mr Flanagan outlining a possible motive or motives. Utilising "intelligence" he had picked up in the pub, these included robbery, the sneaking away of someone's property, acting out an old grievance, hatred of one's neighbour, bad mouthing, a supposed or actual desire to betray one's country, deliberately causing a person to have bad luck, "druidical" business, the commission of an indecent act followed by a cover-up.

'There you have,' he said with some satisfaction, 'the whole array of human wickedness.'

The trial became bogged down in legal difficulties, all brought up by Judge Moran – the nature of any one of which always appeared impossibly intricate and even incomprehensible. At each attempt made by Mr Flanagan or Mr O'Connor to move matters on, he would interrupt to "consult the law", closing his eyes, holding his head in his hand, his thumb in his mouth and meditating deeply, often saying nothing at the end of it all.

Just when things would start going smoothly again he would find something in "ancient law" that contradicted or rendered invalid whatever had just been said, rendering each revised "rule" or "precept" with eyes closed. Complaints were made by both prosecution and defence about the prolongation of what should have been a straightforward case.

The trial entered the late afternoon with very little, if any, progress in legal matters, but with lots of talking, laughter and the buzz of speculation throughout the courtroom. Some women had commenced wailing. Some had started praying. The prevailing temper of the times – a general sense of doom and foreboding, was now being utilised to prepare the appetite for an increased intake of alcohol.

Questioning of witnesses became loud slanging matches with the public joining in. There was no shortage of volunteers to testify one way or another. Fist fights broke out as the atmosphere deteriorated into a sort of general hostility, with people falling all around the sides, beer and whiskey (now having been brought into the courtroom) raised in their hands.

Whether due to harassment from lawyers or crowd – witnesses now were agreeing with everything that was being put to them. Slanders against Patsy received standing ovations. "Friends" either damned him by faint praise, or related his good deeds in such a way that they became in the mind heinous crimes; thus casting the worst possible light on him, whom a minority, now, still believed if not entirely innocent, at least deserving of a milder punishment and certainly not the life imprisonment or capital punishment that was certainly coming his way. "Praise" of Patsy or declarations of his innocence were booed whenever attempted, with the biggest cheers of all for the most iniquitous descriptions of his truculent, lawless, unreformed character.

The presence of the "fairy", as well as the little grey man (who most there took to be the room orderly), seemed to be weighing heavily on the judge. He was now, it would seem, speaking only for the benefit of an invisible audience. Others thought that his strange behaviour was due to his having drunk too much whiskey. His physical appearance – which at the start of the day had been so colourful, flamboyant, full of the zest of life, proud, full of the flower of tradition, had now so deteriorated that they had all become gradually aware that he was no longer a man in his prime but someone who had gone beyond his present age, and was looking decidedly at least forty years older. He was now some old fellow who looked as if he might not be "all there". His black cloak had become a shabby, torn rag; the fancy pins and brooches that had been displayed were all gone; his hair was no longer a distinguished grey but an unkempt mass of white, with a long ragged beard of similar colour. Was it even him at all, there, some wondered now.

Judge Moran looked at his watch; it was the hour of re-opening of the pubs.

He called for Patsy to step forward. He asked if there was anybody present who had any objections to make regarding the conduct of the trial or any reason or reasons why he should not pass sentence.

'At long last I get my chance to say something,' said Patsy who, apart from his opening statement, had remained silent all day, not having moved from his chair. He had just finished reading his book, which he had found to be totally engrossing.

'It would be better for you if you said nothing,' said the judge, 'for you would not be the first man to put his own neck into the rope.'

The verdict was an enthusiastic guilty. There were cheers and stamping of feet.

Judge Moran was breathing very heavily. His body was shaking with the effort of speaking. His face had become twisted out of all recognition. His hair seemed to have all fallen out and what remained was only a mass of solid dandruff covering his head and shoulders. His gown hung on him like a filthy rag. He looked down where he still could hear, but not see, the little fellow he was going to defy. The unseen entity was shouting at him, saying that what was going to happen must not happen!

He would ignore the threats and do what was best for Patsy and the country.

Judge Moran's finest hour was at hand.

Death by hanging.

With great difficulty – he seemed to be in pain – he put the "black cap" on his now near-bald head (he'd had to ask around for a black cloth).

But the words would not come out. The obstruction in his throat prevented him from speaking. He had another panic attack as his throat enlarged to an unnatural size.

Everybody looked at Patsy. The fellow seemed totally unconcerned, his mind apparently a million miles away in some reverie of the intellect or imagination, and quite indifferent to his fate.

"Poor Patsy. Poor, poor Patsy," Judge Moran found himself saying. The words were coming as if they were being forced out between his clenched teeth.

Something odd was happening, now. Surely not...? What was this...on his face? What was this loud groaning? His whole body had seized up. Gradually, he came to realise that he was weeping.

He could not hang Patsy Murphy!

The news had already left the building and was travelling at great speed over the rooftops, mountains, lakes and bogs as the cheering began, nearly lifting the roof.

At long last they could get on with the ceremony.

Father Murphy had rushed into the courtroom, from the little anteroom where he had gone to say his prayers.

'The banns are all done,' he shouted, barely audible above the commotion.

Patsy looked at Eileen who had rushed up to his side. He was speechless. He was not sure what was happening. He only knew that he felt relief, for he realised now that he had, indeed, been facing the rope. Everything else was a blur and the roar of bedlam.

Without further ado the vows were exchanged in front of Father Murphy and the judge. The couple were carried shoulder-high out of the courtroom to the church opposite. There the marriage ceremony was completed. The happy couple ran out rather than walked to where there was a waiting horse and carriage.

It was said at the time that nobody knew who had paid for the transport. The other strange thing was that the horse, its harness and carriage were all black. More fit for a funeral than a wedding, someone commented.

The crowd outside were still recounting the enjoyable and shambolic events of the day. Individuals were continuing to argue and fight with each other, women were still weeping and wailing for no good reason, children were still getting into mischief and learned, respectable people were still discussing murder, marriage and revenge in a great release of pent-up, scandalised talk.

It was only Father Murphy who noticed the unusually strong wind that came round the street in front of the church as they waved off Patsy and his bride. It caused skirts to rise, hats and caps to fly off, the city's statues to sway and wobble, the horses to become frisky and a car with a drunken driver swerve to avoid an invisible obstacle and crash into the courthouse door, narrowly missing a large group of unaware, distracted people.

A large, exceedingly ugly, red blotch had appeared on Judge Moran's face towards the end of that afternoon of the trial. It proved to be permanent. Some speculated that this was a "fairy stroke". It could be interpreted either as a punishment or a "thank you" – in lieu perhaps of some harsher punishment. Even when he later went on to achieve his great ambition and obtain a seat on the top bench up in the capital city, the mark never left him. It caused the many people – humble peasants and VIPs, foreign emissaries, wealthy businessmen, artists and the whole collection of famous and not-so-famous people who were fated to meet him always to excuse themselves at the first opportunity, and studiously avoid the man if possible thereafter.

A strange sort of "luck", or "bad luck" depending on one's viewpoint, dogged him for the rest of his life. He was never again able to play the part of the strict enforcer. He became a "softee" (it was said he had "gone weak in the head"), so that the worst and most demeaned criminal types flocked to have their cases heard at his court (though they, too, would use every ruse to avoid having to look him in the face). It was this quality of "the merciful" and unwillingness to convict – that lay like a curse on him – that ensured he would end his days as the most loathed, hated and laughed at high official in the land.

In later years, during the landmark public inquiry into corruption in the judicial system as reflected in the many miscarriages of justice over the years, alongside the gung-ho attitude and behaviour on the part of an establishment that was, apparently, for many years answerable to no one, the Patsy Murphy case became a *cause célèbre* as typifying the debased conditions of the times. A great commotion and controversy had arisen upon the death of this man, due to the vast wealth that he had acquired and associated problems of inheritance and redistribution. There was, in the case of the conduct of his marriage ceremony, on the legality of which so many issues hinged, systematic and prolonged abuse of innocent, hapless witnesses on the day of the legal "tying of knots" that had made them feel that they, too, were in the dock. What was termed "evidence of character" had been only hearsay and a mishmash of ancient tradition, folklore and superstitious beliefs. The elderly Judge Moran would, when hauled before the commission, state that he could remember nothing of a trial, its procedures or outcome, and least of all could he recollect anything relating to either his own behaviour or to his contemporaneous decisions. He doubted if he had even been in the city on that particular day.

The tribunal thereupon declared Pasty's marriage to Eileen O'Rafferty invalid, in the legal if not the moral sense. This was two years after the death of both parties, but as the tribunal chairman declared – justice can be retrospect. This conclusion left Patsy's many descendants with innumerable problems due to the implications of the divorce (or more accurately, the non-existence of the marriage) and complications for the distribution of Patsy's immensely increased wealth – for it had increased more after his death than before – a miracle in itself – amongst a plethora of children left by both invalidly married persons and the presence of other children whose exact parentage was not recorded.

Five

THE MARRIED COUPLE'S carriage pulled up outside the Railway Hotel, a somewhat rundown-looking establishment. The coach driver disembarked and opened the carriage door.

'The honeymoon hotel!'

'Bejasus, it is,' said Patsy angrily, getting out and pushing him to one side. He jumped up on the coach driver's seat and took the reins.

'Get ye going,' he shouted, and the carriage moved off, the door still open.

They went down the street at a strong gallop.

Inside, Eileen sat back to enjoy the bumpy ride, a smile, as well as nervousness fixed on her face. As the rain came down, and with the increasing commotion and noise outside – loud horns blaring, shouting, the sound of ambulance or police car bells – she leaned over and pulled the door shut. It was to be an all-night journey with regular stops at the side of the road for rest and refreshment.

After an hour Patsy pulled up on a quiet road. He got into the carriage (the rainfall was continuous), and had a first chat with his bride.

'We will have our honeymoon at the farm. The cows cannot milk themselves, you know.'

'I'll help you, Patsy. You can take it easy now. There is another pair of hands to do the work.'

A long silence followed. Something told Eileen to stay quiet; to let him brood. After some time he attempted, but failed, to say some words.

'Take yer time, Patsy. There's plenty of time,' she said.

'There's something I need to tell you…'

'Yes, Patsy.'

Silence.

'I'll get to it in time.'

'Yes, Patsy.'

'Just wait a minute. Till I get the words.'

'There's no hurry in the world, Patsy.'

Silence.

She saw him struggle with himself. He crouched over. He folded his arms around his middle as if that would force the words out. His mouth was moving but no words came. Eventually there was a groan – but no decipherable sense. After some more minutes of this grunting and fidgeting he suddenly brightened:

'That horse will need water. I'll look out on the way for a little stream.'

'Yes, Patsy,' said Eileen, disappointed.

As he opened the door he accidentally brushed her side.

'Oh, sorry. I'm so sorry. That was an accident.'

'You are my husband now. You can feel free to knock into me.'

'I was brought up to respect women.'

'That is a good sign in a man. You are of the old school, Patsy.'

'I am indeed,' he replied, glad that she was agreeing with everything he said.

Heavy rain meant that visibility was nil, but they carried along at quite a good speed. Patsy was gifted with night vision – or at least he was on that night. Many times he had to pull the reins sharply to the right or left, thus avoiding imminent collision or disaster of some kind. It was on the second stop that Eileen suggested they light up the oil lamps in the glass boxes at the side of the carriage, at least for the sake of the many vehicles that passed, loudly sounding their horns and often braking suddenly or swerving;

from the sound of it some of them had ended up in the ditch.

Patsy took out his box of matches and lit the lamps, muttering under his breath that there was no need for lights. And they didn't want the whole world to know their business.

'Oh, it's so romantic, Patsy,' she said happily.

He did not respond.

'Have you remembered what it was you wanted to say?' she asked him when he got back inside to dry off from the rain.

'Well...I don't want to talk about it just yet,' he replied grumpily.

Silence once more.

'But didn't you think the wedding was a bit of a surprise?' he asked after a while.

'What do you mean, my beloved Patsy?'

'I thought I was on trial for murder.'

'What do you mean?'

'The judge and all that. Those gabby lawmen. The guard. My near escape from the death penalty. And the Little People, bless them, standing up to that tyrant judge?'

'Little People! Tyrant judge! You mean the marriage registrar! And didn't Jim O'Connor gave me away in great style. And Dan Flanagan the best MC ever. Garda O'Hourigan did a wonderful job as your best man. Sure, stop your raving, Patsy.'

'It didn't seem to me to be like that at all. All those things they were saying about me. And all that talk about me covering up a murder for years. An unrepentant murderer they said I was. And I fully prepared to admit my guilt!'

'That was just idle chat and gossip. It was the craic, Patsy. Some interfering do-gooders were deliberately over-praising you in front of me. Just to get a dig in, I suppose. Jealousy!'

Was Patsy a bit of a simpleton, she now asked herself? But what would it matter if he was?

'By the way, don't be saying too much about the Little People, Patsy. Or they will call you a Man of the Sídh.'

'Sure do I care what they call me?'

'Garda O'Hourigan had everyone in stitches telling them about those bones in your field turning out to be sheep bones.'

'Sheep bones? They were human bones. What are you on about? Who is telling all these lies?'

'Ah, to be sure, you're right, Patsy. They're all clowns and eegits. Pay no more attention to them.'

'They told me I was going to court. I didn't think I would be attending a wedding today. And I sure didn't think it would be my own wedding!'

'Didn't the registrar, Mr Moran and Father Murphy have everything fixed up between them? And isn't Mr Moran on his way to be a top judge? They have your best interests at heart. Now what was it you were going to tell me, Patsy?'

'Nothing.'

As the rain continued, Patsy put his head out the door and shouted, 'Gee up.'

The horse commenced galloping along the road, driverless.

'Patsy, are you sure he can find his way?'

'Surely. The Little People will direct him.'

The story of the driverless "death coach" (although some said it was driven by a "headless ghoul") that rampaged through the countryside that night was repeated many a time and dark evening thereafter, in pub and home, field and workplace in that part of the country. A good number of people had dropped dead roundabout that time. Cows stopped giving their best milk. Bees abandoned their hives and went on stinging rampages. Schoolmasters increased the tempo of their beatings. Politicians promised to end emigration. Priests and religious prophesised the end of the world, with the dire certainty that not one inhabitant of Erin would be saved. Love, health and happiness declined, with a steady drift away from the virtues, especially by the young. Mothers sacrificed their sons and daughters. Fathers abandoned the homestead for the nearest pub.

All these things happened about the time that the death coach was seen rushing through the countryside.

More than one witness reported seeing the death coach heading for Rathcloon. One or two brave souls said they saw it go up Patsy Murphy's lane.

As the horse and carriage trotted up to the house, Patsy at last was able to find the words to express to Eileen what had been on his mind.

After a long spit through the carriage window of a mouthful of tobacco juice, he said, 'There is another woman in the house.'

Eileen was taken aback, stuck for words.

'What…?'

'A young lady.'

'What is she doing there…?'

'She is the daughter of the king of England. The fairies and I brought her here.'

Eileen was determined that they were not going to have their first argument before they had even crossed the threshold. She kept her temper and spoke as coolly as possible: 'The daughter of the King of England!'

'An unknown, unwanted daughter. I am sworn to secrecy, as you are now, too.'

'How did she travel here?'

'I went with the sídh through the night sky in what I thought at first was a dream. We came down in the grounds of a wonderful palace. There was a great ball going on inside. All the princes and princesses of the kingdom were there dancing and feasting. Except this one who, my fairy guide told me, was imprisoned in a dungeon cell. She was more beautiful than all the others, but she had a fatal flaw – the sidheóg told me. She was astray in the head. Mortals who are like that, he told me, are blessed with many gifts. If I would release her form her imprisonment and take her back with me, they would guarantee that bad luck would never strike me again.'

'And it hasn't, Patsy, it hasn't. You got married today!'

'Hold your whist, girl, you don't know what you are saying. She will be no trouble. She is just happy to be away from her wicked relatives. You will see her wandering the fields. You must always address her as "Your Highness", and give a little bow. She would want to live in the cowshed, though I try to tell her otherwise, and that is where she will be right now. She likes to do little jobs about the place. She is no trouble at all.'

They disembarked in the darkness, and Eileen waited on the doorstep as Patsy unharnessed the horse and put him in the barn. (He never returned horse or coach to the rightful owner, and nobody ever came around enquiring.) As they settled in for the night, Patsy explained that all was chaos as he had not expected to be bringing back company with him. Eileen insisted on joining him in the bed, whereon they both collapsed into an exhausted sleep.

Father Murphy was having great trouble saying his prayers. Indeed he could not even get started. He knelt in the church before Mass and tried "the usual". Nothing happened. Even when he had managed to overcome his main distraction and banish the image of Widow O'Rafferty from his mind, he still could not pray. The prayers he was attempting were set prayers, never altered or varied throughout a long life. They had always been the foolproof armoury against the wiles of the devil. If only he could say them now, all would be fine. He knew all he had to do was just begin to recite the words; that would be enough to get the whole process going. But the words were submerged below. Hard as he tried to get to them, he failed. His whole consciousness was in a state of immobility. His "interior" life was imprisoned by some power greater than prayer! He gave up trying to concentrate. He told himself just to "relax and let be".

His mind coursed over the day of Patsy's wedding; and the words that had passed between himself and the widow. She had such insight! She seemed even to know about his troubles, saying to him it must be a quiet life at the presbytery and wasn't it very invigorating to be able to get out and go to weddings, funerals and the like. Just as he was often thinking! Every word she uttered had a deep resonance.

'How are you, Father?'

How did she know that he was feeling "low"?

'Isn't it wonderful to see two young people beginning their life together?'

She too, perhaps, was imagining a day like that again for herself!

'You must come soon again and visit my humble home.'

The very thing in the world that he wanted to do!

Perhaps, he thought now, she had been sent as an antidote to the loneliness that had only increased as the years went by. None of the old remedies for "pallor of the spirit" seemed to work anymore. One would have thought that – at his age – "wishing for company" would have been a thing of the past. How could he desire human company, indeed, when that of the holy spirits was there all the time – just waiting to be asked? And how could he, really, have anything in common with a country woman, unversed in matters of theology and philosophy, plain of speech and simple of mind?

Try as he might to dispel the thought, theology and philosophy paled into insignificance in comparison with the loveliness, wisdom and intelligence that was the Widow O'Rafferty! He would give up prayer, faith, religion itself, for just one minute more of basking in that wonderful woman's munificence!

Could he ask the Lord for that favour?

Was it blasphemous to praise such as she? The church came alive now with the thought of her! The light itself was lighter. The dim walls were bright. The plain windows were thoroughfares to heaven. An inner communication with the universe came to him as he knelt there. He looked at the statues, and especially at that of the local holy man, St Finbar. It might be his imagination, but was he smiling at him? He had always felt some empathy with St Finbar, a fellow countryman, a local boy.

'I'm in a spot of bother here, St Finbar,' he said in a light voice.

When the saint replied with cautionary, friendly words, he was not too surprised.

'Be quiet and hold your tongue, Michael. Listen to some good words of advice.'

★

The grandeur of design and planning of the new city of BailenahEoropa had exceeded everyone's expectation. Brazil and Co, the architects, had "gone to town" on the layout, insisting on wide, straight streets called "boreenevards" that were part of something that was an entirely new concept for the country – a sensible, orderly arrangement of streets in a grid pattern. This planning novelty was claimed by Señor Brazil, the chief architect, to be the counter to the anarchic and chaotic pre-European civilisation of the island, an inferior civilisation that had spawned all those "counter-cultural" settlements of the past with their cobbled maze of crooked streets, winding lanes and irregular walls that had constrained the native culture, making it both feckless and impotent. The glass and steel buildings were so high that their roofs were completely out of sight. Each glass cube or obelisk, a maze of mirrors, reflected the sky, sun and moon, stars, cloud, land and water. A new mental ailment or "physic condition" was to arise in this city's inhabitants that was labelled "Jerusalem syndrome" whereby previously non-spiritual folk – atheists, agnostics, sceptics, materialists and the like – were so taken up with their surroundings that they would break into spontaneous song as they walked the streets, become transfixed to the spot whilst gazing skywards, and go on eventually to found or join a multitude of cults and sects that eulogised the city (soon to be called the Eighth Wonder of the World) not as a mere mortal creation, but as a place of impossible, indeed miraculous prosperity and happiness.

The city was built in such a way that it was impossible to tell where the city ended and the countryside began. The original terrain had presented a great challenge to Señor Brazil, who considered the eradication of the original, primitive landscape a mission in itself. This almost religious zeal to eradicate the past became an obsession; it was almost impossible to get him and his acolytes off the subject of the backwardness of the country and the need to reform its people at the many meetings and important conferences that prepared the groundwork for the new city.

He had first visited the area in the company of Enterprise Minister

Michael Fitzgerald, TD, who had pointed out Rathcloon and environs to him as the "El Dorado" of Erin, just waiting for exploitation. Señor Brazil, who claimed to have built the world's most modern city in the middle of the South American jungle – a city that also had the capacity to "fly like a supersonic airliner" (Michael believed this latter claim to be something of a vain boast; and explorers were never able to find or confirm the existence of such a city.) – had looked at the village with its one shop, petrol pump and small, grey cottages and shaken his head.

'Wad a misery place.'

The surrounding countryside of twisting lanes, treacherous bog, a small hill that Michael referred to as an "eyesore", tiny, hedge-enclosed, undulating fields (nowhere was there anywhere flat, Señor Brazil had complained) devoid of livestock and activity, small whitewashed or grey farm buildings (dwelling houses could not be distinguished from outhouses) huddled away to conceal themselves from the prying eye, gave the whole area a forlorn, haunted look. Even Michael himself had confessed that he, too, had similar negative feelings and nodded in agreement when the internationally renowned urban architect proceeded to make extremely derogatory, libellous remarks about the people of Erin.

'I have build a brand-new city in the middle of the American wilderness. Much, much bigger, wilder country than this! I have fight snakes, rebels, Indians, outlaws, diseases, drought, corrupt officials, useless workers. My city is now the pride of a great continent. This place? Ah! There is something cursed here. There is much to destroy before we plan to build.'

'This document I have,' said Michael, building on this latterly more positive attitude of Señor Brazil, 'is cabinet approval for the public financing of an international airport to be built on that land right there in front of you...'

'The swamp?'

'Not a swamp. We call it bogland. Do you see Dunmor church steeple over there in the distance? Many believe that a miracle took place some time ago in that church. A statue was observed not only moving around but speaking to people. This was witnessed and confirmed by no less a person than the present bishop of this area, a good friend of mine. Our far-sighted government believes that an airport will bring multitudes from all over the world to worship at the spot. Some of my fellow government ministers are of peasant stock and very superstitious. They feel that they will be building up a spiritual reward for themselves if they approve the scheme, as well as gaining in popularity with the electorate. Even if it never amounts to a great success, they will still bask in the glory of having proposed such an ambitious, grand and even unworldly scheme! What the people admire in this country is not the same as what they admire in other countries, Señor. But you and I will hold them to their word – if we can come up with a convincing looking, cost-cutting, architectural plan for the area. We will build, Señor, the cosmopolitan metropolis of BailenahEoropa at rock-bottom prices, with public funding covering the losses and private funding receiving all profits. You can even claim before the world that you rescued the surviving inhabitants of a poor, backward, obscure land whose existence you were not even aware of before, from superstition, ignorance and economic backwardness. Television programmes, films and books will be made about your revolutionary development. The land will be drained and levelled, which will be the subject of handsome praise, grand speeches and worthy newspaper articles. That hill and all the others will disappear. I have always hated them; they get in the way of the view and block direct routes. The people will have no further use for the bogland, for they are going over to electricity and they will not be needing turf anymore. They give away their land for nothing, anyway, saying that it is like the lifting of a curse. My company already owns much of it.'

'An international airport – here!'

'The greatest power in the land has given its blessing. If you don't believe me, ask Bishop Murphy. I will arrange for you to meet the bishop. He knows this area and its people like the back of his hand. Once he has given the go-ahead, no government or power can stand in the way.'

They shook hands, Señor Brazil not being particularly pleased with the spittle that Michael put on both their palms as the seal of agreement.

The peasants are certainly in control in this country, Señor Brazil reflected.

There was no doubt now but that *the luck* had turned against the Little People. Knowing that that they had not been able to prevent Patsy's wedding, all that was left to do was to save face. The few simple giants still around, such as Patsy, were being led up the garden path and there was nothing they could do about it. They decided to accept the fact of Patsy's marriage and try to get along with his new wife. Indeed they could even celebrate something; for this was one of those rare occasions when a giant showed true altruism, as Patsy had, both in his giving refuge to Bridie Murphy as well as his agreeing to share his comfortable bed with a relative stranger, Eileen O'Rafferty. (The most generous, hardened, brave and sophisticated of the sídh would never have found it possible to share a bed.)

Contrary to popular belief, they really were on the side of all who showed good will. They could share in the giants' sorrows and triumphs, even if sometimes only to indulge in enjoyable fits of Schadenfreude as well as bouts of drunken celebration. Manifestations of virtuous deeds were the occasion for those legendary open-air celebrations in fairyland that often became audible and visible to humans. Dancing, singing, loud playing of flute and fiddle and boisterous hurling matches between the reds and the blues that went on non-stop for twenty-four hours, were renowned in folklore for their noisy, unusual manifestations of joy. Even if this particular occasion did not merit quite such a celebration, Patsy's kindness was still the silver lining in a dark cloud.

It was imperative now that Eileen should begin the week well, for there was nothing worse and more humiliating than a failed scheme followed by the determined pursuit of a lost cause. It was best to believe that all was for the best. They would ensure that Mrs Murphy's first week was an eventful one, and perhaps also show her into the bargain that grand plans for modernisation had a way of falling apart in the real world of the countryside. Their plan now was to give Eileen a "buzz in the head" so that such indignities as having to sleep in a damp bed, waking up to find a frog in her shoe, and that her husband has been keeping another woman in the house, would all be OK by her. She would greatly surprise herself at being able to put up with things that previously would have filled her with horror!

Little pleasant surprises should continue to cheer her all through the week – a husband who showed unrestrained pleasure in having his tin mug of tea handed to him (a pot of té always on the hob) with long, hard hand-grips that crushed the bone; grunts and belches in appreciation of the grub that would always be ready at any hour of the day or night; surprise and wonder in finding that his clothes were always put away to dry when he went to put them on, expressed by long, loud expletives; the sound of him singing loudly to himself and spitting out his "baccy" – would at least hint at the possibility that her husband was on the way to an acceptance of the married state. Furthermore, the presence of a "maid" to help in all things – and indeed to do all the unpleasant work that might be considered unsuitable for a lady of the house – was a real bonus. All this would build up her sense of accomplishment and so happy would she be at her success in keeping Patsy happy, all ideas about improving the house would recede into the background; indeed she would find herself accepting and defending the status quo as resolutely as any "old woman", in case any change caused a disturbance to the present state of happiness. It would all seem to her a dream too good to be true.

So when she awoke to hear Pasty cursing the fact that there was no room in the bed, she laughed heartily and thought his behaviour was very amusing.

'Our first day together, Patsy!'

'The cows, the cows,' he cried, not sure either of his whereabouts, the identity of his bed companion, or even what he was meant to be doing.

'Sure the cows will be fine.'

'Who...what are you doing here?'

'I'm your brand-new wife, Patsy. Your life will be an easy one from now on. What would you like for breakfast?'

'Breakfast...?'

It was at that moment that a knock was heard on the door and Bridie Murphy entered, bearing a tray with breakfast for two.

'What have you got there, Your Highness?' asked Patsy.

''Tis breakfast for you and the lady, sir. May the tea whet yer mouths and the porridge satisfy all yer longing.'

'And what land are ye a princess of?' asked Eileen politely, showing respect.

'I come from a kingdom that I am not permitted to speak much about. I am the daughter of the king of England. But I was treated badly by him and imprisoned in a dungeon. It is one of the wonders of the world and a kindness of providence that I was carried away to this safe haven of Patsy Murphy's farm. Good fortune is bespoken also in that I share with him – with the great man Patsy of whom there is no equal – the same name of Murphy.'

'Oh, that is a wonderful tale you tell,' said Eileen.

The poor girl was clearly out of her mind. She certainly presented no challenge or threat to her own relationship with Patsy, or to their marriage.

And Patsy obviously knew how to humour her. Eileen decided that she would just follow him in everything – particularly in the way he dealt with Bridie and spoke to her. Imagine having breakfast all prepared by a servant and enjoying it in bed with a new husband on the first morning of a lifelong marriage-to-be! If only her friends and relatives could see her now. How could life get any better? When Patsy muttered again about the cows needing milking, the princess said in the happiest of tones, 'I have them milked already.'

The look of bemusement on Patsy's face bespoke that here was a man newly surprised by life, and particularly by the realisation that he was no longer master in his own house.

★

Sean Murphy was spending his days talking to himself. Here he was cooped up in some God-forsaken place where they were all off their heads. He felt no bitterness or impatience, even though his own presence there was as a result of a complete misunderstanding. He was so sorry for the other residents. They were victims of a range of delusions, and he had decided to make it his business to try to restore these unfortunates to some semblance of sanity before he left. The men in the white coats, who called themselves guardians, were the most stricken of all, although they did not realise it. They held themselves to be the sole possessors of the knowledge of reality. "All *you* see and experience is only illusion," they proclaimed; "listen to what we say, for *that* is reality." There was no clearer sign of madness than this. The most pitiable of all was the man who always locked himself into his room for most of the day. The sign on his door read *Dr O'Boyle, MD, Dip Psych, Administrator.* There was probably a whole heap of delusions in those perplexing letters. Another sign on the door read, *Do Not Disturb Under Any Circumstances.*

Whenever Dr O'Boyle appeared, usually about 12.30 p.m. when everybody else was tucking into dinner, he would walk around glumly, keeping his distance from guardian and inmate alike. Being drawn into conversation was apparently the one thing he greatly feared. This realisation on the part of Sean of the fellow's great shyness and introspective, withdrawn nature, was the reason he always made a point of getting Dr O'Boyle's attention and then drawing him into conversation on whatever topic might come to mind at that moment. These attempts sometimes failed, with the guardians intervening to put a stop to Sean's well-meaning efforts and escorting him, sometimes roughly, back to his place.

There were the men in dark uniforms, who appeared at regular intervals bringing with them a seemingly never-ending supply of willing and unwilling captives and – for one reason or another – carrying others off out of the place. These men had a bit of a reputation for violence and for this reason, he was more astute and careful when questioning them as to the nature of their particular concepts of "reality", their views on Dr O'Boyle staying locked up all day, their opinions as to the mystery of the doctor's real identity and – more circumspectly – what they did with the residents they took away. Whenever he put these points to those burly men, he was always careful firstly to greet them with a self-mocking, sort of fool's smile along with flamboyant hand gestures to assure them that he, too, was not perhaps quite all right in the head, posed no threat and therefore was not requiring yet to be taken away for some common sense to be "knocked into him".

Today he had just left, despairingly, another discussion session with the men in white coats. One "expert" had proposed the idea that violent urges, frustration and hostility were really positive, beneficial emotions whose expression should not be suppressed, but actively and deliberately encouraged. Such expressions of one's feelings, he said, would release society and sick individuals from their inhibitions and produce a freer, more spiritual world. There was something wrong with a person, the expert went on, who refrained from – or worse was incapable of – demonstrating these qualities. Sean had tried to show him that he was not only deluded, but that his views posed a threat to public order and the safety of innocent and non-innocent alike. For his troubles, he became a recipient there and then of some of those supposedly beneficial, violent, hateful words and "aggression".

He went to Dr O'Boyle's room to see if the fellow had considered any responses to ideas and suggestions he had put forward. In particular, he wondered whether O'Boyle had now come to accept that the Little People not only existed, but were a force to reckon with locally, and in the world at large. Hopefully, he had taken Sean's advice to observe closely the way certain objects moved around the building, sometimes disappearing, without human intervention. Similarly, items had gone from people's pockets. When a scapegoat, accused of being the "motivator" of the disappearances, was punished Sean observed that the "disappearances" still continued thereafter.

He hammered on O'Boyle's door, knowing from experience that a gentle knock would bring no response. Unfortunately the door remained closed, so once again he found he had no option but to put his weight against it and shove. This time it worked – the door gave way.

O'Boyle had a look of great alarm on his face.

'I have come to pass on a warning from the Little People.'

'I have told you before. There are no such things as...Little People,' said the doctor, from behind his desk.

'Believe me when I say that they are aware of your insulting comments. They only refrain from revenge because of my own words of restraint.'

Sean was staring straight ahead, like a seer in a trance. His voice rose:

'I had another dream last night. It was given to me as a warning. People are going to turn from traditional ways. The land will disappear, to be covered by an abomination, a great city that will stretch as far as the eye can see. It will outdo even the Place Without Blessings that is called Dubh Linn. Nature's power of regeneration will be no more. Alien laws will return to oppress the land. People will be barred from walking on grass, forbidden to live in the countryside! From breathing in the fresh air, from chewing or smoking tobacco, from drinking, cursing, carrying on, from speaking out as they please...'

'I have never heard such utter rubbish!'

Sean kicked Dr O'Boyle's desk and waved his arm, accidentally striking the doctor on the head. The men arrived at that moment and Sean was escorted out of the room.

'If you let me out of this place, I will cause no more trouble.'

'Ask the Little People to get you out,' said a big man at his side.

That night Sean planned revenge. He still had his wishes. Was it worthwhile wasting his time in this place? It was like talking to the wall here. But, at the same time, a salutary measure of humiliation for them, a sharp lesson, would also be appropriate before he left. He would make contact with his friends and get their advice. He closed his eyes and drummed his fingers on the wall. He had worked out, through experimenting during long hours of isolation, that this was the best way to get in touch. The acquisition of this skill compensated for all the insults he received. Soon he was fast asleep. He drifted into other worlds – where everything was moving, shifting, a great deep – obviating the need for thought or deed. At last he heard the singing and music that had become so reassuring. It was always just when he had given up any hope of hearing it again that he would hear it! Within a few moments he was in touch with the good folk. But it was not to be a happy meeting this time, for they seemed to be annoyed with him.

'You said I had more wishes!'

'It is our prerogative. You have become too ambitious. Too worldly. Your will has become more important than your wishes. Now you want to save Erin!'

'What's wrong with that? In any case, the people here do not understand a thing I say. They do not believe that I foresee the future. I am wasting my time here...'

'Your time...?'

Their laughter was loud and prolonged.

'I want to leave.'

'O hear, Seanín. Abandon desires, thoughts, answers, human advice! Instead question! Doubt! Disbelieve! Fail! Failure is everything! It is your destiny!'

'You should punish those unbelievers. They say you and your world represent what is bad in culture and history. Some say you are never to experience the joys of paradise. They think themselves...superior!'

'They will punish themselves. That is the best sort of punishment. We will make sure that they make their mistakes. We encourage them in all their follies. Let them curse us. It is music to our ears.'

'Give me another wish.'

'You should only use a wish in exceptional circumstances. What you want is not important. We cannot stop you wishing to leave this place. But we can persuade you that it would be a wish wasted. Would you like to have a wish wasted?'

'Should I save it then for a more important occasion?'

'As you've said. But it is not in our power to stop you wishing.'

Sean said that he would have to think about it. But it would do no harm, he said, if they took it upon themselves to add some potion to the food or drink of the guardians here that would at least make them feel discomfited, if not extremely sick.

In the meantime, there was another matter he wanted advice on.

There had been the recent visit of Liam Lawler (Caoilte) of the Fianna. As well as a courtesy call, he had brought tidings of the ongoing war against "foreign influences". Caoilte had said that they faced a renewed battle against the Fomorians, which called for new tactics to counteract the enemy's changed strategy.

Sean had been surprised by the visit. They had spent a few moments in familiarities. He thought that Liam wasn't looking too bad, despite spending his life in the midst of war and conflict.

'The life must be agreeing with you, Liam.'

'If only you knew the hardships we have to put up with in the business of defending this land. Though, I must say, you are not looking too bad yourself. The grub here must be agreeing with you. I have come to ask you a question. When are you going to join us?'

'I am busy at the moment.'

'What do you do in here all day?'

'I am doing a lot of thinking.'

'Thinking?'

'Yes.'

'About what?'

'Reality and non-reality. But more importantly – I am trying to control my thoughts, for they are getting more and more powerful, coming up all the time with great power about this and that and everything. There is nothing that I have not thought about, now. Some of them are so mighty they have a mind of their own. Those ones escape – who knows where they end up and what they do. It's a fight to organize and rule them. My life here is a constant struggle, of strong thoughts against weak thoughts, of correct thoughts against incorrect thoughts.'

'Be the hokey. That sounds serious. Ours is a war of thinkers, too, Sean'.

His voice rose, for he was thinking that he and Sean might, indeed, be of the same mind after all.

'It is a war of our thoughts against their thoughts, our beliefs against their beliefs, our ideas against their ideas. The Fomorians are no longer satisfied with rampaging, looting and pillaging. They want the lot now, Sean. They want to take over our way of thinking. They hide in the woods and the backstreets of the bailes, pretending to be just part of the landscape. But suddenly the tree, bush or pillar comes to life grabbing the unwary passer-by and instilling in him, or her, their alien ideology. They have agents in every walk of life, some of whom you could mistake for your neighbour or best friend. Maybe even your husband or wife. Within the Fianna, we have a special team for detecting agents who may be in our midst. We have to be as subtle as they are; as cunning and crafty as snakes and go along with them, pretending not to know of their schemes, so that they become careless and reveal themselves...'

He looked around the common room.

'Your best chance of getting out of this place is to come in with us. Anyone,' he said, lowering his voice, 'who has once resided in this place is tainted forever with the stigma. You will never get a job in this land, Sean. You will have to emigrate to distant parts in order to find any sort of work. You will always have to hide your past. If it ever came out, in the future, that you had spent time here, you would be finished. And they always find out. Then you would have to emigrate further away, to an even more distant land. But you can still win glory with the Fianna!'

Liam asked him again, pleading, to come and join them for the final battle. No one knew for sure, yet, where or when it would take place. Recent actions had been designed to weaken the one-eyed, one-armed monster as he sneaked and hacked his way through the land. But eventually they would have to take him on face-to-face, in hand-to-hand combat. The final battle – according to the bards – might not even be just a clash of arms, but also take the form of a struggle of a spiritual nature. A contest of Herculean proportions. His thoughts on this fight would be welcome; Finn McCumhail considered the atheist mind the best and clearest mind of all. The old man had said that he was proud to have known such a fine unbeliever as Sean Murphy, and that there could be no greater preparation for a life in the Fianna than your time in this institution.

'I will think hard about all this, Liam, and send you my decision. Give my regards to Finn McCumhail. Tell him that his confidence in me will not be in vain.'

'You said right, Seanín. But you will not join the Fianna. You will stay in this place, a sacred spot that has preserved the last blessings. Even the sídh find shelter here whenever we need to venture into the outskirts of the big Baile. Here, where you are powerless, you will have great power! Here, where you are derided and scorned, your unseen influence will extend to the great spaces. You will have more power than those power-brokers and decision-makers who think they rule the land. That is the way power works – without you or anyone knowing it is there, amongst the weak, the poor, the vanquished.'

'I do not wish to stay here.'

'What you wish is neither here nor there. Do you wish to leave?'

A trick, thought Sean. He did not answer.

'Well, Seanín, here is that advice you asked for. Tell Finn McCumhail and his second in command that there will come a day when they will learn that their enemy is not the Fomorian. The Fomorian is known to us of old. His brute strength and ignorance have been an easy target for warriors. They have spent generations fighting the Great Ugly Giant with steadfastness and single mindedness, little realising that they were fighting their own shadow. The Fomorians have served their purpose well. We will see to it that they have their reward – for the dirges and the memories of their misdeeds will last till the end of time. Tell Finn that the Fianna's mistake was to become proud. They reverted to imitating the druids – our old enemy. They, too, have taken to excluding the very best – the ignorant, foolhardy and weak – from their ranks, relying instead on the clever, astute and strong. The works of the druids did not last. Their kingdom was taken from them. The same will happen to the Fianna if they do not change. And change is something almost impossible for them now. There is only one weapon left for them to use against their enemy – kindness. It alone might succeed. It is a weapon that perhaps they have never tried using before. The sídh practise it occasionally by default, by not always punishing evildoers according to their desserts. But it is not possible for us to practise it all the time, or even full-heartedly. It can be the Fianna's weapon of last resort. They must use it unsparingly. So long, Seanín. Goodbye...for now!'

'Oh,' thought Sean, 'Kindness! It is impossible to… . How…?'

Suddenly, it seemed his thoughts were leaving his head again, flying out in all directions, like airborne "bombs". He could almost see them – swift, silent, dark objects travelling at the speed of light with their payload, though what exactly distinguished each one from the other he was unsure.

Soon afterwards, after he had left the room and joined the others for breakfast (for he had been up all night) he discovered that they had all had a dream about him during the night. And each one now said to him: "You told me this… . You gave me a message… . You said that…"

He was the centre of attention during the meal. Everybody was talking to him, about him, at him. The men in white coats and even Dr O'Boyle, who had come out of his room early, were looking at him strangely and, for once, keeping their peace. He noticed embarrassment on O'Boyle's face whenever he looked at him, the doctor quickly turning his eyes away. Then he realised that it was more than embarrassment. It was shame. The shamefaced doctor was doing everything to avoid avoiding looking Sean in the eye. For he knew that Sean had been with the Little People during the night, and realised now how wrong and ignorant he had been.

The big man in the white coat was asking everybody to quieten things down – to no avail. He said that so much talking was very bad for their health, a sure sign of sickness. It would put their treatment back for months. Day trips would have to be cancelled again. (Nobody now could remember when the last one took place.)

Everyone from that day on looked upon Sean in a different light. It seemed that they continued to have powerful dreams about him, some positive, and some not so positive. He acquired the status of a "character", someone whom people looked up to, queued to have a word with. He was given right of way in doorways, his words were remembered, repeated and commented upon. For the men in white coats and Dr O'Boyle, he had now become their chief problem. His categorisation was upgraded so that Sean was now placed in the ranks of those sufferers who were said to live completely in another world – with whom no further communication was possible for the foreseeable future.

One afternoon Sean, feeling homesick, began thinking about Uncle Patsy down on the farm. At that same moment, Patsy began thinking about his nephew, Sean, up in that place called St Dismal's in Dubh Linn, which was said by some to be an even higher place of learning than the university. Patsy had been wondering to himself what he was going to do about all these women around the place; being made to take off *all* his clothes and wash every day in an old tin tub in full view of the women. They made him stand in the cold water for ages. No longer able to chew his tobacco in peace; to curse or belch; being tucked up in bed every night like a baby!

'I'm sure now my nephew and good friend, Sean, would know what to do. His wisdom has grown since he entered that top university, called St Dismal's. Didn't he send me the princess? And didn't the sídh deliver all his messages. What was that he said, or wrote?

> *'Uncle Patsy – You will be the father of a great progeny. Your sons will all go by the name of Patsy Murphy so that your name will never be removed from the face of the earth. Your empire will extend over many townlands; your sons will be there to defend you if they come to take your land.'*

That is what Sean told him though he didn't know how, or when or where Sean had told him this. That evening Patsy began to talk, unceasingly, in front of the fire about "his sons", Patsy Óg, Patsy Mór, Patsy Mall, Patsy Caol, Patsy Láidir, Patsy Ramsach, Patsy Cliste, etc. The two ladies did not know what to make of his talk, or what had come over him. For the next week he went around talking about his imaginary progeny and the different, huge estates that each would be master of. He had even, temporarily, given up chewing and spitting tobacco and was pulling instead on an old pipe that had belonged to his father and grandfather before him.

Eileen took him aside and spoke sternly to him.

'Stop talking this nonsense at once, Patsy, and behaving like an old idiot, before we become the laughing stock of Rathcloon. What are you talking about – all these children that are in your imagination? Who would bring a child into this house of hardship? It would be worse than the workhouse for them. You should be ashamed of yourself for wanting to bring young children into the world right now. I have asked a man I know to come here and take a look at the place. We can talk about babies when everything is fixed up.'

'We have no money to fix up the house.'

'This person is giving us a loan.'

'Who is this man?'

'Michael Fitzgerald. A very good businessman.'

Sean's thoughts, for some reason, as he sat on the floor in the corridor outside O'Boyle's office, turned involuntarily to Father Murphy, the parish priest whom he and most others had studiously avoided during their school days. (For he had the habit of grabbing an individual and, along with going over every detail of the subject's life, including every single misdeed committed in the recent and distant past, never failed to give a long lecture on how to behave at every stage of the "long road ahead". Included also, for the most unfortunate, was a complete history of Erin.) Sean remembered now the time he went to confession to Father Murphy and in order to impress him had admitted "intentional murder". He had been, to his great embarrassment, given a mediocre punishment and laughed out of the confessional box. It was the memory of this that had come to his mind at that moment, making him feel once again the shame of the whole thing. The crime had certainly not been worth the penance.

The same Father Murphy was at that moment on the bus heading home after the meeting at the bishop's palace. Even though it had been a hectic, fraught meeting, what came into his mind at that moment was a young fellow who had once confessed murder to him. He wondered now how he was getting on these days. Probably gone to England. He felt a sudden, urgent need to pray; somehow to enable the lad not to get himself into more serious trouble. He offered up a sincere prayer. He then proceeded once more to reflect on the day's events.

To say that he had received a "dressing down" was putting it mildly. The bishop had not wanted to talk about anything else but the "drink problem". (Canon Carey's "psychological advice" had been so long and complicated, the bishop had decided that drink must be the real problem.) Everything Father Murphy said, explained, tried to inform him about, was down to the drink. It was difficult at first even to get through to the elderly prelate. He was an amalgam of conflicting types. He was the kind old countryman – promoter of

Gaelic games, hearty celebrator of rural traditions, participant in convivial gatherings of old stagers, "new things" and all the rich mixture of folk that goes to make up any backward, God-forsaken spot; ever welcoming of the sick, infirm, poor and downright criminal, and a hearty enemy of townspeople. A true Christian, he had been called by many a bad type. Above all – he was renowned as the teller of clerical jokes, a fame that made all of a pessimistic disposition avoid him like the plague, whilst those who listened but could not see the funny side always had to laugh uproariously. The dark side of his character revolved around his preoccupation with hell. He was an expert on the lower reaches of the abode of the damned and on who dwelt there. Most clergy and rich men were there. Some of his best friends had ended up there. The higher reaches of hell he scorned. Nobody of any worth would want to go there. It was reserved for despicable low-grade sinners such as cheating racehorse trainers, bent jockeys, fallen women, corrupt lawyers, politicians on the make, bank robbers, murderers and the like. But for those who ended up in the lower reaches there was a sure notoriety and the pleasure of interesting company for a seemingly very long time. Idealists gone rotten. Holy men who had indulged just a little. Schoolteachers who had misled the young. Writers, poets, painters and musicians who had used their creativity to promote profane material. The great sinners revelled in the most terrible of pains. Not for them simply "the worm that turns" or the "fire"; there was the real torment of knowing that all their ideals had gone for nothing. Nothing was surer to send a person to the lower reaches than high hopes, worthwhile ambition, good will and, particularly, a sense of the aesthetic. The bishop's sermons on hell were well known throughout the land. Many came from near and far to hear them. The Little People were eavesdroppers. Reports were brought around the country by the little grey man. Those of a nervous disposition were the bishop's most attentive listeners. A few thought he was too soft; they said that he held back on the full intensity of the "pains", not giving them their full due, due to softness. This guaranteed him a place down there for himself as the worse sort of heretic – one who pretends to be orthodox. Meanwhile, the "higher" reaches of hell faded into obscurity throughout the land as a result of his sermons, joining limbo as just a shadowy place with little substance, a place that nobody worried about; and even for some a desirable place at the end of one's days.

This man would not listen to any of Father Murphy's explanations for having requested "dirty books", dallying with hidden powers (albeit of the less dangerous type), having a large number of bottles of whiskey in the presbytery, and being one parishioner (Patsy Murphy) short in the collection plate.

'I have always admired you, Michael, as a down-to-earth, man of the people. Like myself. You have learning, but do not let on to the faithful, knowing that extraneous knowledge is something that is usually disturbing to them. Your love of whiskey, too, is good. If only it hadn't become a talking point. Above all – you are not an ambitious priest, content with your lot and to serve in a humble parish. But if I was asked what is your best quality, I would say your obedience. For there is nothing a bishop wants more than an obedient clergy. Therefore, I am sure that you will not take it the wrong way when I say to you that you could do with a little rest. A few months in Dubh Linn. Or even a few years on the missions. I have good contacts in South America...'

'I am sorry to interrupt you, Your Lordship, but there is something else that I have to tell you. I was keeping it till last. I have a message for you from St Finbar.'

'St Finbar! Now there is a good man. Nothing wrong in that direction. Is it something you have read?'

'No. His statue came to life when I was praying in church. He spoke to me. He said that I was to tell you that I am to be the next bishop.'

'Were you drunk?'

'I was as sober as a judge, and you know I do not lie.'

The bishop's mind raced back over the various infamous occasions in history when the Lord or even His Good Mother had tripped up a sensible bishop by sending along the most preposterous of messengers with the most outrageous of demands. Never a polite request, mind you. Plain, unabashed cheek.

The bishop would be cagey. He would not be tripped up, not even by all the powers of heaven.

'Then it is a serious matter. What is your proof that St Finbar spoke to you?'

The words, miraculously, came straight into Father Murphy's head.

Ask him if he is a prophet.

'Are you a prophet?'

'Bedad, no!'

Erin is in need of a prophet.

'Erin is in need of a prophet.'

'Is it now? Who says so?'

St Finbar.

'St Finbar.'

'I shouldn't have asked.'

Tell him the lot.

'The words are coming out of my mouth like the river of life – and whence they come and whither they go I can tell not. Only that I speak that which is given to me to say – and the truth shall be in it. I will be bishop, come what may, and heaven help him who stands in the way.'

The bishop reflected, 'I can't let this man go out of the diocese talking like that. The best place for him at the moment is back in his parish.'

'Michael, you can go home. I have thought the better of it. Maybe you are a prophet. Who is one to say?'

You must resign your see, and I must be the bishop. It is not my will, but that of St Finbar himself.

'You must resign your see, and I must be the bishop. It is not my will, but that of St Finbar himself.'

As the humble (or lately humble) parish priest left the palace the final words of the bishop, now become extremely irate and hostile – for St Finbar's request he interpreted as some kind of threat or challenge to his authority – sounded in the old priest's head like music; at once terrifying and furious, yet inexplicably consoling and rewarding for one who had lived his life in the shadows, up to this point:

'And if I find out there are any shenanigans going on in your parish, the lower reaches of hell will be too good for you.'

Michael Fitzgerald, ebullient at the success of one business deal after another (making money was so easy), had now taken to mixing with the big wigs; and had quickly forgotten all his old acquaintances: family, friends, relations and all who had been part of his unremarkable, insignificant past. In particular, he had already completely forgotten all about the humiliation of his rejection by the Fianna. Therefore it came as an unpleasant surprise to him, as he sat in the lounge bar with a solicitor on one side and a "dealer" on the other to be suddenly reminded, as if from nowhere, of the day when he had proved not good enough for that august body of great men.

You will never, never forget. You dare not forget. If you try to forget, it will pursue you like a hound that tears and consumes your flesh.

'Be the hokey, what's going on in my head? This brandy and port is quare stuff, surely. I shouldn't be drinking it, showing off to these guys who are secretly laughing at me behind my back – a raw youth trying to enter the world of big men.'

He was surprised at his own…thoughts. It was as if they were not his own. Extraneous words again sounded in his head.

Humility! Mend your ways now before it is too late.

He could hear his companions laughing at him under their breath. He was suddenly feeling a deep uneasiness that often comes just when one is enjoying oneself and feeling on the top of the world. Everything went cloudy. A lassitude set in, not dissimilar to that which occurs as the first flow of alcohol wears off. He felt as though much time had passed; that all his achievements were so much dross. That he was living now in another time, in the future. To his companions, it seemed as if he had gone into a trance. They looked at his empty glass of brandy. It had been number three.

'Why am I here, being treated like a common criminal? Why should I be feeling guilty? Me – who has brought unheard of prosperity to this land! Hundreds of thousands of people depend on me for their livelihood. Didn't I become the most noted politician in the country? My business expertise was previously unknown for its like in Erin. I took this country and put it in the front rank of nations. I saved Erin.'

The charge is treason.

'What? Who makes such a ridiculous charge?'

Michael had shouted these words, alarming his two companions.

We do.

He was startled.

'Who is it that's there?' he asked, suddenly afraid, for he knew not – now – how they all came to be here, or where he was, or who was present. The mist was getting thicker and was about to encompass them. He could not see the rest of the pub or its refurbishments. Panic came.

We do not dwell in your world. Are ye admitting yer guilt now? For all the things that ye are going to do? There is no time in eternity.

'The day I admit any guilt is the day I cut my own throat.'

His two companions became more alarmed, for once in their lives surprised and unsure. They were staring at him, looking around to see whom he might be addressing. But Michael's eyes were fixed only on the empty space between Mr O'Connor, the solicitor and Mr Doolan, businessman and political fixer.

The way things are going that day is not far off. Will ye undo all the wrong ye have done? Will ye unlevel the fields? Will ye restore their living places. Will ye go back and return things to how they were.

'It's impossible to go back,' he said.

Oh, to go back. Go back. How many want to go back!

The words were echoing in Michael's head. He was asking himself

– was it all in his imagination? The panic lessened. He suddenly felt inexplicably nostalgic and sorrowful as he reflected on a life that had already passed, a long and successful career that had passed its zenith. He felt like an old man. He never knew that he could feel so emotional! It was almost a joyful feeling.

He shouted out, 'All right. I ducked and dodged. I avoided my responsibilities. I cut corners. I betrayed friends. I gave bribes. I made crooked contracts. I offended many. I admit it all.'

The two men started to laugh their heads off. Then the darkness became total and he could see nothing. Panic returned, and he became agitated, his knees knocking and his body shaking and trembling. He started talking at an extremely fast rate, about fairies, fields, gripes, hedges, hills and other various features of the countryside; he related the origins of Erin's first inhabitants; the reasons for their oppression and suffering over millennia; their present legal rights, their fate in modern Erin; the consequences for them and the public at large of all the wrongs that he and others had committed, were committing or would soon be about to commit.

He started weeping uncontrollably. The words dried up.

The two men could not understand why the original, convivial proceedings had veered off course like this, with the young fellow Fitzgerald having become suddenly taken up in some sort of mad delirium.

As the weeping eventually subsided, they both became silent, awaiting the end of this "fit" that had overtaken their young friend.

The solicitor and dealer put their hands on his shoulders and made signs to the publican for some hot coffee and milk. The lad began to quieten down. The haze around him had begun to lift. The serious matter of supposed future financial shenanigans, the mad talk about the fairies and all that stuff now seemed to be just a bad dream, even to Michael, as he smiled back at the men, who themselves were smiling somewhat ironically as Michael gratefully drank the coffee (and milk), telling himself and everyone in the place that he would never drink brandy and port again (or at least not so much at one time).

O'Connor and Doolan left him in the pub to recover fully.

'Take it easy,' they said as they went out the saloon-bar door.

O'Connor and Doolan were often to wonder about that episode. They were careful never to mention the incident again when they were in the company of Michael Fitzgerald, TD. But this "breakdown" gave them a hold over Michael so that later, when he went on to become one of the most powerful, respected figures in the land in his own right – and they themselves looked to him as their economic mentor and political fixer – they were able to think back to that day in the pub, look knowingly at each other, and relate to all and sundry the story of the serious flaw that was in Michael Fitzgerald's character. And somehow Michael always knew, whenever he was mixing with the people of his native county – or even with the big names up in Dubh Linn – that there was a possibility that, behind his back, he was a bit of a laughing stock.

Six

THE YEARS SEEMED to have vanished leaving nothing behind; no evidence that they had ever existed. The seasons, too, always seemed to fail to fulfil their promise so that the giants would always comment "maybe next season" and became inured to their passing and philosophical about the passage of time, accepting that life itself was a mirage.

Many famous giant events took place, but these too were like brief bursts of lightning; traumatic for the moment but ultimately forgettable. Complex social problems, scientific developments and questions of deepest philosophy arose, and were barely comprehended before they, too, were forgotten. People talked together – and before a riposte or reply could be delivered, or even thought up, those they had been addressing (or who had been addressing them) also were gone, never to be seen or heard of again. Mother Time harried and flummoxed the world of the giants, refusing to do their bidding; whilst in the case of the little folk this same time only went backwards and, as ever before, served only to confirm them in their age-old beliefs, prejudices and opinions.

And as Michael grew in status and wealth, his attitude and mindset changing so much for the better when he married a good woman who bore him rebellious children not deformed in any way and nagged him so that he gave up sowing his wild oats and began to think about how he could help the country; and he did not have to show off to anyone anymore and he watched for any opportunity to grab more land and after a while he felt supremely confident and realised that he did not have to let the millionaires make all the money and run off with the big contracts but that he could control all that himself; and he took up golf.

And Patsy Murphy grew in stature with the number of children he and Eileen were bringing into the world and his farmhouse became a show house with people from all over the country coming in droves to view "the perfect house with all the mod cons"; not to mention the music sessions, parties and the craic put on by Mrs Murphy with the most generous hospitality ever seen anywhere in the land. She had developed an economical scheme of killing all their livestock on the premises, saving thousands in middle-men fees and providing cheap food for the unceasing flow of guests, visitors and clients alike. This business was to expand later into a family firm that was to provide fuel, alcohol and tobacco and other services such as informal, non-fee banking at very low prices. Great also was the credit heaped upon her and Mr Murphy for their looking after the poor girl of the simple mind who believed that she was a princess and who loved nothing better than to spend all day in the fields talking to herself and the fairies.

In his heart and head Patsy felt doomed; and he knew that if it were not for the presence of the daughter of the King of England he would have been destroyed by the Little People long ago. The hospitality he provided for the noble lady, he was constantly telling himself, was the reason the fairies left him alone. Perhaps they even praised him, despite the hames he had made of the farm and the land. And even that might not have been too bad; hedges had certainly been removed; the fields were larger; a bit of drainage was done; but you could still recognise the place and wasn't Foirnocht Hill standing there yet, the great landmark that it was?

And Father Murphy was surprised and not surprised to hear of the awful accident that befell the bishop when he fell off his horse whilst out hunting with the toffs, when he had hit his head so hard on a tree trunk that even his accompanying curate had shaken his head and said, 'The last rites are useless,' or to hear that the bishop had left a letter strongly advocating that the upcoming vacancy in the local episcopate be filled by the one man in the country capable of facing the challenges of modern times: dirty books, hard drinking, superstition, television, politics conducted for personal financial gain; modern dancing, hasty marriages (under the age of fifty or whilst the old man and woman were still alive), the flow of good young blood overseas, modern vehicles, including bicycles, especially if driven dangerously, new agricultural implements, money, talk, foreign countries, non-native sports; and above all, any politician or person who falsely and boastingly claimed that he/she could bring about an economic miracle in a country where hunger had been for too long too familiar a visitor. The man to see off all these challenges – said the bishop – was Father Murphy.

The bishop had become very detached and fatalistic in his latter days. He had also become absorbed in a heightened, personal fear of hell. It was as if he knew that the end was near. Everybody had blamed him when a papal investigation of the events in Father Murphy's parish church was announced, along with the banning of all pilgrimages to the church. The injunction was ignored. Indeed it served only to increase the zeal of the masses, who had begun calling for Father Murphy's elevation to the episcopate (at the very least) as well as exile for the bishop. The bishop's acquiescence to these events and to his fate was increased when Father Murphy relayed to him a goodwill message from none other than St Finbar himself, something that was to give him incalculable consolation in his last days. It was also said that in his latter months the bishop had become less religious, taken to secular activities in a big way, drinking, enjoying himself and taking up hunting.

Meanwhile, Father Murphy's town and district had gained the enviable reputation as a place of supernatural wonders – of a moving and talking statue; of a public appearance by St Finbar himself in the middle of the churchyard, in solid stone, observed by no fewer than five thousand people. This remarkable sight became all the more remarkable when the statue of the great St Patrick soon also appeared outside, having left its customary position inside the church. Many claimed to have heard not only the voice of Finbar, but of Patrick too, and to a man/woman they claimed that the two had given warning of terrible times ahead for the whole country.

The parish priest always addressed the crowds when they appeared, and warned against sensationalism. It was also a God-given opportunity to get going on his "hobby horses".

'The only thing that will save this land from heathenism, I have been told by voices from above, is not only for the laity to repent, but also the clergy! Bishops and archbishops, curates and parish priests, mother superiors, prioresses and abbots, must admit their terrible crimes that cry out to heaven for vengeance – not getting out enough, being constrained in conversation, criticising fellow clergy who like a drop of whiskey or go to the races, annoying politicians and newspaper editors with phone calls and letters, accusing their flock of crimes they did not commit, and many more. Your parish priest is only too happy to admit to his serious sins – demanding money, encouraging parishioners to read unsuitable books; whiskey, straying thoughts.'

Many fell down on their knees and confessed enthusiastically, publicly and loudly their own sins and crimes.

Some people claimed that Father Murphy even spoke with the accent of St Finbar. Others said it was with the voice of St Patrick. While many proclaimed Father Murphy the hero of the hour, a prophet, the man to save the country, others (a minority) said that he was telling lies; that he had misinterpreted what the saints had really said, that they had heard the *exact* words spoken and that it was not anything like what Father Murphy had been saying.

University professors who investigated the events, agnostic to a man/woman, said that it was all simply superstition and that "ley lines" in that area were responsible. Or perhaps people were just seeing things that weren't there.

St Finbar had also called for an airport to be built in the vicinity. There was a call for a new cathedral to replace the parish church in Dunmor, and that the diocese HQ be moved there. Hotels, restaurants followed as surely as dry weather after rain. Roads would have to be widened.

These were challenging times that saw the Fianna, too, experiencing traumatic events. Their numbers had declined over the years as the young saw other opportunities for advancement. This decline had extended to the public's perception of the glorious band of warriors; many even believing that they did not exist anymore. Their name had become reduced to a mere legendary, mythical existence for a large section of the population. This was one reason why Finn and Caoilte had decided to launch a new war around the extremities of the island, in what became known as the War of the Shadows. For what they identified as the enemy, and focussed their attacks on, always lay in the darkness. Even in the most fraught of battles the enemy's outline was barely discernible. In the full light of day it was impossible to see exactly what one was facing. The whole island was surrounded by these threatening shadows. A shadow was all the more threatening for its insubstantiality. Although the Fomorians had supposedly withdrawn to their northern fastness, the Fianna did not believe for one moment that they had abandoned the battle. Initially, the renewed warfare had involved the defenders in a variety of new and untried techniques, in what was essentially guerrilla warfare. (The Fianna of old had always insisted on face-to-face combat.) The new tactics represented a two-edged sword – to confront the shadows – and to persuade the population to become even more afraid of the shadows. Crouching behind boulders, bushes and so forth (and thereby creating shadows of their own), blocking highways and byways with their renowned, massive body bulks, particularly backsides, in the darkness of the evenings and the early mornings, so that nothing could pass, or making strangers and unregistered travellers fearful of attempting to pass so that they turned back; making use of natural disasters such as avalanches and the dropping of heavy boulders from great heights onto bridges, roads and track-ways to discourage travelling in general and so reduce Fomorian mobility; deep holes concealed along route-ways for the careless Fomorian; making loud, frightening noises in the dark; wild shouting across streets and back lanes whilst remaining concealed; name-calling. All of these methods were used. Their efficiency was still being assessed, for they never seemed to trap, kill or draw out the Fomorians.

And as for the mass of the population, it just seemed to become accustomed to living amongst the shadows, to hearing loud, unexplained noises and experiencing unexplained disturbances and frightening happenings in the course of the day and night. Indeed, it became so that quiet nights were for many the nights when they couldn't sleep!

They said that the Fomorians themselves were also using new techniques that were more insidious than the old-fashioned spear, blade or knuckleduster. Caoilte became adept at analysing the new tactics. He pointed to the main Fomorian "softening-up" weapon – persuading everyone that they did not exist. The genius of this strategy was that the Fomorians did not have to appear at all. Indeed it seemed as if their shadows, too, were gone or going, thus making people lose interest in any sort of proactive or sustained resistance.

Caoilte noticed that Finn was often falling into a deep sleep, whose duration increased over time so that he was incommunicado frequently for days on end. He took the opportunity to persuade the dispirited old guard to let him have a try at the leadership. (The old days of the two slugging it out to decide the leadership were gone, Caoilte had sighed.) He offered a whole range of new approaches, pointing out that the old ones were clearly producing no results. The old men muttered about "new fangled ideas" and that "the world is for the young, now" in a dismissive way and yet were glad that the burden was off their shoulders.

New talk about "positive images", "freedom of action" and "individual expression" took the place of discussion of battle tactics until eventually debate, sharing ideas, creative expression etc. became more important than planning or carrying out the war. The war of the shadows petered out, with hardly any engagements now taking place. Defeats – a defeat these days was when a shadow failed to appear and the warriors had to walk ingloriously home – became the accepted thing and were even beginning to be glorified as "the struggle is more important than the outcome", "defeat brings its own victory", and "dignified tactical retreats signify victory at a higher, or deeper level". Defeat and failure were being promoted officially as good and were no longer to be feared, for in war there are no victors – only losers. The next phase consisted of discussion sessions on "reconciliation", "seeing the other side" and "feeling the pain of the Fomorian". Finally came the momentous day when Caoilte suggested that they actually make a friendly approach to the Fomorians.

Later, when word got out that Fianna were being seen drinking with Fomorians and getting involved in mutual business ventures, social action and even entertainments, a backlash set in from the public. Eventually, Fianna familiarity with the old enemy, not to mention the many scandals of overindulgence, crookery and the carrying out of physical assaults on innocent members of the public rather than on Fomorians or Fomorian sympathisers, brought the attention of the powers that be to bear on the new, subversive activities of the old, once trusted warrior band. Eventually, Caoilte and company were hauled before the courts.

Meanwhile there was a meeting of the *gentry* under the oak tree in the large field outside Rathcloon village. Fairies and leprechauns came from every part of the region to attend this important conference, and the underground passages were crowded even before the main hosting had arrived! As usual, a watch was placed to ensure that no one entered who was from the tribe of Aon. This was a desultory lot who always gave problems to the main body of sídh. They roamed the land in indecent attire (unapproved colours, buttons undone). Their life's mission, apart from that of embarrassing their own folk, appeared to be solely to cause trouble to giants who dressed particularly well or respectably – and especially those who overdressed – accosting or insulting them as they made their way to important social functions or family occasions. Their favourite tactic was to arrange for dirt to be splattered over someone's expensive clothes on occasions such as a wedding or funeral. They had been officially banned from all *gentry* company for having once helped the Fomorians against the giants.

As was customary, the declared acting king for the day was a very insignificant fairy – on this occasion a smelly fellow who was shunned for his bad habit of washing himself in water. He spoke quickly, wafting away his body smell at the same time with his left hand:

First matter – Revenge on Dr O'Boyle and his hirelings who do not respect a wise one – Seanín. Now they will see and hear strange things! They will experience, for a time, what their captives experience. They will understand the wise, and even more so, the unwise.

There was loud acclaim. The cows grazing nearby lifted their heads, snorted and ran round in circles..

Next matter – Patsy Murphy and the problem of the Theory of Relativity.

Patsy had these days become the most well read man around. There was not a book on philosophy, theology, history, politics, sociology, science or arts that he had not at least mastered the gist of, if not read right through. Every bookshop in the land had become accustomed to his letters and phone calls requesting books. He had a special arrangement with Dunmor Library for access to their index and reserved library. His knowledge now knew no bounds, and Father Murphy and Garda O'Hourigan had long given up trying to have a sensible conversation with him.

'Tell me, now, Guard O'Hourigan – what do ye make of the relativity theory?' he would begin a conversation of an evening in the back room, well away from the screaming leanbhs (babies).

'I have not thought about it. How are the cows?'

'The Little People are annoyed with me for having learnt this theory, which is called "General and Special Theory", but which they call sídh wisdom or fairy knowledge. Indeed, they are very angry. "There'll be no more understanding of your special position," they tell me; "unless you give up talking about relativity. That is information that has always been the preserve of the sídh. We can't have giants talking about these things", they say, "because if they do, they will start to think like us, prognosticate like us, and act like us. Leave it to those scientists to worry about. They don't really understand it like yerself, and only give misleading interpretations. Their ignorance suits us fine."'

'Begob, ye are a wise man, Patsy.'

We must find a way of putting a stop to Patsy Murphy's theorising. Already there are signs that the whole Rathcloon area is discussing these subjects. In the pub, on the playing field, on the farms and in the workplaces – in the schools even – giants are trying out little experiments with time and space. They are dangerously near to understanding that both these supposed solidities are only relative. There is a real chance that soon they will acquire some of the powers that rightly belong to us. What a thing! Mortals able to ignore the age old laws of earth and move about like us as quick and as light as a whisper! Wherever and whenever they like! No! Yesterday it was reported that a farmer was trying to make his plough horses work two drills at a time! And the curses and swearing out of him when at first he didn't succeed! But then he sits down and reasons to himself about what the bold Patsy had told him and the next thing is he has mastered one of the arts of relativity as he realises that it is all in the thinking. Before you could say "Fomorianist" he just goes ahead and ploughs his first drill and when he finishes, he sits down and thinks. He congratulates himself on a fine piece of work and when he looks back – lo and behold not one but many drills are completed! In fact, as he sits there, he sees the whole field completely ploughed up, and congratulates himself once again on being the greatest ploughman in the country, clapping himself on the back over and over again, helping himself to a swig from his container, and smoking his fine tobacco. A finer workman in all the land there never has been, the giant continues to tell himself. It makes the rest of the day's work extremely enjoyable and sweet. 'No effort at all,' he boasts to the wife when he gets back home.

On the hurling field the Rathcloon players have been practising pucking the ball at their own goalpost, in preparation for an experimental match against Bailebreoite. We know that this way they will learn the secret of success through confusing the opponent, such as has guaranteed sídh victories in every hurling match ever undertaken against Waverers, Wasters, Messers, Mashers, Chancers, Teetotallers.

Then the schoolchildren, too, are taken up with the excitement, refusing to line up at school for their master, undermining his every attempt at order and claiming that they know more about geometry than he will ever know. What a thing! Every man giant, woman and child in the district is walking, cycling and even driving those great mechanicals in every sort of wobbly way, as though they were travelling blithely through the great chaos, believing now that the straight road is for the fool and uneducated, and the wide and crooked way the path of learning and wisdom. That is knowledge that is our preserve. Oh for the times when every man, woman and child feared to swerve or to leave the straight and narrow.

Next matter – Father Murphy and his new clothes. He was getting a new hat! His power was going to get stronger and not just in the district of Rathcloon, but beyond. A change in attire or fashion always bespoke new and dangerous adventures, for they knew from experience that the putting on of new or different clothes meant that a mortal always gained new powers. It had been a long time since a friend of the sídh, such as Father Murphy, had gone on to great things. Indeed only the very young sídh could remember a previous occasion of promotion to such a high office of "one of their own". Now, what with all the to-do about Dunmor churchyard and Mikey no longer there to run things, it could lead to the arrival of a meddler, of the kind who held the giants for days, even months on end in a state of fear and trepidation; whose sermons always ended with everyone going out and throwing stones at any helpless leprechaun they might spot, calling them devils and worse, and praying that they be cast into the lower parts of the nether world.

That very evening the same Doctor O'Boyle had a brainwave. There had suddenly come to his mind, as he sat in his office dreading the next walk-around, a brilliant idea about how to get that long-earned rest. The board had worked him like a slave; he reckoned that the last time he had had more than a day off work was twenty years previously when he had got married. (When he had been granted an unprecedented two days' leave, something he had never been allowed to forget.) They had always refused him a holiday, declaring that his work was a vocation and not an ordinary job. He was captain of a ship that was always in danger of sinking, and that he could not desert. Oh, how he had always envied his patients! They seemed to have everything going for them in life. Free food and board. No responsibility for life's decisions, even being exempt from the difficult moral ones. The medicine they took seemed to make many of them happy, and to have all kinds of wonderful and unusual experiences.

He now decided that he would join them, at least temporarily. He began taking a number of tablets, including the experimental ones sent by the company in America with whom they had a secret business deal. It was quite disappointing that at first he felt or experienced nothing out of the ordinary. He had to up the dosage.

He then began to hear a voice, telling him different things. He was told that he was to take a rest from his job. He could see, amongst the flashing lights, little green men. They were all about the place, meddling with the canteen food and putting potions in the drinks.

He was taken off duty by the second in charge, whose long-held suspicions about his boss were now confirmed. O'Boyle was conveyed to the most secluded room in the institution and his next of kin informed.

Patsy Murphy's learning and its dolorous spread into the community – for it was not only relativity but subjects such as astrology, atheism, transistors, the beliefs of tribes in faraway lands, the hidden mineral wealth of Erin, spaceships, were all being endlessly expounded upon, with a number of adventurous folk carrying out some very dangerous experimentation, such as in mountain climbing, and in activities on water and even in the air – was dealt with by the simple procedure of putting on him a straightforward spell called "full of the blarney".

He had discovered, when relating an account of how he had first come across the king of England's daughter, that people were sitting spellbound, listening to his words. This gave him such a feeling of satisfaction that he immediately decided to devote the rest of his leisure time to story-telling. He gave up complaining about his wife's hectic social life and began enjoying himself, too, seemingly losing many years in age (something that happened to Father Murphy also, when he became bishop and people commented that he looked "twenty years younger"). Especially now when he realised that he had, on top of everything else, the gift of the gab, which made everyone sit or move closer and stand by the fireplace as soon as he opened his mouth. Eventually, wherever he went around the county thereafter there would be immediate calls for "an seanchaí" to take a seat and speak. His repertoire of stories and legends was miraculously complete, and indeed he talked no more of relativity after that time. He became a contented man at the secondary level of happiness (the first level being the preserve of those who lived alone). He let his land go to waste. Indeed, the Little People were delighted that there seemed to be a deliberate neglect of the land, in comparison with all the grand land improvement schemes going on elsewhere in the district. Too late did they realise that this was a deliberate ploy by certain parties both to undervalue the estate, and also to use it as a cover for other money-making activities.

Garda O'Hourigan was feeling quite forlorn, if not desolate. The days of glory were long past. Everybody had forgotten about his role in the murder investigation. His best friend, Patsy Murphy, was married and seemingly content to live in the midst of women. It was a betrayal. Their old friendship (though it had been a friendship struck up late in the day) was still a valued friendship for all that. Indeed, its value was all the greater for its brevity and its complication by the murder charge. Now all that was over. And so too, apparently, was the friendship. There was no sign of that promotion or removal to another county. The worst thing of all was that the crime rate had dropped even further. Indeed, it was so low as to be considered non-existent. Neither the old crimes, or the "new" crimes he had taken such care and effort to list and watch out for, were being committed. He had not left the barracks for months. He had taken to having all his messages delivered to the door. What was the point? He had also long since given up riding his bicycle, after that traumatic ride he had had that time when his bike had taken him on a wild chase across the country.

His letters to headquarters claiming a one hundred per cent success rate in crime eradication were never answered. Indeed, there had been no communication from that quarter since the murder charge was dropped. He sat at his desk now and thought glumly about his future. It was no good "beating crime", he told himself. It got you nowhere. He reflected bitterly that perhaps if Rathcloon had the worst crime in the country he would be receiving plaudits and medals from the top brass. The trouble was – they were all so simple around here they did not know how to commit a real or serious crime. He could teach them a thing or two! He could start lessons in the subject. He could even go and do the crimes himself, in the proper and correct manner!

Well now, there would be no harm in him going out and committing one crime, just for educational purposes. It might also wake headquarters up to the importance of his work here in Rathcloon. He would think about it.

He thought about it day and night, for a week. At first he just played with the idea, but by the second week he found himself busily – and enjoying it immensely – planning his first big robbery. This was carried out on the wealthiest farm in the district – that of Major Moore. The yardman came to work one morning and found Garda O'Hourigan standing there, declaring that he had "intelligence" about a raid on the premises. Sure enough, they discovered some valuable tools missing. He received great praise and thanks from the major himself, for the quickness and efficiency of his work, and the guard drove off in his newly acquired van ('Headquarters won't give me a squad car, so I have had to fork out of me own pocket.') with the assurance that the criminal/s would not get far.

'I have had reports that some big-time gangsters are moving into the area,' he said.

A visit incognito to the regional capital saw him receive a good price for his haul, plus the establishing of useful contacts for any future deals.

On the drive home he saw opportunities for at least five robberies, and any number of other sorts of crime.

Best of all, when he sent in the report of this first robbery to his superiors, he had received an inquiring phone call in return from HQ. He was even asked to keep a special eye on Major Moore's property.

'That is already being done. I might even have to stand guard inside his house, to see if I can catch them on the spot.'

That phone call from HQ had really been the best thing that had happened to him in a very long time.

His joy was slightly marred, nevertheless, by a strange and unsettling phenomenon that suddenly come to plague him just at that same time that he was turning his whole life around and going on to make not just one friend but many new, life-long friends.

It began with a "squeak" here and a "croak" there and he could not figure out where it was coming from. Then one day he spotted a frog sitting on his chair at the kitchen table. He gently removed it outdoors and when he came back in there were at least ten more frogs in the kitchen. Soon they began to appear in the sitting room, bedroom and toilet. Apart from the annoyance, something about it all made him uneasy, and told him to be cautious in how he dealt with the problem. Instead of launching into a major onslaught, he figured that their presence might be some kind of test. He noted an uncanny aspect to their behaviour. In the daytime, they would remain out of sight, and sometimes it was impossible to see even one no matter how hard he looked. Only the occasional croak was heard to remind him of their presence. Then at night, when he would be lying in bed, there would be the sound of thousands of them, and they would appear in every nook and corner. It was exceedingly difficult to walk around at those times, trying to avoid them, for they never moved. In the daytime they always seemed to make the most noise whenever a caller came to the station. It was just to embarrass him, he supposed. Yet he intuitively knew that the best and safest response would be to try and ignore them as much as possible.

When, after three months of recuperation, Dr O'Boyle returned to duty he was a changed man. There was a calmness and a detachment about him that impressed everyone. The staff were particularly protective, even over-protective, guiding him to this place and that place. His deputy took on more responsibilities to give the doctor the chance to recuperate. When his family came to visit for the first time, he showed an impressive independence of spirit and detachment by refusing to see them. He was even going out of his way to talk to the most difficult residents, including Sean, and to listen to their words.

Sean had lately been imparting his unorthodox wisdom in the recreation room; ideas and advice totally at odds with living in the modern world, such as the importance of idling, of not listening to advice, of disbelieving all that one was told; of work and study being the last refuge of scoundrels and wastrels; that telling lies was always better than telling the truth. There had never been such a quiet about the place than during these talks. Many of the staff, including Dr O'Boyle, were convinced this distraction was helping in the running of the place and even in the rehabilitation of some. There were far fewer fights, arguments, of crying hysterically, laughing uncontrollably or claims that one was cured and ready to leave. Everyone was calling Sean "The Doc".

'It is certainly the case,' Sean said one day, his oratory become more profound and indeed ornate with each passing day, 'that the world is controlled by a secret hand. Who or what it is – and it may be a small clique – is pure guesswork. You don't have to look very far to see signs of its existence. Every day and night, month and year, you see the world moving about, rotating on its axis, orbiting the sun, giving us the seasons and days and years in regular succession. Yet the hand that organises all of this is invisible.

In the same way, the business of men, women, cities, towns and countries is conducted in such a way as completely conceals the hand of the one who is organising it. Buses, motor vehicles, bicycles, people moving about in every direction so that if you looked down on it – all that movement and flow of millions of different people and things – you would say that they would be sure to be about to collide in some terrible accident. Yet they never do collide, but carry on safely and swiftly according to fixed rules and regulations devised by a great, manipulating brain. The produce of farmers, tradesfolk, factory workers and fisher folk is visible in the market places and shops. It appears, as if conveyed by a magic hand, in our own homes and places of residence. It would also seem that no one can do anything, obtain anything, sell anything, plan anything, do anything without "permission" in this world. For aren't we always looking over our shoulders to see who is watching; or watching our back in case this unseen hand comes at us with a knife, gun or bludgeon? Yet the instigator of all of this remains out of sight. And those who call themselves "the government" are not the masters! For how could they be? All they do is sit around on their backsides all day talking the hind leg off all the donkeys in Erin, never leaving that big, comfortable building if at all possible.

Why does it not show itself? How can we be sure that the master-hand exists? Because if it wasn't concealing its existence, it would have by now – or long since – have revealed itself, or been revealed by others!'

Everyone, including Dr O'Boyle, clapped.

'Now you know about it too! But watch out – they are dangerous once you get to know about them! Before long, they will come for me. And then maybe for you.'

A number of people began to run about the place, shouting and knocking over whatever got in their way. Some were fearful. Others were very angry and set out to find where the supposed "hand" or "clique" might be hiding.

Naturally enough, it soon became clear to many that Dr O'Boyle and his staff perfectly fitted the picture.

'It has come to this,' said Dr O'Boyle's deputy, as the staff eventually succeeded in quelling the fights, sieges and assaults and restoring order. 'Sean Murphy has become a dangerous madman. We can't do any more for him here. There is no possibility in any case of someone who has once lost his senses and strayed into the realm of insanity, ever recovering or returning to normality.'

Dr O'Boyle murmured some dissent, saying that the outbreak of violence was at worst just the harmless "letting off of steam, and at best a healthy response to a dastardly conspiracy".

'It's a case of either he goes, or you go back to that room,' he was told.

On the morning of his departure Sean was called in by management.

Dr O'Boyle, flanked as usual these day by two burly men-in-white, had a big smile on his face and he was as cheery as a schoolboy. The staff had allowed him one of his favourite, strictly rationed tablets.

'Good news, Sean. You are cured. You are free to go.'

'Thanks,' said Sean, a little surprised.

'There is one thing before you go. We will be very pleased if you agree to do something for us,' said the deputy. 'There is a little bit of an ongoing problem here, because of your bad influence. You could do us all a big favour before you leave by admitting to everyone that you made up all that nonsense about a "secret hand"! The patients are suspicious of everybody now. Pills are of no avail when they are of this frame of mind. This has all been caused by your silly talk.'

'If I say that I lied, they will know then for sure that I told the truth. And it is not possible to deny something that does not exist.'

'Is that all we taught you? Is that all that you have learnt? Gibberish?' asked the deputy.

'He has a point,' said Dr O'Boyle. 'Remember, he was once a philosophy student at the university. Before…'

But his words did little to assuage their anger and impatience, and Sean was ingloriously escorted to the gates by the two burly men.

A man, looking out of a window high up, shouted, 'Look! The secret hand is at work. They have got Sean!'

Sean was checked at the gate by another orderly to see if there was anything in his bag that shouldn't be there, and as the gates clanged noisily shut behind him he felt a little sadness. He waved back goodbye to everybody and went out to rejoin the world.

He walked down the long road in the direction of the city. He was soon being addressed by one of the sídh.

Ye got yer wish, Seanín. Ye'r out.

'I took back that wish.'

Ye can't take back a wish.

'Are you tricking me?'

Just a lesson. There is no such thing as "another wish." Ye will get anything ye wish for.

'I will be more careful from now on.'

That is the lad. Don't wash, Seanín. Let ye get plenty of dirt all over yerself. It will keep ye warm and the bugereens out. Look out for a long coat. Ye need two bags. A good pair of shoes. Ye know where to look. Bridie showed ye! Ye have no worries. No worries at all.

And sure enough, he had not a worry in his head. It was late spring, or early summer. The rain was holding off. He was sure looking forward to getting dirty. They made a person wash so much in that place. Cleanliness was next to godliness, he had heard it said. So what would being dirty make him? He had never yet had occasion to disagree with the Little People. They knew what was what. Even before he had thought about a matter, they had the answer. It must be near midday, now, he mused. It would be lunch time now, back in St Dismal's. He could do with a bite of grub!

Ye will find food anywhere ye look.

True enough. He had often seen apples and bits of bread lying on the city streets, just waiting for the picking. But you couldn't pick up a cup of tea like that. You had to pay for it! Money. He didn't have any.

Ye begs for the money.

Of course. People will just give you a few coppers, if you ask respectfully. A man was approaching. He was middle-aged, walking briskly, his brow furrowed with worry or deep thought.

'Have ye got a spare penny, sir?' asked Sean, surprised at his own forwardness. He would soon come to realise that such forwardness might be seen by others as desperation, or aggression.

The man gave him a quick look, cursed and continued on his way.

Rain started to pour down and Sean realised that he had no overcoat. Indeed, he wore exactly the same clothes he had worn on the day he had entered the institution. Now where was it Bridie had said they gave out free clothes? Where she said you always get something if you beg desperately. It was in Rathmines. He would get a bus into town. He would tell the conductor he had lost all his money. He might take pity on him. He stood at a bus stop and waited. After an hour or two a bus came along. He got on board and sat at the back. After a while the conductor came to him and asked, 'Where to?'

'Do you go through Rathmines?'

'Rathmines is sixpence.'

'I lost all my money. I am sorry.'

'Get off the bus now!'

He was unceremoniously brought by his jacket collar to the door. The bus stopped and he was sent off by a kick from one well-polished official CIE boot. When he pulled himself up off the side of the road he noticed that his hands and clothes were dirty. His face, too, felt as if it had dirt on it.

It was late afternoon by the time he reached Rathmines. For he had got lost a number of times on the way and had not felt like asking anybody for directions. He had been sensing hostility in people. He could see no sign of any place in Rathmines that was likely to give him a free overcoat! He was "drenched to the skin" now. He felt chilled. There was no Bridie around to help him out in his time of need, he told himself now.

He sat down as night arrived in a derelict shed in a waste yard in one of the back streets. Almost immediately he fell asleep – and the strange thing was that despite the chill, wet, hunger and loneliness his sleep was deep and peaceful. He awoke just once during the night with a happy, contented feeling. Deep down, without having even to think or say it, he knew that this was the best, most reinvigorating sleep that he had ever had in his whole life. It was, indeed, the best sleep he would ever have – past, present or future. He fell back asleep, amidst a number of emotions: deep gratitude, a sense of freedom, joy and fulfilment; and something that he could not define or even describe but made him feel that, in the morning, he would wake up and be able to take on the whole world.

It dawned grey and wet. Yet to Sean it was a clear day of blue skies and glorious sunshine. He whistled a tune, its name or origin unknown, and he shook off the dust and dirt and walked out into the open air. Down the back alley he went, and he marvelled to himself at how in such a large city it was possible to find places of refuge where there was no sign of other people or the affairs of a busy world.

He looked about him in wonder. The landscape was arrayed in a multitude of colours: red, orange, yellow, all the colours of the rainbow, even colours that he could not name or recognise. Every colour streamed through its particular landscape so that, for example, not only were the grass verges and trees green but so was the air around them. The blue sky veered downwards so that it penetrated the ground and coloured it as well. The blue air was flowing like a river, with waves as large as those in the sea, so that it was quite easy to think of it as water. There was a yellow colour coming from the sun that splashed itself across the walls of buildings and ran down the street so that the whole thoroughfare was yellow for as far ahead as he could see. Red was coming up from below the ground, and tinged the foundations and lower levels of everything, like the glow of a great fire, dispensing a warm effervescence into the world. Where there was rain water running off the street and down into gutters it was red too! Water-fire, air-fire, earth-fire were the words that came into his head. Red water! Wonderful! Much of the solid world itself – the buildings and walls – was a rich, pleasant brown. This brown seemed to incorporate many of the other colours, so that eventually it was not brown at all but a whirling kaleidoscope of colour that, if one looked at it for too long, became a bright white light that hurt the eyes. The yellow road was leading off in a bewildering variety of directions, some even going upwards and some downwards into the earth. He heard a loud singing and before he knew it he was surrounded by a multitude of the sídh who came to his side and guided him downwards along one of the yellow roads into the ground. He had not wanted to go with them at first, as he had been enjoying the scenery and sunshine. But as soon as he heard all the commotion and saw the bustling, hectic activity below ground his hesitation left him. It was the first time he had ever seen the home of the sídh, he realised. Only privileged mortals were ever invited down there. His guide introduced himself as an old rascal who had reformed and was now an official guide to visiting children and invited wise ones.

'It just shows ye how much I am trusted now. I sometimes operated as the pooka in the County Kildare.'

Now that was an honour and a half, showing a degree of trust unprecedented. For the pooka had the power to be both helpful (in a roundabout way) and incredibly destructive and vindictive.

'Everybody has heard of the Kildare pooka,' said Sean.

'All this activity you see and hear – the crowds of giants and those ones talking all at the same time – is the big election campaign that is now going on in the country. The ruling party is seeking another term. They say they are the only ones fit to govern.'

Sure enough, there were many exceedingly tall men (to Sean, too, they looked like giants) making speeches and he noticed all the election posters of the different parties arrayed around the place – Fianna this, Fianna that and Fianna the other.

'They are not the real Fianna,' said Sean.

'The *real Fianna*! They are no more *Fianna* than I am!' shouted his guide. 'Worthless wretches who dare to steal the name *Fianna*. I would put a stop to their boastful words now if it were not forbidden.'

Sure enough, when Sean paid close attention he could hear the candidates vying with each other in boasting about their achievements and proposed policies. Each party candidate wore a large rosette that represented his party. Sean thought to do his guide's dirty work for him and to throw something at the speakers. Also, he would use some of those new, choice insults he had picked up by listening carefully to fairy chat. Before he could act he heard his guide's command:

'Do not throw anything at the speakers. It is forbidden.'

There'll be a chance later, he told himself. He would show them – teach them not to call themselves Fianna.

'Ye have a chance of getting a good overcoat here,' said the guide.

Sure enough, the speakers had taken off their coats, which were put folded over crates of beer that were lying around all over the place. Some of the crowd were taking bottles from these crates and drinking back the contents with much swagger, happy looks and loud belches. Sean was engrossed in the sight of their red faces, whose mouths were enlarged to allow the intake of a vast quantity of beer with each great gulp. It was like standing at the edge of roaring rapids as rivers of beer rushed past jagged rocks in a great, swirling flow and down deep gorges and over waterfalls of raging white foam, the thunderous noise nearly drowning out the talk and arguing. Sean marvelled at how massive the giants were. It was as if they were continually growing in size with their talk. He felt as small as a fairy just looking at them.

'Ye are one of us,' said his guide. 'That is why they look so tall.'

Sean went over to one of the crates. He used his right hand to lift a bottle out and with his left hand took an overcoat. Folding the overcoat over his arm, he took the cap off the bottle by hitting it against the crate. He drank back the contents whilst gazing at the speaker nearest him, shouting out at intervals when the speaker paused.

'Good on ye, man. Good man.'

The little fella was laughing his hat off at Sean's antics, and kicking him in the leg and egging him on. Sean felt emboldened at this encouragement, and he proceeded to question the giant about his "policies".

'Do ye promise free food for the poor?'

'I do. And more besides. I promise them a job. A good job in a factory, not one of those underpaid, slavery jobs they have to do like picking potatoes in foreign fields and clearing up the slops after the rich have had their fill.'

'Good man. Good on ye. And how are ye going to go about doing that? Will it be out of yer own pocket?'

Another kick on the leg from the fairy.

'I am not a rich man myself. My poor parents nearly died from starvation bringing me up. They were so poor they envied the poor mice they used to chase for the bit of cheese that they would be carrying away. I cried myself to sleep every night from the hunger. The rain came in through the roof and gave us all pneumonia and tuberculosis...'

'Ask him where he put all the money he stole from poor boys by beating them up and threatening and blackmailing them,' said the guide.

'Where did you put all the money you stole from poor boys by beating them up and threatening and blackmailing them?'

The giant went silent and stared down at his questioner. Some other giants surrounded him and bent down and began to shoulder him from side to side. It was as if he was a plaything in a sport or game. But Sean felt no discomfort or fear because he knew that he could call on his guide at any time for help. This time, though, he would handle the situation himself. His small size was his card, as he easily slipped out of their way and went on to the next speaker.

This man was talking about the Fomorians, saying how his party had driven them out of the country and if it were not for him and his colleagues they would all be slaves to those cruel tyrants by now.

'It was the real Fianna who drove out the Fomorians! Ye were clinging to yer mothers' apron strings while the real boys were doing all the fighting,' Sean shouted.

His guide was clearly pleased with this jibe, kicking his leg again.

'Are you a member of the real Fianna yourself?' asked the politician in a sarcastic tone that bespoke someone not easily put off by a heckler.

'Are ye?'

'Erin Abú! Erin Abú! Erin Abú!' the man shouted, angrily.

Other giants standing around joined in his chanting until their cries drowned out all other sounds. Their voices became louder, more loud than one would have thought possible, until Sean had to put his hands to his ears. He cried out in exasperation, 'Oh shut up, ye lot of clowns!'

There was a stunned silence, then curses of bafflement and annoyance.

They were all looking down at Sean who had now shrunk to an extremely small size. The single eye of each giant was all Sean could see, so that some parts of the sky were white, other parts yellow. Rivers of red blood were criss-crossing these vast, empty spaces. There were also multiple volcanic moons, grey or green in colour with deep, sinister black holes at their summits out of which no light escaped. Sean was transfixed as he moved ever closer to these black holes. The whole phantasmagoria was whirling around, moving this way and that so that Sean became dizzy. He felt the breath of these giants, too, like a great wind carrying sulphurous odours and pestilence in its wake. There followed more tremendous, thunderous roars of "Erin Abú!" and Sean thought that the world itself was breaking up under the force of their cries. He had finished the bottle and he flung it up at the speaker to shut him up. It fell short by a long way and nobody seemed to notice for they were all so busy staring down at him, asking him questions such as "who are you?"; "who sent you?"; "where do you come from?".

His guide must have worked a magic trick for Sean's legs carried him out of that spot at a great speed. Faster than the speed of light, said the guide, when Sean had commented that for some moments all had gone black.

He now found himself looking at another speaker. This fellow was speaking in a posh accent. He wore very fancy clothes and he had on a fine brown felt hat such as only the most well-off, educated-at-a-top-school and belonging-to-one-of-the-finest-families-in-the-land wore.

He was saying that most giants did not know how to vote properly. They were too easily led astray by the rough, uncouth element in society, who played on their emotions and primitive instincts. They had been hoodwinked over the last forty years and led by their noses into all sorts of stupid schemes and wasteful adventures, completely unaware that they were being made fools of, simply by voting as they were told, advised or encouraged. They knew how to fight with their fists, but the art of politics was unknown to them. When his party got into power they would abolish the vote "as presently devised" and have a more intelligent, complex form of balloting along proper, prudent lines that would cater for the best brains and talent in the country. The poor and lowly would be better catered for by a system where they wouldn't even have to bother to vote at all, but could spend the day happily employed at their work, leisure activities or in the pub. It would, let it be admitted, be a relief to most of them.

'Leave it to those who know best,' he said in a raised voice, that did not quite become a shout, 'and vote for the educated party, the party that knows what is good for you.'

'Go and make a speech yerself, Seanín,' said the guide.

Sean moved forward, still holding the overcoat on his arm, and clambered up a pile of beer crates beside the speaker, balancing himself as best he could. He heard a voice saying 'Look. He has a fine coat. He is one of us.'

Sean began his speech, ignoring the man still talking beside him.

'It's easy seen that that man is a bodach for to be spinning lies and it won't stand him that long itself! Good cause ye have to be angry, as it is after making a fool of ye that he is! Isn't it timely that I got here this blessed morn to spake up on account of me friends the Little People, who are the backbone of this country? Yes – it is for sure, yer honours, within yer privilege to deny me the liberty of free speech. I'll go bail but I will speak only the truth when I say that it is sure and certain not a one who knows me will say that I do not speak the truth and there is not one in the world that will contradict me. Maybe it's wondering ye are – bad luck to yer impudence, please yer majesty, for darin' to interrupt me – how I came here honest and fair of speech on behalf of the little folk? Faith by all accounts I am a poor, humble amadán too, no different from this fella of the fat face and fancy hat, who has no knowledge of the Little People; and the speech of the foreigner – I cannot master it entirely. But I have been given the power of honest speech by the silent folk who have no one to stand up for them on their behalf. Leave that coat there and you'll oblige me, mister! When the little folk see me accosted like this – don't put in yer prate, mister – sorra one will dar' for to come near me...'

The mob held back, forewarned.

'Saving yer presence, mister, sorra care, I care. For the truth to tell, I came over a long road to be here, devil a less! I beg yer pardon for the liberty I took, please yer honour. It is not the bit and the sup that the little folk are wanting after, but no blame on them for wanting that. It is a heavy handful I have of ye when ye will not listen...'

'He has been causing trouble for every speaker,' said a giant. 'Maybe some new party sent him over here.'

'May bitter bad luck attend you night and day for a blackguard bostún of a fellow, wherever you go, for to be bad-mouthing me. It's easy seen that ye know nothing of hardship and sorrow, and it's the bad life that ye do be leading that has given me the power over you. By my soul, I'll go no further then. M'bhrón, ye've had a long while of it there, fooling the poor and robbing them of the little they had so that not even a pratie and a grain o' salt is there on the table for them in the hungry times. The Little People will put a curse on ye if ye trouble me further, for no harm or hurt can ever be put on me! There, see, maybe it's wondering ye are that no one can be in the way of putting an obstacle before me, for I have their protection. For ye know that if ye harm me even in a small way greater still will be the harm that they will put on you. Small blame to them if they have to put a curse on ye all now, so that a great fear will be upon ye and ye lose yer house and land and yer wives leave ye and yer childer know ye no more…'

'Are you a culchie lad, unused to the ways of Dubh Linn?' asked a giant, who quietened down the onlookers with the warning of a quick eye that here was a fellow who it might not be wise to "bate" as the press was in attendance.

'Isn't it timely that I was addressed by a civil question? Good cause I have to be angry, for the way I have been treated. Is it after making a fool of me that ye'd be? Sure enough, a culchie I am to my credit. But I tell ye – attend now to the warning I give ye that ye be no longer taking away the land of the Little People, robbing them of their ancient rights, their rights of way, their sacred brews and distilleries, their places of worship which are not like yer churches; ignoring, suppressing or even denying the existence of their ancient tongue…'

It was after many hours of talk and standing up for the rights of the Little People that Sean first noticed that it was night and that the giants had all gone. He heard the sound of hands clapping and when he looked down there was his guide smiling and chortling.

'That was a speech that will be repeated for thousands of years to come among the sídh! And look – there is your reward.'

Sean looked down at his feet and there was a posh, fine felt hat and in it was a pile of coppers and silver put there by someone or some group unknown.

'Only the best for our Seanín!' laughed the guide.

Seven

WIDOW O'RAFFERTY WAS a constant visitor to Patsy's household. Indeed, you could say she was almost a lodger, for she often "stopped overnight", her stays usually extending to at least a few weeks or months.

This was when she wasn't elsewhere, gallivanting all over the country, paying her respects in all parts of the region, being received in state by respectable people and institutions as the woman who had got the parish priest promoted to bishop. She had come up from nothing – to be the confidante of a bishop! Every house, shop and church she went to gave her the best of welcomes, never complaining about her many visits, for they knew that she was only doing her duty, going around and giving her respects as almost a famous woman. Once a resident of a humble, run-down cottage (to which she now seldom returned) it did not daunt her to be in the grandest of houses and palaces. 'A true prophet of the peasantry,' Bishop Murphy called her on the occasion of his installation drinks party. 'A mature Joan of Arc; the poor widow of the Gospel who only ever thinks of others, never herself, first; a bishop's best friend.'

On that day before all these great events had taken place, when his emotions had overpowered him and the whole world had come alive like never before so that even the act of praying felt like something vital and solid, and he had felt impelled to make a loud confession to the cosmos itself, admitting his failings and expressing his desires – even to the statue of stone that was in front of him –

believing that nothing was more apparent but that the world and its inhabitants would be both blessed and inspired by such honest acknowledgement of weakness – with St Finbar himself publicly acknowledging and approving his prayers – he had left the presbytery and cycled out to Bailebreoite. He did not know at the time why he had felt that sudden, overwhelming impulse to go to Widow O'Rafferty's cottage. His mind was in turmoil and he was still in a state of excessive excitement when he arrived. The two O'Rafferty women fell down on their knees when he came to the door.

'For heaven's sake, women, get up. This is an emergency! Do you know what has happened? A statue has started talking to me! Am I going mad? Widow O'Rafferty, I have to find the answer to something that has been bothering me. How did you know my name was Mikey?'

Widow O'Rafferty had looked him in the eye for the first time. There was still a shyness in her demeanour, but it was diminishing and she spoke to him now not in the usual reverent tone but in a more normal voice.

She had been having dreams about him, she said. She could not help it. She had tried to put him out of her mind. But the more she tried to dismiss him, the more he had persisted in her mind. She was now having "great dreams altogether" about him. She saw him sitting on a throne as a bishop. She saw that he would build a mighty city "where the village of Rathcloon is now", and an airport and all the other things a great city has. The place would be even greater than Dubh Linn. He would do many other great things, even to performing miracles, making the barren fruitful and the lame whole. And he would be the "father" of many children, healthy and handsome, who would revere his name forever. Most impressive and wonderful of all – he would personally defeat the powers of darkness that were about to descend to "destroy all that is ancient in the land, and the power of the Church."

'Listen to the promptings of your heart,' she said to him now, 'and prepare for many pilgrims to come and worship at the spot.'

Father Murphy asked for a chair and sat down in shock. It was exactly as he had been thinking. Here was a turnaround! All those years a priest, of providing pastoral care for every imaginable type of human predicament; absolving sins that, one would think, not even the most wicked or imaginative mind could have conceived of and what's more – wiping them away as if they never existed; of studying the most learned books, reflecting and preaching on all the great theological issues every Sunday of the year so that one would think here is someone who knows all; of rubbing shoulders with all the clergy and hearing from them every sort of strange story and unusual anecdote – and here he was now – completely bewildered by a simple old country woman. How could she know all that? Dogma, pastoral tools, "exercise of supernatural virtue" were of no use here. Spiritual knowledge, so-called intellectual ability, mental and emotional skills were made null in the case of Widow O'Rafferty. The power of prayer, even, was apparently up against the odds.

He had left the cottage with the answer to his original question already forgotten. However he knew, now, the answer to the questions he hadn't asked.

Within days word of the miraculous event at the parish church had spread far and wide, and crowds began to come.

Eileen was delighted with all the help and support she received from her mother, especially in preparing for the innumerable parties and celebrations – so many birthdays, christenings, confirmations, first holy communions, halloweens, ceilidhes, story times with an seanchaí Patsy Murphy, and so on. Patsy had developed the art of story-telling to such a fine degree that he could talk non-stop for a week and few were the listeners who could stay the course. It seemed that his story-telling got longer and more complex as time went on. This was, of course, partly a deliberate ploy by Pasty to clear his house of these unwanted visitors as soon and as quickly as possible.

However, Widow O'Rafferty, good countrywoman that she was, and a good mother furthermore, thought that the whole Murphy household was still far too backward and unambitious. Her daughter had started off the marriage with all the right ideas. But as time went by and the number of children increased, Eileen seemed to lose interest in the farm, concerning herself with domestic comforts above all else. Widow O'Rafferty would frequently broach the subject of making some money from the land with Patsy himself, telling him that some farmers were making money for nothing just from letting their land. Others were amassing fortunes from "factory farming" – where all the livestock were kept indoors, fed mush and left to get fat. The secret of profit was in having exceedingly large numbers of the said article. To cram in as many as possible into as small a space as possible. Then there were "egg farms" – millions of hens locked into boxes where they would lay three eggs each a day. That was cash for nothing. It was like printing money. There was also a rumour going about that a brand-new airport was going to be built in the area, to bring in the crowds who were flocking to the parish church in Dunmor. Whichever lucky farmer owned that land would be in the pink.

'Making millions! It can be done!' she exclaimed excitedly.

'This is a family farm,' said Patsy. 'It is to be passed on from generation to generation. Patsy Óg, the first-born, will be the next farmer! What do we need money for when you have the treasure that is a son and land?'

'The children will starve for a want of money. Cabbage and potatoes is not enough for these young ones today. What will pay for their education? They all go to school now. Where will you find the dowries for the girls when they go for to get married? Who will bury you in a decent grave for nothing? As a respectable farmer and father your grave will do with a proper headstone. My daughter deserves nothing less. It will be higher than all the other headstones around. It will be marble, and will have many decorations. I want the whole O'Rafferty family tree on it. It is said that we are related to Raifteirí an file.'

'Ah, hush, woman, leave it alone. Why do you talk about death in the midst of life? All I want is a bit of peace in the house,' said Patsy.

They were both seated by the fire, as the children played noisily around. Eileen was taking her early-evening rest and Bridie was bringing in the cows.

'I am not a woman to fool around with, Patsy. People who have crossed my path have lived to regret it. I have more influence than most men. If it were not for me, Father Murphy would still be an ordinary parish priest. And if it were not for me, Patsy, you would not have a wonderful wife either! You would have lost everything by now, your good name and even your life. Your marriage saved you from the hangman's rope! For what protects a man's name more, and preserves him in good health – than marriage?'

'I know ye are a strong woman. I would not cross ye.'

She left soon afterwards, to go visiting. Patsy was delighted that she would be away for some time. However, as always, disappointment followed on the heels of hope, and she turned up again the very next afternoon.

Patsy was cleaning out the cow parlour with Bridie, who these days was busy learning all the country songs, with Patsy as her songmaster.

The widow had returned with the big news.

'Ah, it's all right, Patsy, don't look so startled. Did you hear the news on the radio this morning? So many pilgrims are coming to Dunmor that the government says it will build an airport here. Bishop Murphy is campaigning for it.'

'Be the hokey! An airport in Dunmor!'

'No, Patsy. In Rathcloon. An airport in Rathcloon. Where the land is flat.'

Silence. A look of bewilderment passed over Patsy's face. Then panic.

'They can't bring aeroplanes in around here. And build over good land. And in any case there is…a hill.'

'It will have to go.'

'But part of it is on my land. It can't go!'

'You would only have to sell them a little piece of land. They will pay top prices.'

'I don't know what to make of all this.'

Bridie Murphy looked neither right nor left, up nor down, but continued humming her song to herself. The widow looked at the fairy woman with the usual displeasure. But it had long been noticeable, even to Patsy, that she never commented on either Bridie as an individual or Bridie's presence.

'I met the TD Michael Fitzgerald in Dunmor this morning. They say he is for the government. He is making a fortune these days, they say. He is coming out here to meet you. He wants to see how he can help the poor farmer in these trying times.'

'I don't want to see any TD.'

'He could be the next minister for agriculture! Think about that. You would not have to bother with all those schemes they are coming up with these days. You could get exemptions to everything!'

'Bedad, that would be no bad thing. Did he say anything about this airport?'

'He says if anybody wants to build an airport, they will have to go through him. His first wish is to protect Rathcloon and the people of Rathcloon. People before money, is his slogan.'

'His word is as good as his bond?'

'The point is – he has a lot of money. You can't argue with money.'

Patsy let her have the last word. He did, however, venture to ask her (for the first time ever) when she might be going away again.

'After Deputy Fitzgerald has been.'

He came, sure enough, first thing the very next day, without any official invitation. He was wearing the attire of a stud-farm owner and he looked twenty years older than his age. Before Patsy could even open his mouth he was being addressed as if the visitor had known him all his life.

'Well, I hear, Patsy, that you are the best farmer in the county. You don't bother with all those skilled fellows who think they know it all, coming here to tell you how to do your job. And to take your money, if given half the chance! Good on you. I know you are no fool. It is a privilege to meet a true countryman. And a true man of Erin. You're a breed that's dying out, unfortunately. We must move with the times, if we are to save the country. You, Patsy, have a role in saving the old country.'

'This is a crafty fella,' Patsy mused to himself; 'I will have to be careful with him. He is one step ahead of me already. And before we are out of it he will be many more steps ahead. He is about the same age as my nephew, Sean. I wonder if he knows him?'

'Do ye know my nephew, Sean Murphy? From up the road here in Rathcloon.'

Michael made a show of a big effort at remembering. Of course he remembered Sean. Weren't they in the same class together! And didn't Sean insult the Fianna to their face?

'Sean? Sean Murphy? Oh yes. I think I do. He is up in Dubh Linn now, I believe? How is he doing?'

'He's going great guns. Doing philosophy at the university. It's a great subject. I did a bit a reading of it myself. I learnt a few things too, I can tell you!'

'Bedad he is studying philosophy for a long while now, then! It must be ten or more years he's at it. I reckon he will be the best philosopher in Ireland when he comes out.'

'In some countries they study these things for a whole lifetime. It is only at the end of their life that they can say...'

'I heard he was in a spot of bother.'

'The ancient Athenian society placed philosophers above every other profession. Even above politicians.'

'Bedad, you are a wise man, Mr Murphy. There is a rumour, though, that he was once locked up.'

'Ah, he is what is now called a dissident. What we used to call a rebel. The very best. He is against all that society up there in Dubh Linn. More power to him. They have persecuted him, like they did the country people of old. They have pursued him from pillar to post. They are crucifying him.'

'So you have heard that too!'

'The word came to me via a special messenger.'

'Do you know he was accused of a serious crime?'

'The poor fellow has paid for it over and over. He won't say he is sorry. So they wouldn't let him out for a long time, in case he did something like it again. His poor parents have aged twenty years with the worry. They have been left alone in their old age. Their only daughter has gone to America with the shame of it. They don't talk to anybody now.'

'I have never heard such a sad story in all my days. I had no idea things were so bad with him. Well, I will not stand for it, Mr Murphy. I know the right people to deal with this. I will find your nephew in no time, and he will be back here with his people as right as rain before you can say sixpence halfpence.'

'Oh what? Oh could you? There's a girl here who knew him up in Dubh Linn. She often asks after him. She would be over the moon to see him again. Can ye help?'

'I promise you that I will get him freed. I do not make a promise that I do not intend to carry out. That is one thing that you will learn about me, Mr Murphy. Can we sit down somewhere? I want to discuss a little business with you.'

'Oh, of course, Your Honour. Excuse me my indiscretion, I should have realised that you'd be doing with a bit of rest and a sit down what with all the hard work and travel that you must have to do. Come into the parlour. It's quiet in there.'

By the end of the day Patsy had handed over the bottom field, on which part the ancient rath of Foirnocht had stood for ages past, to the bold Michael Fitzgerald. A deal was done whereby no money would be handed over just yet. Money, according to Michael, was a useless commodity to have in the present – it was *future* money that was really worth having. But Patsy and his heirs would have a good share in the new airport that would run just past their place, when it was up and running. And the beauty of this deal was that Patsy did not even have to sell the field to Michael. He had only lent it to him. He could even have the field back if the airport failed to materialise. Patsy couldn't wait to sign the papers, so excited was he by Michael's assurances. And as part of the deal, Sean would be out of Dubh Linn and back home in no time.

There were celebrations galore in the house that night! Money in the future and Sean about to come home. Bridie, however, seemed subdued. When Patsy asked her why she was so quiet, she gave no answer. She did not know herself why she felt like this – the feeling that whatever transpired, things would not work out in the way that everyone hoped.

She had changed much since she came to the country. The knowledgeable, assured city girl had been replaced by a quiet, introspective, though basically good-natured individual who seldom spoke. The events that had led her to coming there – and to be accepted as one of the household – were always considered a bit of a mystery. It had indeed taken some time for her identity and the whereabouts of the "daughter of the king of England" to become known to her relatives in the Rathcloon district. It was unclear if they had indeed known from the beginning the identity of the strange young lady living at Patsy Murphy's; or had even accepted that she was a relative. They had not wanted to ask, to pry, or indeed to know too much. It was quite normal for a newly married couple to take on a servant girl to help in the house, especially for the first few years. If the girl came from a poor background, and received room and board in return for her service, it made even more sense. Everyone benefited from the arrangement. The fact that she was a princess, a "fairy princess" to be exact, explained many things. Even permitting things that should, properly, be frowned upon. She did not go to Mass on Sundays, for example. Fairy princesses were exempt from this. There was no doubt that any public appearance by her in Rathcloon or Dunmor would attract the curiosity of the idle, the curious and the gossip-mongers. It would be very bad for everyone – for the community, the church and the people – should she ever appear out like that. An occasional chat with Father Murphy, and then with his successor, was enough to guarantee the integrity of her religious state.

But nobody ever knew what went on in her head. Few even dared to speak to her. Such princesses did not need to be spoken to – or had a need to express opinions, or needed to be asked questions about their origins, background, upbringing, experiences etc.. For she was a princess. It was enough to hear her hum or even sing in a low voice as she went about her tasks. The children called her Princess and learned that they could not ask her questions, but that they could bully her sometimes. When the children were very young they did of course ask her many questions, to which she always replied yes. This briefest of responses meant that the children acquired from her a great, uncomplicated wisdom – that yes can be the answer to everything; and as the years went by they would say that Princess was the wisest person in the world and that they had learned more from her than from all the adults and teachers they had ever come across.

But it was not true, as Patsy had said, that she was continually asking after Sean Murphy, or had never ceased wondering where he was or what had become of him. In fact she had more or less completely forgotten about him. She was quite happy just to walk the fields and commune with the birds and wildlife and with all of nature. She developed a little habit of talking quietly to the creatures that she encountered in the fields, lanes and hedges. This was how she began to get the reputation of someone who talked to herself. Such "conversations" should never be listened to deliberately by others; indeed they should never even be accidentally overheard.

Her favourite spot was Foirnocht Hill; specifically the rath that adorned its summit. Here she would sit and muse on the "big things", e.g. that man had constructed the buildings, bridges, streets and back lanes of the city of Dubh Linn, but who built the land, the waters and the sky around here? Why is time always just before or behind us, but never in the here and now? Why do people always complain that it's too wet or too dry, too hot or too cold, too dull or too bright? Why does everything change? Why do good things always end and bad things continue? Why, since she could remember back to times long ago, couldn't she remember coming up the hill to where she was now? Why did Patsy chew tobacco so foul that he had to spit it out? Why do cows always walk home in a straight line behind each other, never departing from the track even by a single step?

The hill gave her a view over all the land. It stood out as an island of dry land in the middle of a large, wet bog. This sense of being on an island made her feel completely secure and happy. Just to be there was bliss.

She often recalled her excitement when Sean had brought her the letter from Patsy Murphy, inviting her down to see the place as he was in "the marriage stakes". And she might be interested in finding out how she and he might get along together. Sean had certainly given her good references, he wrote! She sounded just like the sort of person he could have great chats with. She had wasted no time in locking up the flat, collecting her belongings and heading down on the first bus available. She had called in to see Sean in St Dismal's before she left.

'Are you sure your uncle will want to see me?'

'Definite. I know him very well. Your best chance to be allowed to stay there is to be always very quiet. He does not like to be told what to do. He has never been engaged, or anything like that. It would be best to always let him have his way whatever he wants to do, or say. Don't boss him or interfere in his business. I do know he has a problem driving home the cows. It's a job he hates. Say that you'd like to drive home the cows. That's all. That will warm him to you.

'Sean. I want you to know something. No matter what things they say about you, I think you are all right. When I went to Mrs Byrne to get your stuff, you know what she said? She hadn't touched any of your stuff since you were taken away. That it would only be wearing gloves that she would touch anything belonging to you, and then only if it was absolutely necessary. She said that she had the room blessed by a priest called Father McDoon immediately after you left. But nobody still goes in there yet.'

'It is only right and proper that my old room be treated with the greatest of respect. For it is there that I first met the Little People,' said Sean.

On coming down to Rathcloon on the Dunmor bus and getting off at the head of the lane that led to Patsy's farmhouse, she had felt even greater excitement (as if that was at all possible). As she walked up the lane to his house, she already knew that she would never leave this spot again. She was coming home. Even Pasty was an irrelevance. The smell in the air was the first thing. She remembered it from the time she was a baby. It was now a late evening in early June; the light was strong and birds and livestock were making their presence felt with all kinds of sounds. There was no noise of traffic. She told herself, in her Dubh Linn dialect, that she would kill to remain there!

'Begob, Sean described ye right down to the ground,' said Patsy, who came to the door after her much knocking and with the shy, quiet collie hiding behind him. He was pleased that she had come with just one small bag and no coat; it meant she was clearly a woman of simple tastes.

There was a handshake.

'And to be sure he was right about you too. It is an honour to be invited here. I hope I don't get in your way.'

'Ach, you won't. In fact, I have a spot of bother going on at the moment. I have a court case coming up. It's a murder charge against me. They found the body in the top field. Ye can bring in the cows while I am away.'

'I can drive home the cows every morning and evening, if you like.'

Patsy's jaw opened. He looked confused for a moment. After a short silence, he asked, 'What! Do you mean that?'

'No bother.'

He led her inside and Bridie did not even notice that he made no effort to help her with her bag, coat or umbrella.

That night was the "night of the big dream". Both of them had the same dream, they had discovered the next morning. Bridie had gone to sleep in the hastily made bed in Patsy's old bedroom, adjoining the main bedroom. It was where Patsy had slept from childhood, until his widowed mother went to her eternal reward. Bridie had closed her eyes in bliss, feeling so much at home in the cobwebbed, airy, damp room where she was sure she could hear a frog croaking a welcome. At the very same moment as Patsy was dreaming the same thing, she found herself back in her flat in Dubh Linn, with somebody knocking on the door. She felt a little frightened, for the rowdies often came by and caused a ruckus. When they had had drink taken they were a cause for concern.

'Where's yer boyfriend?' they were shouting, hooting and cursing at the same time.

They banged on the door. Then they began kicking it.

The rumour had gone around town that "her boyfriend" was a quare fella and had been arrested by the "polis" for relieving himself against the sacred monument known as Nelson's Pillar. This had caused the immediate collapse of that monument. There was no doubting the terrible danger to Dubh Linn's young and particularly to its womenfolk from this roving heathen whose whereabouts, as was typical of his kind, remained unknown at any one moment of time. Everyone was on the lookout for him, with young and old alike warned not to approach him but to go to the nearest Garda station (or, in the case of children, report to the nearest responsible adult). Schools and churches were notified. A strange young man approaching the young or the devout at the gate or in the streets nearby was to be viewed as an emergency. Flight was the wisest course of action. Word had also gone round that the same fella had been seen in Corporation Buildings. He had attempted to corrupt some young people on the stairwell. He had been up to see his fancy woman, who lived in the same building. Now a gang of louts was taking the law into their own hands.

The door was kicked in and the gang rushed into the kitchen. Bridie was now hiding under the sheets in the bedroom, scarcely daring to peer out in the darkness. She could hear a commotion in the kitchen. Apparently they were helping themselves to food and drink. Loud laughter broke out. There was much talk. Rude talk. Dirty talk. They were whispering. She could only imagine what they were whispering about. Giggles followed, and then a long silence. She heard a noise at the door and her heart began to beat at a frantic pace. Her mind went blank as fear engulfed her. Then, to her horror, she heard the door slowly creak open and a chink of light appear. She could feel and hear her heart as it beat even faster; so fast that she thought she was going to die. Suddenly a face appeared, looming over the end of her bed. It was unrecognisable, covered in hair and appeared to have a fixed, wide grin with great dirty teeth. It was the head of a monster. She screamed. At that very moment, just as the monster was about to leap on her, Sean appeared in the room, standing in the doorway. The light came on. The room was full of people, arguing with Sean, then threatening him. But they were afraid to lay hands on him. One of the raucous crowd spoke.

'Why did ya pee on the pillar?'

'I am proud of what I did. I would do it again, if it was still there. I felt great after it. Now leave this lady alone and get out of here. Or I will put a curse on ye. She is the daughter of the king of England.'

'The king of England's daughter!' they all cried.

'She must not be touched. Not a hair on her head must be harmed,' Sean shouted.

'Not a hair on her head must be harmed! It has all been a great misunderstanding. A great mistake. Now leave her with us. We will take care of her. We will treat her with the respect she deserves. Go now, for we will have to kill you if you don't go.'

They moved closer and surrounded the bed.

With that, a great cry was heard and Sean swooped down like a bird and lifted Bridie from her bed. He flew with her through the roof of the building, and the next moment they were up above the Corporation Buildings, Bridie held securely in Sean's arms, and both riding on the back of a great eagle. They hovered for a while, then swooped low over the streets before heading off in the direction of the moon. It felt such a natural thing to be doing, flying through the air, that Bridie felt no fear or worry. Indeed she felt quite comfortable, even at peace and knew deep in her heart that Sean would bring her down safely again. They descended at Patsy's farmhouse as dawn was breaking. She was left standing alone at the door, for there was now no sign of Sean.

'I wish ye the very best,' had been Sean's last words.

Patsy came out and greeted her, saying that he was expecting her.

'I am the King of England's daughter,' she said.

'I know,' he replied.

From that moment on there was a deep understanding between the two. Deeper even than that between husband and wife. Both Patsy and Bridie knew that she had been crowned a princess by the sídh; that worldly concerns would no longer weigh on her; that whenever or wherever she wished she could call on the help of the sídh; and at the end of her days she would be taken away by them to that happy land where no tears are shed.

Bishop Murphy was aware that he had reached the highest position possible in the religious/spiritual sphere. No pope or prince of the church was above one who held the episcopal office. Here he was sitting in his big room in the "palace" with the power to command not just souls but whole principalities and powers; to order matters above in heaven even; to instruct no less a Person than the Lord Himself on what was what! Even indeed to tell politicians what to say or do! If he called the radio station, he would be on air within the hour. If he spoke to a national newspaper editor, his views would be on the front page the next day. He would probably be able to get on that new craze, television, to air his views, too.

Despite all the testimonies and tokens of respect, praise, prayers, gifts and petitions, he had the feeling in the early days that he was balancing perilously on the edge of the great abyss, caught up, whether voluntarily or involuntarily, in a subtle war between the powers of light and darkness.

And the suspicion was that it was the powers not of light but of darkness that had been instrumental in his rise to eminence. For wasn't it he himself who had instituted, and encouraged the cult of the statue of St Finbar – and finally as bishop officially guaranteed its divine origin in an official declaration that not even Rome could overturn? He had not made the slightest effort to discredit the talk amongst the faithful that he was the recipient of great supernatural revelations. Even the normally cynical clergy were in awe of him.

It made him tremble and perspire even now, as he sat in his official chair signing canonical documents, many of which he did not understand, especially as they were written in Latin, which he could not be bothered to read. He sighed and pined for the old, simple days.

He had shed private tears of remorse over his weakness in being willing to accept not simply praise and encouragement, but something worse – the comfort of human companionship. He had ended up going out to the widow's cottage and chatting with her three or four times a week, absorbed in her country wisdom and, let it be admitted, her fulsome praise of himself. He had indeed tried often enough to detach himself from this influence, to no avail.

She had put him right on so many things. She it was who alerted him to some new personal habits that had become marked features – such as continually blowing his nose loudly for no reason and wiping it in public. She had put a stop to that. She had also somehow become aware of his keeping stocks of Baby Power. He had ceased that lifelong habit, too. She had helped him overcome his recent giddiness whilst riding his bike, by giving him one of her handkerchiefs to hold in his hand as he cycled along.

He had once, proudly, told her he had never once cried from the time he was a child – and then he had cried uncontrollably in her presence!

And she had such a down-to-earth approach to spiritual matters! Whilst he was agonising with his conscience, wondering if he was facing divine condemnation, she would laughingly tease him saying, 'You must be someone important for St Finbar to be speaking to you!' And even more satisfyingly, 'I can see you as a bishop.'

It was something that he had never even dreamed of before. Suddenly, it all made sense. Of course he could be a bishop! Weren't all the powers of heaven telling him so, giving him all these marvellous signs? Weren't the vast crowds of devout and not-so-devout coming now on pilgrimages to his church – and queuing up to have words with him – a wonderful sign? He was thinking that the widow possessed great spiritual wisdom – as is so often the case with the poor and simple. He began listening more carefully to her talk on matters appertaining to the laity and religious affairs. Everybody in the area, she said, was saying that he was a great man. A prophet. He clearly had an important mission to carry out. He should have no qualms about encouraging pilgrims to come to Dunmor church. And the more opposition there was to this – especially by holy people – the better, for that would be a sure sign of the miracle's authenticity.

Like all humble people, she was a great spiritual director without even knowing it. Her wisdom, as far as he was concerned, knew no bounds. All the books in his library did not contain the wisdom of Widow O'Rafferty. She even told him that he was too much into book learning. Books could not help him understand life or people. He turned to scorning book knowledge and any reliance on "learning". What did those scholars know? He was ashamed of keeping so many books. He would get rid of them.

Father Murphy had despatched his books on a bonfire at the back of the presbytery – ignoring the protestations of Mrs Dunne. She had physically intervened and tried to prevent the conflagration, burning herself in extracting half-burnt papers from the fire. As he watched, he thought that he was hearing, above the crackling of the flames, the mocking laughter and angry scorn of many wicked spirits.

He had long since got used to wearing all the extra bits and pieces and other extravaganza of his job. He had moved on from the early days, losing all that false humility, forgetting all those scruples and becoming self-assured in all things. He had become a practical man.

Religion wasn't a dream – it was about improving society. Apart from the now dying controversy over St Finbar's statue, and the still unexplained, mysterious spiritual aspects of the Dunmor church phenomenon (the claiming of a number of miracles on the positive side, whilst cynics pointed to a corresponding nationwide sharp decline in religious practice as a negative), there had been other, major positive improvements. Wasn't there a huge international airport now at Rathcloon? And BailenahEoropa was growing in size by the day. That was the biggest miracle of all – for the whole thing had been started off by those first pilgrims coming and spending their few pence in the souvenir shops.

And wasn't he in a position now to help all his friends? Mrs Dunne, housekeeper to Dunmor's new parish priest, was enjoying her renown and prestige for having been the housekeeper of a priest who became a bishop. She even overshadowed the new PP in esteem and authority. The parish brought all their troubles to her. Her poor, alcoholic daughter was installed securely in the most modern of homes for the disabled, with wonderful drugs to take her mind off the drink. And to top it all, when Mrs Dunne unfortunately became reliant on the drink herself, he had seen to it that she, too, was taken into care in the same modern home as her daughter. All those acts of charity that he had dreamed of performing whilst a simple priest, he could now carry out.

There had been talk of him being the next cardinal. He was nearly old enough. Even the pope had called by to congratulate him.

He would laugh to himself every now and then when he remembered the old days – the stories about the fairies, the hush as someone related strange happenings in a remote house or field, at Halloween or in the middle of the night. Oh, weren't we simple and naive in those days, he would laugh to himself, or with some important visitor or researcher. As for Widow O'Rafferty – to prevent scandal or talk he had cut off all contact with her. He had heard that she was having a great time travelling around and living off her reputation as a friend of the bishop – well, good luck to her. But friendship could be a dangerous thing. It was something he could now do well without. Friendship was for people who had time on their hands, people who did not have to make important decisions; and especially who did not have to hold and upkeep such an important office as a bishopric. He was a little bit ashamed now, for having let her have such a sway over him; and he would pretend to himself that he had never been friends of the woman.

And as for those so-called powers of darkness that had worried him so much in the past – they had certainly been put in their place – defeated by the new, prosperous, educated populace of Erin.

It only remained to him now to do something about those banned practices and superstitious devotions that continued to take place at Dunmor church, and which the Church in her wisdom considered no longer good for her image; though thankfully it was now only a small remnant of mostly old people who still clung to the "sacred spot".

The chance finally to abolish the reputed "apparition" site at Dunmor, along with the decrepit old church building itself, came when he had a visit from none other than the Minister for Enterprise, (and co-campaigner for the Rathcloon development in the old days).

They had greeted each other like old friends, or more accurately, two co-conspirators.

'Minister Fitzgerald is here to see you, Your Lordship,' said the monsignor/secretary, wondering to himself how much he would be able to hear through the keyhole.

'Ah, Michael! The great man. Send him in.'

'Good to see you again, Your Lordship. Thanks for fitting me into your busy schedule. I wouldn't be here taking up your time unless there was good news.'

'And how is the family, Michael?'

'A few ups and downs, but that is the way. The young these days don't think like we used to. And the women have become fearfully independent. The mansion is a bit too big for me – now that I am living on my own. But that is the way – Erin and the times have moved on. You and I have our feet in both worlds, Your Lordship

– the old and the new. That is why we have wisdom, whilst all the rest have only knowledge. I have come about that old problem – the so-called apparition site at Dunmor. I know it was very helpful to us in the early days – to have all those pilgrims coming – and the name of Dunmor becoming a commonplace throughout the world. It put us on the map. But as you know, it is now standing in the way of our plans to extend the new city into Dunmor and beyond – and replace the whole lot with brand new housing and industry…'

'Haven't I been thinking hard these past few months about your offer? But closing Dunmor church and banning pilgrimages is easier said than done. Don't you think it hasn't been a real conundrum for me? For who first heard the statue speak? What will they think if their bishop now says he was deluded, or even lying? I have got to go about things the right way. Nevertheless, I have made by mind up, providing the deal we discussed becomes a reality. As regards St Finbar and his now somewhat dated messages – well, all I can do is quote from Scripture: "When we are children we think as children think. But when we are adults, we must…" Now theology has moved on. No more of this introspective, self-indulgent navel-gazing that some die-hards still see as spirituality.

'But – there is still strong opposition to any interfering with the St Finbar devotions – and particularly with the statue. Mrs O'Rafferty is a leading, formidable opponent. Indeed, I have had to pretend that I am on her side. I always say it's others higher up in the Church who are for closing it down.'

'That is probably very wise. Why I have come here today is that there has been a development in my efforts to get private funding for that new cathedral with all the mod-cons, to replace Dunmor parish church. Well, Your Lordship, I have succeeded!'

'Great news, Michael! Wonderful news! I never had any doubt that you would come up with the goods.'

'Where Dunmor is small, this building will be immense – the biggest church in Erin. Not even the Dubh Linn cathedrals will give it a run. Where Dunmor is bleak, this will be bright, with a glass roof and glass walls. Where Dunmor lacks basic comforts, this will have all the amenities. It will be multi-purpose, and will have three different levels for different functions. It will have a St Finbar theme section. We will build it as a showpiece at a major ring road junction, where everybody will have access. It is a winner. At no cost to your good selves. All you have to do is put a stop to all this silly opposition to closing down Dunmor church. And ban all pilgrimages officially.'

'Who are the donors?'

'They are good religious people who wish to remain anonymous.'

'I respect their wishes. And I can definitely announce the new St Finbar's cathedral? No strings attached.'

'No strings attached.'

Michael walked back to his state car with a spring in his step. In the driver's seat his chauffeur was lying sideways, asleep and reeking of alcohol. This was a great surprise to Michael, for he was certain that the man, who was proud of his job and had boasted to everyone about being a driver to the great Michael Fitzgerald, was known as a staunch teetotaller. Michael had to push him into the passenger seat and take control of the Mercedes himself. It had been quite a while since he had had to drive, he mused. Perhaps Tommy had a problem at home. He would ask him when he woke up.

The car glided out of the palace grounds. Michael commented to himself that this new model was certainly the smoothest car he had ever been in. It was to his surprise that he found the sign for Dubh Linn to be pointing in a direction that he was sure could not be correct. Still, there were so many new roads now perhaps it was some kind of diversion. Strange, though, the way the car was now seeming to drive itself. It was as if he wasn't needed at the controls. The road was as smooth as the air itself. He felt like closing his eyes and letting the most up-to-date, computerised car technology do the rest. Suddenly the vehicle accelerated to a speed that must have been at least 100 or 140 k.p.h., sweeping down the road as dusk set in. It was wonderful what they put into cars these days. He would close his eyes and have a nap.

He was immediately in dreamland, and was floating down through the clouds to earth. Then his dream became a nightmare. He could not tell if he was awake or asleep. He had landed not back in the Mercedes but aboard a horse that he knew somehow was none other than Fast Lad, the first horse he had ever owned. They were trotting out onto the track, in the pouring rain, black clouds making it more like night than day, his skin as wet as that of a fish. He was astride the animal in his own racing colours of red and white, and barely staying in the saddle for he had never ridden a horse in his life. It was evident that there was great excitement in the crowd in the stands. They were clapping, cheering, shouting and some were booing and it took him some time to figure out that it was all directed at him. He could see Fast Lad's name on the bookies' boards – it was two-to-one-on the favourite. The shouting grew louder:

"You can't lose, you mustn't lose – or else!"

"But...he is useless. He never bred anything in stud...!"

A shout was heard: "We have put our shirts on him."

The next moment he was being carried at a steady gallop down the course to the starting line. He lay as flat as he could, clinging to the horse's neck with both arms while all the other jockeys laughed, jeered and shouted insults. He had never felt so afraid, so vulnerable, so panicky in his life. Fear, insecurity, alarm had been completely unknown to him before. So powerful were these emotions now that he wanted to weep; to call for help; to call even for his mother – but no sound came out.

Fast Lad was ignoring Michael's pulling on the reins and continual silent pleas to slow down. The bumping and knocking on his bottom was now exceedingly painful: *bop bop bop bop bop bop bop bop bop bop bop bop bop* went bottom and saddle like a leprechaun's hammer as the pain, the redness and eventually blood bespoke a raw wound; so exceedingly painful that it felt as if some sadistic torturer was at work.

'I wouldn't like to be in your boots if you lose this race,' said a jockey as they lined up with the rest of the field. Still unable to speak so intent was he on trying not to fall off – for the drop to the floor appeared to him to be from an exceeding great height with the likelihood of also finding himself under many horse's hooves – he appealed to the jockey for help with pleading eyes. The fellow laughed at him and said, 'You haven't a chance.'

A bugle was heard and they were off! To his horror, as they thundered down the course (there were so many other horses in the race it would have been impossible to count them from close up), he saw a fence looming up in the near distance.

'No! It can't be,' he shouted, for his voice had returned. 'Fast Lad is not a chaser! He has top pedigree blood!'

'He's a mule!' laughed his fellow-jockey tormentor. 'And he's the father of mules.'

They approached the jump and he could feel a change taking place in the rhythm. Fast Lad was preparing for his first jump ever. They were at the front of the field, so if he fell every other horse would be on top of him.

They took off and Michael felt himself somersaulting high up in the air. He came straight back down again onto his mount, landing on his very sore bottom.

'No bother,' laughed the talkative jockey, 'but wait till the next one! Then the water jump! And then the Great Ditch!'

His laughter was louder even than the thunder of the horses' hooves.

Michael dropped the reins and held on very tightly to the mane for the next terrifying ordeal. His jumping companion told him not to worry. 'The next is the lowest jump in the race.'

But in fact it appeared in the far distance to be as high as the Tower of Babel.

'Ha ha ha. It's called the Tower of Babel. It's the lowest fence in the race. It only looks small from a distance. It gets higher the closer you get to it. The Tower of Babel! Ha ha ha.'

The Tower of Babel was in fact the highest fence it was possible to imagine. It was so high it had lanes of traffic running underneath it; he could see motor vehicles of every description, lorries, buses and juggernauts rushing through its tunnels. It dominated the horizon, the top disappearing into the clouds. He could not see how it could possibly be getting smaller the closer one got. The fellow was a liar! He felt great anger and he turned to shout abuse at him.

'You lying no-good chancer!' he shouted. But there was no sign of him now. Only other grim-faced riders who all looked as if they were in as much difficulty and as fearful as himself. And no wonder! With fences like these! He was so angry now that he felt almost cocky. He kept his head down and decided not to look at the fast-approaching fence. He closed his eyes and held on tight, for he could feel that dreaded change in rhythm coming again. Up they went sailing through the air and Michael made a little prayer that he would be flung far above and beyond the mêlée. Perhaps he might land on his front, side or back this time and not on his sore bottom.

'Please, Lord. Please!' he prayed.

To no avail. This time he hit the deck even harder and it felt as though his backside was on fire.

'Only number two, only number two! Forty to go,' laughed the joker, who was at his side again.

'We'll see about that,' Michael shouted grimly.

'The next jump,' he was informed by a voice turned suddenly cold and officious, 'is a water jump. One of the easier ones. It has all the natural water of Erin that ever fell down from the clouds. If a jock falls into it, he is never seen again. You must hold on tightly, for it is a very dangerous obstacle. Heed my words, like a good man.'

'Mother, mother!' cried Michael as they lumbered towards the third jump. He could already hear the sound of rushing water ahead and a roar that could only be a mighty waterfall.

Up and over they went like a ship sailing through the sky; and then down into the water for Fast Lad was finding the going hard.

'Up, up, you stupid beast,' shouted Michael. 'Up! Get up out of it, you mule!'

Somehow they managed to pull themselves out, and then off again to catch up on the field. Soon they were back up with the leaders, and his helpful friend had a few more words of advice for him.

'Ye had a narrow escape there. There is a mighty long way to go, my friend. Ye must pace yerself. The next jump is the Quartermaster.'

Michael dared not look ahead.

'After the Quartermaster, there is the Tower Block, followed by the Sky Scraper, then the Long Runway, the Tunnel, the Housing Estate, the Cathedral, the Spire, the new Shopping Centre. Oh, there's a whole gamut o' them all the way to the back of the course and then we pick them up again for the cavalry charge back to the first and then all the way around again another three times....'

'Oh please have mercy!'

'Ye are not so cocky now! Go on! Give me yer cheek. Give me some of yer cheek. Give me yer cheek again! Ye cheeky, no-good lout. Where is yer cheek now, ye heathen?'

The Quartermaster proved to be the worst jump thus far. It felt like it took a lifetime to get over it. Or more accurately, to get through it, for its outer part was a massive concrete wall, totally beyond the capability of any living creature to jump. Michael and Fast Lad crashed though the wall. As blocks of concrete came hurtling down through the sky he put a protective arm around his head, which bore the brunt of the rock-fall. But they were not through it yet. The second stage was an electrified high-security barrier that was higher even than the concrete wall. Michael, unbeknownst to himself, was patting Fast Lad on the neck and murmuring words of encouragement.

'Good lad, you can do it. Just one last, good jump and we will be over and out of this race, for I am not jumping anymore.'

Such was the electric shock they both received that Fast Lad catapulted himself over the fence, in a leap worthy of any Grand National steeplechaser.

'Are ye still on that critter? I'd have thought ye'd be both on the flat of yer backs by now,' said his tormentor, as they galloped along.

Michael, despite his best efforts, had not been able to pull Fast Lad to a halt.

'Yer mule is very stubborn. He won't stop for ye? Has he it in him, d'ye think, to be a winner? How much did you pay for him now? Would ye recommend him to all the brood mares in the land? Are ye proud of him? Is he the best horse in Erin?'

As the race proceeded and the jumps got even worse, Michael was wishing that he could just die. He prayed that Fast Lad might break a leg or collapse from a heart attack. Each time they passed the stands missiles were flung at them with shouted instructions to hurry up, as he was now some way behind the leading horses.

He had given up worrying about anything; whether he lived or died, whether he was first or last in the race; whether the crowd attacked, mauled or killed him if and when he eventually made it back to the enclosure. For there was no doubt now that Fast Lad would be the last horse to finish the race. He could remember little of the rest of the race, other than that it had been a prolonged ordeal with each succeeding jump worse than the one before. He had given up caring by the time of the last jump. This was a leap over the highest mountain range in Erin – the MacGillycuddy's Reeks.

As he trotted back the last few furlongs – trotting being more excruciating than galloping or even jumping – he could hear the roars of anger and outrage. As they pulled in to face the gauntlet of irate racegoers, Fast Lad suddenly reared up and threw Michael off. He fell to the ground under the feet of his mount and was trampled upon. What the horse had started, the crowd completed.

The kicking and thumping went on forever, until he felt that he did not have an unbroken bone in his body. He must have been bawling too, for eventually that sound came to his own ears.

'Get out of that car at once. Get out!'

He looked up and saw a torch shining in the window. He could see a garda uniform in the darkness. The man was knocking on the glass with his fist.

Michael struggled to sit up straight and before he knew what was happening, he was being pulled out of the car.

'Look at the cut of him. The way he was driving is enough to ban him for life. He doesn't know how lucky he is.'

'Or the public. Look, Sergeant. There's someone else in the car. On the floor. He looks in a bad state too.'

'Both of them – stinking of drink.'

'It's Mr Fitzgerald, Sergeant O'Hourigan. The government minister!,' whispered the guard.

'You think I didn't know that before I even pulled him in? We will have to handle this one carefully. First of all, a breath test.'

They gave the test to Michael, all the time pretending that they did not know who he was.

'Jiminy Cricket – talk about being over the limit.'

Michael had found his voice by this time and protested, 'But I have not been drinking...'

'Look at the state of your clothes. And you are covered in blood and bruises. This man down there on the floor has also been beaten up. It might be dangerous to move him. Oh...wait now! Is it yerself that's in it...? Is it you, for sure, Mr Michael Fitzgerald TD? This is your old friend here from the old days, Sergeant O'Hourigan. Thanks be to the Lord that it was me who pulled you in, sir. You were in a right state, sir. Here, take a sit down and have a rest. Would you like a cigarette? Here, Guard, give the gentleman a cigarette.'

Michael only slowly recovered his senses. He still did not know if he felt good or bad. Mainly it was a feeling of numbness. But he was definitely beginning to feel a little more normal. The two guards were pulling the chauffeur out of the vehicle and Michael shouted, 'He is drunk. He is the cause of it.'

'And half dead,' replied the sergeant.

'A private chat, sir,' said O'Hourigan, taking Michael by the arm and guiding him a little further away.

'You were very lucky I caught up with you, sir. Do you know where you were nearly ending up?'

'I was on my way to Dubh Linn.'

'You were nearly ending up in Rathcloon. Bandit country! Now that would have been a fine thing, for you to be taken hostage. The wild Murphys. And the godfathers of crime operate around these parts too. You would not be the first one to disappear.'

Michael's heart began to thump. The Murphys! They had declared him enemy number one after a deal went wrong years before.

'I'd consider it a favour if you get me out of here,' he said to O'Hourigan, almost pleadingly.

'I can see you've had a bit of a hard time, sir.'

'I have been through hell and back, I can tell you.'

'Get in the Merc. I'll drive you home. Your troubles are over.'

Eight

BAILENAHEOROPA HAD APPEARED suddenly in the boglands around Dunmor. The Little People first had an inkling of something going on when they began to hear the sound of loud mechanical "horses" ploughing overhead and all around them. At first they accepted that this might be just one of those rogue, so-called clean-up operations that, by removing everything useful, usually ended up making a worse mess. Or even a worthless job that might, however, provide them with some unexpected bonus such as a newly flooded field, an exquisite set of new tunnels to fool around in, a clearance of some previously giant-polluted area to be replaced by interesting, landscaped gardens, fruit trees, a stream diverted to become a strong river, or even a new wood. But this time something strange was going on. The work developed into a large-scale operation such as they had never seen before. The work went on day and night, with no sign of it ever stopping. Strange, unfamiliar giants appeared, talking in languages they didn't understand.

Then they realised that if this went on they were going to have to do some evacuations of their widespread depositions – possessions collected over millennia, as well as their stable of white steeds, pets, hidden crocks of gold, etc. This had only ever been necessitated in the past when a church was built, a new road constructed or an old one widened to cater for increased traffic as they inevitably ran over sacred spots. Patsy's farm was dangerously near to the new developments. In the nearby fields there was much activity, with large slabs of stone being laid down. Then mechanical birds began to land on the ground. Something else was going on too, they noticed, because a crowd of people began to appear at regular intervals on Foirnocht Hill, shouting and waving placards with lots of noisy arguments. Gardaí appeared and attacked the crowds with their hitting sticks. This series of events continued to happen at regular intervals.

Then one day the unbelievable happened. The roof over their heads came crashing down. They had to flee at once in front of the big mechanical horses as their home was destroyed. They went to hide in the huge new pipes that were being laid in the ground, and waited till evening. When things had quietened down, they went up to have a look.

Foirnocht Hill and its rath were no more!

There must have been something greater than mere giant ignorance behind such a crime. Dark powers were at work. However, mortals would have to pay, at the very least for being accessories.

The Little People found a new halting site in a secret location. They went to sleep in exhaustion and sorrow, for a length of time which they did not measure. They did not wake up because they did not feel like waking up. When one temporarily came to his senses, he remembered what had happened, closed his eyes at once and went back to sleep. None had the energy or the will to wake up or arise. It was only after such a time that moss, woodlice, beetles and fungi began to creep over their bodies that they knew it was time not only to wake up, but to move from that place. When they looked outside, what they saw was unbelievable.

A huge city of glass covered the land for as far as one could see. It covered even the sky. Fantastic lines of carriages were moving along high up in the air, ferrying uncountable numbers of giants who sat in silence as if struck dumb. There was a deadness in the faces of those giants that they could see up close. Their eyes were blank. No laughter, talk or song. The giants were all in a great hurry, walking in straight, direct lines to their destination. Such order was a disquieting sight for the happy-go-lucky sídh. No more did the giants look around them, to the right or left, up or down, to admire a wild flower or to laugh at a farmer stuck in a hole, to feel sorrow at the sight of a broken flower or of dark, gloomy clouds in the distance. The columns of giants, walking in straight lines apparently oblivious of their surroundings, appeared to have succumbed to a condition that was irreversible, for not one single individual strayed from his/her course.

Later, some (increasingly idle) sídh attempted from a distance to influence the rigid walk of these giants and make their routes less direct. One method was deploying the rarely used power of fairy hypnotism, which enabled them toalter perceived messages or images subtly – such as those on advertising billboards – to distract the passer-by. This had to be done with great care. For it often caused not a creative distraction, an increase in imagination and "dream vision", but some accident, minor or major. It was a number of serious instances of the latter that had made them some time ago give up this activity, for no sídh may deliberately endanger an innocent mortal. However, the practice was revived and it did often successfully make the looker "see what was not there" and thus impede the progress of his/her walk.

Here and there two or more giants were fighting. Unlike the brawls of old, these fights went on interminably, as if there could be no winner or truce.

Large mechanical birds – of a much larger size than they had ever seen – were alighting or taking off from the newly levelled land near Patsy's farm. Everywhere they looked they saw annoying, view-blocking signs with the words *Michael Fitzgerald Enterprises*.

At every entry and exit point mechanical monsters were constantly going in and going out. In the past they had been able to see clearly the giants riding these; but now it was difficult to see up to the top of them, or inside them. It was not clear who was in charge of these great moving mechanicals; and this phenomenon of ghost operators extended to many other objects and features in this new place – many seemed to have no giant in charge, as if they were operating by themselves! Lights came on or went off by no visible hand. Sounds, voices, singing, music – all could be heard coming from no obvious or visible source. They shuddered at the eeriness of it all. Already "urban myths" were appearing by the cartload. For instance, it was said that whilst inside their homes the giants sat around all the time and did not have to do any housework, it being done for them by some mechanical or magical means. They even had strange ways of working at their places of employment. Sometimes they did not leave their seat all day. Others spent the whole time talking to no one that they could see; and this continuous talking was called "work". Another very strange phenomenon was the much increased cohabiting by male and female giants but with no new children appearing as a result! The decline in the fertility of the giants was to become a cause of great concern to the Little People, for they wondered if the power of nature itself was diminishing.

A strange quiet came over the place later in the evenings. The population disappeared! Large areas which in the daytime were busy with huge crowds, became deserted. These central areas still remained lit up by the "fire posts", however, and one could see inside the buildings (many were without walls) and all their interior goods. It was a wonder for them to see these buildings without walls. In the outlying areas of the agglomeration there were rows upon rows of houses for as far as the eye could see, where most of the population lived. These buildings were so numerous they ran up into the sky. Nowhere was there any green area visible. These outlying areas were all deserted too, for the residents went into the houses in the evening and did not come out again until the morning.

They wondered if it was the same place at all that they had known since time immemorial. They asked the shaman what all this meant – and he did not say anything, just shrugged his shoulders and carried on walking. (Shamans never stayed in the same spot for longer than a few moments, due to the various spells they were either weaving or being weaved into, in lieu of the danger of becoming seriously entangled in some strong or even evil spell. Hence it was difficult to pin them down to any sustained, serious conversation.)

They asked the forgetful ones (those who had overdosed on toxic mushrooms and never spoke). These chaps were always wandering abroad, getting lost, or forgetting to return home until turning up moons late on the back of some eagle, crow or other bird; or even in the mouth of a fox or cat. Nobody knew what went on in their heads as they went living rough around the habitations of the giants. This involved creeping into posh mansions at night and helping themselves to the choicest food and drink (all they ever "got" was the flavour). Top restaurants were also a favourite haunt. They would play about in the wardrobes of bedrooms, feeling the silk and satin. They would go into clothes-wear shops and try on baby and small children's outfits. They sought out displays of expensive silver and played about in cups, goblets and other silver or gold utensils. This was seen as the lowest kind of down-and-out behaviour by the rest of the sídh. Some shamans went so far as to claim that the forgetful ones were a symptom of the deterioration of the race. One shaman claimed that he had received a "revelation from the unknown deity" ordering a clean-up campaign against mushroom-taking. This shaman went around proclaiming that, 'Mushrooms are a vegetable!' That of course went against accepted beliefs, rituals and traditions. So the same chap was thereafter seen as a subversive, marginalised in society and he and his campaign mocked.

It was thought that perhaps the shock of this destruction of the old landscape might force the forgetful ones to say at least a few words. Who knew what wisdom they would have learnt during all that silence and wandering? One did speak, on being pressed very hard. However, his speech was indistinct, croaking, almost a cough. He had shrunk in size so that even for one of the sídh he was tiny! He looked straight ahead as he "croaked" – and it was necessary to get a shaman to try and explain exactly what he was saying. These were his words:

'The giants have imagined all this up out of their great poverty of spirit. They think that this dreamworld they have concocted –

and it comes out of their most base, infantile impulses – will compensate for their loss of song, story and soul. They believe that the glass world really exists. That it will last forever. That nothing in the natural world or the underworld can destroy it. They believe that the Little People do not exist. They laugh at the sídh. They destroy raths and sacred trees. They even think that they will not have to pay.'

One leprechaun came into the huge pipe where they were all meeting. The pipe had apparently been deliberately discarded and left on a rubbish heap in a remote corner of a large, derelict field. Such rubbish piles, of course, would prove to be temporary. He was very forlorn and threw his skin bag, which contained his shoe-mending kit, on the ground. He was talking to himself, saying that making and mending shoes – even the pretence of doing so – was no longer worth the effort. For when the lesser sídh made themselves visible these days they were liable not to put on the old-style shoes, but visit the factories and shops of the giants and put on baby shoes; insultingly going to the senior leprechauns and demanding that they adapt, shorten or enlarge these as the case may be. These degenerates had succumbed to the temptation of places where there were amazing quantities of goods and chattels piled up, and had increasingly been drawn there. He himself had witnessed the incredible sight of countless pairs of shoes and other goods lying ownerless in the wall-less buildings.

The discontent of this leprechaun struck a chord amongst the assembled gentlefolk. Their dismay grew at the destruction of so many old things; at the rapid advance of the new technological age where giant technology was replacing everything familiar; and more particularly the corruption of impressionable sídh who were falling into temptation and being led into *desiring goods in the manner of the mortals*!

There was only one thing for it.

A risky, brave, even foolhardy course of action was decided upon after a lengthy session of music, song, dance and nectar drinking.

In the cold light of intoxication the best, and most daring, decisions are made. It was something unheard of before. A ploy that would have been condemned by every member of the nether world in the past. But the past did not exist. The past was the present. The present was the future. So despite what scholars and folklorists believe, it was indeed possible for the Little People to decide to do something that broke their unbreakable code. And when they did this thing that was unusual, heretical, disgraceful, disloyal, irresponsible, shameful, pitiable, sacrilegious, dishonourable, disreputable, unworthy, they always felt that they were succeeding, even if only for a brief moment, in turning back the tide of the future.

They had decided to make a direct approach to their old friend, Mikey Murphy. Or as he was better known now – Bishop Murphy. In other words, directly contact a member of the clergy – and a bishop at that.

Mikey could well give them advice on how to counteract temptation. He was the professional when it came to understanding and preventing the corruption of the weak and ignorant; indeed of the wise and strong.

He also had the power to deal with the L of D – the one whose name they dared not utter.

For who else would be behind the earth-moving, shifting, sky iconoclasm of recent times but the common enemy of mortal and sídh? Mikey would, in his capacity as an important representative of the unknown deity, have the know how and means whereby to offer them some protection.

Oh yes, they knew Mikey could give them short shrift, and had done so a number of times when they had come calling in the vicinity, never directly addressing him but trying to make their presence felt in the forlorn hope that they might, somehow, get a blessing from him. And they also owed him a few favours. He had helped them settle Patsy Murphy down when the farmer was on the verge of succumbing to the wiles of science and veterinary medicine and allowing a number of his cows to be put down. There would have followed additional pressure for him to get rid of his ducks, hens, goats and even the few sheep he kept, for the purpose of "sanitising" his cow herd against natural conditions that those busybodies called diseases. They had first made him witless by constantly interfering with his cows' trek home. This ensured that he was in a foul mood each time the vet called. Mikey had then taken poor Patsy's mind off cows completely by encouraging him to read, and by advising him not to think so much about his cows. They were certainly alarmed at first when he began reading serious subjects – but relaxed when they realised he was only doing this so that he could criticise and reject everything the experts wrote in their books. Mikey had also seen to it that Patsy would be more self-assertive when the inevitable happened and he ended up having a woman about the place – and this again was achieved through the medium of books.

There was the business over the statue. It had started as a joke. They had wanted to pull his leg when he was in his sups and had gone to pray in the church. Interfering directly with those at prayer was a no-go area; but in this instance a prank was possible because he had drink taken and was in a highly emotional state.

He had returned from a visit to the only mortal whom they genuinely feared and would never cross – Widow O'Rafferty. They knew her very well indeed. When the widow was a child she'd had the ability to see all the sídh. She never had to make the pretence of being able to spot a leprechaun or a ghost or the Pooka as other children did in order to impress peers or elders. Unlike everybody else, she never claimed that she "believed" in fairydom. For she saw them all the time and knew all about them. They were no more remarkable to her than any wild creature; their activities no more interesting than the antics of a collection of March hares, a conference of crows in August or the frolicking of yearling cattle at dusk; no more distracting than any wild flower or hovering insect.

But what impressed the sídh most about her, and made them wary, was something else. She had the uncanny ability to see what others seldom clearly see – the *weakness* in every creature, sídh, mortal or animal. This allowed her to have, despite her lack of education, much basic common sense, along with a knowledge of the world that surpassed even that of the cleverest, most educated mind.

What made matters worse – alongside this ability to detect weakness went a corresponding tendency to *pity*, and thus to interfering in the affairs of others. And for the sídh if there was anything worse than being the subject of laughter, it was being pitied!

She knew that the sídh's hold on reality was slight. That their ability to influence the material world depended on the whims of mortals and the weakness of fools. That their visible presence in the world was gradually becoming rarer, because of a lack of belief. That the one thing the sídh could not bear was to be laughed at. Any domestic crime – such as throwing waste water out the door – she could freely commit. For they dared not enact a punishment for fear of her scorn.

On that first day, when Mikey Murphy had visited her cottage to ask for the hand of her daughter in marriage on behalf of Patsy Murphy, after the initial awe and nervousness, she had soon detected his loneliness. It was the way he had suddenly looked off into the middle distance when she asked him if he would like a sup. Indeed, as soon as she spoke – or looked at him – he would stare away, as if deep in thought, or perusing some remote, all-absorbing religious or contemplative scene. She had a sudden, irresistible urge to make him lose the shyness. She would make him feel at home. She knew from the church notice board that his name was Michael. (It would be a salutary reminder for Father Murphy that he was still mortal, as he had indeed forgotten – from lack of use – his own baptismal name.) Sure enough, the show of friendliness worked tricks and he became a regular visitor thereafter to enjoy the easy, sociable chat. As he became less reserved and more outgoing, he spoke about the frustrations of the job. She knew that she was listening to someone whose gifts were being wasted in Dunmor. He had been satisfying a huge brain with the poor fare of book-reading – even if they were books of the highest intellectual calibre. She knew that he was meant for more than that. For what good was book reading, unless it led to something practical or material? He should be a bishop at the very least.

So, as Mikey had come under her spell and began to think great things of himself, the Little People planned to have a bit of fun – and achieve something useful at the same time. They would attempt to make him see the weakness of his willpower and the corruptibility of his imagination, and thus accept that he could, after all, be subject to the wiles of another mortal. And worse still – of a woman. Then he would be their man again. He would remain a humble priest. He would be content once more with his lot.

But their scheming had all gone astray. They had no problems in making the statue appear to move and say, 'Mikey – shame on you. Letting yerself be led along like that by a woman.'

However, something else had already happened with Mikey, for he did not seem to think it remarkable or even unusual that the statue had moved or that he had heard it speak (as they had hoped). Instead, there was a sudden booming sound and flashing lights all over the place. Mikey doubled, trebled, quadrupled in size before their very eyes so that he was now without doubt the biggest giant they had ever seen. He was superior in ranking (they would laugh later) for bulk and awesome strength even to the "super giants" of old – the Finn McCumhail (and not any imposter), the Great McMahon, the One-Eyed Fomorian, the Slavish MacHamish. As they watched, his face glowed with such a brightness that they had to look away. They felt emanating from him the white heat of the sun, so that they had to retreat. His eyes were bright suns in their own right, and out of them came an energy stronger than that contained in multiple universes. All around him the world waxed and melted with the heat which – although it burned – did not destroy. The deafening noise of the thunder was painful to their ears, yet all they could hear was silence. An atmosphere of an unknown spirituality – that took the form of dense smoke or cloud – was above Mikey and then engulfed him and his surroundings so that they were unable to observe what was happening.

However, they could hear him talking, though the gist of his speech was untranslatable. They memorised it and kept it for posterity (for that hopeful day when some scholar or future genius would be able to provide translations of mortal prayers):

'Wind and Fire, Heavenly Light, Living Water, Rock of Ages. Do not let me fall for the sinful suggestions of the Ancient Adversary and become proud. I abandon my will, so that I can do all. I become nothing, so that I can be everything. You who want nothing, who needs nothing, accept my sinful, repentant, miserable, pitiable soul. I was buried, but now I am arisen. I was dead, but now I am alive. I was wise to the world, but now I am foolish. Your strength is in all that is weak, poor and infirm. The deaf hear, the blind see, the dumb speak your praises...'

Is he talking to him? the sídh were asking one another.

Is it him? He's talking to him! It must be him. Who else? The one and only!

It was Patrick the Moderniser who had ruined it all for them. They had never been able to break into, change or improve in any way the religion of the giants since. What they could understand of it was that it was about a giant (him) who had walked the earth in recent times and who worked good magic, cured the sick and cleaned up the neighbourhood generally. His name, try as they did, they could not pronounce. They knew that the giants spoke to him all the time – that he was still living somewhere in the land though only a few knew where, or could see him.

More particularly, they had been led to believe, from some of the preachers of the new religion, that *all* were free to talk to him. Even the birds of the air and the animals of the field – all who asked would receive his friendship and help! When they had first tried to speak to *him*, with this understanding that he listened to everybody, and that they would not be punished for their forwardness, they had been puzzled by the fact that he did not reply. At least not in words.

Instead, it seemed he started playing games with them.

One such game was called lobbing the red ball. A red ball would fall from the sky and bounce around. Initially the sport was to catch the ball. But after a long length of time they realised that this was probably impossible, so they modified the game into seeing who could achieve the nearest thing to a "catch". A point was scored by the one who seemed to be nearest to touching the ball, even for a single instant and with even the furthest extremity of the body.

A variation on this was called "hopping the ball", whereby the participants would endeavour to leap over the red ball as it bounced around, the aim being not to let it come in contact with any part of the body. These games led to the enjoyable spectacle of hundreds and thousands of sídh jumping around in a field in chaotic frenzy – a scene that led to some misunderstandings amongst mortals regarding the nature of sídh activity. Many came to believe that they held regular battles, or partook of a game that used extreme physical force.

Another game that was played when they attempted to talk to "him" was "riding the rainbow". A rainbow was always guaranteed to appear at such times of "shouting", "hollering" and "yelping", which was the nearest thing to praying they achieved. A pot of gold, jewels and precious stones would be spotted at the end of the rainbow. They would attempt to reach the same, but of course reaching it proved an impossible, illusionary task. This led to amazing trials of speed between the more athletic folk in determined attempts to reach the end of the rainbow; and also to much "metaphysical" discussion about rainbows.

Eventually it occurred to some that perhaps the rainbow was not "over there" but right here where they already were! This in turn led to all sorts of other games. The most challenging one was where they would take various measurements of the visible part of the rainbow to figure out where – and how – their present position was in relation to the rainbow's apparent presence. Whenever one of them became certain that he was indeed in the right position, he would get himself into whatever sort of abstruse, even impossible position was necessary in order to "ride down the rainbow". Acrobatics and contortions of the most challenging kind, crossing over into the dangerous, were performed in this game.

Others proclaimed that the sport did not call for such antics – that it was a matter of sitting down in a comfortable spot and "meditating" and "contemplating" the problem of the rainbow. Insight would come to those who mastered the arts of meditation and contemplation. Some claimed that extreme joy and pleasure could be experienced through these acts of mental reflection. Other "seers" claimed that they had actually ridden down the rainbow, reached the pot of gold and savoured its contents. The invaluable jewels, precious stones and gold they carried around with them all the time – for "those with eyes to see".

So it had appeared that the power of Mikey Murphy at that time had become so immense that he breathed life into dead and inanimate objects. His uncharacteristic cheerfulness and buoyancy transferred to all around him. The world reflected back the sound of his laughter and his jolly talk. The rocks, walls, ground and hills came to life in the over-abundance of his exuberance. People began commenting on how cheerful not just Father Murphy but everybody was looking. The whole world was alive and a wonderful place to live in. Such was the joy and happiness Father Murphy radiated that normally staid, serious people – even the glummest or most morose – were no longer their old selves but were full of life and bonhomie.

Their parish priest was happy – and this was some kind of miracle in itself. They felt that the whole world was singing and dancing with them – that they were joining in what had become an unprecedented, great universal celebration of existence.

It was the first time in their lives they actually knew what it was to be cheerful. All this contrasted with the previous gloom and pessimism that had characterised the population for so long. It had been the norm to talk down life, ambition and any kind of hope or expectation. The parish priest was both the conductor and conveyer of these fatalistic emotions. Now here, for the first time, was a PP who was suddenly effusive and positive, suggesting that life was not only good but was going to get better. And what was more remarkable – suggesting that life itself, as presently constituted – was really worth living.

Other miracles wrought by him – though he never claimed them for himself – included making the stones move and talk (many were reporting manifestations of inanimate matter "coming to life"). Some said that perhaps such things had always happened. It was just that they hadn't noticed before how alive the world really was. The marvels brought crowds aplenty from far and wide to the blessed spot. Never had a place known so many blessings.

The little folk had a great time tricking folk out of their precious possessions – silly frivolities they could well do without – and leading them astray with all kinds of antics that had the sídh laughing day and night – and the gaiety of the time under the hills was immense. When Mikey was called away to be bishop the sídh were, to put it mildly, flustered.

Who would they send to Bishop Murphy? Not a shaman, for he would be given short shrift. Not a solitary fairy, for he had a bad reputation amongst the giants. Not a forgetful one, obviously. The one they sent had to be not only smart, tough and brave, but also possess full protection against religion.

That was Freagra – the one who had the answer to everything.

Freagra was in some ways a laughing stock amongst the sídh; they would shut their ears whenever he spoke. His self-proclaimed ability to tell exactly what was always going to happen took the paradoxical form of a tightly shut-mouth and a continual, sleepy nodding. (This movement of his head seemed to be a permanent feature; he was more often nodding than not.) Freagra always knew when it was going to rain. When a downpour, a sun-burst, a fall of snow, a shower of hailstones or just the dawning of an ordinary, nondescript day came to pass it was always greeted with "Aha", a quiet sigh of satisfaction followed by the words "Just as I said".

His ability to foretell the weather was the least of his talents. He claimed that he had foreseen every disaster, triumph, tragedy and joyful event that had ever taken place in the fairy or mortal world. And the reason the world was continually being disturbed by earthquakes, landslides, floods, infestations by insects and other pestilent plant or animal life; polluted by poisons in both running water and stagnant pools and blighted by those great "eclipses" whereby the sun, moon and stars could no longer be seen as clearly as they had been by the "first" sídh – was because they were always expecting such terrible phenomena! If only they would think positively!

There were his many self-formulated theories to explain why everything happened. He knew why the giants only *appeared* so big and frightening. It was because they were merely figments of the fairy imagination, personifying their secret fears and suppressed feelings of inferiority. It was true that he himself had enjoyed many ephemeral conversations with the same mythical beings – but he had always reminded himself in the course of such chats and debates – with what were in any case decidedly inferior intellects – that he was engaging in a purely metaphysical process; though one certainly of great symbolic significance as well as being a productive, creative exercise that reflected/related to those primitive instincts in the sídh that accounted for all that was best in their culture and way of life.

Their inability to understand, explain, infiltrate or influence in any way the "religion" of the so-called giants was easily explained, according to Freagra. For what was interpreted as religion was simply the giants' – and their own – lack of understanding of the open sky, due to its vast expanse, inaccessibility and the random and sometimes dangerous objects that fell from it. The superstitious mumbo jumbo reflected nothing more than their own still unresolved problems with, and attitude to, the sky, the subject indeed of many eccentric, false theories. The gods, chants, spells and rituals that they imagined they were observing in the giants' world were, in fact, only the shadows of those similar, supposedly indispensible rituals in their own shaman culture that sídh of a nervous disposition believed would, against all the evidence, ward off sky-danger.

This was the no-nonsense, level-headed fellow they decided to send to Bishop Murphy, for they felt that he alone of all the sídh would be fully protected against the dangers emanating from religion, priest and bishop.

He set out full of bounce, excited at the adventure ahead. He sat atop an emigrant's suitcase at the back of the bus – where he knew he would not be disturbed, for folk made a point of never looking directly at an emigrant or his/her baggage for fear of bad luck.

The monsignor reported to Bishop Murphy that a prankster of some sort had been knocking on the door the last two evenings and then running away. Neither he nor the gardener had seen anybody on either occasion.

'A prankster? Have you seen him? How do you know it's a prankster? Maybe it's someone in desperate need. Someone too scared, or too shy, to ask straight out for help. If it happens again, stand there and call out after him.'

'Yes, Your Lordship.'

The monsignor had grown accustomed to the bishop's unworldly ways.

'It's our duty to offer Christian kindness and hospitality to everyone. As it is, too few decent, humble people have the courage to walk up the drive and pay their respects. It's like living in a fortress here, cut off from the world and people. The Lord always frowned upon such places – Herod's palace, the Praesidium, the Temple forecourt. Only irascible chancers and the worst drunks ever come here.'

'Yes, I agree, Your Lordship. We should present a more accessible face to the world. Heaven knows that it is in bad enough need of that.'

There was another knock that evening. The bishop heard it too. The monsignor stood on the doorstep and half-heartedly shouted:

'Hello! Come here. What do you want? His Lordship wants to help you.'

A little voice answered from some bushes nearby, 'I want to see His Lordship.'

'Step out of that bush and let me see you. Are you a beggar man?'

'Beggar man! How dare ye insult me. I will have yer hide for that. Apologise at once.'

'I did not mean to offend you. What important matter brings you here? The bishop is a busy man.'

'I'm a busy fellow, too. I do not kowtow to bishops. Where I come from, there are no bishops. Ye can tell him that. And I want nothing from him, for there is nothing that he can give me, except some good advice, which is what brings me here.'

'You will have to show yourself, my good fellow. I cannot go back in and say to his Lordship that I have been talking to the shadows. Are you not man enough to show yourself?'

'Man enough! Ye will rue that remark. Go in and tell him to come out.'

'Not till I see you.'

'Don't be looking over there. Look down at the ground.'

Barely discernible at the bottom of the laurel bush ten yards away was a tiny figure in green trousers, red coat and red cocked hat.

'I see now why you wouldn't show yourself! You're as tiny as a mouse. If I were you, I'd be hiding myself too.'

'Have a good laugh then. Because ye won't be laughing again for a long while.'

'Wait there. I'll go in and tell him a mighty strong fellow is waiting for him outside. Don't be running away now, for the fear or terror of meeting a bishop, a dog or a cat.'

He went inside, closing the door and locking it as a precaution. He went with a spring in his step to the study.

'I don't want him to be wasting your time, Your Lordship. It is the tiniest fellow you ever saw in your life. An aggressive little urchin, full of cheek and backchat and fight, like a lot of undersized people. I cannot allow him indoors for fear that he would be fearfully rude to you.'

'Did he say what he wanted?'

'Only some good advice. Of course that will be his opening line. Then it will be – a pound for this, ten shillings for that and a guinea for the poor relatives. And a good meal into the bargain.'

'What are we here for, if not to feed the hungry sheep? The Lord said: let the hungry, the oppressed, the powerless, the sick and unwanted come to Me, and I will feed them with good things.'

Bishop Murphy sighed and smiled.

'Let him into the reception room and I will be down in a minute.'

'You had better bring your best pair of spectacles. Better still – bring a telescope, or you will miss him otherwise.'

Bishop Murphy blew his top.

'What sort of a way is that to talk about the poor? How dare you slight – insult – make fun of another Christian when you call yourself a man of the cloth! How can you look at yourself in the mirror when all you will see there is a hypocrite of the first order. I am ashamed of you. I don't blame you – mind you – for you have been cooped up here for too long. You have seen nothing of real life. We bishops are to blame, for relying too much on your typing and secretarial skills and undoubted diligence. But Judas was a diligent secretary. Remember that. And to make fun of someone because of his size…! His God-given nature as bestowed on him by his creator! It is a most unchristian thing to do. Get a grip on yourself. For it is a serious sin to be of such a frame of mind.'

'I am sorry if I sounded offensive. I did not mean to be. You will see and hear for yourself in a moment why I spoke like that.'

He went back out to the door, unlocked it and looked around.

'He says you can come in now. Take your hat off, if you don't mind.'

'Take me hat off! Take me hat off!'

The diminutive speaker laughed his head off, repeating the monsignor's command over and over.

As he walked in the door, hat unremoved, he was still laughing: 'Take me hat off! Take me hat off!'

'Erin is producing them yet. Come in here now and sit down. Behave yourself.'

'Come in here now and sit down. Behave yourself,' repeated the little fellow.

His Lordship was called and came to the room some five minutes later. He asked the monsignor to stay outside, as it might be a confidential matter. He went in the room and closed the door, looking around at the same time to see the beggar. He could not see him anywhere.

'Where are you hiding now, you rascal. It is not many who dare to be brazen in front of a bishop. Show yourself, or be gone with you.'

'I'm here, Mikey Murphy of old Dunmor. Sure where is yer hat? They tell me ye wear a great thing altogether, a mighty, massive topper that outdoes that of a king. Good on ye. Can ye show it to me, or is it all a load of old tripe, and ye wear nothing more fancy than a sodden, snotty handkerchief?'

'Well, the cheek of you! Where are you hiding? Don't be afraid. I will not harm you. Is it help you want? I never turn away a poor man.'

'Ha ha ha. Poor man! I am richer than ye, fellow. I know more than ye. I was old when yer grandfather was just a bold boy. Who would ever have believed that one of the Murphys from the back of Mulindoon would have ended up a bishop. Did ye have any help in getting the job? Was it a relative pulling strings? Did ye do a favour for someone?'

'You cheeky fellow. I can see you now. I admire your courage, and I think you must be a desperate person to be talking like that. Is it your God-given impediment – that hard cross you have to bear with your stunted size – that causes you to be bitter? If we all made too much of our impediments, the world would be an unhappy place. How can I help you now?'

Bishop Murphy was beginning to think now he was seeing and talking to a fairy, one of the sídh, whose existence the Church had never fully recognised. It was all put down to the superstition – and worse – of a sinful people. If he had been back in the presbytery in Dunmor, he would have had less of a problem than he faced now. It would have been a simple, pastoral conundrum that a little sprinkling of holy water, a charitable prayer, followed by stern words of dismissal and strong advice would have easily sorted out. But as a bishop he could not afford to be seen dealing with, even *thinking* that he might be dealing with the gentle folk. His private beliefs, or any sort of speculation, could not intrude into the majesty of his office, an office which should not be tarnished with the slightest taint or suggestion of dabbling in the nether world. In other words, he was now no longer the simple, humble priest but Bishop Murphy, an emissary of High Heaven and an enemy of the profane and unholy. Therefore the first approach would have to be to attempt to deal with this fellow not as if he was just an ordinary, sinful member of the public, or more precisely as he would deal with an agnostic, atheist, a Protestant. In other words, with clean hands, a prayerful mind and a pure disposition.

'Is me size an issue for ye then? Do ye have a problem with small fellas? Is it in yer religion to mock those not as big as ye?'

'Oh dear, of course not. I'd hesitate to say, now, that it is indeed not a God-given blessing you being such a small creature, given that I have my doubts that you have a mortal soul...'

'Ye arrogant, presumptuous fool. Who says ye can talk to me like that? Doubts...a mortal soul...! Ye call yerself a holy bishop, ye insulting wretch. I'm as good as ye are.'

'Forgive me. I've no doubt you are.... But I have a doubt. Maybe, in the larger scheme of things – in some strange, distant way that is unknown – you are even better than us. That is not for me to say. But I have to be sure I'm offering the proper spiritual services to those qualified to receive them. It is no good wasting graces on... . And it may do harm.'

He was in a tight spot, professionally and otherwise, not sure if he was in the process of committing some great sin against the Holy Ghost; or an even greater one against charity.

'Wasting.... So I am not worthy of yer charity, should I ever want it. How dare ye boast about charity, kindness and all those things ye go on about unendingly in yer church and yer holy books. Are ye a big hypocrite?'

His voice went back to a whine again.

'Why do ye treat a poor, lost fellow like me so badly? Ye treat me worse than if I was the greatest ruffian in Erin. No – ye treat the bad ones with more respect, telling them that they are forgiven and will go to Tír na nÓg; but a cacha like me does not even get a short prayer. Ye big hypocrite!'

Freaga got down on his knees and held his hands up, the palms joined together as he had seen them do in and about the churches. He put on a pleading voice:

'Bless me, Father, Bless me, a mhic.'

'Are you one of the gentle folk? Are you a solitary fairy?'

'Do ye hear that, ye listening at the door? Yer boss is refusing to bless a poor beggar. This is how he behaves when he thinks no one is listening or watching. This is how he two-times the downtrodden of the earth. Come on in and tell yer boss to be true to his principles. How can ye obey him, when he betrays all he believes in, refusing to use his good graces to help a poor beggar? Who only cries out for some small...meagre...*some tiny portion of the crumbs that fall from the table...?*'

'Cut it out now or I will sprinkle you with holy water. Silence! Now what is the business that brings you here? In what way can we be of help to you?'

The little fellow got up off the floor and brushed his trousers down.

'We – the royal we! Ah, "we" can help me in a way "we" think we're not helping me. And ye'r not helping me in the way ye think ye are. The first question is – what do ye tell yer folk to do to resist temptation?'

'Now why might you be asking a question like that?'

'Because my folk are succumbing to temptations these latter days. The stuff you put on display... . It should never be seen at all. Those terrible things they take – do – copy – oh, so terrible! Is that what ye mean by...sin?'

'Well, the only way to be safe from temptation is a way that is not open to you at all.'

'Some holy fellow! I hope yer man is listening.'

'However, I can say this. Go back to your folk and tell them that from now on they must cut themselves off from the world of mortals, and stay confined within the boundaries that were originally given to them. There – under the hills and at the bottom of the lakes and seas, you will not be tempted for you will be avoiding all "occasion of sin". That is the only way. For in the past you have mimicked every wicked thing that sinners have done. It is a failing with ye.'

'I will take that message back, ye heathen. And now let we get down to business. That what ye call – the signs of the times.'

'Some respect is due to my office. Even from you. Apologise now. And withdraw the "heathen" word.'

'Oh! Oh! I'm sorry. I'm so sorry. I'm so, so sorry. Is that OK then?'

'Will you withdraw "heathen"?'

'I do withdraw. I do apologise. Most sincerely. Please tell us the signs of the times. If I go back empty handed, I will be a laughing stock.'

He began to wail, in that high, squeaky voice that was half a cough. It was probably meant for other listening ears as well.

'I'm being murdered! He's murdering me! Aieee! Help! Boo, huu, huu.'

'Cut it out you rascal. I will help you. For what harm have you ever done to me? Or could ever do to me?'

The wailing stopped immediately.

Bishop Murphy collected his thoughts.

'The signs of the times are – women no longer smoking pipes; young people not going fishing; licences required for fishing; simpletons and ignoramuses on the television and wireless; emigrants not promising to come back home again; women riding men's bicycles; people travelling around the country by bus, car, train, scooter, taking in the view in order to impress friend and foe alike with their travel lore; clergy having doubts; farmers admitting making money; unexplained lights moving across the night sky; hay fields cut early; cattle without horns; bulls redundant; amateur dramatics being taken seriously; men of Erin achieving fame and notoriety abroad; messages delivered to the wrong addresses; anaesthetics being used in operations; enforcement of the drinking laws; toilets indoors; pets on leads; mastery of the umbrella; medical treatment for flat feet, buck teeth, squinting eye and fits become standard; left-handed people not enforced to become right-handed; tidy town competitions to include villages; upkeep of gardens; modification to steeple chase jumps and courses to facilitate horse and jockey; no more cattle, sheep and pig selling on fair greens and town streets; shoelace-tying a universal skill; hair oils for men not considered effeminate; cheaper meat; a brew called lager; respect for the law; scientific names for cloud types; collecting rubbish in large containers; decline in morals; laughing at devout people; acceptance that fairies and fairydom are figments of the imagination.'

'Oh. That is so? They don't believe in "we" now?'

'That's the case. There are occasional manifestations of your world that some newshounds still might put in the papers for sensation seekers; but these are soon forgotten. And some people still pretend they believe in you. Children play games using symbols and legends from your world. But that is all that is left.'

'If we don't exist, how do ye talk to we?'

'Your influence must diminish gradually, gently, like a world wakening from a dream. There must be mutual respect between the past and the present.'

Freagra looked down from the side table upon which he sat, staring at the floor, crestfallen. He shook his head slowly from side to side.

'Then it is the work of the L of D. That…has always wanted to destroy us. This ye can confirm for me. That…he…has won. That we no longer exist.'

Bishop Murphy reflected that there was a bit of a trick in this question. He could not afford to be made a fool of, even by a nonentity – for *that* story would certainly go the rounds for generations, if not for all time.

'Well, you exist in a sense.'

'How ye mean?'

'Strictly speaking, you have no place in the world. Men have, in the past, indulged your whimsies, not with the express permission of religion, but at least without outright condemnation. But that was only to allow the poor people some entertainment in their lives; lives that were short, hard and troubled; something to indulge their fancy during interminably long winter evenings, when the harvest was poor; or even to add spice to their entertainment when things went well. But sure who needs all that now?'

'Ye are as tricky as we are! Good on ye. That is what I like. Sure, ye have said nothing. What does...Mother...say about us...our destiny?'

'That you were excluded from Paradise, but that you are not the worst, so your punishment is less. That your time will end, like ours. That the One Above is in charge – not the One Below – his power and time, too, are limited. He could not do anything, even to the sídh, unless it was permitted. You may tell your folk – there is no need to fear the Evil One, unless you do evil. Nor fear the changes. They must happen. There is nothing that you can do, or must do. Just go back to your old dwelling places, and accept all.'

'How did ye get yer job?'

'By the powers that be.'

'Why did they put ye in here – in the top job?'

'To save Erin.'

'Ye sound proud. Are ye succeeding?'

'I am constantly phoning the television and radio station. I write to the newspapers. I am making a stand against all that offends religion, morals and the good name of Erin. My name is to be reckoned with now, and many no-gooders fear to hear it mentioned. It is, I suppose, what is called progress.'

'But are ye saving yer...that...re...l...i...g...? Is him helping ye?'

'We can only hope. It is said that on the last day there will only be a few believers in the One Above left on earth.'

'Ye're wasting yer time, then?'

Another trick question. It was time to send the fellow home.

'Be off with you now. You've heard everything you need to know. And don't interfere with anything or anybody on your way.'

'I must hand it to ye. But as ye say – yer power is going too, like ours. Ye're not much more fortunate than we. Goodbye!'

As Freagra went to the door it opened of its own accord. The monsignor was approaching, pretending that he had not been eavesdropping.

'Oh, it's yerself! Did ye hear what that man in there said? Accused, found guilty, sentenced! No defence. I've never come across a more judgemental fellow in me whole life. Ye have a very long nose on ye there. And it's going to get longer.'

The monsignor couldn't help immediately feeling his nose, for he had never thought of it as a particularly noteworthy feature before. As he led the visitor to the front door he was still feeling his nose. He chuckled to himself at the idiocy of his action and, all at once, he felt it growing longer. Imagination! He became sombre – worry set in – and his nose stopped growing. This was how the monsignor came never to laugh again – for he discovered that whenever he felt like a good guffaw, a snigger or even a slight, quiet smile his nose would start to grow. This embarrassing affliction he was never able to mention to anybody, not even to his doctor or spiritual advisor. It was one of those things that a person decides just has to be suffered quietly all of one's days. He spoke determinedly:

'Goodbye to you now. Consider yourself privileged for having had an audience with the bishop. Show some gratitude.'

With a kick of his feet Freagra threw up so much dust that he was obscured from sight. When the monsignor looked down again there was no sight of the little fellow. He went back inside, somewhat nonplussed. The uncomfortable feeling about his nose had begun to cause him a niggling disquiet about the visitor. He immediately decided to ask the bishop some questions.

'Our visitor was a very small man, indeed. He looked a bit upset on the way out. He claimed that you treated him badly.'

'You should never listen to anything their type says.'

The monsignor, for once, did not refrain from expressing his anger and annoyance.

'How can you say that? Isn't he entitled to the same rights as any of us? Just as you lectured me not one hour ago. To think that you gave me a telling to for exactly the same fault!'

'Didn't you see what type of fellow he was?'

'I don't understand.'

'Don't you...? How can I...? He was not like us.'

'Do you mean he was a perverted individual? Or had a screw loose somewhere? Or had something odd about him? A quare fellow?'

'Yes...sort of.'

'Well then, didn't he deserve our compassion and help as a fellow sinner and sufferer? Just as you said to me.'

'Some of these individuals... . They don't have a proper soul. They exist in the twilight world, somewhere between dusk and darkness, night and dawn. Lost beings. They can't be helped. Not even by us. The good Lord did not die for them. They do not deserve even the title of sinner. They are distractions and should always be ignored. I do not know why we in Erin have been favoured, or cursed, by the presence of so many of these...superfluous beings. Do not be too familiar with them. Do not hope for their salvation. Do not help them or show them charity. Do not pray for them.'

When the monsignor, later that evening, had recalled every one of those words and assiduously recorded them in his diary, he set about preparing a confidential paper on his typewriter that he would send off to the Congregation for the Clergy in Rome, detailing His Lordship's heretical beliefs, unchristian character and denial of pastoral care to the most needy and handicapped people in society.

That was why, when the bishops made their Ad Limina visit to Rome a year or two later, the Pope had reason to call Bishop Murphy aside and say to him: "I must admonish you for your lack of charity towards the Little People of your diocese. In future, give them that pastoral care you give to others."

Of course the bishop had no idea why he received this reprimand. He had been struck dumb with shock and surprise. For nothing the pontiff says is ever casual, accidental, or of small import. He would certainly have to learn again how to show respect and charity to all – regardless of "character", reputation, worldly status or place of origin.

When the sídh heard about the pope's words (via the little grey man) needless to say there was hysterical laughter all over, ructions of delight and "I told ye so" and general celebration and intoxication that lifted the roof of every sídh habitation in Erin.

Nine

SEAN MURPHY WAS accompanied each evening to his residence in the city's finest park by an escort of the sídh. The procession generally extended for half an Irish mile, on both sides of the road or pavement. Musicians played and there was often a chorus of song. Any number of impediments were put in the path of giants who got in the way.

Trip-ups, inexplicable walking into posts, splashing of mud and water on the clothes of such unerring accuracy – even from vehicles quite far away – meant many were led to think it deliberate; sudden, involuntary decisions by pedestrians, cyclists and other travellers to stop and turn back, caused by some troublesome memory problem, such as a realisation that an important item has been left behind or some crucial job left undone – or even just a crazed, impetuous urge to retrace one's steps and route for no good reason; collisions with other travellers where the cause is a decision that one immediately realises was extremely foolish and which now brings what feels like an eternity of regretful reflection, thus worsening the deleterious effects of the coming, inevitable impact; and even worse for morale – collisions caused by an inability to give way to some approaching traveller on foot, bicycle or motor vehicle, preceded by a prolonged exercise of voluntary giving way that only leads to the opposing party always performing an exact copy of one's steps so that that particular collision is accompanied by strong emotions of Schadenfruede, self-righteousness and hypocritical apology that makes it all the more painful for everyone – all gave Sean cause to smile as he noted the satisfaction of the sídh at gaining some sort of upper hand on the streets of Baile Átha Cliath itself.

The finery and trumpery of this party of diminutive show-offs helped to compensate, to some extent, for the paucity of comforts and exposed nature of his home; at least in the first year or two, until he had learned how to make his habitation more comfortable. His "hide" was now less exposed and less obvious to passers-by, off-duty soldiers, escaped wild animals from the zoo, drunkards and various vermin. Indeed this construction of ash branches intertwined with evergreen bush eventually became a master construction, the would-be envy of every shanty dweller in the world.

In time he was able to dispense with the escort, and he had in fact asked that he be granted a time of freedom in which he might pursue some of his own interests. They were only too glad to creep away, for they had always been uncomfortable in the built-up surroundings.

He was spending his time these days researching, studying and cogitating in final preparation for the production of his life's main work – an accounting of why the world is as it is. This, in an arrangement with his little friends, was to be presented eventually at a speech-giving day in fairydom; the official invitation to which he had already received and accepted. It would be on this great occasion that he would be presented with the qualification and high honour known as Bard of the sídh.

On his travels around the streets, public places and fine residences of Dubh Linn, he had reason to note the lack of good manners, the absence of happiness and the wayward aggression of many of its denizens. He had come to the conclusion after much reflection, enforced chats with various uniformed officialdom, idle cogitation, star-gazing and climbing over walls, that there was a great deal of unhappiness in the world. He felt exceedingly sorry for the inhabitants of Dubh Linn, and often wished to give them advice on how to be content. The very fact of their unwillingness to listen, or to be made happy, was the sure mark of their discontent. That was why he took to singing and humming as he went his way. It was more to cheer up others rather than as any sort of self or artistic expression. Even that, too, failed in its objective, for there was apparently a law also against trying to make people cheerful.

One day he found himself embarking on the relatively long walk to the Green. He did not know at the time why he had decided to go there, but he assumed it was to feed the ducks with the crusts of bread he had just picked up in the street. As he was passing Leinster House, home of the politicians, he stopped to allow a limousine to pass through the gates. The stout, grey-haired official in the back, who was clearly someone high up in government, was staring at him. The man's face went pale. That was nothing particularly unusual for Sean, who had often wondered what it was that made people stare at him. Strangely, the face of the man was familiar. Then he realised: it was Michael Fitzgerald of Dunmor! Whom the sídh had told him so much about! He had, apparently, destroyed Foirnocht Hill, amongst many other landscape features not only in Rathcloon, but around the country. It had been prophesied that he would meet him again; and that he would get a chance not only to admonish the "great man", but to try and persuade him to undo the many wrongs he had perpetrated. Sean decided to hang around the gate until Michael came out again. This meant that he spent the whole of the day there, making himself as inconspicuous as possible (no singing), going around the corner and coming back again. Eventually, as dusk set in, a limousine approached the gate and Sean walked briskly to a position close to the exit to see if his "friend" had reappeared. Sure enough, there he was, in the back seat, staring out the window at him. The car sped off as a guard came and asked Sean (again) to move on.

However, Sean was back again the next day, the day after that, and every day after that to greet Michael on all his comings and goings. Once or twice he attempted to get close up to the vehicle, but he was always pulled away by the guards. Eventually, his vigil had to become surreptitious and innovative to avoid, hoodwink and finally wear down the patience of those who guarded the gate.

On just one occasion, when the guards happened to be a bit sleepy, he had got right up to the vehicle. He banged on the window with his fist and shouted, 'Michael! Michael! It's me, Sean!'

There was a rush of men and he was whisked away once more, up to the far end of Kildare Street.

As he sat now tied to a chair in a locked room somewhere in the area of Rathcloon/Dunmor, Michael Fitzgerald was thinking about how he came to be on an unfamiliar back road in the early hours of the morning, waiting for Sgt O'Hourigan to come back with help. Instead, a gang of blackguards had turned up, wearing balaclavas and threatening him with shillelaghs. Not a word had been spoken as they took him out of the car and blindfolded him, apart from an order to behave himself and do as he was told. He knew that a ransom demand had been put out the next day – and that "someone had better turn up with the money or else". For good measure, there was also a demand for the government to recompense the people of Rathcloon for "all the robbery that had been done to them".

Yet, he had always had luck on his side. After all, his whole life had been strangely blessed with success, money and job satisfaction. He thought to himself now that perhaps a little prayer might do some good. He had never been particularly religious. He had been too busy helping others, and helping the country. But now a humble prayer, perhaps acknowledging his shortcomings and promising to do better in future, might stand him in good stead. He closed his eyes, held his breath for a moment, and started to pray that he be released soon from the fix he was in. He did not seem to get much satisfaction or relief from this. Instead, for some reason, the image of Sean Murphy came to his mind. It was almost as if the fellow was standing there before him. And now he remembered something that Sean had said, that time in Dubh Linn when they had met.

The embarrassment and desperation caused by that stalking of his official car by a bearded, unkempt "street person" was nearly as bad as that caused by his present predicament. The gaunt face he already knew, deep down, belonged to Sean Murphy, Patsy Murphy's nephew.

He forgot the praying now and sighed deeply, 'I don't know what made me want to talk to him!'

He was speaking out loud, not caring who might hear him, for the quiet of that place was getting to him: 'I eventually asked the guards to bring Sean into the police post for a cup of tea.

Sure, let's find out what's on the poor fellow's mind, I said. Perhaps we can persuade him to give up on his mad enterprise.

He was brought unwillingly in, anyway, and made to sit on a chair to which he had to be securely tied so violently did he resist the guards. We were amazed at the strength of the slight, emaciated fellow.

I came in and stood beside Sean, who looked a bit angry at being tied up like a criminal, or a wild animal.

'Well, at last we get to meet. Are you a fan of politicians, that makes you hang around outside here all day?' I said, pretending that I did not know who he was.'

Michael went silent now, straining to hear if anyone had been there, listening. There was not a sound from outside. His "cell" might as well be in Siberia, or deep underneath the ground.

He continued to recall the events of that day at Leinster House, but in silence now.

Sean had made another, half-hearted effort to free himself from the chair. It was all for pure show. (Little did they know that if he had wished to exert his full strength, there was no way they could have held him there. He could easily have brought the whole building down with one blow, and knocked sideways every politician in the place. But the time for that would come soon enough.)

'It's yourself,' Sean said in a voice that was unused to much talk, so that his throat hurt with the effort of speaking. 'They tell me that you have changed the whole countryside. I have a warning for you. One day you will need our help. If you call, we will come to help you.'

'Aren't you Sean Murphy of Rathcloon? They said you were a

brains-box. Finn McCumhail asked you to join his men. But off you went to Dubh Linn instead. And that was the last that was ever heard of you. You have ended up on the street! Are you on the bottle?'

'I am a person of consequence in the world, I tell you, Michael Fitzgerald, and I have some very influential friends. I am due to graduate soon from the finest university in the world, in the universe. A secret university where only the best bards, filí, brehons, druids and the strongest giants enrol. You would not believe some of the powers I have, if I told them to you. But enough of that. For even the highest qualification from the sídh university is nothing compared to the honour of membership of the Fianna. However, I foresaw that I would have to fight Finn eventually for the leadership. I did not wish to humiliate the old man. Too many of Erin's heroes have ended their days in disgrace.'

'Well, they are in disgrace now, I can tell you. Finn is in an old folks' home and Caoilte is reduced to being a regular prison visitor where all his top men are. The rest are scattered.'

'Well, that is bad news! Caoilte came to me once, telling me of all his great plans. I've heard that he turned out to be a bit of a disappointment. He wanted to recruit only the best brains. He saw the Fianna as a career – not as a vocation. That was their downfall. But the good news is – there is a new Fianna.'

Although Michael had been telling himself that he was listening to a madman, his ears pricked up now. He turned to the guards and gave them a big grin, letting them know that he was just humouring the fellow.

'A new Fianna! Well, that is something! Where are they now?'

'That would be telling! They stay hidden, their membership a secret. They are working at this moment to undo the harm that has been done by your good self and many other great men up and down the land.'

Michael was nodding in a wise manner, pretending that he understood it all. Still something bothered and irritated him. He determined to get to the bottom of what Sean was saying. Sure enough, it could only be fantasy. And weren't they choc-a-bloc with subversive groups already, without the need for one more? But could there be something behind what Sean was saying? Was he referring to something that really did exist, whatever sort of fantasy and wishful thinking it was all wrapped up in? Something that was there all right, below the surface? For it was within the realms of possibility that "street talk" might have an uncanny knack of revealing exactly those undercurrents in society that even the most astute and learned never detect. They would pick up all the stray conversation. Hear all the cursings, praisings and worries of the population as it moved about its daily business. They would be able to read people's faces, with the accuracy conditioned by seeing people as they really are.

'I suppose it's become something that takes account of these modern times. An up-to-date Fianna?'

'Oh sure, I wouldn't be knowing anything about the new Fianna.'

Fitzgerald asked the guards to leave them alone for a while, whispering that the fellow might be a bit put off by the presence of uniformed gardaí.

'Sure they're gone now, Sean. You can speak your mind. Would you like me to get you fixed up in a nice warm bed-and-breakfast. With free food and drink thrown in?'

'Sure what would I be needing with all that? Don't I live in the finest palace in Erin, with servants to do my bidding and grant me my every wish if I ever call on them?'

'Tell me more about the new Fianna, Sean, and I promise you that no harm will ever come to you on the streets of Dubh Linn. Sure, I can order the most wicked men in the city to do my bidding. My best pal is the minister for justice.'

'All right, Michael, for old time's sake. And I would not be wanting the Special Branch breathing down my neck again. I am the leader of the new Fianna. If ever you are in trouble, Michael, just shout out "Send the Fianna!"'

He went silent. Michael realised that that was about all Sean had to say about the new Fianna. There was a knock on the door.

'The cup of tea has arrived,' a voice said.

'Come in.'

The two guards re-entered, one holding a cup of tea.

'I am sure he's a harmless fellow at heart,' said Michael, still musing over Sean's last words.

'Maybe we should let him loose,' said a guard.

As Sean (unbound) sipped his tea Michael said quietly to the policemen, 'Let him go after I've gone. I'm sure they must have a file on him somewhere. I will check with the Branch.'

"Send the Fianna". Those words came back to him now, and feeling the right fool he was, and ignoring all his misgivings and best instincts, he said them out loud.

As nothing happened he said them again, and then a third time. All at once everything went blurred and a huge lump came to his throat. He had the sensation of drowning. How could he ever have expected such stupid words to have any effect? Was he losing his senses? And hadn't he seen Sean's Special Branch file, in any case. Far from being a king living in a palace, he had been arrested for attempting to corrupt the young. He should have known it. It's no wonder he never settled down into becoming a respectable member of society. He should be given a good hiding. Knock some decency into him. The police always kept an eye on him, monitoring where he went and whatever antics he got up to. Sure, he was too dirty and unkempt even for the secure units. Nobody would want him in there. It could ruin his own career if it became known that he ever had any association with him. The way scandals take off these days. He began to feel drowsy. He had trouble keeping his eyes from closing, so heavy did his eyelids feel. It was as if someone was pushing them down, and keeping them down against his best efforts. Double darkness – with the blindfold. The men must have come into the room again, he suddenly realised, because he could hear footsteps and shuffling about. Muttering and whispering. He was sure that they were giggling. Laughing at him. Playing games with him as you would with a child, or a helpless fool. He was beginning to feel anger now where before there had been fear, anxiety, despondency and confusion.

He had never heard any of them speak clearly. Just once the blindfold had been taken off and a hoarse, muffled voice ordered him to look only at a piece of paper put in front of him. It had been a ransom note. He was told to sign it. Then the blindfold was put back on again.

There was something funny about the way the guys were acting now. Their voices were kind of squeaky. Was he imagining it all? He felt slow-witted, as if he was, indeed, asleep. A triple darkness. Black, black, black. A ludicrous thought suddenly occurred to him. Could they be the "new Fianna"? His heart leapt. Hope rose in him. It felt as if there was a huge crowd – a horde of tiny beings with funny voices – in the room. Had they come to help him? To rescue him? Set him free! Oh, please!

He began to speak quickly, excitedly:

'I have known the bold Sean Murphy of old. He was my good companion in the halcyon days of youth. The respect I have for Sean Murphy of Rathcloon is greater than the respect I have for any other person, living or dead. He is both a hero in the world of the warrior and great men, and a humble servant of the poor, outcast and misbegotten. It is my one wish to emulate Sean. To be like him in all things. To give away to the poor all the wealth I have in the world and to spend my last days as a poor beggar wandering the roads of Erin. Like King Sean. I wish to give back all the land that I have stolen from the people of Rathcloon and roundabouts. In particular, I wish to give back that piece of land that was once Foirnocht hill. I will resite the airport and erect there a new hill and a protected natural wilderness that will be better than the hill that was there. It will be a home and place of refuge for all the wildlife that was killed or displaced by my own greedy self. I repent. I give it all away to you now. Here. Give me a piece of paper. I will sign it all over to you.'

He heard their voices rise like a great swell of the sea, followed by rolls of high pitched laughter. He laughed himself:

'Ah, Sean told me I would be OK.'

In the farmhouse kitchen at Patsy Murphy's (a visitor from the past would not have recognised it as the kitchen of Patsy Murphy) a family conference was being held. Patsy had decided that the time had come for him to choose his heir. In one corner, in her wheelchair, was Widow O'Rafferty, supervising events, giving orders, reprimands, requesting this, that and the other. Everyone was ignoring her. To have come to this! Her days of glory over! Eileen was telling her to be quiet; that she would get a sup of whiskey shortly; that if she drank it too early, she'd fall asleep immediately and miss everything. Oh, the humiliation! The sheer...unfairness! Once, she had roamed the land, visited everyone of note between Dunmor and the west coast. Now? She was a prisoner. She'd be lucky to get pushed outside to enjoy some fresh air. She might as well be dead.

Patsy himself was dressed like King Solomon. He had on the best suit in all Ireland. The cost of it alone would have paid for the latest, high-powered excavator. It came from London. His fine silk shirt came from the Far East. His bow tie was from New York and his linen handkerchief was of the finest Irish manufacture. His shoes were from Italy. His socks were from Milan. His fine hat was from Paris. His cufflinks were from Amsterdam. He felt very comfortable in his best clothes; indeed these days he was never out of his finery.

Bridie was helping, cleaning, carrying and taking away. She knew not to sing while others were present, to keep quiet and to smile silently at the questions of children.

Eileen was supervising the table and spread. She had become adept at salads, fried chicken, flavoured rice dishes and buffet arrangements. She knew about red and white wine. She could easily guess who wanted white wine, red wine, lager and other such foreign drinks. She knew the best bottles of wine and who to bring them out for.

For her part, she had seen all her dreams come true. Indeed, she was now feeling increasingly nostalgic for the old days, and had begun in these latter times to speak mistily of the great poverty and the humble cottage that she had been born into. Like Abraham Lincoln, De Valera and Cinderella, her early poverty had stood her in good stead, given her strength of character and in some ways she wished she was back there again, living from hand to mouth, in close contact with nature and the real world. The young had it too easy these days. The discontent that had lately come into her life was to increase – so that at the end she would become a morose old biddy, lamenting the passing of the hard old times and cursing her good fortune.

The sons and daughters, with their children, were all present by mid-afternoon, with only Patsy Mall still being awaited. Patsy Mall was the slow one, a bit simple, easy-going and apparently not concerned with life, advancement or getting married. They knew that he would eventually appear, at the doorway, chewing tobacco and looking a bit nonplussed.

Three hired toughs (sent with recommendation by Sergeant O'Hourigan) had been employed to keep order amongst Patsy's constantly arguing and fighting sons. Everybody was searched for consignments of weapons, which were banned in the house, due to the fact that drink always put everybody in their worst fighting mood.

Because of the laying down of strict rules of behaviour by Eileen on this occasion, and the professional security regime that was in place, there was an unusual air of quiet and calm as everyone tucked into their food and drink. The problematical question of Patsy's succession had been put on hold for an hour or two. Even the grandchildren could not understand the peace and quiet. There was something wrong; and they set about putting matters to right and getting back some sense of normality by breaking cups and plates, kicking doors, windows or one another, chasing the cats, pulling the dog around by its tail and other such devilment, to the approval and amusement of the parents.

'Whist awhile now, everybody. Granddad is going to give a short speech,' said Eileen, when everybody had become bored with the chatter and much of the food had been consumed.

'Short speech! He never knows when to stop!' laughed Patsy Láidir.

Everyone knew it was safe to laugh out loud then, for Patsy Láidir was the one who was the recognised "chief bully" of the family.

It was true that Patsy's speeches had become even more notorious over time. He had become so fond of the sound of his own voice that he was always to be found chatting away like Billy-o. This was how he had acquired the reputation of being a great storyteller (which was a euphemism for "bore"). His unending, thick talk was incomprehensible to most; but if one listened closely and had plenty of drink taken it was said that his talk could have a hypnotic, pleasant effect; even to sounding like music or a song that had some mystical, yet familiar refrain. The fact was that so accustomed to the solitary life had been Patsy before his marriage; so well-acquainted with the silence of long days and nights, months and seasons, years and decades, and so traumatically had his tongue been untied by the arrival of numerous people in his house on the occasion of his marriage, that the same tongue had taken on an energy and life of its own. In fact, although his words seldom matched what he wanted to say, his vocabulary had developed by a sort of osmosis into a complexity of its own. He could discuss all the learned things he had read about in books, and relate even his own original solutions to problems which, in some cases at least, possibly involved real scientific breakthroughs in certain fields (or so he would claim), while at the same time everybody thought he was talking about something else. An example of this process took place now. He had been asked to speak first because it was custom and because it was seen as the only way to get him out of the way when the real business started. Láidir would shut him up at the convenient moment, and Patsy would not even realise that he had stopped (or been stopped) talking.

He began relating a story now – in that strange, stilted, even pseudo-educated accent that employed a vocabulary of highfaluting words picked up from books during that phase of his life when he was a heavy reader – about a mysterious local woman by the name of Missus Biddy Joyce, whom some knew as a bit of a recluse spinster and who, he said, had had to go and live in exile after being evicted by her neighbours from her dainty roadside cottage somewhere in the local vicinity. Patsy had much inside information about this woman, whom he had first heard about from none other than Bishop Murphy himself, in the days when he was parish priest in Dunmor. He had given Patsy many warnings about Biddy, and in particular about her fondness for dangerous *incontinent* ideas. She herself had the cheek to claim that she had received special enlightenment from the gods. Instead of realising her sinfulness, she had boasted of possessing the powers of these same gods, and was unabashed in admitting even the worst vice of all – pride. In fact her great pride was a source of further pride to her! Her work revolved around the worst sort of debauchery. She was forever holding impromptu concerts in her home, singing songs of her own concoction. And as regards entertaining folk her talent generally had the opposite effect. There was only one word that could describe it – *useless*. He related the story of how she had been led into her life of apostasy and debauchery by the Jesuits. The people of Erin were fortunate that these "black popes" had never managed to get their hands on the ordinary children of Erin, concerning themselves mainly with educating and influencing only an extremely small minority – the brainy and well-to-do. How Biddy ever came to be one of their protégés was a mystery. As a result of their brainwashing, she had learned to *follow her own conscience* – a heretical notion promulgated by the Jesuits. She was fond of recounting lewd and unnatural descriptions of the human body in the belief that there was something sacred in dirty, foul language and filthy images. Her cottage became the centre of obscene festivals where readings, discussions and exhortations to even greater obscenities took place, attracting both the worst and the best brains in the land, as well as all the loose types. Her base words, descriptive passages and unique phrases became common usage amongst the intelligentsia and the pseudo-intelligentsia, and could even be heard being passed around in some of the smaller towns and villages throughout the land. The clerk, schoolteacher and occasional well-read shopkeeper might be heard repeating her words, albeit in private amongst select companions. Language was made dirty by her. It had happened at the waking of a man named Finnegan that her fetid talk became too much even for her most loyal acolytes, as she had performed the prayers and obsequies around the poor man's dead body using foul words never heard before. They could no longer tolerate or even understand her bad language. It was too much even for them.

'However' – said Patsy, raising the level of his voice – 'I have come to believe that Biddy has been misunderstood. I will prove that she was, in fact, the noblest, purest, most compassionate, kindest and bravest person Erin ever produced. I will begin by relating how in fact, instead of belittling the dead at the wake by the use of strange words and unheard of phrases, she was in fact engaged in fulsome praise of Finnegan's physical, mental and spiritual qualities. The poor man's memory was not only not debased, but his reputation actually improved by the fact that Finnegan was dead, and his body and spirit in the very process of decaying and decomposing. Decomposition can be something wonderful and inspiring, not to mention productive of future life and growth, as we farmers know well enough...'

'The end!' shouted Láidir. The obligatory loud clapping and cheering followed, with drinks being raised to old Patsy's health.

'You can't get him away from gossiping about the neighbours,' laughed Eileen, who made a note to question her husband later about the identity of this Biddy Joyce, whom she had never heard of until now.

She whispered into his ear that it was time now for the big moment – deciding who was going to be his heir. The boys were behaving themselves and he should not say anything upsetting, but instead be full of praise for every single one of them. It might even be possible to get the whole business over with quickly so that they could go back to enjoying their drink. At that moment everyone went silent and looked in the direction of Patsy and Eileen. Patsy Óg (young), Láidir (strong), Cliste (clever), Caol (thin), Ramhar (fat), Ramsach (frivolous), Bocht (poor), Tapaidh (quick), Bródúil (proud), Saibhir (rich), Umhal (humble), Guagach (humorous), Móraigeanta (generous), Brónach (sad), Carthanach (kind), Duáilceach (vicious), Bréan (smelly), Dona (evil), Stuacánach (stubborn), Sochma (easy), Suáilceach (virtuous), and the many other sons and daughters prepared themselves for the big moment. Already, knuckles were being clenched and hair was rising. Patsy gave the opening address.

'As ye all know, it is time that an heir is chosen to take after me after my days are over. It is a matter needful and urgent. When I asked each one of ye, beginning with the oldest, Óg, with pleading in my voice, none of ye volunteered for the position. Not one of ye has the strength, the guts, the sense to agree to become the new master of Toberbeg Farm, that has been in the generations since time immemorial! Pleading, threatening, reasoning – all are of no use. It would seem that the name of Patsy Murphy is no longer to be associated with this place. What would our forefathers say about such a state of affairs? They are turning in their graves at this minute. Sure, ye're a pack of idlers and wasters, prancing about the country in yer big new cars doing this deal and that deal, and ye don't even know one end of a horse from the other. When I was your age, I didn't even know the meaning of the word "rest", "holiday", "entertainment" and all the rest of that modern stuff. I was up before daybreak every morning of the year getting in the cows, no matter what the weather. Sure, I didn't even know what the word "warm" meant! I never knew I was tired because being tired came natural to me. I wasn't afraid of hard work either. Hard work was the best thing about life to me. If I didn't have hard work to do every day I would have dropped dead from the lack of it. Get on with ye's! Yer poor ould cousin, Sean, was better than a dozen of ye put together! He could have a cow milked by the time he had hummed through the first verse of "Danny Boy". And what do you have to do today? Flick on a switch and the job is done for ye!'

He choked on his words. Then he raised his voice to a higher level:

'I have this horsewhip here and I will be using it pretty soon unless someone owns up and says he wants to be my heir.'

He bent down and produced a whip from beneath the table. The children cried with delight and ran forward to touch it.

'There'll be no need for that,' admonished Eileen. 'But I must agree with Patsy and say it is a sad day, indeed, when the sons of the land want nothing more to do with it. That blessed heirloom, the green field, the hedgerow of blackthorn, beech, ash and oak, the watery meadow, the marsh of the screeching curlew, the stream of trout, the solid earth itself, so fought over by our ancestors and heroic martyrs, the precious land of Erin, is wanted by our young ones no longer.'

Her voice was full of sadness. But none of her listeners showed any sign of emotion. They all knew she was acting. Now her tone changed and she glared at them.

'Sure, we can just pick one of them. I have it in my own mind who it should be, for he is the only one left whom we might be able to persuade.'

At that very moment Patsy Mall appeared at the door, as unkempt as ever, a piece of rope in his hand.

'Hallo,' he said shamefacedly. 'I'm sorry I'm late. Have I missed anything?'

'You're just in time, Mall,' said Eileen. 'You are to be the heir of your father, and take over the farm after his days. Congratulations.'

There was initial silence amongst the gathering. Then they all gathered around Mall, clapping him on the back. He smiled broadly, trying to take in the information; what it might mean, etc.

After everyone had finished congratulating him, Láidir went over to him and said, 'Ye had no choice in the matter. Don't go around changing yer mind or anything, or ye will have me to deal with.'

A little later after the table had been cleared Mall was brought over and given a chair at the top. He was surrounded by his brothers, father and "minders" and given instructions on what his future duties would be.

'When the old man retires, ye'll open a bank account in the name of Patsy Mall Murphy. Ye will register the farm as a new business. You will be told what to do by us. If anybody comes asking questions, ye will send him to one of us. If anyone comes threatening ye, send for Sergeant O'Hourigan. Ye'll have no worries. I'll make sure ye get some of that nice, special ice cream you like from the dairy man the next time he comes around, if ye are a good man. Good on ye, Mall. Ye are a lucky man! What! The next thing is – ye will be getting married!'

'Get along with ye, Láidir,' laughed Mall. 'Me – get married?'

'That is the next thing we will be arranging for ye,' said his father.

Sean's attention was taken by the newspaper billboard that announced:

Kidnapped Government Minister
Ransom Demanded

He went over the pile of papers outside the shop and began to read, "Michael Fitzgerald is said to be in good health..."

Before he could continue he was roughly sent away by the newsagent.

He thought back to his last chat with the bold Michael. Sean had been arrested for loitering with intent (a charge subsequently reduced to one of pure loitering), and was sitting in a police cell when Michael entered.

'I've been making some enquiries,' said Michael in a business-like tone; 'and I have taken up your case with the authorities.'

'How are my relatives back home? I haven't heard from one of them for ages.'

'Your sister left for America out of shame, when she heard that you were locked up in an asylum. Your parents do not talk about you anymore. If people make enquiries, they get only silence. It seems they believe that you no longer exist.'

'And Uncle Patsy and Bridie? Did they get married?'

'Who is Bridie? Patsy Murphy got married to Eileen O'Rafferty from Bailebreoite. He is as happy as a skylark. Never was a man so changed for the better by marriage. And they have many children. They are saints, and as if their own many children weren't enough for them, they take in orphans and fosterlings when their own parents don't want them. You wouldn't come across a more charitable, Christian, selfless couple if you searched the length and breadth of the whole world. The good Patsy donated land for the new airport at Rathcloon, which has brought prosperity to a poverty-stricken region. He never asks a penny in payment for any of his good deeds. He only thinks of others – never of himself. He even once asked me if I could find out how you were, and to let him know the story. Mind you, I think he guessed the news might be bad. He said later he'd love to have you back in Rathcloon, if only you hadn't committed those crimes. But I promised him I'd send on his good wishes.'

'Bridie Murphy. She went down to Patsy's years ago and never came back. I thought that she had stayed there.'

'Never heard of her.'

'And so Patsy asked after me! Well, at least he still has faith in his oul' nephew!'

'I wouldn't say that. He said that as you might be a danger to the children, it would not be possible to have you back even for a short visit. For that is all it takes. He said, in fact, that he never wanted to see or hear of you again. I am sorry. I was hoping that I wouldn't have to put it so bluntly.'

'That is sad. I am only a danger to evil-doers. So I have been told anyway.'

'Sure who would tell you such a queer thing? Are you still raving in the head? Be careful now, or they will lock you up for good.'

Michael advised him, now, that the Special Branch would regard any further appearance by him at the gates of Leinster House as subversive activity, and this would lead to their beating him up badly. So it was best that he did not go there again.

'Go anywhere you like – except Leinster House, or within fifty miles of the neighbourhoods of Rathcloon and Dunmor. In all those places you are barred for your own safety.'

Now that was a quare thing altogether, Bridie not being at Patsy's. It seemed that she had disappeared off the face of the earth! And he knew that Patsy had sent him an invitation because he had received a letter from him many years ago in which he had said that he had an important person looking out for him – a government minister by the name of Michael Fitzgerald, who would arrange for his travel back to Rathcloon if he'd like. So Michael had broken a promise and told a lie at one and the same time.

He would contact the Little People now and find out what was going on. It had been a long time since he had been in touch. As with life, time went by and one tended to forget things – even important things. Great events in his life, that once preoccupied him for days, weeks and months on end, had become hazy, even unreal at times, as if they had never taken place.

Such as what exactly happened during that stampede of wild horses down O'Connell Street, when he had used the expertise gained from helping Uncle Patsy with the cows to attempt to bring the mad rush to a halt; thus, possibly, saving many lives – only to end up once again, for his troubles, in a police cell.

So many winters and summers of contemplation, leading him to the conclusion that seasons did not come in sequence but appeared, in fact, at one and the same time together.

So many faces rushing past – preoccupied, lethargic, troubled, tranquil, sad, happy, angry, serene, apathetic, resolute. Who were they? Where had they all been coming from? Where had they all gone? Even yet there were crowds of people rushing along on the same journey.

So many lorries packed with crates of stout and beer. Where had the party been? Who had drunk it all?

So many bodies lifted out of the river. Some had fallen in; some had jumped in; some were pushed in. Whatever the time of day or night or season it seemed that there would always be bodies in the river. Remembered only dimly now, like a bad dream, was his heroic quest to save a drowning man by jumping into the river, only to find himself (a non-swimmer) being hauled out by pulley and rope and being told to apologise for attempting to rescue a supposedly "non-existent" drowning man.

So many electoral campaigns – the only occasion when he found that he had an important role in the city, when he would be paid by person or persons unknown to tear down the posters of election candidates.

So many Christmases, when northmen appeared in pairs to hector, entreaty, cajole and threaten the riff-raff, dissolute and simple-minded to abandon the old ways and accompany them back "up north" where a life of ease, prosperity, respectability and happiness awaited them. Everybody in that remarkable place, which Sean had never heard of before, were extremely fortunate in living there and suffered none of the hardships normal people suffer. There was a great blessing from above on the place, to coincide with the curse of equal magnitude that lay on the people and places "down here". (The strange thing was – when once, on a particularly bad night of unabating freezing wind and rain he did agree to take up their offer – they had immediately turned their backs on him and departed.)

So many changes of clothes, each garment fit for royalty and proudly kept as long as possible, until it no longer could hold together and had to be sadly consigned to hang on a bush or tree branch where it would finish out its days as a reminder to all of its departed owner's high status and immense prestige.

So many years spent preparing and committing to memory his great speech. This would, when ready and the time was right, be delivered to the assembled sídh on the great and solemn occasion of their next centennial Árd Fheis, at a location still to be decided.

(Sean had originally suggested the lord mayor's Mansion House, in the early hours when nobody would be about, but as this place was in Dubh Linn it was out of the question as far as the majority of the sídh were concerned.)

So easy was it now to forget things that he even had to ask himself how he went about contacting the sídh. Then he remembered: the requirement for repetitive action. He walked along the pavement until he came to a spot where there was a crack in the concrete. It was quite a wide crack. This he walked around three times in the clockwise direction. As nothing happened, he walked away, to return again within a few moments to repeat the action. He kept this up for some time. Then he walked away from the spot, found a low wall and sat down to await developments. As darkness fell there had still been no word. He felt disappointment and, indeed, some panic. He had always relied on the knowledge that he could call on them in time of need. Not that he was in the habit of doing so, for there were few "times of need". He fell asleep. In his dream he was calling out: 'It's Seanín! Why don't you answer, Seanín?' He heard his voice echoing down long tunnels. Then he seemed to fall into an even deeper sleep. A sleep such as he hadn't experienced for a long time. Real unconsciousness. No dreaming. Yet when he awoke the next morning, and sat up on the pavement which had been his bed, there was still neither sight nor sound of them. It was a disappointment. He swore at them, and shouted aloud that he would give them a piece of his mind if they didn't show up soon.

That appeared to do the trick for the next moment he heard a voice:

'Don't be swearing at us, Seanín. It's not our fault. It's not easy to get around these days. BailenahEoropa is getting bigger still, and we can't use the old, familiar boreens. They've become "paths" and there are giant dwellings on either side. We have been barred from using them by you know who!! Why have you called on us now, Seanín, after all this long time, when we have been having so much trouble in our own domain, and tears are being shed aplenty? Your cries have been heard down here, old boy. The Pooka and Freagra ask after ye.'

'It's not my fault either that I can't remember how to call on you. I can't even remember why it was I had to call you now. It has something to do with Michael Fitzgerald, who has been telling me lies about Bridie and Uncle Patsy. I lost a good friend when I lost Bridie. And here I have been supposing that Uncle Patsy died years ago, for I had not heard from him and when I went every so often to check the post at Harold's Cross where the crow used to leave his letters in a hole in a tree, there were never any crows hanging around. So what else am I to presume but that he was dead? Now I know from what Mr Fitzgerald says, and he is not and never was a friend of mine, that he is alive and well and still living on the farm in Rathcloon after all these years. And there must be a whole heap of other things that have been going on unbeknownst to me, over the years, so that I have missed out on important occasions and for all I know, they might be believing that I am dead too or else wondering why it was I was so inconsiderate, unfeeling or downright dismannerly for not ever enquiring after them or attempting to find out how they were in health or dishealth, or how things were going with them generally. This man has a lot to answer for because he broke a promise to Uncle Patsy and he also told me a lie – or maybe more than one lie. Now I want to know from you what has been up in Rathcloon, and why this man Fitzgerald lied to me and what he has against me and for what reason. And is the rumour true that I've been hearing that he is being held by person or persons unknown and will not be released until he had paid his dues?

'I will not sleep easy either this night or any other night until you answer my questions.'

'Oh that is a load of troubles indeed, Seanín, and more than we can be handling at the moment, what with the whole sídh preoccupied with the upcoming Árd Fheis that is to make a decision about the future. Sure, it is likely that we will be having to leave this forsaken island and find a last *but last place* of refuge somewhere peaceable and safe. Sure, that is the very conference ye yerself are invited to, so that we can learn from yer wisdom. I can give ye news of Rathcloon, but why are ye concerned about this Michael Fitzgerald? He is certainly well known to us indeed. He is our great enemy.'

'Well, I made a promise to the same man that I would send the new Fianna to him if ever he was in trouble. At the time I still had not even started recruitment. Although I regret making that promise, there is nothing I can do about it now and it must be fulfilled. This has been another *geas* on my life, and I know that the fate of this fellow is somehow bound up with mine. I must go to him now and help him out of whatever trouble he is in. Thereabouts I will find some benefit that will serve my own cause.'

'The new Fianna? Has the old one left the field then?'

There was high-pitched laughter, rising and waning as if it was close-by and yet distant at the same time.

'The old Fianna is dead. The leadership has been locked up and the rest dispersed. Now it is time for the sídh to join me in a last great battle. Together we will liberate this land from its enemies. You can help me find this renegade who, it is said, is being held for ransom. Together we can free him not just from the imprisonment of his body, but of his mind and spirit. We can do one act of kindness together, and thus save Erin. Who knows but your own fate will be changed to something wonderful after this great deed, such as the old Fianna never once did in all the centuries they carried out other wondrous, glorious deeds, but none as glorious as this.'

'If ye go to Rathcloon, ye will soon discover where he is. Yer nose will lead ye to the spot. As for our help, it is always with ye. Every wish ye makes comes true for ye. We notice that ye have made very few wishes in the courses of the moon and sun. Ye have shown wisdom in this. It matters little to us now what becomes of Michael Fitzgerald, for we have got the best of him. We will be with ye as ye make the journey to Rathcloon. It will be a long and hard journey, for ye are not used to travel and it is a long time since ye left there. Ye will not recognise the place. But our guidance will be enough for ye. Head out at the next sunrise.'

Cheered by his reconnection with the sídh, Sean spent the day preparing for his journey south, figuring out the direction and how he would get out of the city. He went back to the park and tidied up his place. He hid certain possessions that he would require when he returned, and he placed the main part of his home in a horizontal position in the middle of a large shrubbery nearby. Then early next day he took himself to Busáras and got onto the bus that he was told was "going his way".

The bus had got as far as Inchicore before he was put off, which wasn't bad going. He knew now the route he had to take. He walked as far as Clondalkin, and then sat at the side of the road to get his breath.

Seanín. Ye'll never make it in time the way ye are going. Ye will have to get a bicycle, as nobody is going to give ye a lift. Go and find or beg an old bike in Clondalkin. The giants here are a generous sort. (Or at least they used to be.) But if ye don't succeed, try the lorries.

He went around knocking on doors, asking the various people if they had an old bike to spare, as he had to get down the country urgently. Most of the people hadn't a spare bicycle or, as might be expected to be the case if they did have one, they weren't in a position to let him have it. A few were sympathetic to his plight although the majority were only keen for him to depart. He struck lucky at number 13. The people who came to the door were very friendly, happy and jovial. They said that they would be only too glad to help him out, laughing their heads off at the same time. Sean had to smile, even if he didn't know what was so terribly funny. At this stage, he also had a bit of a following; a crowd of youngsters who were marching behind him as he went from house to house. His "friends" now took him down a road to where "there was a lovely car that he could drive all the way to Dunmor".

'That is very kind of you,' he said to them as he took his seat in what was a wreck that had once been a car but now was without wheels and engine. The crowd, grown large by now, was cheering and laughing and ignored his requests for help to get it started. After a while they all went away. As he was about to get out two large men appeared with crowbars in their hands, looking very angry. They cursed and swore at him and pulled him out roughly from the vehicle.

'Do ye own this car? Why are you sitting in our car?'

Sean recognised them as those men of the road who had a reputation for being big soft babies. They always went about in groups in case they were attacked, looking fearfully over their shoulders and always gaping round about them. When they fought they were unable to protect themselves with their fists but always had to use crude weaponry. Sean would often laugh at their weak, unimaginative fighting methods. Although, like himself, they loved the open air they refused to sleep outdoors but always had to be put up in nice, comfortable caravans. They were never happy with ordinary possessions, but were always on the look-out for rubbish. They accumulated so much of this rubbish that they either secreted it away in special hiding places or had to go away leaving much of it behind them. He himself had a good knowledge of these hiding places, and often spent many a happy hour going through the discarded stuff for the simple pleasure and wonderment of looking at it. Clearly, now, this car was another example of the rubbish that they collected, and therefore there had never been any chance of him driving it down to Rathcloon. Yet they were still angry at him just for sitting in their old crock and they roughly hauled him down the road to their camp site in order to punish him, as they were shouting, with a sound beating. He was beginning to feel a bit annoyed now, not only because they were squeezing his arms and kicking him from behind but because of what he was hearing now from the Little People:

Those giants knew it was an old crock. They were just laughing at ye; making a fool of ye. Ye will have to defend yerself against these bullies now. For they will show ye no mercy.

The crowd came into the central area and Sean noticed that all the dogs and children were running away. The doors of the caravans were suddenly closed. A number of even bigger men came towards him holding long, thick sticks.

Sean saw red. His body suddenly seized up like it was a block of ice. The hairs of his body shot forward and not merely specks or droplets of blood but whole streams came shooting out from every tip and bristle. His head whirled round so that he could see in every direction at once. A sudden, great pain seized him between his two eyes and they became one gigantic eye. His eye withdrew far into his head and then shot out again with the power and thunder of a great stellar explosion in the depths of space.

At this point, to a neutral observer, Sean simply lay in a heap on the ground with multiple injuries and with no hope of ever arising again. What the observer would have interpreted as the product of pain, weakness, defeat, humiliation was, however, the beginning of a warrior frenzy such as Sean had not entered into since he had played his last game of hurling so long ago in Dunmor. The observer might not even have noticed the first signs of this: his ears turning red. Most would have seen it as blood – the result of some internal injury. In fact Sean was now hearing the hum of the fury – which grew louder and louder until he could hear nothing else. At that moment he felt himself to be as small as the smallest pea or grain of sand in existence, so small as to be invisible to the naked eye. This was the greatest of all strengths to have against a powerful enemy. It gave the individual an invincibility and invisibility that no mortal, or any weaponry, scheming or devising could ever overcome. The roar was of such a force now that it raised him off the ground (he realised that they thought they were letting him get up so as to be able to knock him back down again).

As he straightened up he suddenly saw the massed armies of the sídh on their white, red-eyed steeds beyond the camp, under all their different banners – red, orange, yellow, green, blue, indigo, violet – ready to strike in support when the time came. He was no longer alone. He was filled with renewed spirit and encouragement. He no longer felt any pain. His jaws became bared to the ear and his lips were drawn back to the eye-teeth. A scream escaped his mouth and he grabbed a metal bar off one of the men who had been using it to beat him. As he looked at it, it suddenly became transformed in his hand into Cuchulin's feared weapon of choice – the *ga boilg* – that was feared even by Erin's bravest warriors. It had seven barbs and he only had to point it for it to hit its target. With one strike he split the nearest man in double across the belly. A number of further strikes and every warrior near him became two, smaller warriors. Each time he withdrew the rod he pulled out the inner organs of his victim. The sight and smell of blood gave him greater strength; he fed on each morsel of flesh as though it was the choicest food. Suddenly he was flying through the air, landing on the heads, shoulders and backs of his enemies like a carrion crow that feeds on the dead. Standing on just the small toe of his left foot he struck at every man in sight with his deadly, supernatural spear, sending them bawling to their mommas or to their deaths. Digging deep into their heads with the fingers of his left hand, he pulled out the eyes of his victims and flung them to the vultures that had started to appear. At each hit he gave the warrior cry, and every man the length and breadth of Erin shivered with fear and dread at that moment. It is said that one hundred and fifty of the road men's finest fell that day, and their women still weep.

When Sean had calmed down somewhat and took in his surroundings as the roar of battle died away, he saw devastation all round. The only sounds were the cries of the wounded, the weeping of those who mourned and the chatter of the wild creatures feeding off the dead. A huge, greater silence hung over it all. Sean turned to face the sídh and bowed to them, signalling that he was offering the victory to them. He moved off the campsite, followed at a respectful distance by the invisible armies of the hillocks, lakes and seas, and headed off in the direction of the sun. He thought, or imagined as he turned the corner, that he heard laughter coming from the camp; but when he listened carefully he realised it was the sound that is indistinguishable between laughter and weeping.

His wounds he healed with weeds. It is said that the word of this battle went before him; and no man dared to stand in his way as he made the long journey to Rathcloon over minor roads, lanes and back-ways that were not direct or easy to travel, the main roads being forbidden to pedestrians and hitchhikers.

Ten

CAOILTE WENT TO see Finn in the Home on the outskirts of Dunmor. After his "bargaining plea" with the government on the charge of conspiring to establish a state within a state, which had kept him out of jail, Caoilte had lost much face with his own colleagues, former colleagues and the public. The terms had included handing over to the (official) state much of the property, titles and various legal entities that had once been the Fianna's preserve. It was no good harking back to the old days, he told himself and others, or dwell on the great old "hard times", or to bask in those mighty, wondrous achievements of yore. For one thing, the past was the past and the future has not yet been. Modern Erin was only concerned with the present. And everything had to be paid for now, including old or bad debts, past injuries, old wrongs. There was no such thing anymore as a "free lunch", or immunity from the official law.

'Hello, Finn. It's Caoilte. How are you keeping? I hope they're treating you well in here.'

It took the old man some time to look up and answer. His eyes were glazed.

'Caoilte! Is it you?'

'Yes. Sorry I couldn't come before now. Business. We are branching out into new fields. The old Fianna will rise again yet!'

'Ah!'

'I'm sorry to hear they stole your camán.'

'What camán?'

Finn finally was able to focus on Caoilte.

'And how is young Sean?' he asked, after a while.

'Sean?'

'Sean Murphy. The Sea-Hound. The only one to pass all the tests.'

There was annoyance in Finn's voice. How could Caoilte have forgotten him?

'Pass all the tests? Sure, didn't he walk away?'

'That's the point! He's the only one to do that. For it, he won my undying admiration. That's the man!'

Caoilte thought to himself that Finn was in his dotage. He had known this already, but to see positive proof was a shock. There was no point, he thought, in disillusioning the old man. He appeared not even to have any idea about the destruction of the Fianna.

'Oh, Sean. The last I heard of him he was in jail. Do you remember Michael Fitzgerald? He nearly became one of us. He told me about Sean. He said that he was living the life of a tramp up in Dubh Linn.'

'He is our best warrior. He has spent his life successfully warding off the false prophets, the crooked politicians, the drunken soldiers, the greedy businessmen, the unlearned scholars, the non-believers. He took them on and stopped their devilment in its tracks. How did he do that? Simply by not becoming one of them – the hardest thing in the world. Nobody knew he was Fianna. Nobody knew he was working for us, maintaining the purity of our soldierly way of life when all the rest had reverted to softer ways. He knew he could never be rid of the *geas* I put on him.'

'I thought I was your best man, Finn,' said Caoilte, surprised and somewhat disappointed.

'And you are my best man. But Sean is better than that! He is a tramp! A bum! A down-and-out! A hobo! A wandering "bard"! He has no letters after his name. No official titles. His name is not even entered in the official registers of the land, if you exclude, probably, the criminal records. Nobody knows him. Nobody respects him. Nobody will remember him. Most have no idea even of his existence.

Wonderful! What would I give to be in his shoes, to be out there in the wild, instead of in here in this luxurious pad with every meal provided and all expenses paid!'

Caoilte was taken aback at the vehemence, the certitude, the apparent madness of Finn's words. Yet it was almost as if the fellow had not lost his senses, but gained them.

Finn was sighing heavily: 'All is not lost, Caoilte. We still have Sean. Emulate him! Go and find him. Take to the road! We should never have built houses. They represent the end of civilisation. If you do that, the Fianna will no longer just have one hero – Finn – but three! The name of Finn McCumhail will no longer be alone in its honoured place in the Annals. It will be Sean and Caoilte from then on, too!'

'Ah, it is a hard thing you ask of me.'

'I am not asking you. I am telling you. If you do not obey, you will be under a *geas*.'

Caoilte thought back to the beginning of his time in the Fianna. The prospect ahead had been so promising. They had been geared up to face any and every challenge. They had taken on the world. Caoilte had a plan no less than for himself to rule to the far ends of the earth. Erin was only a stepping stone to a much greater empire. The Fianna would have become the defenders of all mankind. The world would pay tribute to them. Now here they were with scarcely a bed between them to lie down on at night, constantly on the move to escape their creditors, and the butt of every risible joke and slander that could be conceived – that should be used only against the most despicable, most disreputable, most despised set of people in the land. And here was his hero, Finn McCumhail, living in the lap of luxury and telling him that he had it too soft and should go out and learn what hardship is. Thinking back on it all now, what did Finn ever actually do, apart from live off his great reputation? A reputation that originated far back in an age that none living now could remember – or how, where or why the reputation arose. Who was to say that it was genuine – an accurate record of truly brave deeds done against overwhelming odds? In fact, when you thought about it, most of his actions would have been quite impossible physically. Flinging a sod the size of Manannan's Isle into the Irish sea? What we know now about geological methods surely put the lie to that. (Not that he would ever say so to his face!) Or constructing that huge causeway to Alba in order to meet some notorious Fomorian giant? Well, the logic of that spoke for itself, what with the geomorphologic explanations given in standard textbooks these days. Or those mountain passes cut out with his sword? He could see the nonsense of it all now. There was an old tale, he remembered now, of when Finn had fled in terror at the sight of Cuchulain – not the lad he liked to tease with the name but the real Cuchulain. It was said that he ran into a woman's house in terror and hid in the baby's cot. The woman had to deal with Cuchulain. This was a tale that was always said by his supporters to have been a piece of black propaganda put about by Finn's enemies. But Caoilte wondered about that now, too. And surely that famed reputation for wisdom, supposedly linked to Finn's unusual, childish habit of sucking his thumb (it was in his mouth even now) did not stand up in the cold light of reality? For look at the state of the Fianna! Nothing Caoilte did after he took over could have stopped the rot. And here was the big brave hero sitting in an easy chair in front of the television, with the cheek to lecture *him* about hardship! A nurse came in at that moment and put a bib on him and asked him if he was ready for his cocoa. Finn shouted with delight – 'Oh, lovely. Cocoa time!'

The scales fell from Caoilte's eyes at that moment. Anger surged through him. He saw now that all heroism was phoney. It was myth promulgated for political purposes. The bigger the fib the more likely it was to be believed. The hero himself had to be an utter fraudster; a wreck of a human being; a phoney, a low-down no-good if he was to be truly accepted as a hero.

Finn took his thumb out from his mouth in order to take his drink. Caoilte looked at the famous "source of wisdom" and was shocked. It was white, shrivelled, shrunken to the bone, as if all the blood had been sucked out of it. The edges were nicotine-stained.

After shock came revulsion. The old man was now no longer even aware of his visitor's presence, but was contentedly sipping his mug of cocoa.

Caoilte got up from his chair and walked slowly away, the grey, thin features of this slightly built man accentuated now by disillusionment and despair. The tears were already coming as he went out the door. As he walked towards the car park grief had taken over. His pace slowed. It was as if his whole body was in pain. He stumbled rather than walked the rest of the way. Once inside the vehicle all he could do was to hold on to the steering as emotion took over. Fortunately there was nobody in the vicinity to see him in this state. His tears clouded up the windows, mercifully obscuring him from the outside world – for he was to stay there for the rest of the evening.

He thought back to all that he had (idealistically) done for Finn. Of the many occasions he had taken to the field of battle to defend his reputation, in the process decapitating many foe and destroying the livestock of the poor, taking away the wives of warriors and giving them to their enemies, showing no mercy to the wild animals, the child or the calf. All for the good name of Finn. He had entered into degrading, humiliating contracts with contemptuous kings, scheming druids and devilish royal wives in order to protect the freedom of the Fianna. All for the good name of Finn. He had travelled the length and breadth of the land recruiting the young with promises of greatness and eternal honour in Tír na nÓg, in return for no more than their goods, their obedience and their purity of heart, mind and body. All for the good name of Finn.

In the darkness of the night he got out of the car. The tears were still running down his face so that, it was said, permanent marks were left there deeper than the deepest ravines in Erin, and the waters went away to become in Tír na nÓg a river greater in both width and length than the Shannon.

He straightened up and looked into the dark, cloudy sky and tried to think what he might do. He bristled with annoyance and was filled again with anger when he thought of Finn's instruction to go and find Sean Murphy. His great pet! He turned to get back into the car. However, something made him stop. He was unable to make himself open the door. An internal struggle was beginning and he suddenly realised that he was unable to do away with thoughts of Sean Murphy. Try as hard as he did, standing there for the next hour making numerous strenuous attempts to open that door and get back into his seat and drive away from that spot and Finn forever, he could not do it.

He turned away and started to walk off into the night, Finn's words now coming back into his head like the pounding of a drum.

The party at Patsy's was now in its third day. Most had forgotten the original reason for the celebrations, and all had now deserted the fine wines and sherries for the more normal if lacklustre fare of whiskey and stout. Bishop Murphy, aka Mikey Murphy, had appeared at the door wearing a large overcoat that discreetly covered his official "uniform". You would have thought it was an undertaker standing there, or a solicitor or even a landlord's agent. Widow O'Rafferty had insisted he come; and whilst he would normally have turned down the invitation, or just not turned up at all, the simple fact was that he was not that sort of man, or bishop, anymore.

The reprimand from the pope had set him thinking hard. The whole world knew that he had received, in person, a rebuke from the pontiff! How knowledge of his supposed negligence could have reached as far as the Eternal City was a mystery. That His Holiness should consider a mere backwater bishop worthy of such personal chastisement was surely something remarkable. He had gone over again and again the events that had taken place over the years since he became bishop. As hard as he wracked his brains, he could not figure out where he had gone wrong; where he had failed in his duty; where he had not foreseen a challenge. He asked himself over and over again how could he have handled anything differently? Even the hot potato of the St Finbar statue had been settled to the satisfaction of all. Wasn't everyone delighted with the proposed new church and its St Finbar theme park, including the widow herself?

Yet he knew that he had failed. He had failed, probably, the one great challenge of which he had long been forewarned. He had been thinking that some great, important matter concerning Mother Church would have presented itself – and he would have, with much forbearance, wisdom, pre-sight and utilising all the supernatural virtues, dealt bravely and succinctly with the problem. The Church would have arisen from the mire of controversy glorious and renewed. He would have accepted the congratulations with humility.

It might, on the other hand, have been some slight, minor thing. Something that he would not even have noticed in the normal course of events. How he had been tormented by this question! Perhaps it was part of his punishment never to know in this life what his failure was! In the meantime, he must endeavour, for the remainder of his mortal existence, never again to be opinionated, diplomatic, careful, sensible, wise, cautious, brave, or even fair and just. For he had exercised these qualities aplenty and yet they had not apparently led him to make the right decisions, or even enabled him to judge important things correctly. Thus, he had come all the way to Patsy's party just for the fun of it, abandoning all scruples and darn the consequences. For that was surely the lesson to be learnt from the whole affair!

'Mikey! Mikey!'

He heard the cries of the widow and he went straight over to her.

'Widow O'Rafferty! You are looking very well. Sure, you're are as fit as a boxer.'

'They wouldn't let me go to visit you! They keep me locked up here as a prisoner. Can you let me out of this thing? I can easily walk as good as the next one. They are all lying about me, saying that I have this and that illness and that I am not long for this world. There is a plot against me.'

'Sure, I know you are your own best judge. Here, let me undo the strap and get you out of this thing. There – it's done. Stand up and walk!'

There was a mêlée of people in the main part of the house, and in the middle of it a man was shouting, 'Every bit of it! Every bit of it!'

'Ah, ye're a good man. A good man, Michael Fitzgerald. There is none as good as ye,' Patsy was saying, slapping him on the back.

'Look! Granny's walking!'

'Bishop Murphy ordered her to get up off her wheelchair!'

'And now she's walking again! After all these years!'

The children's excitement was immense. They had seen a miracle take place before their eyes.

Patsy went over to the bishop and patted him on the shoulder.

'Well done, Bishop Murphy. It proves all that they have said about you. And put a lie to those who say you are a fraud.'

'Well, in fact, I think the widow could walk all the time,' said Bishop Murphy.

'Oh no! Not at all. She lost the use of her legs a long time ago. It was proven by the many good doctors who came here to treat her. None of them could make her walk. You have done a miracle.'

It was also a remarkable fact that, now that the miracle had been done, not much more was made of it; everybody returned to their drinks and the music was turned up and, indeed, there was even annoyance on the faces of Patsy and Eileen as if something had happened, or was happening, that was spoiling the party a bit for them.

Sergeant O'Hourigan arrived, full of bounce and singing aloud an old "Come all ye" even before he had got in the door. There was nothing he loved better these days than a party in Rathcloon – or in what had been old Rathcloon but was now a much more modern place and, indeed, was where the best people now desired to live. Even himself had one of the biggest houses there. But none of all that was the point of his good humour and bonhomie now. It was that he was the hero of the hour. He had rescued Michael Fitzgerald from captivity; saved the minister's life and rescued the good name of Erin. Michael had promised him the top police job in Dubh Linn.

'And I am a man who does not break his promises,' Michael was saying to one and all in the middle of the room.

'How do ye be keeping yerself these days?' asked the widow.

'I'm sorry I haven't been in touch lately, Widow. I have come to apologise to you for giving you a bit of a cold shoulder over these recent times. I am so bogged down with official matters I don't have time for much else. That's what public office does to even the most well-meaning person. However, I can make amends. You are invited to the next bishops' spree. And isn't it wonderful about Michael Fitzgerald! We had all more or less given him up for good. Especially when you think about the ruthlessness of these new-style criminals. It's a bit of a miracle in itself.'

'And he's been promising the lads, in thanks for them getting him released, to give them shares in his business!'

'That is gratitude and kindness personified.'

'I do wonder if his head has been turned a bit by being kidnapped? He says he wants to rebuild Foirnocht Hill. That is a little hill that was on Patsy's land.'

'That is a very strange wish. Any idea what has put it into his head?'

'Sure it's early days. He has only just come in. "First port of call", he calls us. He hasn't even told the Taoiseach yet. He's buzzing all over with talk. It's the relief, I'd say.'

'I can only say,' said Michael, still talking continuously, 'that we should also remember the Little People in all of this. They, too, had a major role to play. My promises were as much to them as to you, the rescuers.'

'Three cheers for the little folk,' shouted Patsy Láidir. 'Three cheers for the fairies who got Mr Fitzgerald free.'

'It won't do any harm to fulfil an extra little promise I made to them. I heard that they were upset that I knocked down Foirnocht hill. It was a special place for them, apparently. Well, it would be a good thing to put it back up again.'

'Now that is not such a sensible thing at all,' said Patsy Láidir. 'Who told you that?'

'They did! They told me to put it back up.'

'I don't remember anything about that being said.'

'Well, you weren't there all the time they were talking to me.'

'It would be a terrible waste of money. After all, you told them that if you were released, you would direct investment into the projects of the Murphy Company of Rathcloon. Sure, the fairies love Rathcloon. It's their national headquarters. But they are probably happier living in more modern accommodation nowadays. And how would you re-build a hill anyway?'

'I guess I'll ask my engineers. It would be quite easy to get a sufficient quantity of earth.... There is so much of it being moved around these days...'

'But that land is an airport runway now!' said Patsy Cliste.

'Well, perhaps we could rebuild the hill a little further away. I'm sure they wouldn't mind if it was a mile or two down the road.'

Michael was beginning to get a little hot under the collar. Indeed, for him it was more important to keep his promise about Foirnocht Hill, than all the other promises he had to make out loud in front of the rescue team as a condition of his release. It was true that he never got to see the sídh; but they were there all right, just as Sean had promised, for he had heard the patter of their little feet on the floor and their tiny voices were very clear.

'I don't remember you promising to rebuild Foirnocht Hill,' said Patsy Cliste. 'And you can't rebuild the secret tunnels and all the hiding places that they would have had in the hill anyway. But if you want to rebuild a silly old hill, go ahead and build it! Who cares anyway!'

They all laughed and cheered and told him to go ahead and rebuild the hill, as it could do no harm to anybody.

Michael seemed lost in his thoughts and oblivious to their shouting and laughing.

'It can be done, it can be done,' he was saying to himself. 'I will start on it right away. Maybe I could get a plan somewhere. A plan of a sídh hillock. The inside of a rath. Somebody must know. But…they won't accept it on any other spot. I know it! It will *have* to be on the original site. I will have to move the…airport.'

Patsy took centre stage again and said that he wanted to make a speech, for the drink was now getting to him.

'Another one!' they laughed.

'It's a fine day today that we have got Patsy Mall to be the new master of Toberbeg Farm. And we all wish him the very best for the future – and I can only hope that it is not too long before I pass on and am in a position to hand over.'

'Oh, don't say that!' cried Eileen, and it was difficult to know whether she was amused or shocked. She had grown more fond of the man as the years had passed, missing now even his tobacco-chewing and spitting, a habit he had long since been forced to discontinue.

'But there is one man whom we are all forgetting here today…'

'Who? Who is that? Tell us, Patsy.'

'That man is not here now, and he has not been here for a very long time indeed. Even Michael, up in Dubh Linn in that important position an' all, couldn't help him or bring him back home. The poor lad was a rebel and a freedom fighter up there amongst that crowd of…turncoats, and they locked him up.'

'Bad, very bad, Patsy.'

'Well, there is none of ye here that ever met him, bar one; but ye will have been hearing me speak about him from time to time all right.'

'Is it Sean, Patsy? Sean Murphy?'

'Well, he was the one who used to come up here to the farm

good weather and bad and milk the cows. He was the one who never complained about the hard work that needs to be done on a farm. I never had to worry about anything when he was around. The hay crop was as good as in when he turned up, rainy weather or not. I never lost a crop when he was helping.'

Tears appeared in Patsy's eyes and he had to pause. He took out his handkerchief and blew his nose.

'Sure, I can't help getting a little emotional. He was like a son to me.'

His words stuck in his throat. He had to grip the edge of the table.

'Easy now, Patsy. Easy,' said Eileen.

He recovered his voice and continued:

'There was no greater man under the sun. No matter what bad things he has done up there, it doesn't matter to me. I don't care if he ever killed someone. For that person would have been deserving of it. Or robbed a bank, or attacked a police station.'

'For true!' they shouted.

'There is nobody better that I would like to be here now, celebrating with us on this great family occasion. It would be a treat for an old man's eyes to see the lad – and I am sure he still looks as young as a pup and is as fit as a fiddle yet. Just to see him standing here in the midst of us drinking a drop of the hard stuff and singing a song!'

'For sure. One day he will be here!' they cried.

'I make him a pledge now, from out of my heart. I state here before you all that if Sean were to come in that door now I would make him my son and heir. Wouldn't I, Mall? You wouldn't mind, would you, Mall?'

Mall slowly looked up and said, 'He can have the lot.'

They all cheered. Then there was total silence as each reflected on the generosity and high ideals of both Patsys – indeed of the whole Murphy family.

'The weather is breaking up,' said Láidir at the sound of thunder outside.

There was banging on the door and Eileen shivered.

'The wind!!'

The door was pushed open with some force. A man who looked like a ghost was standing there, weather-beaten, clothes in tatters, white-haired and pale. His face bespoke bewilderment. The wind was driving in the rain behind him.

'Who are you?' asked Láidir, the first one to find his voice.

'Sean Murphy.'

His voice was so deep that it seemed to take ages for him to say the words.

Sean was immediately taken into the back room by Patsy's sons and put in a chair. A glass of whiskey was brought to him. A gesture from Patsy and they all left, leaving him alone with his nephew. Patsy was sighing and muttering and wringing his hands.

'I never thought that you would turn up now. How did you get into this state? Look at the cut of ye! Anyone would be ashamed to be called your uncle.'

'You would look like this if you had spent the last month on the road, in every weather, having to get your food from the bushes and rubbish bins along the way.'

'Begorrah! And you a Murphy!'

'I came back to help you all down here, for I heard that there was a bit of trouble. And to see how yourself was, my parents, and Bridie. How is Bridie?'

'Never mind about her now.'

Patsy's face had a deep, worried look.

'Were ye listening at the door?'

'I heard the noise of a celebration and feast and I heard you talking.'

'What did ye hear?'

'I could never mistake the sweet voice of my old uncle.'

'Take a sip of whiskey. It'll make ye feel better. I'll be back in a minute.'

He went outside and spoke to Láidir.

'I'm not sure but I think he heard my speech. What will we do?

The bishop heard me make that pledge, too. It'll be all over the country in no time.'

'Let's get Cliste in on this. Cliste – come over here!'

They went into a huddle and tried to figure a way out of their predicament. Patsy was saying how shocked and disgusted he was by the state of Sean. The lad had obviously been mixing with untrustworthy types and had lost any semblance of self-respect, dignity or honour that might originally have been there. Most likely behind him were a crowd of no-goods who were just waiting to come down and join him in drinking binges and stealing forays into local properties and premises.

'Leave it to me,' said Cliste, the only one who did not look worried and was keeping his cool. He went into the backroom with a fresh glass of whiskey for Sean.

'Sean. I'm your cousin, Cliste. I've heard a lot about you. You have been very lucky to get up to Dubh Linn and enjoy the bright lights. Sure, we have all tried but just can't get out of here. We're all stuck in the bog. It's no life for a man. The farming business is on its way out. Do you know, there are no cows or animals here at all, now. It's all lorries, diggers and heavy machinery these days. Sure, you wouldn't know what to do with yourself if you stayed here.'

Sean dropped his head and took another sip of whiskey. A look of sadness came over him.

'I heard that Michael Fitzgerald was in trouble. I'd promised him I would help if he ever got into serious bother. Do you know where he might be now?'

Cliste was taken aback. He tried to hide his concern as he said, 'Sure, what would we know about him?'

Sean did not reply, for he was beginning to feel that this was a bit like a police interrogation session that he was undergoing. He became angry.

'Sure, I can't wait to be out of here. Is Bridie around? Once I see Bridie I'm off.'

'I'll see if Bridie is anywhere around. Michael Fitzgerald is here with us right at this moment. He's in the there enjoying himself and having the craic. He's a little the worse for his experience, saying that he was with the fairies. Wherever he was, there is no getting sense from him. Who would ever listen to what the man says now? He must have had a sort of...nervous breakdown.'

He left Sean, saying he was going to get him another nice whiskey.

'He knew about Michael Fitzgerald!' Cliste whispered to Láidir.

'Be the hokey!'

'He wants to see Auntie Bridie. He says he'll leave after he sees her.'

'I don't think they'll be too pleased to let him see her. But I'll have a word.'

'We'll have to tell him to make a little speech – to say he is disowning this place, the farm and all his relatives.'

'Leave it to me,' said Láidir.

'No. I'd better take care of it,' said Cliste.

Sean sat on an upturned bucket in what had been the cowshed talking to Bridie. She was standing in her working shawls, looking at Sean with surprise and bafflement.

She had not put on a single year since he last saw her, Sean thought.

'How have you been keeping?' she asked.

'Not too bad. I have those good friends who help me out from time to time.'

'Do you still see...them?'

'When I am settled in a place, I don't usually call on them. When I am on the move, they always make a point of turning up, giving advice, nagging, telling me what is going to happen.'

'That is good!'

"Why are they keeping you in here?' he asked in a concerned voice.

'I prefer to be in here than in that house, since they changed everything.'

'What do you mean?'

'The cows, sheep, dog, hens – they're all gone. It's not like since I first came. Patsy has changed, too. He has become a different man. When I first came, he took great care of me, and we had great laughs. Even Eileen put up with me, and I helped her around the house. I looked after the children. Then they started wearing those fancy clothes. That was the cause of it...'

'The cause of it... .What do you mean?'

'Wearing the fancy clothes turned their heads. They became different people. Grandees. They were looking at themselves in the mirror all the time. Do I look OK in this? Does this look good on me? Is this OK to wear? It was all that they were concerned with after that.'

'So why do they make you live in this shed?'

'They were ashamed of the clothes that I wore. I refused to get into new clothes. They are like the things they used to wear up in Dubh Linn. I wanted to continue to wear the countrywoman's outfit. And I stick to my guns. Visitors will be shocked to see you in those, they said. Let them be shocked, I said. You will have to remain out of sight, they said. That's OK by me, I said. In the end, this shed is the best place for me. At least that is what I used to think. Then, later, I began to think that they were treating me unfairly, for they wouldn't hardly let me out at all. I felt like a prisoner. I was told that if I ever went outside without their permission, they would be very angry with me, and would consider it a breach of trust and a sign of ingratitude. After all we have done for you they said, and you can't even spare us the shame and embarrassment you cause us.'

'This is terrible! Well, come away with me. I am heading off for the fair hills.'

Bridie went silent. Then she began to cry.

'I'm...afraid.'

'Bridie Murphy afraid! Not the Bridie Murphy I knew!'

'They'll kill me if I try to leave here. They'll say that I'll be seen in the area and people will say, "That's the Murphy girl. Isn't she a disgrace!" '

Sean went quiet and reflected. He remembered back to the time he had asked her out for an evening. She said she couldn't and made an excuse. Every time after that she had some reason for not going out. Then he remembered her saying that there was "something in both their stars" that made them very good friends, but that it would also make them a bad husband and wife. She had said it as a joke, but he had thought about it time and again. He wondered now was she giving him the cold shoulder once more? How could he be sure she was telling him the truth? Or was she using the truth as a way to send him away and at the same time not hurt his feelings? Was she a prisoner, or was she a happy woman who would not dream of giving up her present comforts for a life of hardship on the road with Sean Murphy?

There was only one way to find out.

'Will you marry me, Bridie?'

'Quick! Quick! Leave here at once. Someone's coming. If they know I've been talking to you for too long they'll suspect that I am up to something; that I am planning to leave with you. I will have to put on an act now. Forgive me, Sean.'

As Sean was leaving the shed she started to shout, 'Get out of here and never come back. I never want to see you again.'

Cliste appeared and took Sean back inside to say his farewells.

He shook hands with Michael Fitzgerald.

'The Fianna took good care of you, like I said we would,' said Sean.

'Tell them that I owe them everything. I am going to spend the rest of my life making amends,' he replied.

'Goodbye now, to you all. I leave you all, and Toberbeg Farm, in the good hands of Patsy and Mall Murphy, knowing that you will do everything to stop the roads and help the land recover its good health. Bridie Murphy says she's very happy here, and she wants nothing more to do with me. I know now that I am, at long last, a free man. I can go now and live with no *geas* over me. Good health to you all.'

★

'I thought I was a goner,' said Michael to the bishop. 'I said my prayers, I can assure you!'

'Good man. That is the best thing to do in that situation.'

'I heard them in the room, you know.'

'I know.'

'I gave up everything. I am handing over all my land and property in this area to the Murphy family, as decent, honourable and respectable members of the local community. My prized stud farm is going to be auctioned off and the proceeds are going to pay for a retirement home to be set up for unwanted...horses...'

His voice became sorrowful. 'Horses. They started me off in this game, you know. They gave me the leg up in my business career. Yet I...didn't show them...any kindness...sending them off to the knackers...'

'I know.'

'If only I had my life all over again.'

'We all would love that.'

'The little men saved me. There is no getting away from that. And all I can do to repay them is to offer to rebuild Foirnocht Hill! It is small reward for them.'

'It is the best you can do. May I ask you something, now, if you don't mind?'

'Of course not. What is that?'

'Did you see the little men?'

'I only heard them.'

'Did you hear the name Freagra mentioned by any chance?'

'Freagra? I...can't say I did for sure. Who is he?'

'If the fairies were there helping you, I would imagine Freagra would have been there too.'

He had spoken quietly, in case anyone else was listening. He became momentarily agitated, apparently reflecting on some private, personal matter, sounding disappointed that "Freagra" had not been there. He coughed to clear his throat and asked, 'So tell me – how were you actually freed?'

'The fairies came in very quietly. I had called for them out loud, as Sean Murphy once told me how to. They didn't come at once. I had to call out three times. Then they arrived en masse. They filled the room. They told me how upset they were with me. Then I made my promises to them, in order to undo old wrongs. In fact, I knew inside that I would have to do this in order to get freed. It is only right and fair, and I did it voluntarily. There was no coercion. One of them came up close to me and whispered: *We're giving ye papers to sign, and after that ye will be free.* I heard him as clear as day.'

'In a squeaky voice?'

'Yes.'

'A high or low squeaky voice?'

Michael thought for a while.

'I'd say it was – a deepish sort of squeaky voice. Like this – eeh, eeeh, eeeeh!'

'And then they untied you and took off the blindfold?'

'Yes. And the papers were on a little table in front of me. I signed them immediately. There was nobody in the room, for the one who untied me and undid the blindfold was behind me. Then I was told to wait there, not to move, and they would send for help. Can I tell you, Bishop Murphy, the relief that I felt when Sergeant O'Hourigan arrived with the Murphys?'

'It must have been a great relief.'

'I owe them my life, too, because the Little People had told me to stay dead quiet as there was a danger the kidnappers would come back.'

Patsy Láidir came over and said that there had been a call from the Taoiseach himself, to enquire after Michael's health, to give him his congratulations, and to enquire when he would be seeing him back up in Dubh Linn. I told him that you were here relaxing and recovering from the experience. I said that we were taking good care of you. That you were among friends.'

'You are that!'

'Your friend and colleague, the Minister for Justice, Mr McGoon, is up there waiting for you too. He came on the phone and said that he has a lot of questions to ask you. I'd be careful of that man, if I were you. He might be wanting your job for one of his other friends, and be planning to stab you in the back.'

'Ah, no. He is a hard man. But an honest man.'

'An honest man! They are the worst.'

Láidir went away and Bishop Murphy put a calming hand on Michael's shoulders. For some reason, he felt that the senior politician and himself were entering a new phase in their lives; a phase where wisdom was old hat, for they both now knew that there was something higher than wisdom.

'I happen to know about the Little People myself, Michael. Believe me, I take every word you say seriously, and I do not question your integrity in the matter.'

'Thank you, Bishop. Some of them were beginning to laugh at me here.'

'Now listen here to me. It is OK to go by that story while you are here with your friends. But you will have to change it when you go out of here. You cannot go to the press and say that the fairies rescued you. It would not only be bad for your career. It would be the end of the government, and the country will become a laughing stock in the world-wide community of nations. I can just see it now...them pointing to our flag outside the United Nations in New York. Our erstwhile political neighbour of bad faith next door...'

'We will all have to sit down together now and get our story straight,' said Michael, beginning to face the future; anxious indeed to rid himself of the whole business, to resign his seat, give away his goods and head, like Sean, for the open road. Perhaps they would meet up...

Sean left the house and walked down the lane to the main road. He turned left, heading for the mountains he could see in the distance. He had received information that the time was fast approaching for his centennial speech to the assembled sídh. It would be some time before he reached quieter lanes where traffic was not so heavy and noisy and where people became fewer. In fact it took him two days to get back into the real countryside. He walked day and night, accompanied by his good friends. As he turned up a steep mountain track, another walker came along a different track and turned along the same route, some distance behind Sean and out of sight. Night fell and the two wanderers geared themselves up for the cold and wet. Sean, being more accustomed to harsh weather conditions and able to do now without the need for any coat, hat or weather-proof clothing, merely hunched his head down in his open-necked shirt, whilst Caoilte twisted and fumbled with his coat, scarf and hat, still learning the tricks of the trade. (He had – at least – reached the stage of remembering never to wash.) It was near to midnight when Sean realised that someone was coming behind him, some way down the mountain, for he had heard a pebble being dislodged, following its sound as it rolled all the way to the bottom of the ravine. Confirmation of the presence of someone else came when he heard a number of sheep become startled and scattering; a vague shadow darker than surrounding shadows moving around the turn in the hill; a smell not belonging to the countryside coming to his nostrils; a plague of bats, a longer silence in the night than was natural, a slight deflection in the draught coming behind him, a tinge of another's flatulence in the air.

At the same time, Caoilte was becoming aware of someone ahead of him. At first he thought that he had been listening to the natural sounds of a typical mountain, probably volcanic in origin and subject to earthquakes, though he had not noticed any sounds or disturbances when he had first begun the climb. For he could feel the ground shaking under his feet. At times it was scarcely a tremor and at other moments it was a quake so big that it caused him to lose his footing. Then, the path became more and more difficult for the deep grooves and hollows that were appearing. He soon noticed that these were spaced at regular intervals. Then he realised that they must be gigantic footprints. But this was impossible, for the size was far in excess of that of a human footprint. Some of the inundations were deep enough to trap a less wary walker; others were less deep where the rock was harder. Caoilte soon realised that there was, indeed, something powerful and large moving ahead of him. He tried to think of some explanation. He thought of all the wild animals that there might be; feral goats, herds of wild horses for instance. But then there was also now this continuous rumbling noise, like thunder. But it was not coming from the sky. It was coming from within the mountain. It was what he imagined might be the sound of an imminent volcanic eruption. It was getting louder all the time, increasing in tempo. Then suddenly it all stopped. There was total silence.

He carried on walking warily, wondering to himself what could have been making all the noise and why the disturbances had so suddenly stopped. He hoped that, whatever happened, the top of the mountain was not going to blow off!

He was still finding it difficult to keep to the trail in the darkness. Yet he felt some satisfaction, even pride, in the fact that he was increasingly getting to "know the ropes" of living rough, for he was stumbling less now.

A stream of moonlight came through a gap in the clouds. Then more clouds cleared away and the mountainside was bathed in white light. He took in deep breaths at the beauty of it all. He paused to survey his surroundings and as he looked towards the top of the mountain, wondering if he would see anything that could have caused the noise and tremors, his heart nearly stopped with the shock.

The clouds were streaming across the sky as if being blown by some great wind. He could see now that they were not the colour of clouds but were in fact fair or golden strands of hair. Then the whole sky lit up and he saw something else that glued him to the spot. Two suns were glowing from above. After the initial wonder he realised that they were the eyes of a giant. This giant now turned to look down on Caoilte. He heard what he thought was thunder again but realised, as he took in the words, that it was the voice of the giant:

'Caoilte – come. There's work to be done.'

★

The much vaunted, great rebellion of the sidh began. It had been planned by those sidh who were "idealistic" and who had always nursed a secret desire to influence the mortal world positively. These particular fairies admired the qualities in mortals that suggested "selflessness". They were particularly taken with the practice of "kindness" – something that really mystified and impressed them. Other puzzling qualities in their erstwhile antagonists – for example, a tendency to experience a sudden, inexplicable sense of shame on the part of some lout, thug or heathen on looking at himself in the mirror; or a strange sensitivity called embarrassment arising in a normally thick-skinned, hard-hearted individual causing him to intervene and prevent a foolish or mistaken act – encouraged the "idealistic" fairy folk to make a stand with the mortals against the dark forces that threatened Erin. It involved whole hosts of sidh on white steeds, armed to the teeth with every spell, rushing across the plains and valleys of Erin to seek out and attack those forces they perceived to be making the giants selfish and insensitive.

The progress of the great crusade was manifested in the world of the giants in scarcely noticeable events – a sudden, heavy shower from a blue, cloudless sky, the bending of blades of grass on a windless afternoon, a brief blotting out of the sun by a passing, solitary cloud.

OTHER NOVELS BY BARRY SWAN
PUBLISHED BY VALLEY PRESS

www.valleypress.co.uk

THE DESERTED VILLAGE, Barry Swan
ISBN 978-0-9530768-0-2

This novel was runner-up in the Rymans' New Writers' Awards, a UK-wide competition for novelists.

Background of the Novel: A lost village is discovered in a remote part of Co Wicklow in the 1960s. The author goes in search of it, and spends a year following one of its former inhabitants, Dan O'Toole, who has made his way to Dublin. There, in that nexus of civilization, Dan associated with a group of similar incomers, who tolerated him apparently for his ability to croon obscure songs. Soon they were all to find themselves seeking refuge from the authorities, and after tasting the "hospitality" of other high-culture spots of the island they eventually make their way to Dan's village, the long-lost settlement of Bailedecoinin. Here they are given a refuge of sorts.

The following are what reviewers have said about the novel:

"This is a strange mixture of romp, fantasy and humour that reminds me of a very Irish low-key Damon Runyon..." *Claire Toynbee*
"It was a pleasant surprise to read and judge work of such talent by writers. It makes you wonder why they haven't been published before." *Lord Asa Briggs*

AMERIGO VESPUCCI, Barry Swan
ISBN 978-0-9530768-1-9

This novel recounts the story of Fada, a very tall Kerry man who, in about 1485 AD, has to leave home for "political" reasons and heads for Dublin. He does not stay long there. He gets rid of the awkward nephew who is following him about and somehow or other soon finds himself in France. There he meets the "rogues", a bunch of streetwise characters, but Fada outwits them all, sometimes by brute force. He is befriended by Pedro, who makes the historic decision of introducing him to Amerigo Vespucci.

THE INTELLIGENCE MAN, Barry Swan
ISBN 978-0-9530768-2-6

Gerry McArthur, teacher and espionage master controller, has arrived in Jaman on another seemingly monotonous, mundane pedagogic task; but the tedium is diminished by the dangers of this new mission. Everyone knows he really works for the CIA. However for all intents and purposes he is an insignificant, run-down academic with delusions of self-importance.

Gerry McArthur has many fantasies, but it seems they are coming true. The US President really is mad. Someone is outwitting the CIA. But even more importantly, Gerry McArthur must realise the dangers of the Super-Coconut before it's too late.

"Barry Swan's latest book has it all: the mystery of a good spy novel, the dark heat of the tropics he knows so well, and the wit of a born humorist to make sense of it all. Altogether, an impressive achievement." *Dean Irwin, Producer ABC News*

THE MADNESS OF EAMON MORIARTY, Barry Swan
ISBN 978-0-9530768-3-3

This is the story of the god Economy whom the sophisticated Ancients banned from appearing in the cosmic pantheon. Whilst Zeus, Apollo, Ares, Aphrodite and many more were celebrated in poetry and song, scabrous Economy, a poor, elemental sort of fellow, found himself put out of sight by the intellectual, artistic and religious establishment. This was even though, or perhaps because of the embarrassing fact that it was he who made the world go round. With his estrangement from all the other gods, and pursued vindictively by Demeter (goddess of Agriculture) and Pan (god of Pastures and Forests), he had to go and live for a long time in the backwoods.

A humorous allegory where human institutions, seen through the eyes of a madman, become more real the madder they seem. The hero is called Economy, and he seems to have stepped into the modern world from the primeval slime of a classical childhood in a place some believe is Cork. Try as he does to become sane, the hero fails to ward off the terrifying visitations of politicians, social workers, philosophers and others as he becomes the helpless victim in their nightmarish world. He has a hard job working his way through the nuts and bolts of contemporary society, inadvertently loosening some of them on the way.

THE HEAVENLY REALM, Barry Swan
ISBN 978-0-9530768-4-0 Sequel to THE INTELLIGENCE MAN

Brother Gerry, ex-teacher, ex-husband, is a monk in a controversial monastic community on the tropical isle of Jaman. Things here are not what they should be. There is a high security perimeter fence. Instead of saints he has for company ex-crooks, odd balls, charlatans and religious fanatics. The more he tries to make sense of God in this place, the more his reliable "voices" assail him with logical counter-arguments. As his sanity tips, the monastery comes under fire, literally, for its secretive use of a mysterious 'power' that threatens the whole world (not to mention the government).

Background: In the 1970s ferment amongst different Rastafarian groups led to experimentation with every variety of religious experience from Gnosticism to Orthodoxy. Some in this "lost culture" brought themselves by "reasonings" to the fold of Orthodoxy. One group, the Zion Coptic Church, its leadership revitalized by white hippie converts, achieved great success, reflected in their material wealth which attracted attention (they were supposedly among the largest landholders in Jaman). They roused the ire of the authorities who pursued them relentlessly, imprisoning the Coptic leadership. Even their enemies respected their religious commitment, incorporating the best of Rastafarian culture into church life, and their retention of dreadlocks and nyabinghi drumming helped them gain many converts. The Coptics insist that they are the new Jews, a legitimate Orthodox jurisdiction with Catholics among the founders.